| DATE DUE | | | |
|---|---|---|---|
| | | | |
| | | | |
| | | | |
| | | | |
| | | | |
| | | | |
| | | | |
| | | | |
| | | | |
| | | | |
| | | | |
| | | | |

# CURSIVE

ALEX WYNDHAM BAKER

**A Cutting Edge Press Hardback**

Published in 2012 by Cutting Edge Press

www.CuttingEdgePress.co.uk



Printed and bound by CPI Group (UK) Ltd, Croydon, CR0 4YY

**Hardback ISBN: 978-1-908122-20-9**
**Paperback ISBN: 978-1-908122-21-6**
**E-PUB ISBN: 978-1-908122-22-3**

# Acknowledgements

Serafina Clarke, Danny Broderick, Roselle Angwin, Mark Baker, Nicky Eaton, Juliet Antill, Laura Colquhoun, Jimmy Greenwood, Celia Catchpole and Sebastian Bulmer for their feedback; Conny Tedder, Cath Taylor, Joss Wilbraham, Annabelle Redfern and Sophie Barker for their help; Justin Rose, Alistair Redman, Charlie Allsopp, Jamie Buckley, Vic Orr-Ewing, Sveva Gallmann, Lara Colenso and Jonny Biggins for their encouragement; Ed and Henry Holdsworth-Hunt for their Hoopoe Yurt haven, Neil Freebairn for his exhaustive editing, Steve Baker for the snappy cover, shiatsu ninja Mitsutoshi Fujimura for getting me back on my feet, and Katharine McGowan; love found. Athankya.

'Though lovers be lost, love shall not.'

*Dylan Thomas*

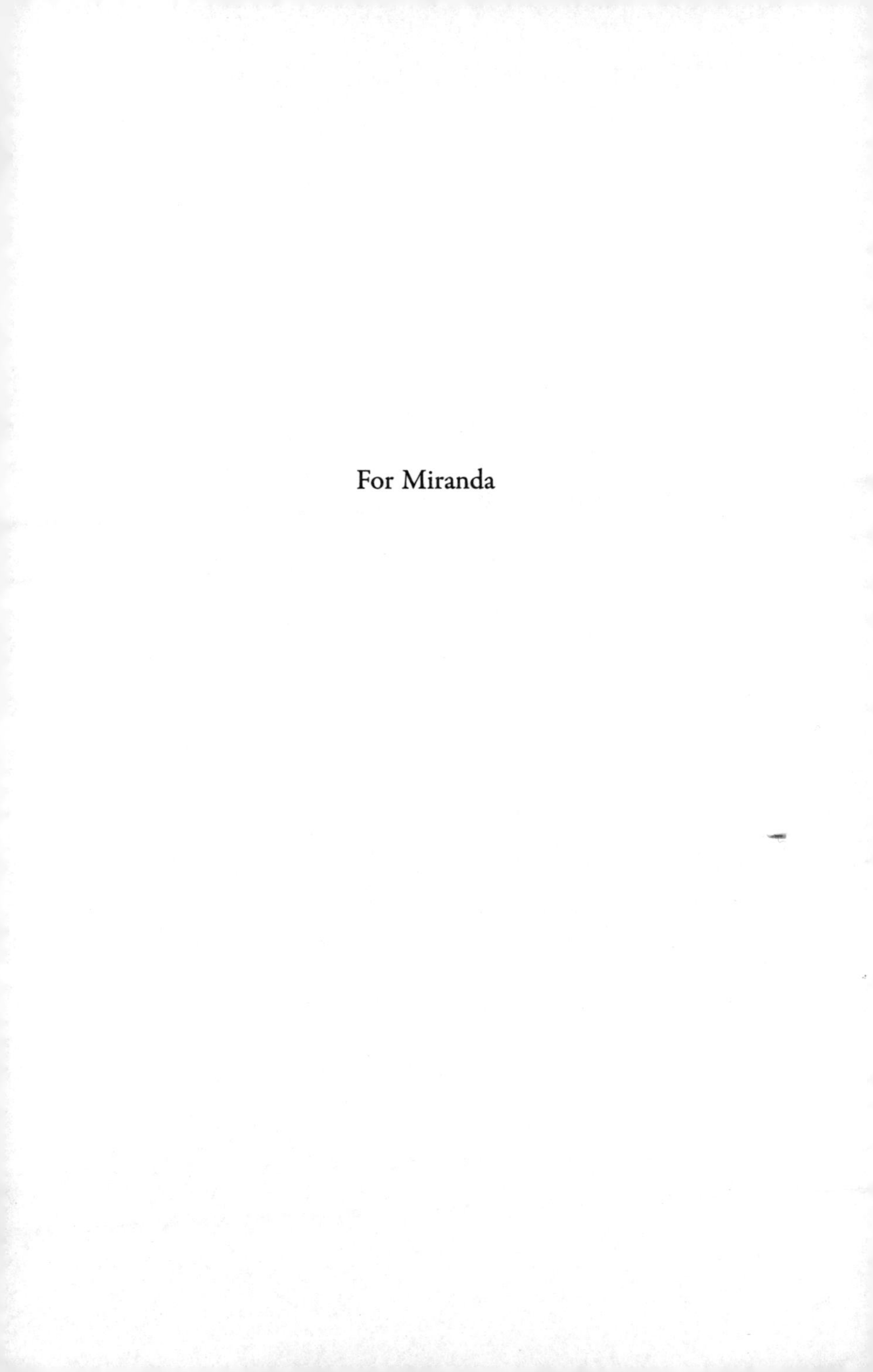

For Miranda

# Chapter 1

*Sunday, 26th September, 1933*
*S.S. Apollonia*
*The Atlantic Ocean*

*My love,*

*One down, three hundred and sixty four to go.*

*I feel exiled, packed off to the colonies like a convict sentenced for a crime he knows nothing of, and must stop counting the seconds, hours and days or go quite mad.*

*Leaving you was without doubt the hardest thing I've ever had to do. Your brave smile, your beautiful upturned face standing out amid all that chaos like a dropped coin in the street, is still clear in my mind's eye and will remain so until I have you back in my arms once more.*

*I stood there at the stern long after you vanished, swallowed up by that damned fog into which England quickly disappeared, staring down into the churning wake and silently praying that I'll be brought back to you safe and sound.*

*Oblivious to both cold and passengers alike, I pictured a golden thread stretching out between us, thinning but tangible, connecting us yet. Keep this fixed clearly in your mind, my love, perhaps the image will help us both get through these coming months – we must use any means at our disposal, no matter how tenuous.*

*Eventually the mist cleared taking everything with it, an illusionist's cloak leaving nothing but grey sea and sky, and you were gone.*

*Staring north, the shrieks of seagulls fading with the light, I was roused from my thoughts by a brusque crewman offering to show me to my cabin. I duly followed, to find my quarters not quite up to the description of 'well-appointed comfort with all the conveniences of home'. It's rather difficult to acclimatise to this claustrophobic box. Darkly panelled, furnished frugally with bunk, bureau, table and washbasin, and musty with mothballs, this is to be home for the next month, God help me. A small, brass-framed porthole lets in minimal light and affords a limited view of rolling seas during the day, waves merging one with another with hypnotic monotony.*

*Am I complaining? Yes, I damned well am. You'd think that the Company, with all its influence, power and wealth, might have at least stretched to a berth on a liner, our freight for Mombasa notwithstanding.*

*In remotely heavy sea anything not nailed down drifts disconcertingly across the room only to surge back again at the next swell, and I've learnt to hang on to my chipped enamel mug. A 'fiddle', a detachable rim around the table, prevents what's on it from heading off it, and shaving can prove understandably challenging, if not dangerous. I might forgo it.*

*Maddox, the ham-whiskered chap who showed me to my cabin, clearly holds all landlubbers in disdain and has yet to utter a civil word to me, depositing a jug of hot water outside my room each morning in exchange for the bed pan (admittedly not the most favourable of trades) and delivering my meals with similar distemper, so far the only contact I've had with anyone aboard.*

*My solitude is not entirely out of choice, since spectacular 'mal de mer', from which I can find no respite, floored me almost as soon as we left Portsmouth; perpetual nausea and a listless lethargy have further dampened my spirits, my love, and my confinement is only relieved by occasional turns about the deck, hat jammed low and collar turned up.*

*There's a sixty-foot walkway that runs the length of each side, with an observation deck up a flight of iron stairs set below the bridge, as well as areas bow and stern where one may ponder, depending on mood, where one's going, or where one's been.*

*I sit amidships.*

*I understand your Pa is only doing what he thinks he should, and that he of course has nothing but your best interests at heart, but still I can't completely forgive him for this predicament. I know, we've talked much about it, but to sever a bond such as ours I find bloody hard to accept. I'm quite sure that the formidable austerity, ruthless acumen and adamantine self-discipline that have made him who he is and engenders so much respect in others prevents him from recognising the tender, plumbless depth of our feelings for each other. Had he the slightest inkling of our love he'd surely praise the Lord, count his blessings and throw a lavish bash for everyone he knows to celebrate the fact that his only daughter had found happiness.*

*Would he, more pertinently, have set the same task for a suitor with proven heritage, and – I'd swap it in an instant – more than just an anonymous trust fund to their name?*

*I only wish your mother had more sway over him. She's clearly as bowed by the weight of his iron will as I now am. Should I have stood up to him? Told him to hell with his proviso and eloped with you? Certainly asking for your hand was unbelievably nerve-racking – what happened to the customary 'yes', slap on the back, brandy and cigar? As to what he actually thinks of me, I hesitate to think. Regardless of your assurances, the man's a tyrant and a bully.*

*Unfortunately one that holds all the cards; had he commanded me fly to the moon I would be diligently gluing on feathers. Let's pray that with this ludicrous escapade behind me I'll have earned if not his respect at least his approval, as well as his beloved daughter.*

*Please do what you can to soften him up while I am away; behind the gruff exterior, I know his love for you exceeds all else.*

*But enough. We must grin and bear it, stoically, and I need to toughen up (perhaps he thinks so too?) or shall be undone. 'What doesn't kill you', and all. Besides, what's a year when we have our whole lives ahead of us? And what a story to tell our grandchildren in the future, God willing – the triumph of love over adversity – it's all really rather romantic. I feel poised at the beginning of a great adventure, chivalric and noble, like the knights in those Arthurian myths you're so fond of, setting off into the unknown with a sword at my waist, ready to take on dragons. Well, large lizards anyway. I'll admit I'm a little apprehensive – not of what might happen to me, but that for any one of a thousand reasons my mind can conjure up I'm somehow lost to you.*

*How I miss you already.*

*We promised to be strong for each other, resolute throughout this separation; I'll try to keep my side of the bargain and relate my adventures as best I can. I shall treat these letters as I would a journal – a log, as my salty peers would call it. Since I've no need of recording these events for myself it will be you I bear in mind, my captive audience of one, and such descendents as feign interest in the future.*

*Thank you for the beautiful writing case, you clever thing, and your letter. Both lie before me on my bureau, as does your photograph; how lovely you look amid that wisteria, though rather more demure and more innocent than the Lillian I know and love!*

*Re your letter: of course we must write as often as possible, with whatever trivia. No detail will be too small – just to know you have held the same piece of paper is somehow reassuring; a physical link that transcends the increasing distance between us.*

*Re your petticoat – I shall treasure it always, wicked girl. The smell of it, of you, sets my head spinning, and I'm back in that meadow, the late summer sun on our skin and the intermittent splash of moorhen giving us the jitters. What bliss. And although magical and beyond regret, the memory will undoubtedly make the privation of the year to come all the more difficult to bear, and I only hope we did not take too great a risk my love, since, by-blown as I am, I can well imagine your father's reaction to a grandchild out of wedlock; perhaps more shotgun than wedding!*

*And as for this pen, what a beauty!*

*A Mabie Todd Blackbird no less. How on earth could you afford it? And such exquisite craftsmanship. The marbled effect of the resin shaft is quite lovely, catching the light beautifully as I tilt it this way and that – most distracting. The weight is lightly balanced and the nib perfectly suited to my sinistral scrawl, so that words seem to stream from it unassisted, flowing across the page with the minimum of effort. I now have no excuses and shall write as often as I can. Did you notice – I'm sure you did since it's exactly the sort of thing that appeals to your sentimentality – the tiny reservoir that feeds ink to the point of the nib is heart-shaped? How perfect, then, for these words to come straight from mine, and forgive me if I wax a little lyrical.*

*Now then, I'm in danger of becoming unforgivably maudlin and had better try to get some sleep. Maddox informs me, with what might have been a hint of Schadenfreude, that we should expect 'inclement' weather ahead – 'Nothing to worry a strapping lad like the young master,' the sarky bugger – and I am already terribly short of shut-eye.*

*I love you – the thought of twelve months without you weighs heavy. Be strong, my love, and know that one day we'll look back on this from old age with pride that our love never faltered. Besides, at least you and your Ma have time enough to prepare for the big day.*

*Yours always, with all my love,*

*Ralph.*

*P.S. While I remember, did that tall negro standing behind you at the quay approach you? I only mention it because of his unusual appearance and that as we left and amid the pandemonium of our departure he seemed to be the only person not waving off the ship but staring intently at you. Perhaps he had a message to deliver from your father.*

*Anon.*

*Wednesday, 29th September, 1933*
*S.S. Apollonia*
*Bay of Biscay*

*My Love,*

*God, what a hellish few days.*

*Forgive my whining from the previous – 'woe is bloody me', and all that – and please put it down to nerves. I now feel like a seasoned mariner, though of course am far from it, as the experiences I shall relate make clear.*

*The 'inclement weather' Maddox mentioned turned out to be slightly understated.*

*The storm kicked off during the night of the second day, somewhere in the middle of the Bay of Biscay. I'd just managed to drift into an exhausted sleep, so weak from sickness, lack of food and rest I believed I wouldn't wake were hell itself to open for me, when that was precisely what happened.*

*With a bang I found myself dumped onto the floor like a sack of spuds, pitched straight over the rail intended to prevent it.*

*Disorientated and in total darkness I fumbled to my feet, my backside bruised and the floor beneath me yawing to and fro. The engine pitch was irregular – due to the propellers actually lifting clear of the water as we crested the waves, I later found out. I felt my way to the cabin door and yanked it open. The lights in the corridor were flickering, the current faltering, adding further to my nausea, whereupon Maddox appeared from the stairwell, soaked through and swearing profusely, barrelling towards me and shouting at me to remain in my cabin – well that was the gist of it anyway. I did as I was told and spent a miserable few hours in the dark, thrown this way and that. The noise of the wind howling beyond the porthole and the crash of waves against the hull combined with my delirium to produce the most bizarre hallucinations; voices calling out in distress, and at one point piercing screams. I swear I heard scratching, and imagined a thick, bristling carpet of deserting rats scrabbling along the corridor outside.*

*How long this went on for I can't be sure, but long enough to convince myself the ship was going down and that I was going down with it. Visions of drowning swirled before my eyes, clawing in the dark, lost to a fathomless deep. My panic mounting, I decided to risk Maddox's wrath and try to reach the deck, or at least find another soul with whom to share my final moments rather than perish alone.*

*Struggling into some clothes, I threw on my coat and stumbled out of my cabin, the lights by this point had completely failed, and banged on my neighbours' doors but received no response. This struck me as strange, since no one could possibly still be asleep, yet where else could they be?*

*I hauled myself up the stairs to the main deckhouse. Beyond the watertight door the wind-whipped sea raged, and through the porthole I could just make out lights aft within the maelstrom. There was no sign of life on deck; no surprise there, since every few minutes great sheets of water broke over the rail and would have certainly swept anyone unlucky enough to be there at the time straight overboard. Choosing my moment I wrestled open the door and stepped out into the tempest. It swung out of my grasp once the wind had a grip on it and I had to struggle to close it. Keeping pressed close to the superstructure and hanging onto the handrail, I made my way along the deck, drenched in an instant and bowed into the wind as if yoked, but beckoned by the glow of light ahead until, prising open the door, I burst into the main mess, off balance, soaked through, with the tumult bellowing my arrival.*

*The wind and the slam of the door against its jamb made everyone snap up from what they were doing and stare at me agog. In the yellow light and haze of smoke I could vaguely make out people gathered around their tables and in their armchairs. The ceiling lights swung drunkenly from their fittings and chased shadows about the room, while I for my part must have looked completely deranged – unshaven, wild haired and gaunt – having slept and eaten little over the previous three days. Attempting to pull myself together I managed to whisper, 'Bit blustery out, what?', groped for support that wasn't there and crashed to the floor in a dead faint.*

*My next memory is of choking back some liquor and coughing 'til my eyes streamed, concerned faces leaning over me and that peculiar, buoyant sensation one gets after passing out, where everything seems disjointed, somehow thinned.*

*'You all right, old chap?' asked a moustached man kneeling by my side, one hand supporting my neck, his other holding a glass. 'Gave us all a bit of a shock, bursting in like that.' I attempted some*

*apology. 'Not a word, lad. Have another swig on this,' he tipped the brandy to my mouth.*

*'How's your head?' he said. 'You clipped it when you fell.' I registered a dull ache on my temple. 'Take your time, you're fine now.'*

*With his help I sat up straight.*

*'Ready? One, two, and up.' He pulled me to my feet and with his support I struggled out of my coat into an empty armchair near the stove. Someone wrapped a blanket around my shoulders and I drew it tight, blinking and shivering.*

*'Symmonds,' he said, 'Colonel, James. You must be Talbot, the Company wallah.' I shook his proffered hand, taking some comfort in the strength of his grip. 'Here, have another go on this.' I did so gratefully.*

*'Well my boy, I'd always wondered where the expression "hit the deck" came from and I think you might have just enlightened me. My thanks.' He smiled. 'We were all a little worried that you might have passed away during the night but Maddox assured us you were fighting fit.' He glanced around for the blighter. 'Seems you didn't get the skipper's request we all gather here 'til the worst of it's over. No matter, you're here now.'*

*Revived by the brandy, I felt some semblance of normality return and my chattering teeth slowed to an occasional spasm. When he reckoned I was up to it Symmonds made brief introductions. Present were some two dozen passengers: a group of Dutch missionaries bound for the Congo; a doctor, Richards, and his much younger wife who from her drawn complexion I guessed suffered the same malaise as I; a delegation of dour looking agricultural advisors from the Government with us as far as Alexandria – I forget all their names; two Scots sportsmen, Swaine and McAlister, quite sloshed by the look of them, and a sullen looking prospector, Kemp, who wouldn't meet my eye and returned immediately to his book. Another fellow, Davidson, was only with us as far as Gib, with business there to attend to.*

*The show over, they returned to their groups amid mutters of 'Well I never', etc., and I joined Symmonds at his table, a game of solitaire abandoned where my entrance had interrupted him.*

*He ordered one of the stewards to fetch me some dinner and poured us each another stiff one while the wind howled impotently – so it now seemed – outside. The ship creaked around us, strange groans belying great stress while the engines thumped away, but I felt bolstered by the company; the false security but welcome comfort of shared plight and Symmonds' lack of concern for any danger we might face. When I asked whether he was familiar with such conditions he replied that he was, and aboard vessels 'much less sturdy than this one.' Good for him.*

*A plate of stew arrived and we got talking; he asked about me, my background and my contract with what seemed unfeigned interest. Between small mouthfuls I told him what little there was to tell; much of you my love, forgive me, and of your father's stipulation. He by contrast was a gold mine of information. Born in BEA to British parents, he returned to England at the outbreak of the War. Seems he caught some shrapnel attempting to rescue one of his men at Ypres – for which he was duly decorated – and was discharged not long after the armistice. Unable to adjust to Civvy Street – 'just not cut out for the dangers of office life' – he persuaded the army to give him a posting back in BEA, or Kenya, I should say. Since then he has been back and forth on His Majesty's business, though in what capacity he didn't tell me.*

*As soon as I twigged we were heading for the same region I'm afraid I swamped him with questions, Lil, unconcerned if I revealed the extent of my ignorance.*

*I am lucky to have met him. Late into the night he regaled me with tales of the continent and his experiences in the trenches until I quite forgot my illness, the storm outside or the bump on my head. I hope I've made a friend, though admit to being slightly in awe of him. I would guess just shy of forty – though the moustache adds a few years – he's a lean fellow with dark, wiry hair, a shock of white above his right ear – the shrapnel wound? I didn't ask – and a deeply creased face etched by both sun and smile lines, the result, I appreciated, of a wry sense of humour; his eyes meet one's own with an amused gaze that's hard to break or fathom. What a life he's led, Lil. If half his stories are true he has lived the life of four men and still thinks himself young.*

*There was one area upon which he would not expand and I fear I might have put my foot in it rather; when I asked him if he had any family, his eyes dropped and he shook his head slowly, lips pursed. When he looked up, something in his expression had changed, a slight tightening around his mouth, and he soon after made his apologies and went to bed. Alone but for the book-bound prospector, and the storm having calmed, I soon followed suit and finally managed a good night's sleep, no doubt helped by the brandy and the clock around the bonce.*

*Awoke late this morning to blue skies visible through my porthole and emerged on deck to that freshly laundered feeling that follows bad weather; clear, bright heat, calm seas as far as the eye could see and a palpable sense of excitement. Though I saw no sign of Symmonds, it seemed the whole company was out on deck, chatting and smoking at the rail while the crew busied themselves with preparations for docking. I took some air, nodding a sheepish hello to those that I passed, then soon ducked back down below. We are approaching our first port of call, Lisbon, and I shall pick up the pen again once on dry land,*

*I am finding my sea legs. Albeit slowly.*

*Enough for now – I hope all's well at Brampton; please give my love to your Ma, Sarah and the lads, and my regards to your Pa.*

*With all my love,*

*Ralph*

*Thursday, 30th September, 1933*
*S.S. Apollonia*
*Lisbon*

*Dearest Lil,*

*I hope this reaches you with all speed and finds you well.*

*Lisbon, a frenetic mêlée far busier than Portsmouth, shone bright against a distant backdrop of heat-hazy mountains. An impressive fort dominates the town from the hill above and a tumble of whitewashed villas cascade to the sea front. Hard to imagine the entire place was once razed to the ground by an earthquake of Biblical proportions two centuries ago.*

*As a Gomorrah it was slightly disappointing, currently enjoying God's grace by the look of it. We were given twenty-four hours' shore leave – an opportunity to stretch our legs; well earned as far as I was concerned. Once ashore the ground continued to pitch for several hours, exactly as if we were still on board; a phenomenon I'd heard about but never expected to be so profound. We disembarked into stuffy heat and chaotic activity. Mule-drawn carts laden with crates and sacks with switch-wielding drovers, teams of swarthy-armed longshoremen, burly navvies, servicemen in white uniforms, blacks of every hue, merchants' clerks and hawkers – it reminded me of a scene from Hogarth, everyone shouting in numerous different languages and none of them intelligible. Cargo in straining netting was swung ashore from the Apollonia on creaking, cantilevered derricks, to be replaced by other crates of cotton, ironmongery, wheat, etc.*

*I didn't hang around for long.*

*Keen to explore, I decided to climb the hill to the fort, both for the exercise and what promised to be a rewarding view, and was soon pushing through the crowds, away from the overpowering piscine stench I assume pervades all ports, to the relative cool and calm of the main street, past magnificent merchant palaces running up from the sea front between the thighs of a valley steeply terraced with haphazard but beautiful, gaily shuttered villas, and veined with shaded alleys. I stopped at a small shop and through a process of pointing and nodding stocked up on bread, olives, cheese, cured meat and a bottle of wine, a feast that I stuffed in my knapsack. I then swung off the thoroughfare and followed my nose up through cobbled alleys so narrow the upper floor occupants could have shaken hands. The path steepened steadily so I couldn't keep the fort above in line of sight, though I guessed I must be heading in the right direction.*

*Gradually the buildings thinned to poorer dwellings, glimpses through open doors revealing frugal interiors and the occasional nod of their occupants, until I came to a grand stone gateway where the buildings ended and the paved path to the summit began.*

*I paused to recover my breath and mop my brow, enjoying the exertion and breathing in air sweet with pine and broom, then climbed on, winding up behind the hill, my head down and quite preoccupied, emerging in front of enormous outer walls set amid gnarled oaks like old giants, similar to those at home but with smaller, spikier leaves.*

*The great doors were open, swung back on iron hinges and, with no one around to grant or refuse permission, I entered past a plaque that I assume explained the history of the place, and contentedly strolled through ancient fortifications, still intact despite their antiquity, to the ramparts overlooking the town far below.*

*The view more than justified my labours. The port spread herself prettily at my feet, the sea shimmering beyond, alive with light. I could even make out the Apollonia standing out clearly amongst the other ships, her blue and white livery bright against the foreign freighters and gunmetal grey frigates.*

*Finding a shady spot beneath a pine that whispered in the breeze, I spread out my picnic, and was soon pleasantly serenaded with bird song and consoled by the wine. I wish you had been there to share my thoughts, my love – for some reason the view seemed rendered pointless without you to validate it, without the confirmation of small observations, the authentication of shared experience; without you beside me. After the last two years, after all our companionship and our time together, it feels as if something is missing, as if I've had a limb amputated. I no longer feel entirely whole.*

*The wine must have got the better of me for I woke with a start some time later, the sun having dropped significantly. About to collect my things I paused and looking to my right saw I was not alone.*

*Some fifty feet away stood Symmonds in his well-worn fedora, a canvas satchel slung across one shoulder. Why I didn't call out in greeting then and there I still don't know, but I had the intuition that he would not have welcomed the intrusion.*

*Remaining quiet, more or less hidden from view by the grass in which I lay and in the opposite direction to where he looked, I watched him, rather guiltily, as he pulled out a pair of binoculars from the satchel and trained them on the town below – to the port, were I to hazard a guess. After a few minutes he took out a notebook and pencil from his breast pocket and began scribbling away in it, pausing to refresh his memory with the binoculars. Before long he put his book away and turned in my direction. I ducked my head, pulse quickening with shame of discovery, but he can't have noticed me for when I next looked he had gone. I stayed where I was for several more minutes wondering why I'd behaved so furtively, then returned the remains of my lunch to the knapsack and dropped down into the cool dusk.*

*The boarding house where we were to spend the night, El Solar Do Castelo, I found with little difficulty. Barrio Alto, the district in which it resides, is a den of magnificent, unabashed iniquity – shouts rang from the balconies above, shadowy figures loitered in doorways and I was propositioned repeatedly – but I arrived without incident as the last of the light was wrung from the sky. In no mood to fraternise with my fellows and with no sign of my friend, I made my excuses after supper – thick bean soup and a little too much port – and hit the hay, grateful for the stability of the room.*

*That night I was plagued by the most vivid dreams, probably due to the port, part of which remains clear:*

*Symmonds and I are hacking our way through some Godforsaken jungle, beset by insects, stifling humidity and the implied proximity of wild beasts. I'm unafraid, confident that he knows what he's doing, but there's a tension to our labours – what with impending dusk and the need to make camp. Anyway, before long we emerge in a clearing, with the light fading not a moment too soon, when suddenly S. freezes and gestures silence. He's seen something on the far side of the clearing, some fifty yards off. Without taking his eyes from the trees, he unslings his rifle, eases off the safety and works a round into the breach. I follow suit. He motions me to stick close and we pick our way around the clearing's edge, keeping to the shadows, towards a large, pale shape prostrate on the ground. A horse. We draw closer, and hear laboured, rasping breathing – it's obviously in distress. We round the beast, S. lowering his rifle and relaxing a little. The wretched creature is mortally wounded; foam flecks its slack jaws, the eyes are wide and blood pours from an awful gash its head. From its chest protrudes a spiralled, ivory spike the diameter of my arm.*

*We realise it's not a horse but a Unicorn, impaled upon its own horn. It becomes aware of our presence and between bubbling gasps tries to speak. S. crouches down to hear more clearly, the beast gives one last concerted effort and we make out the word it's trying to say:*

*'Run.'*

*At that moment we hear the crash of something approaching through the forest, something large, at speed. 'Go', hisses S., turning grimly to face the direction of the scything undergrowth. 'Go now.' I turn heel and belt off across the clearing into the forest as fast as my legs can carry me. I hear a shot ring out and a shrill cry, and I stop and turn, levelling my rifle in the direction from which I've come, but can see nothing in the thick gloom. Then I hear it – eagerly rushing towards me. I loose off a couple of rounds then turn and run, dropping the rifle in my panic. It's closing in on me, panting audibly with a sickening swiftness of purpose. I leap for a low branch, my momentum swinging me upwards just as tusks or claws slice through the air beneath me and . . .*

*I'm awake, covered in sweat.*

*I've been a little shaken by it all morning, my love, and when I saw S. earlier, told him all about it. He laughed, grabbed my shoulder and asked me to remind him not to take me on safari if I'm so ready to flee in a tight spot. He seemed a little distracted and disappeared soon after breakfast.*

*As I write we're due to join the Apollonia imminently; she weighs anchor at midday. I must give this to Maddox to post – I only wish*

*I could stow away on the mail ship, mi amore. I hate being at the mercy of the postal service but must have faith; efficient international communication is what the Empire is built upon, after all.*

*Be well, my love, I shall write again from Gibraltar.*

*Yours, ever,*

*Ralph*

*P.S. Tell Nick and Anna to expect a letter soon.*

# Chapter 2

*Oxford, England. 1989.*

Surfacing slowly, fragments of her dream scattering like cats, Sam Jefferson had a quick flash of panic that kept her eyes closed while she ran through a mental checklist of the night before, easing herself into her body gingerly, like someone entering a too-cold pool. Her head throbbed, but not too badly, and her mouth felt a little scorched from too many cigarettes. Once satisfied that she could safely recall the evening in its entirety – right up to the front door, first light and birdsong – and she was sure she wouldn't find anyone in bed beside her, she peeled back an eyelid and squinted at the digital clock blinking indifferently on her bedside table.

She was, predictably, running late.

Sitting up, she threw aside the duvet and surveyed the half-packed jumble sale chaos of her room. Sunlight knifed through the thin weft of the Indian bedspread that served as a curtain, catching the lazy Brownian motion of dust motes. She stretched, swung her legs over the side of the bed, pushed herself onto pigeon-toed feet and yawned into the bathroom.

Twenty minutes later she was dressed and ready. She was, she liked to think, low maintenance. She skittered down the stairs, along the hallway littered with unopened final demands and into the kitchen. The lights were on, the stereo hissed and the curtains were drawn. It smelt bad; stale, sweet, congealed. She pulled back the curtain, daylight mercilessly revealing the room with a magician's flourish, and opened the window.

'Jesus H. *Christ*,' said Jay, lifting his head off a freshly drooled-on arm so a trail of spittle sagged from his chin. His eyes were pink, different sizes, and he regarded her unsteadily, leaning on the counter amid the detritus of empty bottles, rancid bongs and overflowing ashtrays. Beyond him in the sitting room two bare feet poked over the arm of the sofa. 'What the *fuck* are you doing?'

'Morning,' she said brightly. 'You two muppets haven't been to bed, have you?'

'Ben's passed out, and I *was* asleep.' There was rebuke in his voice, as if he blamed Ben for crashing out and her for waking him up. 'What happened to you?'

'Left about four,' she said. 'Music get any better?'

'No.'

'But you stayed 'til the end anyway?' She filled the kettle and plugged it in, then yanked open the fridge and grimaced into it. No milk. No anything.

'Yeah.'

This was going nowhere, she thought. Her housemates had both just flunked their finals, swallowed up in the quicksand of having left revision too late and having no solid assessed coursework to cling to. Their living together had only made it worse, as if they were both daring each other to see who could fuck up the most spectacularly, egging each other on. A fortnight of panic-driven cramming on cheap speed before their last exam had been the peak of their achievement, and had actually worked, sort of; they covered the ground, searing through borrowed notes and textbook summaries, and were certainly 'alert' come the morning. But the comedown kicked in too soon, leaving their legs spinning in thin air like in a cartoon, and an hour in they'd made eye contact across the silent, cloistral hall, nodded, stood together and taken the Long Walk outside, footsteps echoing, heads high, condemned men walking to the firing squad of their future, and gone to the pub. They'd been hammering it with nihilistic fervour ever since, just with none of the exhilarated liberation everyone else was enjoying.

'Any idea where Gemma went?' One of their number was Missing In Action, her bed untouched.

'She left with wassisname.' He reached for a vodka bottle, squinted at it and drained the remaining inch. 'Jason. From her course.'

'Look, babe,' she said, 'you need to sleep. There's a couple of Valium by my bed. Why don't you go and get them, give one to Ben and I'll wake you both tomorrow?'

Exam results would go up first thing in the morning. He looked at her sullenly, swaying.

'Only if you join me.' He attempted a beguiling smile but it only made him look depraved.

'No, Jay, Jesus. I've got lunch with the folks – apart from anything else.'

'I've always loved you,' he slurred. 'You know that, don't you Sam?'

'That's very sweet,' she used the neutral, maternal tones of a psychiatric nurse, 'but you're off your nut and haven't slept in days. Now go to bed.' She spoke firmly – she didn't have time for this. The house was trashed and they had to be out of it by Wednesday. She'd already written off the deposit and the phone bill. She knew no one was willing or able to help her clear everything up, that they would all be scrambling out the back door with their bags as their Bengali landlord came in the front, and that a future of rejected credit applications loomed.

She found a pack of Nurofen in a drawer and washed one down with a shot of black coffee, gave Jay a hug and left him to it.

Outside the road radiated heat. Looking down the street she could see thermals shimmering, stirring the air like oil in water, or vodka in tonic. Her head blood pulsed. She felt light, immaterial, slightly giddied by the hot breeze that wound around her legs. Rummaging in her vintage suede bag she produced a pair of outsize Seventies sunglasses and found the keys as she reached her car; a pale blue, rust-speckled Beetle convertible with several dents, a missing offside wing mirror and a faded WWF sticker on the windscreen. She folded the concertina roof back, slid her slight frame into the sticky-hot driver's seat and, muttering her usual 'start-you-fucking-bitch' prayer, turned the ignition. It started first time. Gunning the engine to stop it changing its mind, she pulled a pack of Camel Lights from the dashboard, lit one, punched the Happy Mondays cassette into the slot and pulled out.

As Shaun Ryder hacksawed away over the engine's lusty pitch and the wind restyled her hair, she felt her hangover subside and, always susceptible to the emotion of whatever music she was listening to, succumbed to a mild wave of nostalgia for the undergrad life she was about to give up. With most results out, the party last night had been a final thrash before everyone went their separate ways. She would miss it. Not Oxford per se – though now, mid-summer, it was particularly beautiful; a ripe pulchritude beneath the sandstone austerity of leering gargoyles, rich with colour and fragrant with flowers and the scent of dope smoked openly in the parks, the air thick with pheromones and lingering glances, bars full of anything-goes promiscuity – but the lifestyle; the only arena when you could do whatever you wanted, screw up righteously, with aplomb, and it didn't matter. No one gave a toss. A hedonic, self-indulgent freefall (or 'government-sponsored day care for the privileged', as Rachel called it) where you could shake off the personality construct of childhood and the survival mechanisms of school and totally let loose, let rip, before getting stuck into working life, the allegedly real world.

If you got it out of your system, exorcised the mutinies of youth and came out a good little worker, consumer, breeder, unquestioningly settling into society's prescribed idea of normality. She wasn't convinced she had. She felt she'd only just got going, that she was only just beginning to evolve, to fill out into what she would become a little more – and that the unrelenting production line of school-college-job-marriage-kids needed a hefty spanner lobbed into it.

It was a short drive through the wide, lime-treed streets of the south Oxford suburbs, past raven-gowned graduates pressing mortar boards to their heads, manicured municipal flowerbeds and semi-detached houses where Sunday car-washing rituals were already underway, the soapy froth of run-off and long-forgotten aspiration gurgling consentingly into the storm drains. Once out on the ring road she floored it, ignoring the steering wheel's wobble as the needle hit seventy, and slightly perturbed by the suicidal abandon with which fat bugs exploded on her windscreen, and soon turned off down narrowing lanes beneath canopied beech, sunlight strobing through the leaves.

The car park at the Quill & Ink already brimmed with solid,

sensible family estates, so she had to back up the high-banked lane until she could park under the dappled shade of coppiced hazels. She smoothed her hair in the mirror and clipped off down the track scoping for her Dad's Volvo. No sign. She was relieved. It gave her more time to get her shit together.

She ducked into the pub and let her eyes adjust to the gloom, inhaling the cloyed air laden with cigar smoke and the sweet smell of spilt beer. The din of guffawing banter faltered as she entered, back-lit by the sunshine silhouetting through her dress, and ignoring the lizard-lidded sweep – tits legs tits face – of stuffed-shirt regulars, pushed through to the bar.

'G'day.' Brawny-armed and bullet-headed, the Aussie behind the bar grinned broadly, swaggering towards her as he snapped a dishcloth over his shoulder. 'What can I getcha?' Cute, she thought. She had a thing for pronounced clavicles.

'Bloody Mary, please. Double.' She smiled as she paid, holding his eye when he pushed the glass towards her, the green fronds of celery contrasting deliciously with the deep red of the tomato juice, making her mouth water. 'Thanks.'

She wandered through to the back door where she scanned the garden, chewing on one arm of her shades, one hand shielding her eyes. The bench tables were already full of ad-perfect families, the air eddied with small talk, the warm smell of cut grass and the Doppler hum of wasps. She recognised a few faces from campus but thankfully no one she knew. Couples elbow-leant in the longer meadow grass beyond a two-barred wooden fence. A kid capered about with a multicoloured kite, its bright flutter vivid against the backdrop of beech woods beyond.

Remembering her mother would almost certainly have booked a table, she turned and went back in, caught the eye of a hassled waitress laden with plates who mouthed an 'okay' at her before reappearing a minute later blowing a loose strand of hair from her stress-reddened face. Mum had booked, of course. Their table was in a curved bay window at the end of the low-beamed dining room. She sat down in the recess and lit another cigarette, blowing the smoke through the open window and sipping daintily on her drink.

She was, she realised with momentary epiphany, happy. Not that it was something she sat around mulling over, but she would have said yes, blinking and wrinkling her freckled nose, had anyone asked. She'd gone to Oxford Polytechnic with no higher expectations than to finish her degree in History of Art, head to London, get a job in a small but perfectly formed dealership, use her looks as much as her knowledge to flog the paintings, filter off one of the young guns she'd meet at a club or dinner party, marry him, settle down in Gloucestershire, bang out a couple of kids and end up running an arts and crafts shop on the high street in Stowe-on-the-Wold. As far as she'd thought about it.

However, in her second year, just after the mid-term summer exams, a friend from the Art College took her to a house party out of town where, around midnight, she had slaked her thirst from an innocuous looking jug of cranberry juice in the fridge. As she drained the glass, a mop-haired bohemian walked into the kitchen and stopped, slack-jawed, in his tracks.

'Something the matter?' she asked in alarm.

'Er,' he said, 'whoops', before informing her that she'd just necked enough liquid acid to, if not actually kill an elephant, at least make it think it was a ballerina.

Near dawn, while she was attempting to commune with the sentient, dolphin-like creatures surfacing through the linoleum around her, the widower from the farm cottage next door burst into the house with a loaded shotgun, enraged, overwrought and hysterical because the thudding sub-bass from the 50k rig in the garden had kept him up all night and scared all his beloved but highly-strung budgerigars to death. Literally. While everyone else, realising the precariousness of the situation, scattered for cover, Sam, blinking with open-mouthed incomprehension, was seized by the throat and taken hostage.

She spent the next four hours bound and gagged in the bathroom, sitting on the loo and contemplating her fate down the wavering black orbs of the shotgun's twin barrels. At some point the realisation of her predicament triggered a kind of mystical experience (or psychotic episode, depending on who you talk to) and she witnessed with complete clarity the nature of the universe – arcane, ancient, spooky, balanced, beautiful and perfect – the insignificance of her Self and the interconnectivity and Oneness of Everything.

By the time the hammers were eventually uncocked and she emerged to megaphones, fifteen minutes of fame and the blue strobic whirl of police cars, she had made a deal with the creative entity responsible for all existence; that in return for escaping the situation with her life, she would dedicate the remainder of it to experiencing, revelling in, and celebrating as much of whatever the world had in store for her with complete, unfailing Trust.

That summer, with the crest of the starry-eyed ecstasy wave reaching its zenith, and its goofy, faux-naïf exponents gurning through the crèche of the late eighties, still a decade from the comedown of the new Millennium, it was impossible to go to the sweat-drenched parties in remote barns amid seas of corn and not drop a pill or two, but, though she loved the melting, merging, horny abandon, wary of possible karmic forfeit, she never took more than that. Never fistfuls, like some of her friends.

And although she occasionally revisited the hallowed halls of the hallucinogenic panoply, she never had the doors of perception blown off their hinges quite in the way they had been that first time, never again disappeared down those twin rabbit holes to emerge suspended in chilly, meta-conscious space.

She suspected the only reason the Road of Excess led to the Palace of Wisdom was because half way along it you gave everything up, and that was wise – the drugs paled, lost their appeal, became a kind of deferred experience that didn't gel with her promise, her deal. And the casualties put her off, the friends who pushed it too far, took too much and were clearly not having fun, not having fun at all, for whom the medium became the message or who ran into one fang-snapping ego demon too many out there in the ether and were never quite the same afterwards, never quite got their pallor back. She noticed a change in their faces, a loss of wry smile to the corners of their mouths, that sunbeamed shine to the eye, and it was this that she most wanted to retain, that consensus reality was just a matter of perception.

In her first year she'd put up with the amateurish thrustings of the occasional suitor – boys, she realised, not yet men – all of whom fitted the loose idea she had in her mind of men she might eventually end up with. Destined for the City, earnest but unimaginative, they immediately step-fell into type and promptly stifled her. She'd initially assumed this was normal. However, since her emergence from her crisis chrysalis as a delicate but magnificently coloured butterfly, sex had proven an arena in which she now tentatively spread her wings. Or rather her legs.

It was supposed to be the Summer of Love, after all.

With men she tended to get what she could from them and move on. Not maliciously, though this might have made it more bearable and easier to understand for the unfortunates who willingly shipwrecked themselves on her dewy shoreline. Nor were her liaisons mercenary, far from it; she threw herself into each with the resolve of a skydiver, always hoping this would be The One. But she knew when to pull the d-ring, usually quite quickly when she judged there was nothing more to satisfy her curiosity and the veneer of intrigue had worn off. The contrast between her tousle-headed, little-girl-lost looks and the licentiousness she expressed in the bedroom, born purely from experimental *joie de vivre*, was irresistible, and the straightforwardness and openness with which she entered and exited relationships infuriated her partners. Rendered impotent, they pleaded, emotionally blackmailed and raged then, in order to protect what little remained of that most fragile of things, the male ego, retreated and went quiet.

Though she accepted the video had been a mistake, she bore the successive waves of winks, whispers and salacious gossip around campus with the patience of an admittedly libidinous saint. She would sigh and put it down to a combination of two things: the hypocrisy of a society that rewards screwing around by a man – alpha stud – but castigates a girl – needy slut – for a fraction of the same behaviour, and that boys simply didn't understand her. They mature later, she reasoned, and though they all said they 'got her' at the time, they'd usually say anything when taxiing for take-off. All in all, though she might technically have left the innocence behind, her inquisitive sense of fun meant she never lost the bliss.

In other areas of her life her newfound faith served her well. She listened to and followed her intuition without becoming wholly subservient to its every whim. She listened to her intuition, weighing it against the practicality of day-to-day life without becoming wholly subservient to its every whim and her well-honed common sense prevented bleating acquiescence to emotional exuberance – unlike her friend Tina, a philosophy student and stoner who got so wrapped up in Fatalism that she didn't bother turning up to her finals.

Sam's coursework improved once she decided that since the Universe had chosen the path of her studies for her, pre-contract, she was obliged to follow it. She looked anew at works of art, the lives of their creators and the evolution of the theory behind them as if trying to ascertain why she personally was meant to be studying them, what message she was supposed to learn from the experience. As a result, many of her observations were startlingly original, filtered as they were through her own freshly honed subjectivity, and she managed to pull the nosedive of her first year and a half into a personal third year loop-the-loop. Her final dissertation, 'The Flow of Form, Influence of Nature and the Sociology of the Post Impressionists', was partly based on her recognition of what she had experienced on that first acid trip – the energy rippling, the cellular melding, the interconnectivity of matter – and she saw it captured perfectly in the pointillism of van Gogh. She even received a commendation for it from her usually reticent head of department.

Now, a week after her results – a respectable 2:1 – and with the non-stop party Wurlitzer they'd triggered starting to derail, she was ready to move on, ready for her first big adventure. There were boxes to tick and only one way, as far as she could see, to tick them; she was going travelling. What other way would best bang open the shutters of multi-sensory stimulation, lead her deep into the jungles of experiential richness and submerge her amongst the fellow demersal explorers she wanted – *needed* – to meet?

She was off to India. With Rachel.

They shared a similarly mischievous sense of humour and impulsiveness so that one often goaded the other on to do things they wouldn't have dreamt of doing on their own, especially in Sam's case: podium dancing at steamy underground London clubs, skinny dipping in the Cherwell on a hot afternoon's punting, hitchhiking ticketless to Glastonbury and bluffing their way in, shoplifting designer shades. In the same year as Sam but on the sociology course, Rachel had taken a year out after grammar school in south London to teach English in Cambodia. Jealously, Sam recognised the mind-broadening effect the trip to Asia had had on her friend and admired the street-savvy wit'n'wisdom she emanated.

'Fuck paranoia,' Rachel had told her during an edgy post-party come down, 'I've got *pro*noia.'

'Which is?'

'The sneaking suspicion everyone's out to help you.' They both laughed.

Rachel had suggested they go off together, and though sceptical at first – travelling with someone else initially didn't fit in with her vision of personal horizon-broadening she sought – she quickly realised the obvious benefits of going with a friend who knew how to handle herself. Besides, their connection was empathetically close, due in part to a steamy, drunken night in bed together – undertaken purely for research purposes – that had left them wet faced, spent and giggling.

'Hello darling,' her mother leant over to kiss her cheek, snapping her back to earth with a start and making her stub out her cigarette self-consciously 'Have you been here long?'

'Just arrived,' she said. 'Where are Dad and Gran?'

'He dropped us at the door then went to find somewhere to park. Your poor grandmother's really very frail at the moment. Here she comes now.' Her grandmother picked her way carefully across the room. Sam stood to kiss her and gave her a hug, shocked as ever by the pigeon-thin frame beneath the cotton blouse.

'How are you, my girl?' Her voice was strong and her blue eyes, clear amid their wrinkled matrix of mottled skin, sought and held hers with penetrative inquiry, genuine interest. Slightly fazed by the sensation that her grandmother could mind-read her innermost secrets, she fluffed the answer with a non-committal 'Fine, thanks', immediately regretting not saying more. The waitress came over to take the drinks orders. Her mother fluttered gaily through the issues of the moment – the hosepipe ban in place since the previous summer, the inexorable march of the supermarket and loss of high street identities. Not her mother's usual style and an indication of nerves; something was most definitely 'up', Sam suspected.

Only twenty when she married Sam's father, her mum, Jilly, was closer to her daughter's age than to her husband's by a year. They'd met when she'd been a temping PA at his London head office during one of his rare periods of leave from the engineering consultancy that had taken him all over the world, sometimes for years at a time, and which had always suited his restlessness, the inner solitude that had prevented him from ever considering settling down until into his forties, until she'd made him reconsider it.

Just back from a difficult, sabotage-beset job overseeing a dam construction in the highlands of Venezuela, John – or Jack, as he was known – had been lean and tanned when they met, full of tales of remote mountain tribes and mosquito-ravaged treks into the depths of the jungle. She was attracted by his worldliness, intrigued by his aloof sagacity and impressed by the economical consideration he gave to anything. In particular she was smitten with his strong, weathered hands.

Jilly's father had died a year previously and she'd acknowledged her need for an older man. He joked about their age gap, referring to himself as her Honey Badger, deliberately getting Sugar Daddy wrong to make the generational point, but her youthful optimism, lissom figure and quick smile had broken through his reserve, shaken him from a life-long reverie of the soul and left him with little resistance. Besides, he said when he proposed, Jack and Jilly Jefferson had a certain ring to it.

Now in his sixties but with the demeanour of someone a decade younger, her lightness, the fey grace of a dancer, kept him from atrophying, and Sam had never been conscious of having a dad so much older than those of her friends. He had never known his father, a subject Sam found she could never broach though she'd tried to recently on several occasions – something to do with a posting to Africa – and when she asked about him her dad wouldn't be pressed and just said, 'Ask your gran, she'll tell you all about him.' Somehow though the occasion never arose, the time never seemed right, as if the matter was off limits.

Her dad stooped into the room and squinted as he sought them out, raised hand and eyebrows in greeting and tacked his way through the maze of tables.

'Hi Samantha,' he kissed her forehead, 'everything all right, Mum?'

'Perfect, thank you, darling. We're about to order.' He sat down next to Sam on the window seat and scanned through the extensive wine list.

'Right, since we have something to celebrate,' he gave Sam a grin, 'I think we'll splash out. Everyone ready?' He had a knack of making adroit snap decisions, in restaurants and other areas of his life, a symptom of unwavering, sometimes overbearing self-belief. He beckoned to the waitress.

The expensive Meaume arrived, her father making a show of swilling it around his mouth before accepting it. Glasses filled, he paused theatrically, tapping his with his knife with mock formality. *Chink chink*. People looked and Sam winced with those unique spikes of embarrassment that a child only experiences with their parents and concentrated hard on the pepper grinder.

'To Samantha, well done on her degree and best of luck with her travels.'

'Happy travels, darling.'

'Yes, dear girl, good luck,' her grandmother said. 'Just do remember to come back.' She looked pointedly at her son. 'It can be quite difficult to stop travelling once you start and I wouldn't want to see you turn into an itinerant like your father.'

Sam smiled and murmured, 'I will.' There was an undercurrent to her grandmother's comment, something in the look she'd given Dad, a fleeting, unspoken shadow. Her mother led the conversation off towards various cautionary tales of medical catastrophe, statistical calamity and the numerous dangers facing two young girls travelling in countries without running water and street lighting, countries with guns and drugs and disfiguring mediaeval diseases, working herself into a future of sleepless nights. Sam went through the reassurance list: she had insurance, Rachel knew what she was doing, Balham was probably more dangerous, she had her open return ticket, promised weekly phone calls, and six months really wasn't very long if you thought about it.

'In my day –' her father began.

'Dad,' said Sam, 'please. You didn't exactly have a "day", at least not one you can hold up as anything like normal, did you? You took off at my age and only stopped because you met Mum.'

'It's different for men,' said her mum.

'But does that mean it should be?' said her grandmother, surprising Sam. 'I know I would have jumped at the chance to see something of the world. Lord knows I had incentive enough.' Again Sam felt the energy falter between her folks and the old lady opposite, an empathic judder. 'But I couldn't and didn't. The world wasn't ready. Society wasn't ready.' She sighed. There was a pause as the food arrived.

'You know the Discovery Channel?' said Sam. 'Their strapline is "Explore your world" – what, from your sofa? I want to see some of it first-hand while I can, before,' she hesitated, this tack wasn't ideal, it usually upset her mother, 'before anything happens that might mean I can't.'

Don't, she thought, mention the real reason for her trip; apart from the call of the wild, she was running, responsibility-ducking in response to her gnawing suspicion that the entire world was out of whack, off kilter, overrun by free-fall capitalism, getting stripped of its soul by corporations and heading for ecological, sociological and political disaster. That she wanted nothing to do with the 'greed is good' eighties ethos for which she felt she'd been groomed, and that, in the pre-Gulf war footing and escalating propaganda of that summer, she wanted escape. This was the wrong time, wrong place.

'Yes, of course, darling,' her mum said, assuming the 'anything' Sam had referred to to be 'meeting someone suitable and settling down', and, touching her forearm, 'and we support you all the way. After all, it's not as if you're going away forever, is it?'

After her meal Sam excused herself and slipped out to the emptying garden for a cigarette, watching the now unflustered waitress clearing tables. Her folks weren't really worried, she told herself. As far as they were concerned it was a well-deserved break, something she needed to get out of her system before coming back and fulfilling the lead-weight but unspoken expectations that they had for her. Sam knew though that this was just the first step on the road less travelled, the first machete swing in hewing her own path through the jungle. She watched the kid's kite, now snagged in a tree, struggling like a butterfly in a web.

'I thought I'd find you here,' her grandmother said behind her. 'Let's take a stroll, shall we,' the proffered arm and lack of reproach silencing Sam's embarrassment at being caught smoking. Sam led her slowly through the tables to the edge of the meadow. By the fence there was a bench facing out across the field and Sam helped her grandmother to sit down on it. They sat there in silence for a minute, and Sam sensed static in the air between them signalling something coming, like impending rain.

'I gather you have been asking after your grandfather,' she said, 'and I wanted to give you something before you go that I know he would have wanted you to have.' Her eyes held Sam's unwaveringly.

'I thought Granddad –,' she started.

'Never mind what you thought, girlie,' her grandmother cut her short. 'Your grandfather, God bless him, was a good man – bright, passionate, beautiful in that slender way young men can be – though I sometimes wonder if I ever really knew him at all, we spent so little time together. Barely two years. I must have been your age when I last saw him. Times were different then, not as liberating – not as *liberal*.' She looked at Sam meaningfully, and Sam blushed. 'We were much more constrained by things you probably wouldn't understand, like duty, decorum and obligation, and couldn't flit about as the fancy took us even though we might have wanted to, and even when we knew the duty to be silly.'

She sighed and took a breath as if steadying her resolve.

'And then there were the more serious repercussions of incurring society's scorn, the wrath of committing some sort of impropriety. Having an illegitimate child, for example, could be devastating,' she paused pointedly, 'and could bring unimaginable shame upon families with certain standards and appearances to maintain, however irrelevant such considerations may seem to you. Families like ours at the time.'

Sam knew her father was illegitimate, of course; she had her grandmother's surname. She waited for her to continue.

'Dear Samantha, how I envy you in so many ways, your opportunities and independence, though looking around the world today I must admit to having deep reservations as to where it all might be heading. Life's all so fast, so transient, as if you can't wait to get through it.' She paused. 'I wish I'd had a fraction of your freedom. Who knows, maybe your grandfather might still be here today, with me. I've been alone for so long I don't know anything else.' She trailed off, gazing out across the grass. Before Sam could speak,

'I suppose all I'm trying to say, if there's anything a silly old fool like me can pass on to someone of your generation, it's this; follow your heart. For the love of God, follow it! Regardless of the mistakes you might make. Because of them – since that's precisely how we learn. Just don't repeat them. Make them, learn from them and move on to new ones. You'll find they get fewer, though beware of making none – it usually means you're complacent, doing the "right thing". And life's too damn short to waste doing that.' Her eyes shone wet. Sam wondered if she was referring to the war, wasn't that what happened to him? Lost in action on some anonymous battlefield? Or had she met someone else subsequently and been forbidden from pursuing the relationship?

'As for your grandfather – I loved him. And no, no one else has ever come close, perhaps I never let them,' she said simply, anticipating Sam's thoughts, and they sat there in silence, butterflies glancing through the slanted afternoon light, the sigh of breeze-shuffled leaves punctuated by the mournful call of a wood pigeon deep amid the lucent beech.

'What happened to him?' Sam asked quietly.

'Pa, your great-grandfather, was a difficult man. A man of his time, I suppose. He never took to Ralph, and when he found a reason, an excuse to stop us, he seized it. When I became pregnant – heavens, the drama – and with your grandfather away, he made sure we stayed that way – separated, permanently, forever. People are capable of great cruelty when they actually think they're doing what's best.' She sighed again, a low exhalation. The day ticked on patiently.

'As for what became of him . . . Here.' From her bag she produced an ancient leather writing case, scored with scratches and stained with shapes like continents on an otherworldly map, and placed it in Sam's hands. 'These explain everything. Look after them, won't you? They are the most precious things to me. All I ever heard from him, though Mother didn't tell me about them until many years later, after Pa had died, and by then it was too late. Far, far too late. I – I wanted you to have them before you disappear off and I never see you again.' She silenced Sam's protest with a hand. 'Do let's be realistic, dear girl. I'll be long gone by the time you get back from your adventures, which is absolutely fine and just as it should be. I want you to go. You must go and I think it's wonderful. I've seen you grow up, watched you turn into a beautiful woman and I'm extremely proud of you, what grandmother could ask for more? Just remember what I've said. Promise me.'

'I promise,' said Sam, her voice quavering. She held the case, the leather warm, unsure quite what to do. She undid the buckle and opened the flap. Inside, its four corners slotted into slits cut into the silk lining, was a faded sepia photograph, browned and curled, of a young girl about her own age, smiling coyly amid the well-tended gardens of a large house, the wisteria-cascaded windows of which she could make out in the background. Realising who it was, Sam looked up sharply at her grandmother, but she was staring into the past.

Side pockets, small pouches, held numerous scraps of paper, what looked like tickets and receipts. The main pocket bulged with its contents. Sam gently withdrew a thick bundle of time-cracked envelopes tied with a ribbon of black silk, each with the identical name and address – her grandmother's – across the front in the same sloped, measured hand. Something else caught her eye. Beneath the pocket, in the spine of the case, tucked into a leather hoop worn smooth with use nestled a beautiful fountain pen.

She slipped it out and turned it in her hand, the blue-black shaft marbled with silvery mother-of-pearl that shifted captivatingly beneath her tear-blurred gaze.

# Chapter 3

*Friday, 1st October, 1933*
*S.S. Apollonia*

*My love,*
*Departed Lisbon much refreshed – I did at least – buoyed by a calm sea, clear skies and brief but restorative time ashore. Perhaps you've already received my previous letter – I hope so, and apologies for my dark musings. Don't let me depress you, my angel, I promise to be more cheerful in future. The more I accept what's ahead, the more I – we – can make a go of it and turn it to our advantage.*

*We soon left land behind, the gulls gradually losing interest or stamina to follow (though they did return for a while as we drew close to Algarve, the southernmost tip of Portugal) and all aboard settling into a strange state of suspension – conserving effort, as if treading water. Literally floating, I suppose. Open ocean can be most disconcerting; surrounded as one is by a distant horizon whose bisection of the world can, with a slight squint of the eyelids when the sea is still and the sky cloudless, reduce it to a flat, two-dimensional plane.*

*The solitude too is a curious thing, poetically treated much better than I by centuries of mariners. It plays odd tricks on the mind – I often find myself staring out to sea for hours at a time, completely hypnotised by the lack of a subject for my mind to focus on or anchor itself to. The melodic beat of the engines further lends itself to day-dreaming – I've been caught unawares by a tap on the shoulder from whoever has been trying to get my attention.*

*We are attended by numerous dolphins, to my – and that of other passengers not yet sea-hardy – unfailing delight. They ride the bow wave riotously and I have counted pods of over fifty at one time. They take delight in launching themselves from the water in spectacular, spinning leaps – clearly playing – and I'd swear sporting the broadest grins – a joy to behold.*

*It could be me alone, or a result of our clowning escort (the crew regard dolphins as a good omen), but the atmosphere on board has lifted considerably, and over the last few days I've made some progress in getting to know my fellow voyagers. Well, those as seem predisposed to my approaches, anyway.*

*Small routines have developed amongst us. I for one have established my own little niche – a wicker chair and low table near the stern in the lee of the aft chimney stack, which is tall enough for both the noise to be bearable and the smoke negligible, and which has a lovely view out over the disappearing line of our wake. There I while away the day, neither mooching nor mooning, but reading and writing – as you find me now.*

*Regular spins around the deck provide exercise and the opportunity to bump into anyone who might like to make conversation. I seem to have overcome my seasickness – perhaps due to fresh air and a calm sea – and my appetite has returned. Breakfast – porridge without fail – and lunch – usually soup with bread – are brought to our cabins if we so wish, with supper forming the social focus of the day and the one occasion we're all together.*

*The Dutch missionaries, having found little enthusiasm for their suggestion of daily prayers amongst this Godless bunch, tend to keep to themselves. We respect silence while they take it in turns to say grace, then the meal is served – typically some broth or other followed by boiled ham or fish or meat stew and potatoes. Brandy helps everything along quite nicely, loosening tongues and broadening smiles.*

*I've had little luck with Dr Richards beyond the purely courteous, and get the impression his reserve stems from something rather more surreptitious than simply minding his own business. Any attempts at the most trivial enquiries as to his background, where he's headed, what he thinks about this or that subject, are met with minimal response, guarded at best. There's a flash of reprimand in his swift glances at his pretty, fragile wife when she speaks, even the most innocuous of observations, while she emits light sighs, quite unconsciously, and during the day spends almost as much time as I gazing wistfully to the horizon. They seem ever so mismatched, dearest – he, tall, prematurely balding, permanently brooding; she, delicately boned and almost elfin, quite ill-suited to the demands of equatorial life, to my mind. Their posting is in Mombasa where he is to take up a position at the new hospital.*

*I'd hazard a guess that the voyage is not entirely her choice – we all have our reasons for making decisions we might wish we didn't have to, do we not? He has been most helpful re my seasickness, providing both his wife and me – his only current patients – with calmatives when the pendular lurching of the ship becomes too much.*

*Not wishing to tempt fate, I think I'm becoming acclimatised to it – certainly my sleep has improved, despite some terrific dreams. It requires all my resolve to get up in the morning, which is fine since there is little to fill the day; few on-deck activities – quoits, boules, cards etc. – although a note went up that there will be a boxing tournament next week, mainly for the crew but 'open to all'.*

*Swaine and McAlistair, self-styled 'great white hunters', appear to be having a high old time. The latter quicker witted and of leaner build, both equally tough looking and both in their early forties and ex-army, they served together in the Scots Guards. They seem determined to keep any ghosts of the war at bay by remaining half cut for most of the day and distinctly cock-eyed by the end of it. Their harrowing tales from both battlefield and savannah, I'm sure designed to scare me silly, are recounted at high volume, and I can tell make Symmonds flinch – his experiences in France seem if anything to have made him more compassionate, if somewhat world-weary. By contrast these other two, however closely bonded by what they have been through, seem brutalised by the whole thing, coarsened – perhaps inured to any levity by over-exposure to death. I doubt that either of them could survive long without the bravado and camaraderie of the other, the mutual understanding and, presumably, the solace they find in each other's company; proof, perhaps, that they are still alive while so many of their friends are not.*

*I suppose men deal with such terrible experiences in different ways – I can't begin to imagine how I'd be affected, nor how I'd fare in the field, and am glad our generation will not experience anything similar. They cheerfully talk of slaughter on a scale that is difficult to comprehend (gallows humour?) whether of the wildebeest and elephant herds that fill the African plains or the butchery of the trenches, where whole battalions were wiped out in a matter of minutes, and seem so hardened to the lunacy of such destruction they can't switch it off.*

*They are both married, extraordinarily; to hear them talk about their respective spouses you'd think they were referring to domestic animals. I have no doubt that their boasts regarding all things carnal are well founded in fact, that their time ashore is spent down insalubrious alleys around the port and that their idea of game hunting extends to the fairer sex. Certainly the metaphors are similar;*

*'had her in my sights,' 'brought her down', 'bagged me a beauty' etc. As Dr Richards muttered, they might well catch more than game on this trip of theirs.*

*S. is punctiliously polite in their company, as if wary of provoking conflict – rather as I am with your father, dearest, though S.'s deference is perhaps more urbane than mine . . .*

*While he is without doubt one of the most surly characters I have ever met, Maddox and I have made some ground; there's a droll sense of humour beneath the grumpy exterior that I'm beginning to appreciate and, dare I say it, I think he's grudgingly coming to, if not like me, at least tolerate my naiveté. I try to be as cheerful as possible and express enthusiasm in all matters nautical while he, in turn, has let slip the occasional sign of paternal affection, always couched in the most witheringly sarcastic terms: 'And is the young master able to tie his own shoelaces today or does he intend to break his neck falling down the stairs', or, when I asked for my shirts to be laundered every other day, 'It is important to keep up appearances, isn't it, sir, even when in the middle of the ocean?' He's been aboard for quite a few years now, like so many others who saw action in the war, apparently unable to return to the pastoral life ashore. His loyalty lies with the Captain, Buchanan.*

*Of the Old Man I've had only the occasional glimpse. A tall, white-haired man with that unnerving thousand-yard stare common to servicemen and mariners alike, he keeps himself to himself – either on the bridge or shut away in his cabin. He doesn't eat with us nor anyone else from what I can gather, and Maddox tells me he is a bit of a recluse. He was second in command on the Britannia when she was torpedoed in '18, not far from here, as it happens, and like the Apollonia heading for Gibraltar. He survived twelve hours in the water while his shipmates, 423 of them, perished one by one around him. I imagine returning to these waters must be hard. When his wife and child died during the wretched influenza outbreak the following year, something snapped; he sold up – everything – came out of retirement and took to sea again, shunning all but the most cursory leave, accepting arduously long charters and avoiding the company of others where possible. Maddox clearly venerates the chap and I can only assume we're in good hands. Many of the crew, he tells me, have declined promotion aboard other more prestigious vessels in order to stay with him and the Apollonia, such is the respect he commands.*

*We're quite the bunch of misfits, castaways and fugitives, my love; each of us, it seems, fleeing our individual ghosts, outrunning our past, seeking some form of redemption or God knows what. Answers maybe, though to what questions, who knows? The aftermath of the war is still being fought.*

*You have to wonder at a God that requires – demands – a conflict in which all combatants share the same belief in Him, worship the same incarnation of his divinity, as happened in our "Great" War. Ten million dying for the same deity! At least the Crusades were waged against a heathen foe – though S. says Islam is, like Christianity and Judaism, rooted in Abrahamic and therefore Biblical origin, mutual monotheistic foundation. The Good Lord must have a dark sense of humour, one that the two Scots perhaps share along with our venerable skipper. Symmonds, by contrast, seems to know something different. There's a sparkle in his eyes, another take on it all, and I hope I can discover more of what it might be, since it seems to serve him well.'*

*Goodnight for now. It's late and my eyes are packing in.*

*I'm with you in all but body and shall meet you in our dreams.*

*R.*

*Saturday, 2nd October, 1933*
*S.S. Apollonia*

*Dearest,*
*This morning we were all drawn to the rail by the old whaling cry, 'There she blows!' from Peck, one of the younger crew members, clearly as taken by the sight as the rest of us were. That said, Kemp didn't so much as look up from his book. At first I could see nothing, then she surfaced, her shiny black leviathan back the size of a London tram, and emitted a great plume of foul smelling spray, the finer mist of which was close enough to reach us. She sheltered a calf some twenty feet in length who shadowed her every movement. We were captivated, the ladies all gasping and cooing and the crew coming over all sage and knowledgeable, 'Sperm whale that 'un,' 'Forty foot if she be an inch', and 'She'll be aiming to dive any moment now, mark my word.'*

*McAlister, damn him, must have immediately rushed below, for he appeared with a vicious looking rifle, one of the heavy-bored .450s they use for bringing down elephant. Anyway, he wound the strap around his arm quick smart and was squaring up his aim while we all watched aghast, paralysed with shock.*

*S. reached him as he pulled the trigger. There was a tremendous explosion just as S. knocked the barrel upwards, the bullet disappearing into the blue. A woman screamed. There followed a tense stand-off between them; McAlister, apoplectic, turned white, his eyes narrowed to slits and his mouth started working as if he couldn't express his rage. S. stood his ground and I could tell from the way he was balanced on the balls of his feet he anticipated a wild swing. Before it could develop further Swaine arrived and pulled his friend back, effing and blinding, and led him below.*

*Buchanan later demanded all firearms be brought to his cabin by sundown, thereby ensuring that everyone knew McAlister to be held at fault – by the skipper at least. While my money would definitely be on S. in an open contest, I wouldn't like to have these blighters bearing a grudge; we have a long way to go and any bad blood is only going to fester.*

*The whale escaped unharmed. I for my part was surprised that with their reputed intelligence she allowed us so close. Had we possessed harpoons she would have been in easy range – an observation endorsed, predictably, by Swaine.*

*She disappeared into the deep with a flicked wave of her tail flukes, not dissimilar to the Agincourt Salute, and I like to think it was directed at our trigger-happy friend.*

*Anon,*

*R.*

*Sunday, 3rd October, 1933*
*Gibraltar*

*My dear Lil,*

*We have reached that strange promontory, Gibraltar.*

*We had been tortuously within sight of land for some hours, the beaches of the Spanish coast with their mountainous backdrop to port; the first glimpse of the African Continent to starboard – no more than an ill-defined, watercolour smudge across the horizon to begin with, but resolving into low, purple hills fringed with the pre-dusk lights of clustered Moorish villages as we drew nearer.*

*We eventually docked in near darkness so couldn't appreciate the scale of the rock itself until this morning. With a day to spend, I took a stroll around the town, an odd enclave of Britannia stuck out here on a narrow outcrop between the two great continents. I tracked down the P.O. in the hope that you might have written and, optimistically, that a letter might have reached here by land quicker than the plodding Apollonia has done by sea. My disappointment must have shown (you always say you can read me like a book) for the Post Master suggested I return next week when the next mail is due. We shall be long gone.*

*The people appear to reflect the history of the place – mixed – some of which S. related over lunch in the main square (at a remarkably accurate attempt at recreating an English country pub, complete with real ale, steak pies and a barmaid I was convinced came straight from the Coach and Horses in Feltham); Gibraltar is evidently one of those unfortunate protectorates which empires seem intent on possessing no matter how great the cost. Quite why baffled me at first until S. explained, patiently, the strategic importance of such a naval base.*

*Phoenicians, Carthaginians, Romans, Moors, Spanish and our own dear nation have all sacrificed untold resources (i.e. lives) to secure sovereignty of this barren rock. Indeed, the barrels of hefty guns could be seen poking out from the cliff above us – trained provocatively on the Spanish mainland. I can't help wonder about the nature of diplomacy and whether it has advanced beyond our cave-dwelling days of who's got the biggest stick.*

*Some fifteen hundred feet high, the peak resembles the point of an enormous anvil jutting skywards. Gulls no more than distant specks provide a sense of perspective, and mill about continually as if unwilling or unable to alight upon it. S. tells me the entire massif is riddled with an extensive network of caves, some natural, others not, extending for miles throughout the limestone. Great halls and caverns that run beneath the sea to the mainland, he says, into which men have entered never to return, despite the best efforts of their friends to find them.*

*The atmosphere here is most odd. There's a tangible weight to the air, something oppressive, hidden. Overrun with servicemen, Army and Navy, the port is full of tethered frigates and warships, like so many massive flatirons, much as it must have been before Waterloo.*

*S. had errands to run so left me to my own devices for the afternoon. Seeking to escape the sensation of having accidentally enlisted in a military 'son et lumiére', I walked out of town and up to the old fort, originally Arabic, no doubt scene of many a battle. From there a path ran along the western flank of the cliff towards the southern end of the rock itself, gradually slanting upwards to what I assumed must be the peak. Checking my watch, I decided to see how far it went.*

*I was soon out of breath and beginning to question my motives, but each ridge kept offering the promise of the summit and I, ever gullible, continued, despite the many deceptions. The hot afternoon air was laced with the smell of thyme, broom, hardy-looking lavender and rock rose, which speckled the shrubbery as if strewn by someone gone on before me. After an hour I emerged on the hog-back summit and sat a while, my hat pushed back from my brow; the panorama was breathtaking, Lil! I felt pinned to the sky.*

*I looked south, out across the Straits into Morocco and the slumbering enormity of the African continent, dry and barren between those areas where irrigation cast shards of green, stretching off into the distance in a hue of hazy blues as far as the eye could see. It seemed deceptively close, as if I could reach out and touch it, and I could even make out the doors and windows of flat-roofed houses across the water. S. tells me desperate men have been fooled into trying to swim it, only to wash up on the beaches of Portugal. They obviously haven't read their Homer. This Pillar of Hercules has the diurnal flow of the entire Mediterranean surging past it, creating vast whirlpools capable of swallowing entire ships, according to myth. Fable and fact always seem to overlap.*

*From my high vantage point all seemed calm enough, but the thought of what lay ahead set my mind adrift. That feeling of transition common to ports infuses Gibraltar more tangibly than either Lisbon or Portsmouth. Maybe due to the oddity of its geography, maybe the overt military presence, but I think more because of the gateway – literal and figurative – it represents; it's the nature of Frontier that gives it its edge. There is an inescapable commitment that follows once one consents to continue onwards from here, from one ocean to another, one continent to another, leaving the familiar behind.*

*A sense of no going back.*

*In the distance the hunched spine of the High Atlas mountains curved away from me into the limitless, indefinite afternoon, leading my eye towards the centre of that vast land, drawing me onwards. Behind me, to the north, beyond the mass of the rock upon which I sat, the mountains resumed their stride up into Andalusia, towards you, my love, and I suppose I finally took the mental step that had eluded me thus far, despite my rhetoric to the contrary. Like a condemned man awaiting the call to the guillotine, I have secretly hoped for some reprieve, that there would be a letter from you saying 'Stop! It's all right, it was just a test. Come home to me'; but then and there I felt as if something turned within me, a cogged wheel, a penny dropping, accepting that I'm committed to this path.*

*Maybe it was an adjustment I knew I had to make – a growing-up process – and by passing through the Pillars my voyage gains validity, becomes a genuine rite of passage.*

*The afternoon was getting on, so I rose to my feet and began to edge my way back down the steep slope, the limestone dust turning my boots white and the treacherous skid of loose stones making progress every bit as draining as the climb up.*

*Pausing some distance above the fort to catch my breath I heard a clatter of rocks from above and looked up in time to see several boulders, some bloody large, careening towards me. I threw myself into the lee of rock to my side, pressing myself close as they smashed past me, leaving a pall of dust and a shocked silence. Poking my head out from my hiding place my eye caught a swift movement up above me. I couldn't be sure through the dust, but I swear I spotted someone – youngish, I'd guess, from his size and agility – leap lightly across a narrow crevasse in the mountain and disappear.*

*Roused by the shock of my near miss, I shouted out at the bugger and began to scramble back the way I had come, but soon realised the futility of it – if he wanted to escape me he could do so easily – and collapsed, cursing and out of breath. On top of my indignation at having floundered about like an ass, I had the damnedest feeling that whoever it was had triggered the rock fall deliberately. Quite why anyone would do such a thing I haven't the slightest idea, but the sensation of being watched stayed with me until I reached the main street below, still mocked by gulls. Very odd.*

*Now, as I finish this off to give to the porter, in the low light of my boarding room – The Trafalgar Hotel, naturally – with a full belly and a few glasses of wine, I feel a little better about the whole incident, if still a little foolish. I'll distract myself by trying to conjure up images of you at Brampton, picturing what you're up to: tinkering away in your room, helping Sarah out in the kitchen, maybe taking a walk down to that glorious meadow, perhaps even thinking of me.*

*You occupy my thoughts continually, my love, go well.*
*Yours ever,*
*Ralph*
*x*

*P.S. Our next stop is Malta – some six days off – by which time I shall in all probability be calling you 'me hearty' and resemble a character from a Defoe novel.*

# Chapter 4

*Pokhara, Nepal. 1990.*

'Whoohaa!'

Serle leapt out into the void, his pale butt stark against tanned legs and torso, arms cartoon-cartwheeling through the air to stabilise his fall, bringing his feet together and his arms across his chest as the impact of the water tightened his balls into his belly and drove the air from his lungs. He scrambled up through the pellucid green, surrounded by bubbles and blinking rapturously at the shafts of light that danced about him, breaking the surface with a shout:

'Awesome, man,' he called up at the silhouetted head far above him. 'Just keep your feet together or you'll get enema'd.'

The silhouette withdrew. It was a hell of a drop, fifty feet for sure, he thought, especially if, like Saal, you'd lost your head for heights.

A figure launched itself out, arced down and smashed into the water next to him. Moments later he felt his ankles being grabbed and he disappeared under the surface to re-emerge spluttering and laughing,

'Better than a coffee first thing in the morning,' Saal coughed.

'Better than being whipped with an electric eel while freebasing crack first thing in the morning,' said Serle.

'Better than having a total body wax, being smothered in chilli paste and bungee-jumping into a vat of amyl nitrate . . .'

'. . . first thing in the morning!' they chorused, struggling for the base of the cliff.

Hauling themselves out onto a ledge of smooth, dark granite, they caught their breath, dog-shaking their matted hair. Two fish eagles beat slowly in unison across the mirror-smooth water beyond which the thick woods and paddies behind the village rose steeply into pine-cloaked foothills and the stage-set peaks beyond, so massive they still looked surreal despite the month the boys had spent beneath their looming presence. Beyond them all, the terrible goddess herself, Sagarmatha – Everest – aloof and austere, 'indifferently beckoning all-comers to test their courage and try their luck with one-in-six odds of survival.

'How you feeling?' Serle asked.

'Good, man, kind of raw though – exposed – like I've just come out of hibernation or a chrysalis or something.' He screwed his eyes into the sunlight, small droplets of water glistening on his lashes. 'Those antibiotics, though – Jesus, I feel synthetic. I guess they must wipe everything out and start again.'

'You sure don't look like any butterfly I've ever seen, that's for fucking sure.'

'Well, that looks like a maggot,' Saal said, towel flicking Serle's shock-shrunken cock.

'Bastard!'

They'd met in Ossendrecht on the first day of their conscription, next to each other in the barbers' chairs as they watched, with corrugated brows, their teenage identities disappear under the efficient mow of levelling clippers. When they emerged rubbing their pale pates, they were handed their uniforms and paired off in the buddy system, thrown together by their alphabetically consecutive names, Saal Jansen and Serle Janssen, and destined to spend much longer than the next two months of training together.

'Guess we might as well finish this off.' In their barrack, while everyone shelved their new lives into numbered lockers, Saal dangled a small plastic bag with a corner full of white powder. He glanced around, 'C'mon.'

They leant their heads back against the cubicle wall and breathed as the rush hit them.

'They don't test us, do they?' Serle whispered.

'Nah, there wouldn't be a fucking army if they did.' Both stifled laughter.

'So what regiment have you applied for?'

'Engineers. You?'

'Same. I heard they have the best postings – and there's the slim chance you might actually learn something that will be useful in the real world.'

'Other than how to stand in line, read a map and clean a toilet, you mean?'

During the limited breaks between assault courses, briefing rooms, stodgy meals and catatonic sleep that was never quite enough, they became friends. Serle, from a comfortable suburb in the genteel environs of Hilversum, and just out of the exclusive Naarden private school where he'd been both gifted at sport and mentally agile enough to keep those that envied him familiar, admired Saal's subversive resilience, born from a very different upbringing on an estate littered with burnt cars and spent syringes, a long way south of Amsterdam's last concentric, murky canals.

Saal in turn liked Serle's arrogance; the way he assumed the world had been laid on for his exclusive enjoyment, where pleasures and delights could be sampled at will, accepted or discarded accordingly.

They reacted to the first few months of deliberate, soul-breaking drilling in similar ways but for different reasons; Serle, as if the whole thing was somehow beneath him, Saal with knee-jerk surliness, as he had to the 'disciplining' meted out by his father throughout his childhood. Orders were greeted with mutual smirks, salutes morphed into single fingers once officers' straight backs were turned and responses were fractionally delayed, just lagged enough to be refractory, to annoy, without being overtly insubordinate but enough to provoke slightly harder treatment for them both from the drill sergeant and, when the punishments were dished out to the division as a whole, resentment from the rest of the guys. This only tightened their bond further.

About the same height, physically they were well matched: Serle, pale blue eyes, Aryan, bigger-boned from superior genes and privileged nutrition, looked stronger, but his natural athleticism was evenly matched by Saal's rangy sinuosity. They pushed each other during training; instructors who noticed it played on it, while those that didn't took it for enthusiasm for whatever mindless task they had been set. As a result they got more from the experience than they might have done had they not met, and thrived.

They found themselves hooning around in 4x4s, APCs and speedboats, orienteering through the forests of Utrecht, camping out under the stars, scuba diving, skiing and abseiling down vertiginous cliffs, and they loved it. When the time came for their week of parachute training they were both keen. The hours of drilling – dangling from harnesses in a hangar, drumming in the 'cut away, release' until it was routine – culminated in six jumps, starting with three static-line drops from 3,500 feet. The banter dried as the plane wound up to sufficient altitude, the door was pulled back and they all shuffled along the wire towards the tumultuous rectangle, time condensing to an indistinct blur.

The instructor thumbed up at the green light and Serle tumbled out into the vortex, snapping out arms and legs to stabilise his fall, craning his head back to check his canopy had deployed without any tangles, then, breath held, he looked around, marvelling at the sensation of dangling, life held by a thread, suspended so far above a suddenly dinky earth.

As he would recount often in years to come, he felt the violent flap, like a flag in a strong wind, and saw Saal plummet past him a hundred feet away, a thrashing mass of arms and legs, scrabbling frantically at his chest. He had a 'streamer', the chute collapsed and trailing like a used condom behind him as he hit terminal velocity. As Serle watched, the main chute detached and trailed limply away, freed of Saal's weight. 'Cut away,' he mouthed. Then out loud: 'Release.' Louder: 'Release!' Shouting: 'RELEASE!'

As if on command, the reserve chute flower-bloomed below him, obscuring his friend from view.

Later he found Saal sitting with an instructor, crying and laughing simultaneously, violent spasms convulsing his body. He wouldn't jump again though, refused point blank.

The mind-numbing discipline became a minor price to pay for such exploits. The interminable grinding tedium of the army's by-the-clock minutiae became more bearable. Serle delighted in the violent belch of an M60, revelling in the mindless, destructive power in a way Saal knew well from his delinquent days of adolescent vandalism. Equally, aspects of the daily routine appealed to Saal: the regular meals, the relinquished responsibility of not having to think for yourself, the novelty of structure; situation normal for Serle from years at boarding school.

There was no active duty – no action, anyway – during the year-and-a-half stretch they'd covered, although they did get posted to North Camp near el Gorah on Egypt's Sinai Peninsula for two months to 'assist' with the ten-country Multinational Force based there, and spent the time scuba diving and getting into fist fights with Norwegians.

Back in Holland a month, their demob date approaching fast and their duty to Queen and Country complete, in a couple of weeks they could resume their lives, and although the incentives to carry on into the regular army were intended to appear tempting, neither of them was that stupid.

'Looking forward to getting back to the slum, *broeder*?' *Saal* asked over the foamy head of his beer, 'to all of this?' He cocked his head to take in the characterless bar they were in.

'Just to getting away from you, asshole,' Serle replied, looking past his friend at a couple of girls at the bar.

'Check out those two.' Saal turned, clocked the girls and turned back with a grimace. Their taste in women, like their taste in music and clothes, remained polar.

'Classy,' Saal said and yawned expansively. He studied his friend.

'What is it?' Serle caught his look, irritated at the dig. Saal never went for the chicks like he did and mocked him, saying that he needed to make up for all those frustrated years at school.

'I was thinking,' he said, Serle raised his eyebrows sceptically. 'We've just spent nearly two years working for The Man, man, we've got some cash and there's no pressure to go straight into careers that we won't escape for the next fifty years, agreed?'

'Agreed. And?'

'Well, what are you planning to do after this? Have you even thought about it?'

'Not really. Take some time off I guess, see what comes along.'

'Well mate, I have a plan,' he shifted to block Serle's view of the girls. 'Eyes front, Janssen, for Christ's sake.'

They touched down in the slab heat of Delhi and headed straight for Pahar Gange, the city's blackened heart, a pulsing den of thieves, con artists, traders and hawkers, a maze of alleys, backpacker hangouts and buy anything bazaars that flooded waist-deep with sewage in the monsoon and listlessly sweated out its soul in summer, to the Navrang, a no-frills dive recommended to Saal by a hash-smuggling friend back home. Six seedy floors arranged around an open atrium, it gave anyone busy cling-wrapping ingestible balls of sticky, pungent, hand-rolled hash, *charras*, from the mountains, time to flush them down the latrine in the event of a raid. It also had a shaded flat roof, somewhere to escape the midday heat and stone out beneath a hundred mewling, scavenging kites that spiralled high above on the thick thermals.

It took them a day of tracking sun-curled noticeboard ads until they had an address in the industrial area of Karol Bagh; Prakesh Patel of Patel Motors, a paunchy Sikh with an oil-stained turban and matching beard, arranged everything with slick efficiency and told them to come back in two days' time when the paperwork would be ready. They spent the time partying hard with two Israelis they met; like them, recently out of the army, unlike them, having seen and done things young men shouldn't have to. When they returned, they shelled out four hundred bucks apiece without bothering to haggle and, after several spins up and down the street, thudded out into the permanent rush hour with matching black Enfield Bullets and face-splitting grins.

Heading north to outrun the rains, they rode close together, taking turns to crocodile one past the other, yelling warnings and keeping a wing-mirrored eye on each other, slicing out to overtake, clipping in tight behind the next truck to a blare of air horn. Senses tweaked to the limit, Serle rode recklessly, bending the heavy bike low and accelerating hard out of danger, relishing the solid gear-shift and throttle, and the fat 350cc blatt of the single cylinder. Saal played it more safely, keeping his speed steady, judging manoeuvres further in advance and hanging further back from truck tailgates. Stopping at a roadside dive mid-morning for shaky cigarettes and chai, they stashed their jackets, too heavy in the heat, and compared notes.

'Did you see that fucking kid in the truck, man?' Serle said, grinning, 'I swear he swerved out deliberately.'

'Yeah man, and they don't move when they're coming two abreast, head on, when there's nowhere to go. I don't think our insurance covers this shit.' Saal ran a hand through dust-stiffened hair.

'What's the Hindu deal on the afterlife, I wonder, said Serle. 'They seem keen.' They laughed.

With their lives so precariously in the balance, they learned quickly. One day Serle misjudged an oncoming truck so it clipped his wing-mirror, the glass exploding into a fine spray of needle shards that Saal had to pick patiently out of his face and torso with tweezers. Then Saal had a blow out at 90 which sent him snaking across the road wildly off-kilter, somehow hanging on, his pulse racing, blood adrenalin-sweet. Serle rode ahead to the next village and returned with a young mechanic who hoiked up his dhoti to squat by the bike and fixed the puncture in minutes. One evening, dusk foreshortening the lingering light, cruising along abreast of each other, Saal shouted out just in time for them to skid to a halt at the lip of a six-foot deep pothole as wide as the road, no warning signs save for the rubber burn marks leading straight off the edge.

Northwards, biking for the sake of it – unable, unwilling to get off, to stop, even for chai – up through the arable fertility of Hayana to Chandigarth, then side-winding east into the lean-to foothills of the Himalaya to Shimla, saddle-backed on its high ridge, and on up through swooping switchbacks, misted vistas and pine-mantled mountains until they reached the steep gorges of the Kulu Valley.

Blasting round a corner, they found the road crossed with plodding cows, their dewlaps swinging. Saal whacked on the anchors, slewing to a stop. Serle accelerated, anticipating their bovine predictability and the slow swing of the heavy horns, aiming to slice between the shit-spattered rump of one and the foamy muzzle of the other. It was very close, and he had to lift one hand from the grip and arch in his ribs as a vicious horn tip drifted under his armpit in slow-mo. He pulled over, pushing up his glasses and turning back to Saal, laughing with exhilaration.

'Prick,' Saal muttered as he passed.

In Manali, at the head of the vast glacier-buffed valley, they drew up, simultaneously cut their engines and stiffly dismounted like Cassidy and The Kid. Panda-marked with diesel, they sucked in the air, clear and cool after the fume-choked road. After cursory research, they shipped out of the hippy-haunted town, up through steep orchards to the holy village of Vashisht, whose old timber houses, open-air thermal baths and vast views they took to on sight. Two months passed by, borne away on the milky turbulence of the Beas River, whose relentless force could be felt in the deep knock of boulders shifting on the riverbed like troll marbles, and the opium they'd take before floating naked in the thermal baths, rain needling their skin, smiles beatifying their faces.

At dance parties tucked away in apple groves amongst the hills they dropped acid with crazy Israelis and ranged around in dumbstruck wonder, elfin girls twirling like demons under incandescent stars, the sub bass so heavy it was a physical thing, tangible, overlaid with organic slitherings and slingshot treble that ricocheted off into the shadow-scurried night and they'd lose each other for hours until morning, when Serle would introduce another liquid-eyed girl snuggling sleepily under his blanket.

One day Saal walked in on Serle mid thrust. The girl rolled off and lay there, regarding him placidly, not bothering to cover up, her breasts slightly sheened as they rose and fell.

'Dude,' he said. 'We need to talk.'

'What about, man?'

'Just meet me at the Shanti,' said Saal, flaring irrationally. 'It's midday already.'

Truth was, the drugs were starting to get to him; the endless chillums, the strength of the dope making him anxious, an indefinable edginess that he couldn't shake. And he'd had a tricky trip, without Serle, mishearing snatches of conversation, convinced they were about him, misreading glances from freaks on the dance floor, reading hex stares into casual eye contact. He'd reined it in, just, pulling it together by breathing deep and letting go and star-gazing and letting his psyche play itself out and accepting accepting accepting until his rationality regained control, but echoes of it still made him uncomfortable. And Serle was starting to annoy him.

The café hummed with low chitchat and the flies that stirred the sweet, joint-oiled smoke, buzzing sluggishly, as if as stoned as the customers. Serle came over and sat down opposite.

'Man, I need to get out of here,' said Saal, searching his friend's eyes for some sign of agreement. 'Let's split to Ladakh. That guy Shane we met . . .' Serle frowned. 'The English guy with the bike who just got back, he says the drive's incredible but there's only another couple of months before the road gets snowed out. From there we can hook round east, out through Kashmir and back down. If we're quick. He reckons the political situation there is coming apart at the seams and it won't be safe for much longer.'

'And that's supposed to be a reason to go? Why the –'

'Look,' Saal cut him off. 'I'm going. If you want I'll meet you either back here or in Dharamshala in six weeks.'

They left the next morning.

The drive was so awesome, so *full on* and so gruelling that Serle quickly forgot the green-grassed pastures he'd left behind, even thanking Saal for snapping him out of it.

Up the valley and over the Rohtang Pass out of India and into Tibet in all but name, where steep-cheeked shepherds and traders stopped what they were doing and watched their passing beneath inscrutable frowns and shaggy yaks loomed prehistorically out of the mist.

Above the tree line and sometimes the cloud, the road roughened to Keylong, sporadic clusters of huts thinning until they reached the remote, rugged town. They spent the night there, made some repairs and bought thick jumpers and a jerry can of petrol for the next leg. At dawn they set off again, leaving the last vegetation – poplars and terraced fields – behind. They rode low to the tanks as they belted through the wide desolation, sometimes climbing up vast walls in a succession of fifty tight hairpins before the terrain opened up again, on through an alien landscape of wrenched rock, rent as if sculpted by giants.

Fording the outflows at the snouts of glaciers, hauling the bikes across washed-out road, they went higher and higher until the 5,300-metre pass of Taglang La where the wind howled through shredded prayer flags and they stopped, gasping at the astonishing view through slits in scarves they'd swathed round their heads.

Increasingly Saal led, lost in the melodic beat of the engine, the flow of the landscape and the road ahead, sometimes having to stop for half an hour for Serle to catch up, lying back on the saddle with his boots crossed over the handlebars. Once, when he could still see no sign down the long straight behind him, he back-tracked to find Serle sitting on the roadside, his knee torn open and the spilt bike twisted where it had fallen.

'You okay, man?' said Saal, dismounting, pushing up his shades and pulling down his scarf.

'What does it fucking look like?' Serle spat on his wound.

'What happened?'

'Lost it on the corner. These are fucking *road* bikes man, they're too heavy, the suspension can't take it, one of my seals has blown, the front brake doesn't work and I'm fucked. The next yak herder I see I swear I'm going to swap it for one. Give me the iodine.'

And onwards. The rutted road, sometimes little more than a ledge with a thousand-foot cliff above them and a turquoise ribbon river far below, took them down deep, sinuous gorges with villages perched on improbable promontories appearing around a bend, ancient irrigated terraces of potatoes, and apricot orchards a shocking green against the greys and ochres of the mountains until, at last, the whooping descent onto the glacier-scored Indus plains and the jubilant, throttle-out roar into Leh.

The gentle calm they found in Leh and the meditative repose of the Ladakhis was in stark contrast to the incessant mechanical labouring it took to get there, the tranquillity of the broad, fertile valley surrounded by its fortress of rock a balm to their souls. In the quiet environs of the Kailash Guest House, set in a wheat field out of town amid a sea of flowers – the air crystalline, their steps light – time was disconnected, days concertinaed and everyone they met had the same slightly spaced-out serenity, as if the world far below had ceased to be. They weren't sure whether the sign outside a restaurant entreating passers-by to 'come in and taste the deference' was a typo or not. It was only the threat of early snows that shook them from their dream, and they reluctantly said their goodbyes, remounted, and rode out onto the road to Srinagar.

They reached Dal Lake in four days, the road log-jammed with army trucks, and spent a few nights on an ornately sculpted house boat, resting and eating, sun shimmering off the lily-littered surface, sending rippling light across the ceiling of the boat and casting perfect reflections of the mountains beyond. But despite the water's tranquillity and the generosity of Amil, their languorous host, the vibe was uncomfortable, uncomfortable, taut, a gunshot late at night and sirens in town, and they bickered. Ducking the problem, neither wanting to face parting company, they cited looming visa expiry as reason to move on; a long, truck-honked, twelve-hour schlep out of the mountains, down the highway to Jammu and along through sylvan Dhualadhar foothills to Dharamshala.

By the time they'd settled into a brightly painted joint in Bhagsu, overlooking steep, semi-tropical valleys that appeared to exhale smoke as mist roiled around them, Saal was impatient to leave.

Back in Delhi with just days left on their visas, they dumped the bikes in a lock-up under Connaught Square and left for Nepal, barely talking, both resenting the sudden claustrophobia of public transport, lost in memories of the trip, occasionally commenting with a 'do you remember' this or that, and the shared reminiscence went some way to restoring their friendship, smoothing over the differences, but though neither of them said it, both realised that the cracks were papered over. Superficially. Thin as Rizlas.

The train out of Delhi took them east to Gorakpur where they crossed the border at Sunauli and, after clay cups of steaming chai in the foot-stamp chill of the morning, jumped a bus to Kathmandu up through steepening foothills and contour-line terraces, along precipitous roads, the rusting skeletons of buses that had gone off the edge strewn far below like the crushed carapaces of beetles.

After asking around, they checked into the rickety Century Lodge on Freak Street, whose creaking wooden balconies and tiny panelled rooms etched with graffiti from decades of travellers – 'Reality takes a lot of imagination', 'Gone today, here tomorrow', 'Rehab's for quitters' – further gave the impression of sanctuary, a sabbatical from their holiday. Cockatoos bobbed in the branches of a huge rubber plant in the courtyard, swooping low over guests' heads at breakfast.

Gradually, the momentum of the bike trip ebbed. They stayed there longer than planned and longer than it should have taken to renew their Indian visas, quickly slipping into Kathmandu's *shanti* pace of life. The dusty, rickshaw-racketed alleys, the bars and bakeries, *thanka* art shops, tour guides and relaxed Nepalis were a world away from the tired, spent country they'd left behind, with its pandemoniac over-crowding, embalming clot-and-cloy heat and the bedlam that assaulted you the moment you left your room.

Days slid lazily by; hanging out with other travellers, swapping tales and embroidering myths, enjoying the one-upmanship they could garner from their six months in India compared to the two-week tourists and Gore-Tex-clad trekkers, taking trips out to the monkey-rampaged temple of Swayambhunath and watching the world drift by from the worn steps of the ancient, pagoda'd palaces in Durbar Square.

This, they agreed through a haze of chillum smoke, was what travelling was all about: one long bar crawl with a changing backdrop. Same pattern, different colour.

When the monsoon rains arrived – solid sheets slit from the pendulous belly of the lowering sky – the streets turned to churned mud and knee-deep rivers, the mountains became wreathed in cloud and the funeral pyres of the burning ghats spat and hissed. After two gloomy days of it they splashed out of their leaking rooms and bussed out to Pokhara.

Arriving at the steamy lake-side heat of the one-time hippy trail's end, puff-eyed and constipated from opium, they dug into a shack bar beneath the spreading limbs of a banyan smothering an old stone plinth near the shore-front. Patient enquiries with the barman elicited the name of a more remote place out of town, and they decided on a recce the following morning. They spent the remainder of the day playing pool and drinking beer with *raksi* chasers, the rains already a distant memory.

Shouldering their packs, they headed out of town along the rust-red track that skirted the shore, curving round through terraced paddy fields lumbered with water buffalo, the bright green hills strewn with poppy confetti. The track swung around a small estuary, reeds poking from water rippled with the dip-flit of dragonflies and the lazy rise of fish.

A kilometre further and they came to a grassy promontory jutting out into the lake. At its end, amid a blaze of rhododendron, squatted Green Lodge, a jaunty collection of low wooden huts with corrugated iron roofs around a patch of thick grass. In the middle, a bamboo lean-to shaded mismatched tables and benches. A path dropped steeply from the spur to a jetty, to which a dugout canoe was tethered.

Finally, they stopped, and rolled a joint. Both unshaven, Serle's hair had bleached white and he looked like a Californian surfer, while Saal had darkened, with the beginnings of dreads, looking more feral, more piratical. They were seasoned now, old hands, blending with the texture of the mountains.

'Namaste!' They turned to see a short, wiry man with a quick smile emerge from one of the huts, his hands pressed together in greeting, 'Welcome, good sirs.'

'Namaska ji,' Saal said. 'You have a couple of rooms?'

'Most certainly, sir,' he replied. 'I am completely empty so you have free choice.'

'Great. I'm Saal and this is Serle.' They both shook hands with him.

'Sal and Sal.' He flashed confusion. 'A pleasure to meet you. Rijul, at your service.' He made a little bow. 'Please.' He gestured that they should follow him and showed them the rooms.

An hour later, having settled into a hut each, had a swim and a celebratory chillum, Saal, in tattered khaki shorts, wandered over to the main house with their registration forms, stoned and distracted by the feel of the stiff, broad-leafed grass between his toes. He knocked on the door, which was opened immediately.

'Is everything to your liking?' Rijul asked as he took the papers.

'Ja man, perfect, thanks,' he said, spacing out gently. 'We wondered if we could get something to eat,' gesturing unnecessarily to his mouth with thumb and three fingers.

'Of course,' he beamed. 'I am presenting my wife, Priya.' At this, a slight, shy girl half his age, dressed in a bright swirl of colour, emerged from the door, bowed without making eye contact and disappeared back inside. 'She is a most excellent cook,' he beamed.

'Cool,' Saal replied, a little unsure whether there was some other, lewd connotation in the comment.

Looking back on it a few days later, he recalled a shiver of fever when he dived from the jetty on that first day, taking it to be the chill of the water, though it went much deeper, a flinching judder down his spine.

'Any plans for the day?' he asked Serle rhetorically, their days already blurring with inertia. Serle slowly peeled an egg and dipped it in the small dish of black pepper and salt. Saal looked away as he bit into it. Something about the way he ate got to him, always had; an indolent, gracelessness, open-mouthed and lip-smacking. Especially eggs, the soft mulch of their dense texture.

'Actually, yes. I thought I'd head into town, get some more smokes, a bottle of *rakshi*, maybe have some lunch and see who's around. I'm desperate for a decent coffee.'

'Enjoy.' Saal called his bluff. He knew Serle wanted him along, and that he wouldn't ask. Something in him, not cruelty exactly, a need to flex a muscle, made him play with his ingenuous, less complicated friend.

'Sure you don't want to come?' Serle asked half an hour later as he prepared to set off. 'There might be some chicks around.'

'No man, thanks, I'm going to chill.' He forced a smile. 'Bring me back a blonde.' It had been a while since he'd been laid, not since two Dutch girls they'd managed to talk into bed months ago in Manali; drunken fumblings in their respective rooms, gasps and groans audible through the thin partition.

Right now though, truth be told, he really didn't feel like going anywhere. He felt the first of the cramps jab at his intestine.

'Okay, see you later then,' Serle said, nodded his wrap-arounds onto his nose from where they'd been keeping his hair back, and set off, sandals slapping on the path.

By the time he returned – just after dusk, and drunk – Saal was already moaning, foetal on his bed as consecutive waves of pain pulsed through his abdomen.

'You all right, man?' Serle asked. Saal could smell the sickly sweet liquor on him.

'Cramps,' he replied, with grimaced emphasis. 'I'll be fine. How was town?'

'Cool. Met a couple of English chicks. One's a fox, man, the other's yours.' He paused, 'You need anything?'

'No, dude, thanks.'

'I'm going to crash. Hope you feel better in the morning'.

Next morning it was worse. Serle brought him water and asked Rijul to prepare boiled rice and vegetables but Saal refused, the thought of food triggering another spasm. They both assumed it would just be a three-day gig. The usual spat of diarrhoea draining every ounce of energy as the microbes flourished through the body, but over as quickly as it came. But it wasn't, not this time. His system emptied itself spectacularly that morning, wrenching his intestine at both ends. Still his temperature rose. Saal tried to think back through what he'd eaten when he'd first felt it coming, scrolled for a clue, but nothing.

By the fourth day Serle was beginning to worry. He sat down on the chair next to the bed and they ran through the options.

'If it's not food poisoning, what do you think it is?'

'Don't know,' Saal replied through clenched teeth. 'Dengue?'

'Could be, but don't you need to get bitten to hell by mosquitoes?' Few had managed to get through the holes in his net, though one was enough to keep him awake, their whine more irritating than their bite.

'Malaria?'

'None in Nepal, too high. What about giardia? You definitely smell bad enough.'

'Yeah, cheers.'

According to Rijul, no one caught anything from the lake apart from fish. In the meantime Saal hadn't kept anything down for days now; long, tearing heaves that felt as though his stomach would detach. Even the Dioralyte Serle fixed for him, laden with minerals and salts, provoked instant rejection. He was becoming delirious. His eyes had smudges of blue beneath them, his pallor grey despite the tan, his face looming spectrally in the darkened room whenever Serle entered, balking at the stench, to mop his brow.

On the morning of the seventh day, after a night of violent shaking, yawing from shivering with cold to kicking the blankets off drenched in sweat, half conscious and shouting out incoherently, Serle panicked, told Rijul to keep an eye on him and yomped into town.

Saal didn't even register his friend leaving. During the last twenty-four hours – it could have been longer – his fever wrought upon him strange hallucinations that swept through his vision whether his eyes were open or closed. He found, in a moment of eerie lucidity, that he could rewind his life as if on a VCR and play it from any moment he chose. Initially the images seemed random, dislocated, flashes of scenes – a concrete stairwell, or avenues with gutters knee-deep in leaves. When he saw a man bent over a child huddled on the floor, cringing, he recognised what he was seeing: his father. He remembered that all too well; the hushed tones of his teachers, the strained, set-jawed guilt on his mother's face.

The visions, at first obscure to him because they were not through his eyes, were from an objective, disembodied angle, above and beyond his perspective at the time. Images flooded towards him and he played with them. Forgotten memories peeled backwards, streaming like wind-writhed veins of sand that flicker and shift across a dune.

He watched himself running headlong down a corridor and down the stairs; stroking a cat while he, as a boy, watched TV; cutting off the blonde kid's hair, then, urged on, going too far and cutting the kid; standing over a jackdaw, its gaping, dripping beak, killed by his dangling, culpable catapult. Flashes of joy and grief. Leaping into the lido in summer. His father's coffin, lowered with steady finality into a hole in the snow. Intrigued, he rewound further to scenes that should have been impossible to recall: an infant cradled in a mother's arms; a spinning mobile above a cot; a bloodied baby, fists and eyes clenched at the rude shock of birth. Everything faded into darkness.

Later.

'He's lucky, your friend,' a German accent. 'Another few days and the stomach is perforating, *ja*.'

'But we had the jabs, man.' Serle's voice. 'The whole lot.'

'Then perhaps he would have had it worse. Typhoid is strange, effects people differently. Where were you two weeks ago?'

'Kathmandu. Why?'

'You catch it through the faecal-oral route. You understand? – eating the shit – so somewhere he had contact with someone having it.'

Saal remembered the drawn, gaunt face of the girl in Century Lodge. Faecal-oral; two easy steps from tap to toothbrush. He opened his eyes. Serle was standing in the doorway smoking a cigarette, the sunlight shafting through the smoke in blue swirls. Next to his bed sat a gangly man with short blonde hair and a neat goatee, rummaging in a red plastic case. He looked down and saw that from his wrist snaked a clear plastic tube that ran into a bag of saline solution hanging from the mosquito-net hook.

'Hey, welcome back,' Serle grinned. 'You had me worried, man. This is Kris. I think he just saved your life.'

'Hi,' Kris smiled at him, snapping on latex gloves. 'You have typhoid, my friend, but I give you a shot and take one of these,' he tapped a small white bottle on the bedside table, 'twice a day. You'll be fine.' He leant across and turned off the blue tap on the drip causing a small swirl of blood to coil back up the tube. Taking Saal's wrist in one hand he loosened the housing and popped it out, eased off the tape and withdrew the two-inch long needle. Saal looked away.

'Thanks,' he whispered.

'They're on their way south, down into India,' said Serle. 'An entire goddam mobile hospital with doctors, in a Unimog, straight from Berlin to your bedside. Tell me I'm good.'

'You're good.' He felt the cold inoculation fill his vein.

'*Ja*, we were just about to leave,' said Kris. 'So. Now we go.' He snapped the box shut and stood up. 'Don't take any more shit from anybody!' Kris laughed maniacally and stooped from the hut. Saal could hear them talking outside, a murmur, while he looked around with new-born eyes. Chinks in the wallboards made bright beams in which flies jinked. He propped himself on his elbows. Beyond the rectangle of the door, the garden wantonly displayed itself in rich, thick colours and the lake shimmered and sparkled in the morning sun. Paradise. Reprieve from death was making his neurons thrill. He lay back.

He knew he now owed Serle. Recently the balance of their relationship had shifted subtly, and this clinched it. Throughout their service it had been he, Saal, who instigated the minor acts of rebellion: breaking out of the barracks and jogging into town for the night to stagger back before dawn, clumsily, noisy, or calling in a favour to get a couple of hookers dropped off near their position. His urchin mischiefery had rubbed off quickly, and Serle had learned fast once beyond the walls of his old school and beyond the reach of his parents. Time in the army had filled him out, forcing him to think on his feet, and now, in the last six months, he'd discovered girls. India too had broadened his perspective, broadened both their horizons, but more so for Serle. Saal already knew the world was big and bad, had been through it all his childhood. Now, while Serle was the hero, the stud, he wanted some peace. Their yin-yang personalities circled each other like planets on opposite orbits. It had been a slow revolution.

Once they were dry, they clambered back up to the top of the cliff and dressed. Standing together, the difference in appearance was all the more pronounced; Saal's shadowed eyes sat recessed in his angular face, his hair was lank, his slack limbs had lost their musculature and his clothes hung loose. Serle glowed by comparison, tanned and fit. He'd put on weight since they'd left India, as if he'd relaxed once they'd dismounted, once the competition was put on hold.

'I'm meeting those English chicks I told you about later,' said Serle, 'if you're feeling up to it.' Saal looked blank.

'Which English chicks?'

'The day you got sick, when I came into town, you were pretty out of it. Anyway, they're still around and I've hooked up with them a few times – when off duty, of course.' A note of martyrdom.

'Why not?' said Saal, 'I need to stop in town to call Ma anyway.'

Serle turned to him, lungi slung over one shoulder, his hands on his hips.

'Call your mum? Dude, in the seven months we've been here – no, ever since I've known you – I don't think you've ever called your mum.'

'Yeah. Well –,' he trailed off, looking away. Suddenly he couldn't be bothered to explain, not even sure himself. Something he'd been through while he'd been sick. He stooped to pick up his shades and felt a lurch of dizziness when he straightened. He was far from fully recovered. The antibiotics were strong, like napalm, wiping everything out, good and bad, with a list of side effects that matched the disease – headaches, nausea, insomnia. His strength was slowly returning as he worked up through food types, starting with yogurt and honey – to rebuild the bacillus in his gut – then fruit, then porridge, then rice and veg. He was nearly ready to start eating meat again. He craved steak. Saliva jetted in his mouth when he thought about it. And Serle had been right,; the leap into the lake had been cathartic, marking the Official End to his Illness, and the impact with the water had sluiced off the torpor like a vigorous Tennessee baptism. He felt purged.

'Ready?'

'Ready.'

They walked slowly into town. Colours were unusually vivid to Saal, his senses so raw he marvelled open-mouthed at the flowers, the butterflies, the smells. Small things. Details. He had a sudden insight into the natural, enlightened, heightened awareness he'd heard Sanyassin freaks talk about.

In town he wandered off to find a phone, arranging to meet Serle at the Lake View hotel bar. Pulling the booth door to, he dialled, giving a thumbs-up to the guy at the desk when it began to ring.

'Hi, Ma,' he said. 'It's me.'

'Who?'

'Me, Ma,' he anticipated the delay, 'Saal.'

The surprise in her voice carried through the static interference.

'Yeah, Ma, I've been sick – in Nepal – no, Nepal, north of India. Yeah Serle's fine, he says hi. I had –' His mind went blank, he was sweating in the closeness of the perspex cubicle. 'Shit, Ma, I was seriously ill with –' He couldn't for the life of him remember what it was called. 'Name a serious illness, Ma, I can't –'

She started listing off: AIDS, malaria, cholera, typhoid . . .

'Yeah! Typhoid,' he strained to hear her. 'No, I'm okay now but I lost a lot of weight and if Serle hadn't found this German doctor when he did it could have been bad. Of course I'm taking it easy, Ma. Yeah, I'll give him your love.' 'What about me?' he wanted to shout. He listened to her, the usual stuff, the neighbourhood was going to hell, what was he doing for money. He smiled.

'Ma, look,' he interrupted. 'I wanted to say – What? No. Yes, I will . . . I wanted to say that, look, I'm sorry for not being in touch sooner. Sorry for a lot of things, you know, when I was younger. I know you didn't have it easy, Ma, and I just wanted to say sorry for being such a screw-up. I think I'm – Hello? Hello? Shit!'

The waiting foreigners in the bureau were looking at him, then away when he stared back. He was dripping sweat now, his head swam. He slammed down the receiver and yanked open the door, grateful for the sudden wash of cool air, and leant on the counter, breathing hard.

The Lake View had a set of wooden stairs running up at one end and a walkway that led along the roof to a solid, black-beamed bar, one of the oldest in town, with a panoramic, 180-degree view out across the rippleless water. He creaked along it, lost in thought.

'Hey, *broeder*!' Serle called out. 'Over here.'

Some trick of the light off the water made her stand out, illumed against the drab upholstery of the sofa. Her mussy hair haloed her head, blue-green eyes shone against her freckle-speckled tan. The way she sat, legs languidly folded beneath her, arms draped, reminded him of a cat. Next to her sat another girl, darker, denser, in a vest and khaki cargos, beautiful but earthily so, not lissom like the other. Serle was sitting cross-legged in an armchair next to them, empty glasses on the table, the littered paraphernalia of dope smoking. Self-consciously aware of his sickly demeanour, he straightened as he approached.

'How's your Ma?' Serle asked, in English.

'Cool,' he said, 'she sends her love,' he replied in Dutch.

'Let me introduce you,' he said. 'Saal, this is Rachel.' He indicated the brunette, who smiled and extended a hand. 'And this,' he paused, 'is Sam.'

She unfolded to lean over the table and take his hand.

'Hi.' He met her eye, despite the clear view down the front of her cotton dress.

'Hi.' She held his. Easily. Amused. He felt the dizziness return and sat down heavily in the chair opposite.

'Sorry to hear you've been sick,' said Rachel, 'sounds like a total nightmare.'

'Yeah, well,' he paused, distracted by Sam's eyes upon him, 'I was lucky to have such a good nurse.' He slapped his friend on the shoulder. Serle smiled.

'He used to have a serious weight problem,' said Serle, 'so it wasn't all bad.'

'Yeah man, thank God you were around.'

Serle had been playing the been-there-seen-it-done-it biker card, half way through an embellished account of breaking down in the mountains. Saal listened in, sneaking glances at Sam, trying to ascertain how he'd been portrayed in the story's weave, whether he had been betrayed, made out to be the one who always had to catch up, the one who always accepted the lit smoke, the one who followed over the barrack wall. But all he'd been was ill, as far as he could tell, and Serle had justifiably milked the caring friend angle.

He felt a surge of fraternal affection, and his mood lifted like the sun-lit gadflies that rose like motes from the lake.

They spent the rest of the day together, dragging lunch late into the afternoon, leaving to walk along the lake front to a bar where they watched the sunset haze the mountains pink in the distance. Saal pulled back from the conversation, partly playing it cool, partly because he was the only one not drinking, and partly because he still felt like shit, letting Serle carry the banter – it was what he was good at – dropping in the occasional one-liner to show he was on it, following, content just to listen, laugh and watch Sam when she wasn't looking. She too seemed aloof, often gazing out across the lake when Serle was in mid-flow. Her lightness was captivating. Maybe, Saal prayed, just maybe she saw through him.

'It's a niche market, I admit, but I believe it would work – just as a one-off.' Serle, loose-tongued with drink, was expounding his entrepreneurial idea for a scratch-and-sniff porn mag.

'It's totally sick,' giggled Rachel, 'that's what it is.'

'Maybe in England, but that's nothing in Holland, trust me, there's some really strange people around with stranger, er, interests than you could possibly imagine.' He leered. Mistake, Saal thought.

'I believe you,' she said.

Serle had lost Sam on this one. She stood up and stretched, the breeze flattening the cotton of her dress to her body. Saal felt a ripple of lust, still prone to the rapturous, renascent effect of his recovery. When she walked down to the water's edge and sat down, her knees tucked beneath her chin, he gave it a minute and then wandered down to her.

'May I join you?' he asked

'Sure.' He sat down next to her.

'Beautiful, no?' he asked.

'Mm. Calm.' They sat in silence for a while, not uncomfortably, though Saal was desperately Rolodexing through things to say.

'How long do you think you'll stay?'

'No plans, really. We've got another two months on our visas here, then thought we might scoot down to Goa for a while – for the New Year – after that, who knows? What about you? Your evil friend said you might head that way too, on the bikes.'

It was a plan they'd talked about. 'Your evil friend', not 'Serle'. Good.

'Maybe.' He said, 'I need one more month, chilling, to get strong again. I still feel washed out, like – not physical, like –

how do you say, like a phantom.' She turned to look at him and smiled. He cursed his English.

'Ghost.'

'*Ja*, ghost.'

'It must have been weird, being that sick.'

'Sometimes, when the fever came strong, it felt like dying, out of my body, you know, but not bad – like you say before, calm – and I could see my whole life like it was a film. It was,' he paused, 'interesting. Perhaps how death is like.'

'Yeah, fascinating,' he glanced at her to see if she was playing with him, that famous English sarcasm, but she continued. 'Did you get the whole tunnel-of-light thing?'

'I had something, I can't say what. But it was movement towards something other, something deep, something beautiful. I don't know. Peace.' He made the v-sign and pulled a face, not wanting to commit to the seriousness of her question. They sat there in silence. He could feel the heat from her body and smell the base-notes of her skin. A shooting star blink-streaked across the opaque sky.

'Make a wish.'

'I did already,' he said, looking at her and grinning. 'And it just came true.' She looked him in the eyes, smiling back. He wanted to kiss her.

'Let's talk more,' she said, 'when you're better.' She smiled at him and stood up. 'Rach and I are thinking of moving into your place tomorrow. From what Serle says it sounds perfect, *shanti*, no?'

'It is, especially when you're not in bed all day.'

'But being in bed all day might be what makes it perfect,' she winked, and sashayed back up to the bar.

A week later, and Saal had never felt better. He strolled up the path from the lake, enjoying the morning sun on his still-wet skin, now tanned, without any trace of his typhoidal anaemia, his strength almost fully returned. Sitting down next to Serle at the breakfast table he grinned.

'Beautiful morning,' he said.

'Yeah, dude, especially if you're seeing it through the rosy lenses of love spectacles,' mocked Serle, elbowing him in the ribs so he spilt his coffee down his chin.

'Fuck off, man,' he laughed, 'you're no better. How's it going with Rachel?'

'Great. She can't get enough, man. I just have to lie there. And get this – she *loves* it in the ass.'

Typical, thought Saal, of him to debase it, reduce it to the purely physical. With Sam it was different, more profound. Their connection, often wordless because of and despite the language barrier, had triggered something deep within him, a crocus germinating in the hard earth of his childhood and struggling towards the light:

He was in love.

Serle aside, he'd never felt so at ease in anyone's company, content just to spend time with her, doing anything, no matter how trivial. Doing nothing. In bed too, the his-and-hers fit felt as if one had been designed with the other in mind. Foreplay rarely lasted long, each as eager as the other to slide together. He'd tell her, with seconds to spare, when he was close and she would slow down accordingly, calming him until she was ready, one hand supporting herself on his chest, the other busy between her legs, eyes closed and head tilted back, tight breasts quivering, before bringing them both to a bucking, dam-bust climax that was often so draining they'd wake up half an hour later, her saliva on his chest and his flaccid cock still inside her.

They had spent most of the week in bed, either fucking or reading, rarely venturing further than the hammock from where she would poke her head over the top to make sure no one was around, then gigglingly tug open his shorts, or to the jetty for a sleep-scouring swim, or the shack for meals with Serle and Rachel.

She moved into his hut barely a day after they arrived. Her backpack still lay disgorged on the floor. He watched, head propped on his shoulder, as she carefully placed a leather writing case in the drawer of the bedside table.

'It was my grandfather's,' she told him when he asked. 'Here, look at this.' She pulled out an old blue-black fountain pen and passed it across to him. Unscrewing the lid, he noticed that the shaft seemed to trap the light, shifting and glowing within the marbled opacity of the resin.

'What does this –' He slid his thumb nail under the recessed edge of the refill lever.

'Don't! You'll squirt ink everywhere,' she said, taking it off him. 'Check this out.' She held up the nib to the light and turned it to and fro. 'See the ink well? It's a tiny heart. Pretty, no?'

'Beautiful,' he said, admiring her face, enraptured by her expression when she concentrated, the way she wrinkled her nose. She caught his look and gave him a wicked smile.

'Okay, okay, I'll tell you all about it later,' she said, putting the pen down and pushing him back onto the pillows.

They had all taken the canoe out two days earlier. Passing aboard a picnic lunch prepared by Rujil, they paddled out across the glittering water to the empty beaches on the opposite shore, the girls squealing with exaggerated terror. There they spent the day exploring like kids, pretending they were the first to discover the coves and jungly clearings, following a stream up to where it opened in a deep pool where they got drunk and took mushrooms, stripping naked to splash around, rendered lustless by the psilocybin, frolicking away the day.

To Saal's mind Serle and Rachel, though close, didn't have nearly the mental communion he shared with Sam. Nevertheless, they made a tight-knit foursome; jokes and observations clicked smoothly between them, silences sailed past comfortably. Contentedly hanging out until late afternoon they paddled home, lungi-wrapped, wide-eyed and happy, the food forgotten until they arrived back, ravenous.

Now a week together had sped past and their visas were running out. Serle joined Saal at the breakfast table.

'We should definitely try and hook up with them in Goa,' said Saal, crunching into toast.

'Yeah, absolutely. Maybe even drive down with them from Delhi. Imagine the west coast from Bombay, man, stopping each night on the beach . . .' he trailed off.

'Awesome. I'll ask Sam and see what she thinks,' he said, standing up, 'and I'd better take her her tea.'

'Under the thumb, dude,' said Serle. 'Never thought I'd see the day!'

'Yeah, yeah.' He walked over the grass and pushed open the door to his hut with a toe, pausing while his eyes adjusted to the gloom. Putting the steaming mugs down on the bedside table, he lifted up the net, sat gently on the bed and slid his hand under the sheet, marvelling at the soft, hot skin, stroking up her thigh to the downy tuft of hair and slippery folds. She murmured awake, parting her legs.

'Morning, angel,' he said, 'I brought you some tea.'

'Mm, thank you,' she yawned, still with her eyes closed. 'What time is it?'

'Early,' he leant in to kiss her.

'Come back to bed then.'

Later that day they all traipsed into town for lunch and so Saal and Serle could book their bus tickets back to Kathmandu.

'*Tikke*,' said Saal when he joined them back in the Lake View. 'Okay. The tickets are booked for tomorrow, early.'

'So soon,' said Sam. 'What will we do without you?'

'I'm sure you'll survive.'

'So, we've been talking, and we're going to aim to meet you at the Navrang in ten days' time,' said Rachel between mouthfuls of *momo*. 'I shall pine,' she rolled her eyes at Serle, who squeezed her knee.

'Yeah, we need a few days to get the bikes running. We don't want any breakdowns with you two on board. It would be like the cliché in the films where the guy runs out of petrol.'

'Except that's when he's trying to pull the girl,' said Sam. 'We're pre-pulled. God that sounds awful!'

'What is this "pulling"?' asked Saal.

'Oh, you remember,' said Sam. 'All this –' She started acting out coy – sighing, pouting, beckoning with her finger, looking away, then shyly back again.

'You did the pulling, if I remember right,' he said, laughing.

'Oh really, let me see: "There are spare rooms at our guest house, you should check it out...", "Are you going to stay here long?", or "I never felt so relaxed with anyone before." Come on! That's almost as bad as "Do you come here often?"'

'Well, it's true,' he said, throwing an arm around her neck and pulling her close to kiss her on the side of the head. 'Come on. It's our last day. We should have a party.'

Much later, well after midnight when the bars in town had all closed, they stumbled back around the lake in the dark, laughing loudly and shushing each other. Arriving at Peace Lodge, Serle unrolled his chillum and they tripped down to the jetty for a smoke. Rachel produced a bottle of Four Kings brandy, essentially industrial alcohol with flavouring, and passed it round.

After one swig too many and a long pull on the chillum, Saal felt the white-out coming like a wave breaking in slow motion upon a beach. Lying back on the boards didn't help – the darkness pulsed, even when he closed his eyes. He was still unused to all-day sessions, his stomach not fully recovered from the typhoid and the antibiotics. He closed his eyes again, causing lurching swirls of oily colour to shift in the darkness. He sat up and the stars spun.

'Are you okay, babe?' Sam asked, her voice far away.

Without speaking, he rose unsteadily to his feet, stamped clumsily along the jetty and started up the path. He felt his mouth swim with saliva, and retched into the flowerbed. She appeared at his side, her hand on his heaving shoulder as the last four hours' worth of food and drink left his body.

'I'm going crash,' he slurred, wiping the back of his hand across his mouth.

'Okay, babe, I'll come with you.' Leaning heavily on her, they slalomed up the path and burst into his hut, where he collapsed on the bed like a felled tree. She pulled off his shirt and shorts, pulled the sheet over him and brought him a glass of water, then sat there on the bed stroking his forehead. He passed out.

He woke feeling much clearer headed, the storm having passed. She was not next to him. Must be still at the jetty, he remembered, swinging his feet to the floor, lifting the net and straightening unsteadily. Outside the stars shone brightly. It was later than he'd thought, the first hint of dawn lightening the sky to the east. In the grey light he could see there was no one down at the jetty.

That was when he felt a premonitory pitting in his gut and knew, intuitively, what he'd find when he pushed open the door.

They were all asleep, a tangle of post-coital limbs, open mouths and rise-and-fall chests, her pale face, innocence-softened in sleep, in the middle of a tanned sea of skin, the shock of the image made all the more vivid through the veil of the mosquito net, a soft-focus scene from a baroque bordello. Or a dodgy skin-flick.

He pulled the door to quietly, returned to his hut and sat on his bed breathing hard in shocked gasps – nauseous, unable to shake the image. He turned on the light and picked up his lock-knife from the table, allowing a vision of stabbing and pleading to flit briefly through his mind. It's just ego, he rationalised, just jealousy. He should go and fucking join them, if anything. But no. His emotion, his reaction, what his heart felt, was pain and hurt and rage. He felt like he'd been knifed in the guts. Fuck them. Fuck them both. His eyes fell on her pen where she'd left it on the table. Holding it up, it seemed to gleam dully. He opened the lid and held it in his fist above the tabletop, nib down, then changed his mind, re-screwed the lid and put it in his wash-bag.

He then packed his rucksack, stuffing everything into it roughly through blurred eyes, pulled on jeans and his boots and walked out. Coming around the front, he stopped outside Rujil's door and knocked softly. After a few seconds it opened.

'Is everything all right?' Rujil asked, half asleep, peering out at the raw dawn.

'No, I have to leave. Can I have my passport? Serle will settle the bill.'

Rujil disappeared inside, returning with the canvas bum-bag they'd put their valuables into.

'Thanks. One minute.' He walked a few steps, sat down on the bank and took out the passports. He tucked his into his jacket, opened Serle's, tore out the photo page and returned it to the bag. Then he took their money and stashed it with his passport. Finally their bike keys; pocketing his, he stood up and threw Serle's far out into the lake where they made a soft 'glop' out of sight in the gloom. The ripples reached the bank where he stood staring into the mist.

He took a deep breath, then went back and handed Rujil the bag, hefted his pack and walked off into the new day.

# Chapter 5

*Wednesday, 6th October, 1933*
*S.S. Apollonia*
*The Mediterranean Sea*

*Lil my Darling,*

*Three days into our next leg and Gibraltar, with its peculiar vestiges of home, left long behind. The sea has been calm, flat as a millpond, and the skies have been an uninterrupted blue since we last saw land, merging with the horizon so it feels as if we float through, not on, liquid; at night the mirage is repeated by the reflection of the stars on the sea, as if we are trailing through a sphere, through space.*

*By day the dolphins maintain their vigil – I wonder whether they're the same bunch; I like the idea that they take it in turns, one group handing us over like a baton to the next until we reach our destination safely, their talismanic duties complete.*

*Sorry to send you these in bundles. Perhaps you should pause between each, staggering them so they give some idea of time passing.*

*On which subject; it – time, that is – seems to be accelerating. Perhaps this is due to the monotony of life on board, the routine and the blurring of days, but S., when I mentioned it to him, has provided various theories, none of which I'm particularly convinced by (possibly due to my inability to grasp them fully).*

*The first, that since the formative explosion ('as recently expounded by Lemaître' – never heard of him myself) first hurled the building blocks of matter out into the cosmos, the universe has been expanding at an accelerating, exponential rate, and time, linked to space, has similarly accelerated.*

*Secondly; that at the end of our first year of life, our sum experience is one year. At the end of our second year our sum experience of that year is precisely one half of that. Now, at the grand old age of twenty, the sum of this year's experience is 1/20th the sum of my life, and so appears to zip past faster. I suspect that it's more simply understood thus: the more we experience, the less there is that is new and stimulating to the senses, ergo less registers and sticks in the grey matter – that said, the days are still racing past despite so much happening beyond my ken.*

*The third, and the one I personally reckon to make the most sense, is that as we get older our mental faculties deteriorate – and so we remember less. Ironically therefore, the older we get the less able we are to utilise the wisdom that our age should bring us! The brain, S. tells me, 'is basically a muscle and so should be similarly exercised' – much as you practise scales to keep your angelic singing voice in shape, my love. He seems to be giving mine a vigorous run up an increasingly treacherous mountain daily.*

*I'm out of my depth.*

*More musings as and when I organise them.*

*Yours,*

*R.*

*P.S. Regarding exercise: In a moment of masochistic madness I signed up for the next boxing bout. S. has tried to talk me out of it, but I watched the last one and it seemed tame enough; they have padded gloves and the referee – Maddox – ensures everyone sticks to the rules. He, Symmonds that is, has offered to teach me a few of the basics, 'enough to make sure you lose little more than your dignity and don't ruin those good looks of yours.' To that end he has me running circuits around the deck for an hour every morning (timing me while he relaxes in a deck chair), and doing press-ups and star jumps like an idiot. First he wants me fit, he says, then he'll show me a few 'tricks of the trade'. The exercise is already livening me up. Most invigorating. He has also been sparring with me, all the while encouraging me to 'listen to my instinct', and try to anticipate his moves; trying to sharpen up my reflexes. I haven't yet told him I was quite handy at school.*

*Friday, 8th October, 1933*
*S.S. Apollonia*

*Dearest,*
*We continue steadily – yesterday embalmed in a peculiar mist that has yet to lift, so disorientating to look into that we all migrated to the mess, though probably to be closer to the brandy than to each other. I have an idea of what it must be like to be becalmed, as apparently sailing ships can be for weeks at a time. While we have the impression of movement from the steady thump of the engine – which I scarcely notice any longer – there is none discernible by looking out to sea. Sound is deadened also, even the bow splash muted anywhere but above the prow itself. Very unnerving. We might as well be drifting in cloud. My faith in Buchanan's navigation remains firm, since should we encounter another vessel in this fog, evasion would be unlikely. What other buoy do we have around which to tether our fears?*

*Yesterday on deck, approaching the stern, I heard the sound of a woman crying. I was unable to make out anything in the fog, and whoever it was must have heard me – the sobbing stopped and I heard light footsteps quickly recede. One of the missionaries, perhaps?*

*I trust you are keeping busy, my love, occupying your days and not wistfully whiling away the hours as winter approaches – I remember how bleak Brampton can be as the nights draw in; the monochrome of the bare hills and deadened woods. By contrast, S. (I know he's trying to keep me distracted) tells me the Equator suffers from a listless malaise, a torpor that he attributes to the total lack of seasonal change; dawn arrives soon after six and dusk soon after seven with such constancy that the natives begin their time-keeping at the moment the sun cracks the horizon – seven in the morning they call one, and their dusk they call twelve. The temperature remains a relatively constant 'blistering', apparently, though there are monsoon deluges that create floods of biblical proportions. He claims to miss the rhythm of the English weather, the traditions celebrating the annual festivals, 'the cycle of nature'. I say all this as consolation, sweet angel – as sure as spring will follow Easter, as sure as life will return to the earth, thawing and drawing the sap to the trees once more, so will I return to you.*

*He spoke at length about the Cycle of Life: the course of birth, life, decline and death, as evidenced in nature and our own lives, like a heartbeat of the earth, inexorable as day following night, and yet finite. Even the theory that solar systems, stars and galaxies come and go over countless millennia. Possibly even the universe itself, according to Symmonds. An explosive birth, growing expansion as if maturing into adulthood, then peaking and dying to collapse in upon itself, only to be reborn once again. A great, ponderous heartbeat over unimaginably vast periods of time.*

*Just thinking about all this knocks me out quicker than the sleeping pills. I hope I have retained your interest, dearest. My point is that our plight, while of huge importance to you and me, is of little concern to the universe. As Symmonds said, 'It's not the end of the world', before collapsing in paroxysms of laughter (we had been drinking). These talks with S. make the hours fly by – he is very patient and proving a good friend.*

*Yours, ever,*

*R.*

*P.S. You will laugh at this – the riddle of the rock fall has been solved: There lives on Gib a species of tail-less macaque, the Barbary ape, though quite how it got there is still a bit of a zoological puzzle, by all accounts. It must have been one of these blighters I saw – I hope you find this news as entertaining as Maddox did.*

*Sunday, 10th October, 1933*
*S.S. Apollonia*

*My love,*

*Little to report since I last wrote.*

*The cloying mist, which after two days had cast a somewhat dour mood on all aboard, finally lifted, and with it the gloom that had settled upon the ship. The perpetual twilight itself was enough to drive anyone to drink – which could explain some of the behaviour of my fellow 'matelots'.*

*There have been a few 'incidents', though I rely mainly on what I hear from Maddox, whose confidence I have finally won. Such goings-on are normal aboard a ship on a long voyage, he assures me. After so much time in each other's company, with nowhere to escape to other than the stuffy confines of our cabins, little wonder, frankly. I half expect the splash of someone throwing themselves overboard most days.*

*Aside from numerous disturbances during the nights – shouting and stamping about above decks – meal times have become quite strained. Everyone's heartily tired of the Scots' blue banter; they've already scared off the missionaries and now seem intent on riling the rest. I'm rather entertained though, while I try not to show it.*

*It seems that all is not matrimonially well between Richards and his long-suffering wife. Following some altercation that required the intervention of the good Captain himself – which I did not hear despite my being nearest to their cabin, but which the rest of the ship by all accounts did – she has requested to be put ashore at the next opportunity.*

*M. has implied, without much subtlety, that the reason for the Doctor's flight from England is not as altruistic or philanthropic as it might seem. He has been, I'm told, made cuckold, and recently into their marriage, if not directly preceding it. She, stronger than I had assumed or than she appears, had been perfectly willing to annul their vows and suffer the slings and arrows – for love of the other party – but he would have none of it and, under the guise of saving her reputation, took up the appointment in Mombasa, not for her sake, you understand, but in the interests of saving his own face – apparently it was all over the papers not three months ago.*

*That quote about a woman scorned; I suspect a man would be quite able to raise hell with just as much fervour. And to think I thought our own situation fraught with injustice! It seems Mrs Richards and I are in a similar plight, leaving love behind for an unknown fate, though she has even less choice in the matter than I; a married woman and in the eyes of society the malefactor. Now clearly desperate, she has chosen the only option short of jumping overboard. I'll try to speak to her and offer some sympathy, though the opportunities are few since she's never on deck and rarely looks up from her plate on the few occasions that she joins us for dinner.*

*Later. Late last night in the mess:*

*S., when I brought up the subject, raised his eyes heavenwards and shook his head slowly as if exasperated by my ignorance.*

*'Firstly,' says he, 'one should rarely embroil oneself in the affairs of others, especially if those affairs are of the heart. We only know one part of the picture and, while I applaud your charity, some people are experts at putting on an act to elicit sympathy.' I think that means 'mind your own bloody business.' He continued,*

*'Secondly, the ways of woman are and will ever be a mystery, will always elude man's understanding. Indeed it's our intellect that leaves us floundering, utterly ill-equipped to match or predict their most ostensibly direct mood, emotion, reaction, even chess move. We operate under the auspice of logic.* We men require stricture, the guiding principles of intellectual validity, though the events of the last fifty years might justifiably be viewed as anything but. These are all functions of our governing cerebellum; the left. They, by contrast, and may Aphrodite be praised for it, are *ruled by the right hemisphere of the brain, responsible for the vagaries of intuition, wild mental agility of instinct and the witchy presentiment of the irrational.* They not only physically bring life into being but, since the right hemisphere is that which governs artistic expression, are also more creative. We men, by *reducing everything to reason, often cannot see the wood for the trees.' He poured more brandy, swilling it thoughtfully.*

*'You must understand just how disparate these two ways of thinking actually are; the cycles of the moon, ways of the Earth and the understanding of Mother Nature are much more innate to women, while we seem to regard the planet much as a spoilt child regards a new toy; to be played with until it breaks. If –', he began, then paused and eyed me sceptically. 'Never mind.' He paused again, 'Oh yes, thirdly, and most importantly; never give someone with*

*the means to cause you harm the reason to do so. Our venerable Dr Richards has a chest full of medicines, any number of which could kill you – slowly, painfully and untraceably. He'll clearly go to any lengths to hang onto her so I wouldn't get in his way if I were you.'*

*Well, thus chastised I admit I retreated from any further action. However I am now much more intrigued by his heretical religious and spiritual views, these small glimpses of which are fascinating.*

*I'll endeavour to keep you abreast of developments.*

*Yours ever,*

*R.*

*Monday, 11th October, 1933*
*Malta*

*My love,*

*We reached Malta with a good deal more excitement than previous dockings, presumably due to the length of the leg, our longest since we boarded.*

*Low lying, we were almost upon the islands before any of us properly realised it; the sudden appearance of seagulls our first sign. Dry, treeless hills layered with terraced fields, the highest point is little more than a few hundred feet and it seems to wallow, floating in the water, bare and quite desolate but for the port of Valletta where we 'hove to' around midday. Flat-topped buildings cluttered the sea front, well fortified by the looks of it – once again the military importance of the place seems to have both written its past and sealed its future. S. tells me there are 6,000-year-old structures under water that must have been there before the Atlantic broke through the Straits of Gibraltar.*

*Since then the islands have been crisscrossed by warmongers, merchant traders, pirates and invaders, including Sicilian Normans – imagine – and Napoleon, who having asked for safe passage and the opportunity to re-supply his fleet, promptly turned his guns on his hosts once within the harbour walls.*

*On such treachery are empires built, dearest, and my role as lackey for the incumbent global power is starting to sit a little heavy. As I'm beginning to appreciate, the Company is a sly old wolf in sheep's clothing, created to carry out the political wishes and economic will of the nation; I'm following the footsteps of many a colonialist buccaneer, a flunky to the whim of whiskered ministers, whose dark manoeuvres and machinations remain obscure to their minions. But as you know well, and your father might suspect, I'm not in it out of patriotic duty but simply that it may lead me back to you. A means to an end. You, my love, are that end.*

*The port teemed with a cocktail of nationalities; its importance as a refuelling and supply point for those, like the Apollonia, traversing the Med having dramatically increased since the Suez Canal opened. The usual flotilla of warships filled the harbour, looming threateningly, while naval personnel milled about officiously. S. led me off – he said he wanted to show me something – up the narrow streets above the port to the imposing Co-Cathedral of St John. On entering, I stood there dumbstruck:*

*As my eyes adjusted to the cool gloom the full splendour of the place was revealed. I can scarce do it justice. Built in the late sixteenth century as a shrine to the Grand Masters of the Order of the Knights Hospitaller of St John of Jerusalem – quite a mouthful – who ran the islands as a sort of nation state, the entire floor comprises a marble pavement of memorial tablets, 400 or so in number, to past Masters, each beautifully inlaid and richly wrought with mysterious iconography and arcane symbolism – skeletal Grim Reapers, hourglasses, upturned torches, skulls, swans, heraldic crests, severed heads – like a set of apocalyptic Tarot cards. Inscriptions on each attest to their physical and spiritual duties. The walls were similarly covered in elaborate detail, top to bottom in gloriously gory images of the life and death of the goodly saint by Mattia Preti – a Knight himself – and in the adjoining Oratory of St John was a depiction by Caravaggio of his beheading. Eight satellite chapels signifying the eight branches of the Order also sported intricate carvings that leave the mind reeling.*

*Symmonds, clearly having been there before, stood beside me, arms folded, while I slowly turned to take it all in, I suspect with my mouth hanging open, 'Quite something, ain't it?' he said, then related some of the Knights' bloodstained history; established during the crusades as warrior monks (surely an oxymoron) they had as impressive a reputation for slaughtering the heathen as their related Order, the Knights Templar. After the sudden fall of Jerusalem they withdrew to Rhodes, where they quickly acquired mastery of the seas from their numerous skirmishes with pirates. The Turks finally prised them off in 1520, and they roamed Europe before ending up here in 1530.*

*A six-month siege in 1565 (the Ottomans again) failed, and cost the lives of some 40,000 invaders. The Knights, only 500 of them, held them off, marking the beginning of the end for the Ottoman Empire. Here they remained, building up the islands into a centre for the slave trade and battling the region's marauding freebooters. Then our friend Bonaparte, en route to Egypt in 1798, sacked the island as I mentioned, leaving with anything not nailed down, to wreak havoc for two years in Egypt and Syria. Interestingly, his luck seemed to turn at this point and the campaign ended ignominiously when he abandoned his troops to their fate, returning to France and his subsequent disastrous campaign in Russia. Symmonds, now in full flow, muttered darkly that 'the Knights are not the kind of people one robs like a petty thief' and insinuated that once Napoleon, himself a Freemason, had deceived the Maltese, his days were effectively numbered; the Order wielded spectacular power, quite capable of making or breaking every Royal House in Europe.*

*'How are the mighty fallen,' I said, trying to sound sage, and he looked at me with that same infuriating slight smile,*

*'Oh they're far from finished, my lad,' he said, looking around at the pomp and majesty of the chamber around him. 'They simply operate with less . . .' he paused, searching for the right word, '. . . ostentation.'*

*After that we took a short tour, taking a skiff across the bay to the town of Birgu, where the Knights first settled, and the old fort of St Angelo. Within these massive walls the fit and the wounded, Knight and peasant alike, made their last stand against the Turks, bombarded for weeks from where we'd stood not an hour earlier. As we walked the walls it was easy to picture it; the heat, privation, claustrophobia and fear must have been immense. We climbed to the highest fortifications and sat a while enjoying the view across the sea to the town, had a late lunch down on the shore front, and took in the sights and sounds of the locals going about their business. After that, S. left me – something to do with meeting an architect friend of his – and I didn't see him for the rest of the day.*

*Happy to while away the sunny afternoon, I sat at a table in front of our hotel – Le Meridien Phoneicia, with fantastic views out over the Grand Harbour – then joined Swain and McAlister who were propping up the bar and working their way through its contents, lewdly appraising any local woman that had the misfortune to pass by. Highly amusing at the time, especially after a carafe of wine.*

*Later – slept fitfully that night in the hotel, perhaps missing the engine's constant tone, and dreamt of dank dungeons and the clash of weapons beyond my iron-studded door.*

*R.*

*x*

*Tuesday, 12th October 1933*
*Le Meridien Phoneicia*
*Malta*

*Lil, in haste,*

*This morning there was a knock on my door at the crack of dawn: Symmonds, already dressed. 'Ready?' he asked me.*

*'Ready for what?' I said, bleary headed, more than a little hung-over.*

*'You'll see. Meet me in the lobby in five minutes,' he says, and disappears.*

*Upon stumbling down the wooden stairs, cursing his infuriating secrecy, I was introduced to the lavishly named Señor Ludovico della Rovere – not sure of the spelling – a dapper chap, hair slick with brilliantine, in a linen suit and with a large gold ring on his forefinger engraved with odd glyphs. I quickly downed a coffee and a cognac, and we left the hotel, climbed into a waiting trap and, with a flick of the reins, set off at a clip across the island, the fresh morning air brushing away the cobwebs.*

*Soon we arrived at the southern edge of the island and the prehistoric temples of Hagar Qim. Rovere gabbled away in Italian and S. translated either what he could or what he chose to, I don't know which.*

*This ancient ruin complex, dating back to 3600* BC*, sits perched on an exposed, desolate cliff edge high above the turquoise sea. We wandered through time-worn columns and arched portals, the roofs* *long collapsed, marvelling at the scale of the structures. Huge menhirs enclose apses and chambers with clear evidence – notches in the pillars – that there was another floor above. Archaeologists discovered a wealth of artefacts, including small statuettes to the Goddess herself – unusual figurines with, as our guide indicated in a series of sketches, grossly exaggerated breasts and belly to symbolise her divine fertility. One enormous oval aperture between two twenty-foot-high dolmens symbolises a woman's nether regions (more graphic sketches) that let the solstice sun enter the sanctuary. It seems this great pagan temple has secrets that have been taken to the grave with the shamanic priests who lived here.*

*Our guide then led us on to the Hal Saflieni Hypogeum, a vast network of underground burial chambers into which we stooped, lighting torches tucked away just inside the entrance. The cool of the catacombs was a relief after the building heat of the day and we wound our way down, deep into the cliff through eerie halls, chambers and passages, our footsteps echoing on the old stone. The upper level consists of a large hollow with a central passage and burial chambers cut on each side, some still containing remains of people buried here more recently. The middle level has various chambers very smoothly finished, which give the impression of built masonry – all the more impressive considering the chambers were carved into the living rock using only flint and stone tools. Spiral paintings in red ochre are still clearly visible. One of the niches in the 'Oracle Chamber', as it was translated, has the phenomenon of echoing deep sound spectacularly and, while we rested, S. tried to 'placate the spirits' with a rendition of some Gaelic song or other, the words of which I couldn't understand, their resonance reverberating throughout the chamber.*

*I immediately felt unwell. My breathing shallowed and I suppose my brain, starved of oxygen, played tricks on my senses – the scurry of a shadow here, the whisper of voices in the tunnels there. The flames of the torches seemed to dim, and the words of the song pulsed within the chamber's close confines. I felt my head spin and the walls crowd in on me. I had to get out, Lil, craving open air, and staggered to my feet with my torch, off in the direction from which we came. S. broke off his incantations and called after me, 'Hold on, Ralph!' I shouted back that I needed air and retraced my steps, virtually at a run.*

*Somewhere I took a wrong turn and became completely lost, redoubling my claustrophobia. The flame was barely enough for me to see by. I entered a chamber with signs of recent use; grinning skulls leered from their niches – I swear I didn't hallucinate this, my love – and in shock I tripped and fell, the torch tumbling from my grasp and dying. Now in total darkness I must have blacked out; the last I remember is the fading glow of the flare, then nothing.*

*For the second time since I've met him, I opened my eyes to find Symmonds bent over me. With Rovere leading the way we eventually reached daylight – I gulped it down, the sight of the sea and the sky a sweet relief.*

*S., to his eternal credit, was entirely sympathetic, though I believe I caught the hint of a smirk on the face of his curious friend. We returned to the trap and back to town, I in silence while the other two prattled away as if nothing had happened.*

*Arriving back in Valletta I turned down an invitation to visit the museum – I'd had quite enough antiquity for one day – and retreated to a nearby bistro to write this letter (hence the headed paper) while the adventure is still fresh in my mind.*

*Today, this afternoon, we lift anchor and continue on our way. I'm giving these letters to a young subaltern I met earlier, Ben Nicholson, who's returning to England directly. He'll ensure they reach you personally, since his leave takes him to Newmarket.*

*Later:*

*I took a final walk, a last leg-stretch before the next, long reach to Alexandria, up the vast zigzagging ramparts above the port, enjoying the colours of the orange trees, the birds flitting this way and that, the bustle of people – little things, footnotes to life, trivial I suppose, unless one's going to have them taken away, then they have poignancy. I could feel my eyes sucking in every detail like sponges, savouring each flower, each variation in colour of the stones, every texture in the weave of the dresses of the women, and my ears were tuned to every sound: the bray of mules, birdsong, the clamour from the interior of a dingy house, the shouts of stall holders in the market.*

*I experienced a state of contentment that I've not felt since we left England. I know you will think it the result of the excitement of the morning or the wine at lunch, but it felt like a profound movement of the spirit; a subtle shift in my perception of the world, and one I wholeheartedly welcome. I felt a stirring of understanding for what S. had attempted to explain to me a few days ago when I was complaining of boredom, but that I'd forgotten.*

*'Learn to see the world anew, Ralph, with wonder,' he said, 'since whatever majesty and mystery the world holds for us, whatever we can possibly conceive, is but a fraction – a fraction of a fraction – of the truth. All I can tell you – for now – is that when I let the beauty of the world around me permeate my very soul, I find the quality of my day improves. When I allow myself to truly appreciate whatever vista is presented before me I'm rewarded with a sense of calm and tread a more confident path through the forest. The alternative, all too often, is to hack through it rather as you described in your dream.' With that he became quiet, drawing contentedly on one of his cheroots and gazing into the sunset.*

*Anyway, for a split second, while I sat on the harbour wall, smiling like some kind of fool, I thought I knew what he meant.*

*Just then I spotted Symmonds across the square, emerging from what must have been the museum, Señor Rovere close behind. He shut the door and turned to say goodbye, then they stepped close to each other, so that their right feet and right knees touched. Each took the right hand of the other, and with their left hands clapping their backs, embraced, seeming to whisper – or kiss? – as they did so, quickly enough for me to doubt it. S. then reached into his satchel and gave his friend a thick Manila envelope and they parted, oblivious to my presence. Perturbed for no good reason, I came back to the hotel and packed my belongings – only your writing case, the only object I'd risk my life for were the ship to go down.*

*Now I must leave you, my love, and get this off to Nicholson.*

*I love you with all my heart, my darling. Know that you are in my thoughts constantly. I will send further news from Alexandria.*

*Until such time.*

*Yours ever,*

*Ralph*

*x*

*P.S. My hair is now quite long, to the collar, I've grown something of a beard – which should amuse you – and have become quite tanned, my love – as if I've dunked my head and arms in tea.*

*P.P.S. Also, it appears Mrs Richards is to continue with us – I saw her board as I leant on the rail. She kept her head down, so I couldn't see her face, but I suppose she must have relented.*

# Chapter 6

*Gokana, India. 1991.*

*Keep your eyes open, motherfucker.*

From his vantage point above the beach, leaning back against the sea-sculpted post of the thatched bar, he could see all the way down the shimmering sand to where it rose up the headland and a narrow path wound precipitously around the point. Slender palms swayed gracefully in the breeze, their foliage casting gently shifting shadows along the scimitar shore. Behind the shack, thick jungle wrapped the steep hills impenetrably, while in front, small waves broke flat upon the beach with a patient, rhythmic slap.

From here he could see anyone coming long before they saw him.

He cantilevered his emaciated, six-foot frame vertical, wasted muscles hanging in loose folds from his limbs, the sun-wrinkled skin so dark that the tattoos lacing every inch of his torso were almost indistinguishable, like stains on leather. Gaping snakes writhed up his forearms, fangs and tongues bared at the world. Sanskrit ran from wrist to elbow, while the stalks of thorny roses choked his shoulders and wound down his back. A death's head, cowled beneath the curved blade of a scythe, shadowed one scapular; on the other sat an inverted pentagram crowning the leering goat head of Baphomet. Knotwork tracery spread down his paunched stomach, past the embossed shiny six-inch knife wound and on down into his crotch, beneath the leather loincloth and thong cupping his pendent scrotal sac and cock, to emerge and continue along his withered thighs.

His shins were clear – almost – but the ball of each calf bore an elaborate, multiple-rayed sun and moon respectively. Through all threaded the dark ox-bow narrative and serpentine network of his veins; blackened with sclerosis and irreversibly brittle from thirty years of mainlining black heroin, like rough worm casts beneath his skin. He was running out of sweet spots fast, currently alternating between his toes and the base of his prick. The irony that he might not physically be able to shoot up for much longer and have to stop . . .

– *You mean die, don't you?* –

. . . had not escaped him.

He hooked his leather drawstring bag over his shoulder and swayed into the bar. They knew him well. Tattoo Toni.

*The marked man, ha!*

That was what everyone called him. He couldn't remember when the prefix had become a permanent title but it had stuck. What did he care? As far as he gave a flying fuck . . .

– *You do care* –

. . . he liked it. It went with the territory. Everyone had a nickname: Acid Eric; Blind George, whose girlfriends were always stunning, as if they wanted to escape from what their beauty meant to sighted men; Eight-Fingered Eddie, a natural – kinda – at double bass; Mescaline Bob; Goa Gill; Bombay – or Bullshit, depending on who you listened to – Brian; Myrrh and Mayflower. Only the real bona fide characters, the long-termers, had earned their nicknames. He wasn't just plain Toni; everyone knew who he was . . .

*– You're a feature, brother –*

. . . and although that wasn't necessarily always such a good thing, he reckoned there was a hint of respect in the moniker. Better than Toni the Forger. Toni the Dealer.

*Toni the Murderer. Say it.*

He had changed his real identity so many times he hardly remembered his family name. Anthony Hitzig. Heated. Like the bubbling smack in his crucible spoon.

'*Ek* Kingfisher *ji*,' he drawled.

'*Tikke baba*,' said the barman, Kadal, the youngest son of the fisherman who had built the shack, as he popped the bottle and pushed it over.

'Thanks, chief,' he said, exposing his ruined teeth in a facial-muscle-only smile, a grimace.

*He's laughing at you.*

'Everything okay *ji*?'

'*Shanti baba. Bahot tikke*.' Relax. Everything's okay. The kid's eyes blanked defensively.

'Good. *Acha hey*.' He swigged the lukewarm liquid, belched and wiped his drooping moustache with the back of a black-veined hand, each finger heavy with silver rings inset with semi-precious stones, a lining of gems set into the inside rims where no one would look, then wandered back outside. Sitting back on the log and leaning against the post, he screwed the bottle into the sand and tugged open the strings of the bag. He pulled out a canvas roll containing his works, all he needed, gazed at it, changed his mind . . .

*– For the moment –*

. . . part of him rocking back-and-forth gibbering, whispered

– and lit a Gold Flake instead. On impulse he opened a small, inlaid wooden box and took out a lump of opium, rolled it into a ball and flicked it into his mouth, grimacing at the acridity as he slushed it down with beer.

*You know that's not enough. You know what will happen.*

He'd been around for as long as anyone could remember, thirty years on and off, maybe more, coming and going with the seasons but never away for long. He hadn't been back to Austria for fifteen years and rarely flew out of Asia nowadays. Too many databases and too many photo-fits; not 'Wanted' per se, but definitely 'Detain and Question'.

Hadn't always been this way. Back in the late sixties he'd been one of the original, we-can-make-a-better-world Freak Pioneers, the hundreds of bright-smiled Overlanders who met up in London, Amsterdam or Munich, bounded onto a gaily painted ex-army Bedford ('Peace it together'), beat-up school bus ('Blunderbus'), or converted ambulance ('Ambiance') and hit the road East, joining the old silk route from Istanbul across Turkey through Iran, Afghanistan, Pakistan, Nepal and down into India – to Goa. Where else? Laughing. Skipping.

*But you stopped laughing and you definitely stopped skipping, didn't you?*

On his third run back. Busted in a set-up on the way through Islamabad, before he'd learned to pay off the pigs.

*– Before I taught you anything –*

He hadn't had the $500 they demanded and was locked away where the sun never shone for a year. Longer. Due to some bureaucratic cock-up no one even knew he was in there.

*No one looked, no one cared.*

They got their money's worth though . . .

*– Much, much more –*

. . . and when he came out he was different. Something in his mind had broken, severed. He was never the same after that.

He returned home to the clinical refuge of Salzburg, but his family, already losing their ability to relate to this long-haired, gangly creature espousing vehement rejection of everything they stood for, mood-swinging violently and, late at night, talking to himself in his room, didn't even know him, hardly recognised him, and certainly couldn't handle him. The staid society that he had grown up in and had forged his eagerness to leave in the first place, now drove him, withdrawn, and plagued by screaming, sheet-clawing nightmares, deeper into his fissured pit.

He robbed a chemist's at gunpoint and high-tailed back out to India. The whisper that had kept him going in prison became louder, crowding in on his daily thoughts, snickering, pointing out the compost where others saw flowers, the foolishness where others saw naivety, Satan where others saw Pan, the shadow that defined the light. Only the junk could stop it, rein it in, shut it out, though even back then he could feel the beginnings of his soul's shadow lengthening like a leafless tree's in the afternoon sun. The sun soon went down, and every day turned to night.

Hash runs to Amsterdam and travellers' cheque fraud kept him going until he managed to crack the forging industry – big business in Delhi and Bombay. He quickly discovered he had a natural ability for doctoring passports . . .

– *Aww, you could have been an artist* –

. . . using a freshly cut potato to transfer a stamp from one passport to another, or ironing a vinyl record over an embossed stamp to copy it, or razoring out photos – even, if necessary, down to the painstaking detail of mimicking watermarks. For the right money, about 5,000 US, he could organise a whole new ID, complete with birth certificate, bank statements, driving licence and a home country that would fit the colour of your eyes. He was good. He knew, now, precisely who to pay off and who to intimidate if the competition grew too great, who he could trust in the network – from suppliers of stolen passports to the numerous ex-cons, rat-race refugees and paranoiacs who provided the insatiable demand.

By the mid eighties – his mid-thirties – he'd quit Bombay . . .

– *You didn't quit, you liar, you were told to leave* –

. . . and moved down to Goa full-time with Clara, a French hippy ten years his junior with a similar dependency and with whom he had found reprieve, some shelter – something like love, albeit sexless – from the storm howling inside. Problems shared and all that.

*-Remember how you found her, how you thought she was only sleeping, mottled and blue?-*

But it didn't last, and with her went any reprieve, any chance of loving anything again.

Then it was just him again . . .

– *Always was, always will be, there's no one else you can trust, no one you can depend on* –

. . . in a little place amid the coconut palms up in the hills between Anjuna and Mapusa, ripping off the steady stream of travellers that flocked into Goa's hedonic Mecca. The Devil's Paradise. He was right at home.

Leaning back in the shade he blended into the background, looking like sun-bleached flotsam; anyone glancing across the bar would have double-taken and panned back to check their eyes. He often got that. Despite having more than his fair share of 'distinguishing features', he could, if he wanted, make himself virtually invisible, unnoticeable, by simply willing it. His energy was so depleted it had become reversed, a vacuum, and people, even customs officials, failed to notice his wraith-like presence. He was a black hole from which light could not escape, as if it bent around him, sucked into the pupils of his eyes. He could go days without water and a week without food, sustained by the heroin, supported by it, with a skeletal portrait cracking and blistering in the attic. Like a Sadhu in negative, the junk having replaced his chi with its dark, sliding coils.

It had all been okay until recently. Some slick new *goondas* in from Bombay, rolled T-shirt sleeves, Ray-Bans . . .

– *Armed* –

. . . were on to him, trying to shut him down. The disembowelled dog on his doorstep, revealed in a heavy veil-lift of flies, had been subtle enough warning. So he took the hint, had a quiet, $2,000 word with one of his cop friends . . .

– *Only because you pay him* –

. . . at the station and retreated to Gokarna until it blew over. It was entirely possible the thugs could out-bribe him, in which case he'd have to stay away for longer, maybe for good, but he guessed two grand would be enough *baksheesh* to ensure they were given a bit of hassle for a while, perhaps enough to rethink their patch. Why they even bothered with him was worrying; he was small scale, independent and certainly no threat to their operation. His was a specialist market: gems – emeralds, mainly – passports, liquid acid and top-end hash; Malana cream or this year's *charras* only. Niche requirements . . .

– *So the split peach of a twelve-year-old girl is a 'niche requirement' now, is it?* –

. . . shit that was hard to get unless you'd been in country for years. Things everyone wanted, especially the English and the Israelis, or they needed to go with the old-hand image they were all gagging for, accoutrements that they couldn't get their hands on in the available time they had. 'Ask Tattoo Toni.' You could always find him in the Rose Garden, in the shade, with a good view of the wall door, cross-legged on the harem spread of cushions where you could approach him deferentially, ask one of the scrap-begging courtiers for an audience, and he would 'see what he could do', 'come back tomorrow'.

Gokarna was the perfect fall-back position, the ideal contingency plan. One he had used often before. There were still enough backpackers for him to survive off . . .

– *Like a parasite, sucking* –

. . . but it was off the police radar. Apparently one of countless sacred hotspots dotted around the country, each with its role to play in the Hindu mythological tapestry, the dusty village had the weary torpor of antiquity – even the flies were listless. He had no idea what piece of the story related to the place, and didn't care, but the locals were pious and ignored what went on along the succession of beaches leading off to the south: Kudli, Ohm, Full Moon, Half Moon, Paradise, each separated by a headland and each slightly more secluded the further you walked – fewer shacks, fewer people. After Paradise, the beach curved south into Kerala in an uninterrupted parabola as far as the eye could see.

He was tucked away in Dolphin Bay, misnamed after the porpoises that surfed the waves every morning – Porpoise Bay doesn't work, he thought, though Porpoise Point had a good ring to it – between Half Moon and Paradise, with a freshwater stream gushing out of moss-smothered rocks into a small pool that sprayed the canopy with rainbows. The spring was a bonus, one less thing he had to buy from the food wallahs who walked up and down the scorching sand each day with baskets of fruit, vegetables, rice, dosa, gee, samosas and milk balanced on their heads, calling out to the neo-hippy travellers camping amongst the trees as they approached.

He'd stashed his kitbag in a locker at the station five ks out of town and parked his battered 250cc Rajdoot anonymously off the bazaar's main drag, taking with him only a lungi, a hammock, a couple of thin khadi shirts, sandals, his leather shoulder bag and an old canvas knapsack.

*– They'd never even look, never even notice –*

His . . .

*– Our –*

. . . old camp, his dhuni, lay in the middle of a stand of bamboo and thick bush just up from the fifty-metre-long beach; a warren of tunnels that had been there for years, added to and modified by successions of travellers, open to the stars but shaded during the day, with several sleeping areas, a roughly planked floor in the communal centre and arm-thick bamboo branches sturdy enough to sling hammocks from. When he arrived, there had been a Swedish couple in it, like him living naked (she had been in the middle of smothering herself in pawpaw when he turned up, but he found nothing erotic in the sight of her glistening body) and brightly brimming with New Age good will, but the sight of him jacking up one evening had prompted their departure soon after.

The camp had the advantage of numerous routes in – and out – and invisibility from the small cove, unless you knew where to look or you saw someone slipping behind the boulder that marked the main entrance. The best feature though was the total lack of mosquitoes or sand flies. Usually, he thought, you arrive at a slice of heaven, your own little corner of undisturbed nirvana, scrunch your toes in the sand, marvel at the sunset, then get eaten alive from dusk 'til dawn. Not here, for some reason, even though the beaches north and south were infested. They don't know about it.

*It's a secret.*

Apart from the monkeys that occasionally raided the camp at night, he'd been undisturbed for two weeks.

*Who's this?*

He looked up, narrowing his eyes to slits over his aquiline nose, and saw a figure round the headland and walk slowly down the path to where it met the sand – male, bowed slightly by the weight of his backpack. No one.

*Customer, you mean.*

Maybe they would want some gear, who knows?

*And this?*

Another figure, a girl . . .

*– His girlfriend, obviously –*

. . . a few minutes behind. The walk was a long and hot one at this time of day even without bags, and they were weighed down. Not like him. He could travel light.

*Tourists.*

He had about fifteen minutes before they reached him and this was the last place they could buy a drink.

*You've got plenty of time, do it. Do it.*

He stood and walked up a path behind the bar, turned off and disappeared round a large boulder, the indented back of which formed a secluded u-shape, one he knew well. He spread his lungi on the sand, took off his loincloth and pouch, sat down and took out what he needed from the satchel, lining it all up ritually on the cloth; he took the cap off the needle, sprung an elastic band around the base of his bark-brown cock, tapped a small mound of brownish powder from the plastic bag into a blackened spoon, squirted in lime juice from a small plastic bottle and brought it swiftly to boil with his gas lighter, his hand shaking slightly in anticipation as he stirred it with the needle. Once dissolved, he let it cool, drew the liquid into the barrel of the syringe through a small filter of balled cotton wool, laid his tournique'd prick in the palm of one hand and slowly injected the solution into a vein near the withered fraenulum with the other. His hand steadied as the needle approached the dark vein.

*It always steadies, always does, steadies and calms.*

It was half an hour before he returned but they were still there . . .

*– Told you so –*

. . . sitting at a rickety table, their shoes kicked off on the sandy floor, each sipping on a saccharine Thumbs Up, fanning themselves with laminated menus. The boy had taken off his shirt, exposing a lean, long torso, and looked as if he was regretting the beard in the heat. She was wafting her Hysteric Glamour T-shirt so that, from where he stood, he had tantalising glimpses of paler, swelling skin beneath.

*You're not tantalised though, are you?*

They both stopped what they were doing when they saw him enter . . .

*– Because you look pretty fucking out there, man, like an all-time freak motherfucker, enough to make anyone stop dead in their tracks and wonder who the fuck you are, what's your story, tell me about yourself because I'm not going to believe a fucking word about anything unless I hear it from you and then I'll reconsider everything I have ever heard in my entire life and re-evaluate it all, because you clearly blow everything I thought was normal out of the fucking water –*

. . . and lean languidly on the bar.

'Hi,' he said through the heady whorls that pulsed gently against his brain. He blinked heavily. 'Hot enough for you?'

'Yeah,' she blew out her cheeks, 'too 'ot.'

*French.*

'Too far to walk at this time of day,' said the boy. Germanic. Maybe Austrian.

*Like you.*

'Another beer, Kadal.'

*Good, well done – establish that you live here and that you know the set-up.*

Kadal passed him a beer. 'Thanks, chief.'

*Though how anyone could possibly think you were just on holiday . . .*

'Shush!' he said, out loud.

At this the couple glanced at each other briefly, eyebrows raised.

*Don't talk to me, you idiot, they'll think you're a fucking whack. Cool it. Breathe.*

'You been here long?' the boy asked, trying to be polite.

*See! See! Patronising.*

'A few weeks, but I know the place well. You?'

'Just arrived.'

'I can tell.'

'We biked down from Goa. Man, what an awesome road – that Highway 17 – it's like a river.'

Dutch.

'Yeah – it's a beautiful drive. How were the New Year parties? Good, no?'

'Awesome, oh la la,' the girl said, her accent lilting sexily. 'The best by far was Bamboo Jungle last week: two days and maybe five 'undred people. Crazy!' She rolled her eyes. 'You know Goa.'

*Yes, he knows Goa.*

'But now everything is a bit – what's the word – passed it, hammered, *ja*,' the boy said. 'Everyone has taken too much, the police are getting pissed off and the vibe was getting a little fucking dark, you know what I mean?'

'Ah yes, the come down,' he nodded sagely. 'What goes up must come down, it's basic physics.' He bared his teeth. 'Well, welcome, and cheers. It's the perfect place to relax – chill out for a while.' He raised his bottle and they theirs, three epiglottises bounced in unison. He put the bottle down on the bar. 'I haven't introduced myself – Toni,' he said, leaning over to offer a steady hand.

'Tattoo Toni?' the boy said. 'No way! We heard about you, bro, good to meet you. This is Yvonne,' the girl bobbed her head and smiled, 'and I'm Saal.'

'So, we were sitting in the Shore Bar – packed after the party, everyone still totally out of it – when this cow wanders along the beach, stops directly in front of the bar and kinda goes into a trance, you know?' Saal is animated, high, holding court in the camp. 'No one thinks anything of it, there are fucking cows everywhere. Then someone shouts and points and everyone looks and the cow gives birth there and then! Standing there in front of everyone! Man, people were screaming, clapping, freaking out. Took about fifteen minutes. Most tripped-out thing I ever saw in my whole fucking life, I swear.' They both laughed. Toni winced.

'Wizin 'alf an hour the little fing got up and trotted along after 'iz movver,' said Yvonne. 'Amazing, honestly!' She shook her head as if still in disbelief.

'The owner took it as some kind of blessing on his bar and bought everyone a drink, and the place kicked off for the rest of the day,' Saal said. '*Big* celebration. And that's when we met, didn't we, babe?' He threw an arm round her shoulder and pulled her to him to kiss the side of her head. 'You came up to me and said, 'Holy cow', then fell over giggling. Quite an intro.' She laughed.

Toni was a mass of angles, all knees and knuckled spine, squatting by the fire and stirring an open pan of chai with a stick. Empty tins of condensed milk, bags of tea and sugar and scattered tin crockery covered a raised plank on rocks that made for a work surface. The smoke from the fire, lit blue by the sunbeams, spiralled up into the pick-a-stick bamboo creaking in the onshore breeze.

'Yeah,' said Yvonne, 'and we legged it here, thank God. I was starting to go a little crazy, you know?'

'Stick around too long and you will,' said Toni quietly, face pinched against the acrid smoke, 'eventually.'

*Like you, like you, like you have.* The voice keened.

'A little crazy? You got your ass licked by that pig in that toilet, you mean.' They both grimaced. 'The pig loos, Jesus, that fucker was eager, man.'

'Yeah, you don't eat the bacon in Goa,' he said.

Over the few days they'd been together he tentatively probed them for a potential angle, anything they might want, need, that he could provide. But they seemed content just to be in each other's company – honeymoon period, all shiny-eyed and full of the vigour of lust, love and life.

*It won't last, it never does.*

He felt a pang of spite. He'd had to listen to their lovemaking, the semi-stifled moans in the darkness, once even creeping closer to watch them in the pale moonlight that filtered through the leaves, masturbating to thin emission. They were so young . . .

*– Look at them –*

. . . happy and carefree in a way he couldn't even remember.

*Ignorance is bliss – they know nothing of the world, nothing of how things really are, nothing of sorrow and pain.*

But he did. Saal did.

He'd told Toni, when the two of them walked back to town to get cigarettes, papers and whiskey one morning, anger flashing in his eyes, about how his best friend betrayed him, took the girl he loved just because he could, blowing their friendship away for a fuck. It sounded to Toni as if he was blaming the wrong party.

*It takes two to tango. La-de-de, la-de-da.*

The girl had sounded like a live wire, someone who would leap first then look, justify it as 'living fully in the present' or some such psychobabble bullshit. And women have a merciless set of retractable claws, graphite in their genetic make-up, a cruelty that men can't pull off without guilt-wracked aftermath. He had seen the expression in the face of a Buddha sculpture somewhere. That simultaneous look of infinite compassion yet unremitting, implacable cruelty that few, only the best, sculptors ever managed to achieve, related to the three-fold manifestation of the goddess: lover, mother, crone; creative lust, protective nurture, regenerative destruction, reflecting the wheel of life. His thoughts drifted, hypnotised by the swirling chai. All women possess some aspect of Kali, the terrible goddess of creation and destruction. Men, by contrast, are lapdogs who have long forgotten their true role: to protect, entertain and serve. With forgetting comes desperation for approval, for recognition, for attention, like petulant neglected children so desperate to receive the love of their mother they smash up their toys, in this case the world. He understood. He venerated the goddess still.

*Oh really. How is that exactly? By destroying your body? Let me guess, by emulating holy ascetism and punishing the physical, blackening lung and vein, purging the corporeal to free the spiritual? Immolation? How? Do tell.*

'Toni!' said Saal, too late as the chai frothed over the rim of the pot and hissed onto the coals.

*You're nodding off, you dick, snap out of it.*

'*Scheisse*,' he said, and lifted the pot from the fire.

'You okay, man? You seem a little spaced – even for you,' Saal tried to make light of their host's state but received a quick-fire, dead-eyed stare for his attempt.

'Screw you.' He filled one of the three tiffin cups, stood and walked out of the clearing.

*They're laughing at you.*

He stooped through the bamboo, emerged from behind the boulder and crossed the sand to the shoreline. The lobbed lantern sun dropped towards the sea unimpeded by clouds.

*They're going to give you trouble. Best get them out while you can. Before they make themselves too comfortable.*

They had given no indication of needing anything he had to offer, though they had bought a 3 gram *thola* of *charras* from him.

*Just to make you trust them. They won't be running any gear back home. Too green.*

They had listened to his stories with rapt attention . . .

– *Not believing them, though. Who would?* –

. . . and he had intimated that he could set them up with all the contacts, all the tricks of the trade to make a run profitable, but they were still falling in love-lust, only had each other on their minds.

What he urgently needed was a big deal, a quick, one-shot,

half-kilo deal for five hundred bucks. Or one of his rubies, one of the big ones. Then he could slip quietly back to Mapsua and pick up his stuff from the house, visit Bernard and use the studio, fix up a passport and get out of the country until these *goonda* pricks had given up looking for him.

*Without his beard the boy looks a little like you. Younger, fuller faced, of course, but the cheekbones are the same and the hair is the same. Your accents are even similar.*

It was true they had similar bone structure but he wasn't going to buy the kid's passport off him and could think of no suitable exchange.

*Don't buy it. Take it.*

Returning to the camp to find them gone, he made his way out of one of the back doors, on the coast side away from the beach where overgrown rat-runs led up the steepening hill behind, to where he had buried his stash. He stood and listened for a couple of minutes – nothing – he crouched and scraped away the earth that covered the ply-board, found an edge and lifted it as if opening a chest. The knapsack was where he'd left it.

*Of course.*

He hefted it out. Cross-legged, he tugged open the flap and untied the drawstring neck. Inside lay various canvas rolls and packets. He picked one out, a medical instrument roll surgeons used to use for their scalpels and forceps . . .

*– Yes, let's just have a quick look at them –*

. . . undid the ties and rolled it out on the ground. The pockets bulged like snake bellies. He thumb walked one of the larger lumps up the pocket and an inch-diameter, blood-red ruby rolled out onto his palm and shot shards of pink sunlight across his torso and face. Soon the open roll was littered with stones –

emeralds, sapphires, a scattering of whorish diamonds – iridescent light playing into the leaves above him like rippled light off the surface of a pool, glittering his greed-glazed eyes. Beautiful.

*We need more, though.*

Other packets yielded yet more delights. Glass bottles of liquid LSD; moist blocks of Manali *charras* and Malana cream; sachets of smack; a hundred caps of MDMA and a phial of Australian DMT; ampoules of medical morphine and a dense pad of four thousand Californian blotters. And not just pharmacopoeia: a small, finger-sized ingot of Mayan gold stamped with a resplendent Quetzalcoatl; selected talismans from Tibet, the Hindu Kush, Ethiopia and Central America; a pure quartz chillum that glowed when smoked; a heat-blistered fragment of meteor; an orb of resinous amber with a splayed, perfectly preserved, prehistoric mosquito suspended in its centre; an obsidian blade from an Incan sacrificial dagger. Shit you couldn't get in the Anjuna flea market. He laughed at the thought, rocking slightly on his haunches. Shit you'd be hard pressed to get anywhere. His . . .

– *Our* –

. . . insurance policy. Fifty grand all in . . .

– *More, to the right buyer* –

. . . and all neatly packaged under three kilos. The last parcel was the heaviest. Wrapped in oiled canvas. An old Mauser .35. He unwrapped it and held the gun in one hand, turning it in the light, then put it back on the cloth. Finally, in an outside pocket, an envelope with ten $100 bills.

His dragon hoard lay spread before him.

*Go on. Treat yourself.*

He unrolled the syringes and filled one with morphine from an aluminium-capped glass phial, flipped open an old compact and, peering into the tiny mirror, injected the clean, clear liquid into the side-winding vein that pulsed on his temple. Instantly the earth split, welcoming him as he fell backwards, cruciform, through space with a moan of delight.

*That's better. It'll all be fine, it always is. It'll be fine. Just fine. You'll see.*

*Someone.*

His eyes split and he rolled onto his front to see her, the girl, squatting topless not twenty feet from where he lay, head bowed watching the golden arc pattering into the leafy humus – catching the light much like amber, he noticed – splayed fingers pulling her bikini to one side, the other hand bracing herself on the slope. At his movement she looked up. Their eyes met.

'*Merde*!' the elastic snapped back over her back-lit pudenda and she stood quickly. '*Pardonnez* . . . sorry, I did not see you.' Her eyes flicked left and right to take in the precious spill that surrounded him.

*You know how bad this looks, how fucking bad this is?*

'No problem,' he slurred.

She turned and hurried into the bushes and he rolled onto his back and lay there.

Looking up into the branches above him he saw other, impassive human eyes staring, blinking, straight down on him through the leaves above. He jerked upright, shouting out in shock, 'Yaaaah!'

*It's just a monkey. Attracted by the stones. Relax.*

He heard it rush off through the trees, crash – pause – crash – pause, as it leapt from branch to branch. His pulse raced wildly despite the opiate.

*Not good for you to get that kind of shock. Not good for your heart.*

He felt his pulse throb, spark motes drifted rhythmically across his vision, peripherally edged with electric purples and reds, and he put a hand to his chest, closed his eyes, tried to breathe.

After a while he calmed, the residual morphine smoothing the panic as if stroking his forehead like a concerned parent. He sat up, packed away the stash and placed a large rock on the earth-covered lid.

*She saw. You're going to have to move it all now.*

He walked back down to the camp where, from the orange glow of the cooking fire, he knew they would be waiting.

*She's definitely told him.*

As he entered the dusk-dimmed clearing they looked up.

*Something's wrong. Why are they looking at you like that?*

There was something wrong.

*The syringe. You left the fucking syringe hanging from your fucking head.*

He swiped the white plastic from where it hung, the retracted needle causing a droplet of blood to well from his forehead.

'Just been praying at my temple,' he said . . .

– *Brilliant, but they won't get it* –

. . . trying to spin the situation. But they didn't get the pun and looked away

– *Ashamed for you, embarrassed for you, laughing at you.*

He was getting the fear now, the cold claws of his demons tapping impatiently. He went and sat on a log by the fire but the panic was coming.

*Out. Get out.*

He stood and walked through the mess area and down the tunnel to the entrance, out onto the beach. The sun had set leaving a pale smear above the sea. He walked to the shore and dropped his satchel onto the sand, then waded into the bubbling wavelets that folded towards him across the surface like lace. When the water reached his groin he dived in . . .

*– Feel it wash away, let the sea take it –*

. . . then lay back and watched the stars blink into the blue opacity above him.

*Okay – that was bad, and the monkey freaked you out a bit but you're the fucking boss around here. You're the man. You're the freak that this shit happens to. Where the stories come from. You are the urban myth. A fucking syringe sticking out of your goddam head, man. You couldn't make that shit up. And they'll go back to Pleasantville and tell all their pre-wean friends about this freak loon they met in India. Be cool. We are not going there, we don't want to go there, we don't need to go there.*

Gradually, head back in the blood-warm water, buoyant under the stars and soothed by the lifting swell of the ocean, he pulled himself back.

When he returned, dripping, to the camp, it was just the boy sitting there.

'Oh, dude,' said Saal after a few seconds. 'There were some guys asking after you up at Kudli. Slick-looking Indians. Said they were friends of yours.'

*Whoops. A. Fucking. Daisy.*

'What did you tell them?'

'Said you were here. They said they had something for you. That it was important. Your suppliers or something?'

'You told them I was here?' his already torpid blood stagnated in his atrophied veins. 'You told complete strangers that I was here? You fucking idiot!' He kicked out at a log sending sparks twisting into the evening air.

*Put the fire out.*

'Put the fire out. Now.' He looked quickly around at the

indifferent jungle, panicking. The boy stood and began bulldozing sand onto the fire with his hands. It was extinguished in seconds. 'When was this? What time?'

'Two hours ago, more or less.'

*Oh shit. Quickly. You need to get the stuff and get the fuck out of here.*

'Man, I'm sorry if I messed up. They seemed cool.'

'You have no idea,' he said

*Where's the bitch?*

'Where's the bitch?'

'Hey man, chill the fuck out!'

'Where is she!' he took one stride towards Saal and grabbed his throat.

'She went that way, to our bit,' he choked.

He grabbed the boy's torch and, without turning it on, strode out of the camp, bare feet making little noise, back up to where his treasure was buried. He heard a noise ahead and froze. There. 'Yvonne!' he whispered, loudly. The noise stopped. No answer. He very slowly took another step, then another, edging forward incrementally. He broke a twig, and ahead someone tore off into the bushes, not caring about the noise they made. He shouted out, to give him courage, and charged forward, snapping on the torch as he did so.

*Oh no. No. No.*

'Oh no.'

The plywood lid had been wrenched open and the contents scattered, pale in the torchlight.

*The monkey. It was the fucking monkey.*

He swung the beam frantically through the leaf litter; canvas rolls were strewn amid the vegetation leading off up the hill.

*There, that one. Back.*

He fell to his knees whimpering – empty.

*Almost.*

He felt the pouches. Some, half . . .

*– No, most –*

. . . were still intact.

*No time. Where's the knapsack? Use your satchel. Quickly. Forget the hash, get the stones and the gun.*

He scrabbled among the leaf trash, not caring how much noise he made, and found the roll with the amber and the gold and the obsidian and . . .

*– Leave that, just the gold –*

'No!' he said. 'I'm keeping this one,' and stuffed it into his satchel.

*Okay. Fine. But find the other stones.*

He searched for the loose gems but found nothing more than an opal.

*– Leave them then, there's enough left in the roll. The gun. Get the gun. It's over there.*

He found it, thrown twenty feet away, shining in the leaves without its oilskin.

*And the money in the knapsack.*

He stood and scrambled up the hill where the ape had gone, ranging the torch beam left and right. Nothing. Shit. '*Scheisse*!'

*Come on. We need to get out of here. Forget the money. There's enough stones. There's something else we have to do though, isn't there? Something we need to take care of? A couple of loose ends?*

'No we don't! We can just go. Just disappear, we've done it before.'

*But you need something, remember?*

'But we don't have to kill them, do we?'

*Stop whining and think it through. We need the passport. If they live they'll either end up with the police or the goondas, either of which is bad news for us and probably for them too.*

'So us whacking them is better than whatever might happen to them afterwards? You're fucking nuts.'

*Really? I'm nuts, am I? Remember the last time? How would you have handled that situation differently?*

'Just shut the fuck up.'

*Best thing to do would be to hit them with a big dose. Big enough. That way the pigs will think they just OD'd.*

'Both of them overdosing together? You're losing it.'

*Could have been a bad batch.*

'That they'll assume I sold them!'

*Shoot them. They'll think the goonda did it. We'll go south to Sri Lanka, across to Colombo, get a flight to Bangkok or Hong Kong from there. Forget going back to Goa. This shit has got way out of control and I guarantee you can travel on the kid's passport. Trust me. I'll look after you.*

With his senses straining, he walked back into the camp. They were there, huddled together whispering. They looked up as he appeared and their mouths fell open simultaneously when they saw the gun.

*She's going to scream.*

He strode forward and hit her hard across the face with the gun, turning quickly to point it at Saal as he tried to stand and as she collapsed, hands to her head, gasping strangely.

'Sit down and don't make a sound.'

Saal sat down and leant over her prone, heaving body.

'What the fuck are you doing, man?' he said, fear in his voice.

'Shut up and you'll both be fine. Now get your passport and your money.'

*Quickly.*

'If you screw me around I'll hurt her more.' Saal scrambled to his feet and out of the clearing. Toni could hear him rustling through their bags beyond the bamboo. He returned clutching a money belt. Toni gestured for it impatiently.

*Check it.*

He unzipped the belt and shone the torch into it. Two passports, a wad of rupees, travellers' cheques, some dollars . . .

*– Not enough –*

. . . and something else. He fished in with his free fingers and pulled out a pen . . .

*– Old by the look of it, expensive, take it –*

. . . its shaft and cap opalescent in the torchlight. He dropped it back in the belt and zipped it shut.

*Someone's coming. On the beach – voices. We need to get the fuck out of here right now.*

# Chapter 7

*Thursday, 14th October 1933*
*S.S. Apollonia*
*The Med*

*Dear Lil,*
*I try to picture you and how you might be occupying yourself; I create lengthy conversations with you in my head and often catch myself actually talking to your photograph out loud. This has raised Maddox's (heavy) brow on one occasion – he knocked to ask if everything was all right – first sign of madness and all. I don't care, particularly, what anyone thinks. Let them think me mad.*

*I imagine I'm taking the picture, you standing there in the garden – how glorious that summer setting seems to me now in this heat – as you fuss about your hair and the appropriate expression you should adopt for the captured moment; you have managed 'demure' with the ease of an actress, my darling, and while you might convince others, I know that you are far from it when it suits you!*

*I do love your scorn for convention, and I know how this must stifle you, and long to somehow provide the means, the platform if you like, from which you can make a stand and shout from your soapbox. You can depend on my support, of course. S. has been enlightening me further as to the role of the male of the species and tells me it is 'to protect, entertain and support' – no more than this, we have simply forgotten it.*

*'Women,' he says, 'are the natural custodians of the earth, and under their auspice – which our entire history has been until the last two thousand years of patriarchal religion – there existed a balance and harmony with our environment that we've lost. Admittedly there was often a need for difficult and brutal decisions; if it ensured the survival of the community, infanticide was not uncommon. But better that than the ruthless expansion of humanity at the expense of every resource that supports us and of every form of life that in some way overlaps with or intrudes on a resource we require. Make no mistake, whenever there is competition between man and nature, nature will lose. Temporarily, at least. It's a short-sighted ambition and one ultimately doomed to fail, since we depend on her for our existence. They knew this, the Ancients, and lived in general under principles of respect and reverence for the earth, which they regarded as their mother. Now the gods are of a more economic bent, requiring devotion weighed in gold, land and power. And just look,' he said, his eyes fiery, 'what we've done in the brief millennia since Christ and Mohammed laid down their doctrines; we've achieved nothing but destruction and waged nothing but war, pitting one religion against the other for the sake of power and wealth and control. Would women start wars over anything but the protection of their offspring, the safeguarding of the resources that sustain their families? They would not.'*

*Here I threw in one word, 'Boudicca', but he brushed it off, saying she was no more than defender of her tribe, the Icene, provoked into war by the rape of her daughters by the Romans – itself an act laden with metaphor; their patriarchy versus Icene heathenism – who sought only the sanctity of her land, not the domination of another's. And that if women are to retake control of the reins, crucial to our survival so far as he can tell, 'there will be a time when they must assume the aggressive characteristics of men'.*

*This would have pleased you, my love; your championing of your Mrs Pankhurst and your determination to vote when you're twenty -one, however your Pa might feel about it. But imagine the woman to take on Macdonald. Or Lloyd George. Fearsome indeed. Promise me your interest in politics will end at the ballot box – I'd hate to be married to such a girl and would probably retreat to the bottle.*

*He continued, 'Obviously women are the real progenitors of life, and our "input" minimal – an act not in itself worthy of particular skill or prowess, as I am sure you well appreciate,' – I hope he failed to notice my embarrassment – 'It was, was it not, Eve not Adam who ate first from the Tree of Knowledge?' (a piece of 'propaganda' which he regards as 'the tyre iron with which the church levered heathenism from the rim of popular belief to replace it with their heavier tread'); 'they are innately connected to the earth and the seasons in a way men can never be.'*

*I'm sure you will appreciate this distinction, Miss Jefferson, my Valkyrie!*

*As for your – our – one delicious display of impropriety, thank God for it! The memory is as fresh as the day itself. The reckless abandon, it's all so clear to me, even here; that look in your eyes, as if you were profoundly sad, a look of such deep grief that I had to ask if you were all right, do you remember?*

*'Happier than I had ever dreamed possible,' you replied, then started crying. La petite mort indeed! You do have a propensity for the dramatic, dearest, just one of the many reasons I love you. You feel more than most, my love, testament to your sensitivity.*

*I by contrast often feel bereft of affection, emotionally numb – at least I did until you awoke me, coaxing my heart into flame as if blowing on an ember. I suppose not knowing what I've missed makes it bearable. It's a credit to your upbringing that you're as full, rounded and well-balanced a character as you are. What a fine mother you'll make (there I go again – bringing the subject back to procreation. God, how will I last a year?).*

*You lie with me when I sleep, walk with me as I go about my day, and are in my thoughts continually,*

*Ralph*

*x*

*Friday, 15th October 1933*

*My love,*

*We had another storm yesterday that lasted the night. Maddox made some quip re my ability to keep my food down under such conditions – 'Bed pan as full as the bilges, sir?' – and I was pleased to prove him wrong. I must be adapting to life at sea after all.*

*The air this morning had that same rinsed feel, so refreshing after the mounting humidity of the last few days – crisp. Even Mrs Richards seemed brighter. She made an unusual appearance at breakfast and again at lunch, amiably chatting about this and that, even laughing gaily at a remark I made about the prevalence of facial hair aboard and whether that precluded women from becoming successful mariners. The good Doctor smiled all the while benevolently, like a proud father over his debutant daughter, if that's not too uncharitable, and whatever marital squalls they've had seem to have calmed.*

*Something strange afoot, though: I've finally met the Captain, who collared me around noon today when I was on deck reading, asking if he might join me. He sat down with a world-weary sigh and remained there in silence for some time. I was on the verge of starting up some small talk when he beat me to it; he asked about my appointment with the Company and whether I understood the duties involved well enough, whether I had any relevant experience ('none' is the inescapable answer to that, dearest) and how long my contract would be.*

*He listened politely, but I suspected he had something on his mind. I recalled what I had been told by M. What an idiot I am – gabbling away about my problems to a man whose own make mine appear no more than a minor inconvenience. I said 'Forgive me for banging on' – but he silenced me.*

*'Life is loss,' he said, sharp eyes on mine, 'and I don't say it blithely. Perhaps you have heard something of my past?' I mumbled something non-committal about his outstanding track record and distinguished career, 'Whatever you've heard matters not. The last few decades have not been mankind's proudest, the sheer scale of the carnage and waste will tarnish our time in perpetuity, though I doubt we'll see its like for the individual gallantry, courage and selflessness which man is also capable of. One, it seems, creates or requires the other. Without hardship we cannot know ease.' – he might have said 'peace', I can't be sure – 'It is the nature of things. My only fear is that we didn't learn our lesson.' He thought for a moment. 'You're young, my boy, with much ahead of you. You're on a great adventure, lad, one that many would envy and one that will leave you at a great advantage over many your age. Make the most of it – and try not to dwell on how things might be otherwise.'*

*He paused, and I thought he'd forgotten me. I was about to ask what he meant; was I not already 'making the most of the situation'? The heaviness in his voice too was confounding – not exactly a ray of sunshine himself, our Captain. His tone implied much more than merely his own personal experience, and hinted at storm clouds to come, maybe literally.*

*'Anyways!' he said, so suddenly it made me jump. 'Look here, are you quite all right?'*

*Having already answered the question at the outset I was a little unsure of his tack, and fancied by his tone he wasn't asking after my physical health, but my mental state.*

*'What I mean to say is, there have been reports of, ah, conversations – one-sided conversations – coming from your cabin late at night, and some of the crew are a bit concerned. It's not unusual for men on their first voyage to become a little, well, homesick . . .' He left it hanging open like a loft door.*

*Long and the short of it is this, Lil; that upon hearing me chatting away to you in the middle of the night they have become worried about my sanity.*

*Or so I thought.*

*'Well,' I said, explaining my 'talks' with some embarrassment, 'I suppose I have been preoccupied occasionally and at times downright depressed, but I don't see how my ramblings should cause anyone any alarm.'*

*He looked thoughtful for a second, nodding slowly.*

*'But, son, what they've heard have not been "ramblings", not by a long chalk. What has been reported to me has been the screaming of a madman, cursing fit to bust and what sounds like violent altercation. From your cabin.' I must have looked stupefied, for he reached out and took my shoulder. 'Think no more of it, my boy,' he said. 'Clearly there has been a mistake – some clamour from the engine perhaps. I simply thought I might reassure the men. Obviously you know nothing of it so no more shall be said. Try to enjoy the rest of the voyage.' With that he stood, patted me paternally on the shoulder and strode off, limping almost imperceptibly.*

*That evening, over our customary post-prandial brandies, I asked Symmonds whether he'd heard any ruckus from my corridor. He said he hadn't, though admitted he knew what I was referring to. Apparently there have indeed been strange noises at night, though I haven't heard a thing. He told me to forget about it – easier said than done, especially since, unless my imagination is playing tricks on me, I now notice a slight opacity to the looks I get from the other passengers; sidelong glances I hadn't until now been aware of.*

*Despite his reassurance that nothing would come of it I went to sleep last night most unsettled. I aim to have this out with Maddox and will relate what I discover.*

*Yours, ever,*
*Ralph*
*x*

*P.S. My boxing training has shifted up a gear; S, with his hands padded, now takes my punches, ducking this way and that, all the while yelling at me to move my feet and bend my body at the waist. The crew find it hilarious, no doubt looking forward to the chance to have a crack at a passenger (I see Swaine has put his name down too, so I'm not alone).*

*Saturday, 16th October, 1933*
*S.S. Apollonia*

*Lil, dear heart,*
*The plot thickens.*

*This morning I took the opportunity to interrogate Maddox re the noises emanating from our deck – more specifically, my room. He eyed me up askance, looking uncomfortable.*

*'For God's sake, man,' I said, angrily. 'I'd hoped we'd become friends. Was I wrong?'*

*He paused, 'With respect, there are things at sea that no one can explain – Lord knows I've heard some bizarre goings-on – unusual waves where the sea should be calm, shapes beneath the water, ships vanishing with no report of bad weather. I can't explain the noises but I know what the men think. Sailors are a superstitious bunch – life's down to a throw of the dice out here, with no concern to God nor Devil neither. So men attach significance to omens and signs – the flight of an albatross or the rising of a whale – and when something unusual happens, why they naturally assume it signifies summat.' He took a breath, letting it out slow, puffing out his ruddy cheeks.*

*'Long and short of it is, lad, the men think you might bring bad luck.' He caught my expression, adding hastily, 'Though I, for my part, reckon no such thing. But I have heard the sounds at night, the sound of argument, words indistinguishable, a ranting, you might say. And,' – these words chilled my blood, Lil, I tell you, – 'only one voice. It stops whenever I approach, so I can't pinpoint it.'*

*'Aha. So it could be from any of the half-dozen cabins along this corridor,' says I.*

*'But that's just the point, Sir,' he said. 'The other cabins along this corridor are all similar, and no one could tolerate such a din without commenting on it.'*

*With that he left me alone. Oh Lil. What on earth do I to make of it all? How I wish you were here to quell my disquiet, run your fingers through my hair and lay your cool hand upon my brow. But you are so very far away.*

*I am ill at ease, my good mood of this morning utterly dissipated, and in dread of the approaching night.*

*God give me strength,*

*R.*

*Saturday, 17th October, 1933*
*S.S. Apollonia*

*My Love,*

*Upon waking – restored by what was, as far as I could tell, an uneventful eight hours' sleep and the sunshine quickly chasing all melancholia from my thoughts – I immediately decided to try and dispel this superstitious nonsense, to approach the matter directly rather than let it fester, no? At breakfast, therefore, when the conversation faltered, I brought up the subject before all present,*

*'I say, did anyone by any chance hear anything untoward last night?' I asked as casually as I could manage. There was a protracted silence and the sharing of glances over the rim of teacups. Symmonds, thank God, broke it.*

*'I for one heard a disturbance,' he says, 'which transpired to be nothing more than the groaning of my digestion after that God-awful stew.' Polite laughter followed. 'But of the raised voices to which I assume you refer, not a jot.' That got their attention.*

*'Since I've only recently been informed about this matter, may I ask who if anyone has actually heard it?' I said, looking around the table, primarily at the Dutch since they shared my corridor, while Niils, the somewhat reluctant translator for the group, relayed what I had said. They all solemnly shook their heads. The only other starboard cabin was that occupied by the Richards', separated from my own by a bulkhead and an empty cabin, and they both agreed they had heard nothing. Actually, in retrospect, he answered for them both.*

*On the more desirable, port side of the ship, lay the eight other single passengers:* Symmonds, Kemp, the Scots – neither of whom were present – and the farming bunch. No one, it would seem, was prepared to say they had heard a thing.

*'Well,' I said, 'in the event that I'm further accused of troubling*

*anyone's sleep, please don't hesitate to bang on my door and tell me to belt up!' And with that I threw down my napkin and retired to my cabin, feeling much better for having brought the issue out into the open.*

*After lunch this afternoon I was roused from my habitual nap ('The rest of the world indulges themselves in siestas, lad, and I suspect this contributes to a lack of stuffiness and a relaxed outlook on life the English would benefit from,' – S., of course) by a light knock on the door. 'Who is it?' I asked, but receiving no reply, got up and opened it. Mrs Richards, looking distinctly nervous, was in the corridor, fidgety fingers twining around a handkerchief and glancing down the corridor left and right.*

*'May I come in?' she asked. Well, I'm not completely au fait with proper behaviour at sea but I am quite sure that entertaining a married woman in one's cabin doesn't conform to it. She cut through my hesitation by tutting, pushing past me and gesturing impatiently that I should close the door. I opened my mouth to protest but she put finger to mouth and hissed, 'I need to talk to you, a minute of your time and no more, so please, for heaven's sake, just do it!' Not one to provoke a woman so clearly on the verge of hysteria, I did as I was told, politely offering her a seat – the only one – at the writing table while I myself sat on the bed. She refused.*

*'I think my husband,' she said, coming with impressive directness to the point, 'is poisoning me.' I must have been gaping like a fish, for she continued, 'Or, at the very, least sedating me.'*

*'What makes you so sure?' I asked as calmly as possible, all the while trying to work out how on earth I could get this madwoman out of my cabin without causing a scene.*

*She turned to look out of the porthole for a minute while she composed herself, then continued, her voice trembling.*

*'You will be aware, of course, that things have not been exactly*

*plain sailing between Mr Richards and myself for some time now.' She gave me no time to reply. 'You don't have to deny it. I'm not a complete fool. The story is long and tiresome but the long and short of it is that we should never have been married in the first place. It was a marriage of "convenience"' – she spat out the word – 'though for whom I'll never know. Not me, that's for sure, and certainly not for his peace of mind. I sometimes think he detests the fact that I even breathe the air. No, the convenience is that of society's alone. I – I made an awful mistake. One it seems I am to pay for in full. No, not as the rumours would have it, of having committed adultery –' She turned, and her eyes, shining fiercely in a way I hadn't thought her capable of, met mine '– but in marrying the wrong man. A crime that I'm sure offends God himself.'*

*I began to commiserate, but was once more stopped in my tracks.*

*'I do not want your sympathy, Mr Talbot,' she said, loud enough for me to worry our privacy wouldn't last long. She calmed herself with a long breath. 'I only tell you this so you might consider my suspicions at least possible. He is consumed with jealousy. Dangerously so, I believe, to the point of madness. Before we reached Malta he would lock me in the cabin at night, as he would whenever he had reason to leave me unattended. He has threatened me with violence on numerous occasions and,' she took a breath, 'he told me, in no uncertain terms, that he would kill me if I left him, as I had planned to do as soon we docked. I must have looked shocked. He's capable of it, you can be quite sure of that.' Thinking me sceptical still, she said, 'The man in question, the third party, dear Robbie – with whom I was truly in love, with whom I should have eloped or done something, anything, while there was the opportunity – he died, under circumstances that were plainly suspicious, to me at least.'*

*'What were the circumstances?' I asked. 'If the subject is not too difficult.'*

*'We were due to meet for what I knew had to be our last encounter before my marriage, at our usual place near the Serpentine, under a willow whose trailing branches offered some privacy from passers-by.' She paused, and turned away to the window again, 'But he never came. It was only later that I learned of his fate. In the papers! David – Dr Richards – handed me the open page; I'll never forget the cold look in his eyes, watching me like a bird of prey, monitoring my reaction.' She shivered visibly. 'They said there had been an accident, that he'd failed to maintain the gas mains properly and, upon returning from his afternoon appointment, lit a cigar and ignited a leak in his sitting room, blowing himself to smithereens, destroying his apartment and much of the one above.'*

*'That does happen an awful lot, you know.'*

*'Yes. But I was his afternoon appointment, and he'd have moved heaven and earth to honour it or at least get a message through to me. There is nothing short of death that would have kept him from being there. Therefore, logically, he was already dead.'*

*'Are you telling me your husband murdered your lover?' I asked, incredulous.*

*She rolled her eyes as if dealing with an idiot.*

*'Yes! Initially I merely suspected it and certainly lacked the proof to go to the police – anyway, who would have believed me? I'm not of the same social standing as he and would have been dismissed as hysterical.' That, I thought, I could understand. 'But in Malta he told me – in so many words – what he'd done. He said that if I ever tried to leave him again, I would find myself reunited with "my" Robert sooner than I could possibly have hoped for. If that's not a confession then what is? Naturally I capitulated.'*

*'Naturally,' I said, beginning at last to believe her, especially given the rise of the hairs at the back of my neck. 'And what makes*

*you think he intends you harm, now that you have agreed to stay with him?'*

*'Since then he has stopped. Locking the door, I mean.'*

*'So his trust in you is returning.'*

*She looked at me scathingly.*

*'Not because he is any more convinced of my faithfulness to our union – far from it. Because there is nowhere for me to go, and,' she whispered, 'he puts something in my nightcap to ensure I'm incapable of waking up, let alone leaving the room. I am not a deep sleeper, Mr Talbot, my disposition precludes it. Never in my life have I slept the whole night through – indeed, rarely have I ever slept longer than four or five hours at a time. Now, however, I find I can scarcely leave my bed in the morning; I sleep at least nine hours straight, without interruption, and am possessed by such lethargy during the day it feels as if I'm already half dead.'*

*I thought for a minute upon what she had said, recalling how I myself had noticed her lassitude and remarked on it in these very letters.*

*'Have you tried refusing the drink?' I asked.*

*'Of course! But he insists. He says it's crucial I take it since it contains the quinine and such-and-such minerals that we need to build up a defence against God knows what diseases on the continent.'*

*At that moment I thought I heard a noise in the corridor, and gestured for her to be quiet. We stood there listening, my heart hammering at my ribs, but heard nothing further.*

*'What do you expect from me?' I whispered, somewhat uncharitably, I'm afraid, and admit my first thoughts were for my own safety; Symmonds' words of warning re any embroilment with the Doctor suddenly seeming somewhat prophetic.*

*She faltered, her eyes welled with tears and she shook her head, her slight frame trembling beneath her khaki shirt, quite unable to talk, and I had the impression of a little girl convinced of monsters under her bed.*

*Filled with pity and the realisation that this girl, no older than I, was genuinely terrified, I stood and pulled out the chair so that she could sit down, poured us both a brandy and lit her a cigarette, one draw of which made her cough loudly. Gradually her breathing slowed and some colour returned to her cheeks.*

*'Listen,' I said, in my most consolatory voice, 'there's nothing more to be done at the moment and I'm sure nothing bad will befall you while we're at sea. Let me think about the matter and the best course of action to follow, if any.'*

*I've no experience of this kind of thing, my love, and was stalling for time.*

*'If any? She exclaimed. 'He's trying to kill me, you dolt!'*

*'That would hardly be in his interests, now would it, not with so many witnesses in such close proximity of each other?' I reasoned. 'If he is putting something in your drink, it will be to keep you where he can see you and nothing more, the same as he gives me for seasickness I imagine, and with the recent disturbances we've been having during the night, perhaps you're actually better off.'*

*My levity was not well received.*

*'Fine,' she said, resignation in her voice. 'Thank you for your time, Mr Talbot.' Sarcasm now. 'I had hoped for some solace but see I shall have to look elsewhere.'*

*She stood up, nodded her head curtly and, after listening intently at the door, let herself out with an unconvincing smile. I heard her light steps echo down the corridor to the stairs.*

*There you have it, my angel. It seems this voyage is to be far from uneventful after all. To think I was complaining of boredom just two days ago . . .*

*It was only after she had left that I was struck with the most perplexing aspect of the whole episode: why, of all the people aboard, she chose to unburden herself to me, arguably the least qualified in such matters. I only hope that her suspicions are unfounded, that she's in some way delusional and that her husband's concoction is in fact keeping her mentally calm, on an even keel, so to speak. Perhaps it is she who is mad? She certainly comes across as highly strung. But what if she is right and something does happen to her? Her blood would be on my hands.*

*I must do something. What exactly, I haven't the slightest idea.*

*At least you know my intention so that in the event of my disappearance you're armed with enough evidence for a proper investigation. The first and most obvious step is to talk it through with Symmonds.*

*Later:*

*Symmonds – Jim, as he's requested I call him – has shone his penetrating intellect upon the situation; I managed to catch him after dinner in his cabin. I knocked and he bade me enter. Similar in layout to my own, the walls were covered in charts and maps pinned into the mahogany, and the room smelt strongly of cologne and tobacco smoke. On the bureau sat a rosewood box, inlaid with a curious geometric design comprising of a many-rayed sun set within two intertwined triangles that formed a hexagon – quite beautiful. From a hook near the bed hung a Browning revolver in its holster, somehow having escaped the amnesty imposed by Buchanan. He was seated at his desk, in the act of closing a writing case not dissimilar to the one you gave to me. He assured me I was not disturbing him, waved me to a chair and expressed some surprise that I had not visited him before now, anticipating by insinuation that something must be amiss.*

*'Your suspicions regarding Richards might be uncannily close to*

*the mark,' I began, then ran him quickly through the events of the afternoon.*

*He listened without interruption, lit a cheroot and blew spiralling rings of smoke through each other while he pondered the situation.*

*'You did well to come to me,' he said, 'and I suspect the poor girl may have good cause for alarm, but she is not in danger of her life – yet. You're probably right to assume that he doesn't intend to kill her – certainly jealousy can be all-consuming and occasionally murderous, but only when pushed to the limit, which without the threat of actually losing her to another I doubt he's reached. Jealousy's the twisted relative of love, Ralph, based on possession and emotional usury.*

*Keeping her where he can see her is probably his intention, and he's most likely using lithium to do so, as you guessed, posing no great danger in small doses. I suggest we keep it between ourselves but remain vigilant.' He exhaled contemplatively, blue smoke streaming towards the open porthole. 'As regards the possible murder of this fellow Robbie, there is precious little we can do about it from here, short of presenting Richards to the consulate in Alexandria, and believe me, they are much too busy with other matters to take anything as trivial as a "possible" crime of passion far away in England seriously.'*

*He stood and opened a cupboard, from which he produced a bottle of fifteen-year-old Glenlivet and two tumblers.*

*'Special occasion,' he said, pouring two stiff measures, and in answer to my raised eyebrows, 'Alexandria tomorrow and roughly our halfway point. Symbolically, anyway, for we leave the Med soon after. Cheers, Ralph. Your health. And welcome to Africa.'*

*We proceeded to finish most of the bottle, I remember little of what was said and I slept as if sedated myself.*

*As I write, we are due to arrive any minute – with all the usual activity on deck – and I'll soon set my first footprint upon the sands of Africa.*

*I love you,*

*Ralph*

*x*

*Sunday, 18th October, 1933*
*Alexandria, Egypt*

*Lillian,*

*In haste – I must post these today.*

*We docked in the ancient port of Alexandria – the Pearl of the Med – to little fanfare; the port is so busy as to absorb a vessel of the Apollonia's size without a ripple.*

*From the ship's rail the city stretched away from us as we drew into the Eastern Port, through the mouth of a vast causeway sheltering the harbour and once the site of the Pharos Lighthouse, one of the ancient Seven Wonders of the World. The light itself could apparently be seen for 100 miles.*

*Jim and I had, the previous evening, elected to keep a close eye on the Richards', and at breakfast he suggested we four – plus Kemp as cover, in order not to make the idea seem too incongruous – take in some of the sights since he had a good knowledge of the city. They – he, at any rate – to my surprise agreed and I caught a quick glance of gratitude from Claudia – Mrs Richards. God knows what effect it must have on the spirits to suspect foul play and have to carry on as if all was right as rain. She's made of stalwart stuff, my love – were you to ever meet her you would immediately become friends.*

*I strode confidently down the gangplank and stood on the quayside trying to gauge my immediate impressions. Entering the turbulent currents and eddies of the crowd I realised that I was no longer cast afloat in the stream, buffeted by humanity, but felt more in control of the situation. The sounds and smells no longer intimidated me with their novelty, their unusualness. Now I found I could savour the experience, observe the chaotic events around me, as opposed to being carried along like a lost child at a fairground. Of course my guard remained up – there were the usual scoundrels around – but I fancied I recognised and 'listened to' my instinct; I was aware of my environs, senses alert, tuned to possible theft but not inviting it by appearing an easy target. What I have admired in Jim I now realised I had, to some small degree, attained myself. Perhaps I was merely emboldened for Claudia's benefit.*

*We made our way through the Turkish Quarter, along the causeway linking Pharos Island to the mainland, through medinas bustling with the hubbub of trade and commerce, past coffee shops with men swathed in djellabas – long robes with pointed hoods – playing backgammon, stalls laden with produce, the majority of which I didn't recognise and, in a square clearly given to their exchange, I saw my first camels. These strange, flatulent beasts were crouched on the ground or ruminating thoughtfully, comically oblivious to the animated gesticulations and haggling of their owners and potential buyers as if it was all beneath them. My attention was drawn to one group of men in particular, in deep blue robes and black turbans that covered their entire faces except for slits through which their eyes glinted.*

*'Tuaregs,' said Jim. 'The Blue Men of the Sahara, which they can cross in a month if the trade calls for it. Unusual to see 'em this far east.'*

*Kemp, who seems to suffer excessively from the heat, soon cried off and headed for the hotel. We continued on to the Cecil, a grand affair recently completed, and in whose cool, marbled confines we enjoyed a delicious lunch. After the monotony of the food on board, the menu was a feast: spiced, grilled fish; squid and shrimp in tehina (a spicy sesame paste); and wonderfully named baba ganoush (grilled aubergine) with scented rice and a fresh white wine and followed by honeyed figs and dates. Conversation was somewhat stilted, to say the least. Jim and I kept it moving, but poor Claudia was virtually monosyllabic – understandably – and her husband likewise, other than to express disregard for whatever we might touch on, as if the subject had become too much for him to bear, e.g.:*

*Jim: 'It's hard to imagine just how much knowledge was lost to civilisation with the destruction of the library.'*

*To which Claudia enquired, 'Pray elaborate, Colonel Symmonds, for I know nothing of the city's past.'*

*'Well,' he continued, 'the Alexandria library boasted some 700,000 volumes collected by the Ptolomies until its pillage in* AD *640 under the rule of the Christian bishop, Theophilus, acting on Theodosius' decree concerning pagan monuments. The story runs as follows: John the Grammarian, a famous peripatetic philosopher, being in Alexandria at the time of its capture, and confidante of the Amr, begged him to give him the royal library. The Amr told him that it was not in his power to grant such a request, but promised to write to the Caliph for his consent. The Caliph, on hearing the request, is said to have replied that 'if the books contain the same doctrine with the Koran, they can be of no use, since the Koran contains all necessary truths, and should be destroyed; but if they contain anything contrary to that book, they ought similarly to be destroyed'; and therefore, whatever their contents were, he ordered them burnt. At his order they were distributed among the hundreds of public baths in the city where they kept the fires burning for six months.'*

*Richards interrupted Jim with, 'Shall we have some more tea?' Leaving it at that. Even Claudia rolled her eyes with exasperation.*

*As I say, we struggled.*

*That afternoon we made our way back to our more modest hotel near to the harbour, where you find me now, dearest, pen in hand. The calls to prayer from the local muezzin are merging with those of other mosques to create a richly woven tapestry of Arabic, the room is sweltering despite the open window but the view distracts – across the flat roofs and out to sea, where the lights of fishing boats wink as if reflecting the stars – a view I imagine unchanged for centuries.*

*That's it for today – at any moment I'm expecting Jim, who has promised to show me around the city at night, 'an altogether different beast', he tells me, and must get this to the concierge if it is to be posted first thing.*

*Adieu until Jeddah – a relatively short haul, I gather.*

*All my love,*

*Ralph*

*x*

# Chapter 8

*Hong Kong. 1996.*

Kimberly O'Connor leant on the marble edge of the penthouse balcony and exhaled smoke out over the city thrusting itself vigorously up at her. If status was proportional to height up the hill – and it definitely was – she must be doing all right. And she most definitely was.

Her apartment – okay, *their* apartment, his – was perched loftily up above Mid-Levels, half way up the Victoria Peak where the buildings began to thin as property prices became incomprehensibly, need-to-ask-can't-afford expensive. There was an almost imperceptible background hum from the city below – she imagined whirring ventilation systems, a thousand simultaneous phone calls, the ping of sent emails and the chink of money changing hands – with louder noise layered on top: the throb of car engines, the clank of trams, the jackhammer clash of incessant pile-drivers, the roar of airliners, the klaxons of ships. A city of light and noise, glittering seductively, a mesmerising jewel dangled just out of reach for all but a few. Presumably the dense network of interwoven electromagnetic signals made no sound, but she could still sense it, an endless subliminal exchange of information.

Below her the shiny skyscrapers were so densely packed she couldn't see the ground beneath them. Each seemed to strive to be higher than the others, like trees in a forest competing for sunlight, glittering phallic testaments to corporate virility that filled every inch of space all the way down to the harbour – itself being gradually filled in to create more precious square metres of buildable real estate. Surreal estate, she thought. Implausibly massive freighters like horizontal tower blocks lolled sluggishly on their anchors or toiled laboriously towards the Kowloon docks, attendant tugs straining and klaxons braying for attention.

She flicked the butt off the edge and watched it spiral down the twenty-three storeys until it was lost from sight, replaced it with the straw of her mojito then turned and, a little giddily, sought the shade of a sun-lounger by the plunge pool.

Lying back, she sighed contentedly, delighting in the breeze that goose-bumped her stomach and stiffened her nipples beneath her Dior bikini. Sun and cocktails. Perfect. Not a bad mojito either, she told herself, though after two years in that sodding bar it bloody well ought to be.

Le Jardin, an open-air joint in a soiled cul-de-sac off Lang Kwai Fong. Open air but hardly al fresco, hardly a garden, so oppressively did the surrounding buildings lean in. If you craned your neck you could just make out a rectangle of blue through the bamboo lattice – the garden – and on good days the street-funnelled breeze just about kept the greasy air moving. For herself, she preferred the hermetic honesty of the panoramic, air-conned glitz of almost all other bars, done out to reflect their frank, hand-shrugging pandering to the excess, shiny glamour and ersatz quality of life here. Le Jardin was trying to be Greenwich cool, Soho cool – out of place amid the city's in-your-face corporate and architectural arrogance. And air-con was a bonus. But the pay was good and the owner, a life-buffeted French girl called Sophie, liked and trusted her, taking her under her wing when she first arrived.

She'd come over from Thailand, destitute and desperate, having fled Bangkok in fear for her life. That had been messy, a 'close thing', or some other platitude that understates near-death experiences, a nail-biting taxi to the airport, urging the driver faster – '*Leo, leo mak ka*!' – straight onto the first flight out. The first time she had been frightened, properly, in the year or so she'd spent there. At least Le Jardin wasn't 'protected' by Triads, as far as she knew, and after her run-ins with the Patpong mafia in Bangkok, that was good enough for her. She'd been lucky to make it to the airport, let alone grab her bags from the hotel. She knew of girls who disappeared, permanently, just for attempting to quit, and she knew it wasn't because they'd hung up their stilettos, gone home and started families.

Two years. Blown past like the blurred backdrop in films before blue-screen; juddering and synthetic. With a city this unnatural, so brutally defiant of the laws of nature, what did she expect? So unlike Bangkok's chaotic, earthy squalour, moral and literal, that kept it real, kept it visceral: The shit, piss and tears that fouled the streets, the blackened Stygian waters of the klongs that reeked of musty death, the slums cluttered under the flyovers as if they'd been swept there by a huge municipal broom. Hong Kong itself was sanitised by comparison, chromed and polished, buffed somehow – though ten million people's crap must be going somewhere each day. A veneer, she knew, masking centuries of crime and corruption and avarice, but an impressive one, especially on first arrival; the white-knuckle landing close enough to see into peoples' apartments, the neck-cracking gawp up between the towering glass temples to mammon. And, if you wanted authentic seediness, Kowloon's Walled City, an insalubrious warren with the highest density of humanity on earth – 50,000 people in an area a quarter of a mile square – delivered it; a sunless maze of brothels, opium dens, cocaine parlours and black-market factories that could make Patpong look like earthly paradise. She'd only been there once – with a bloke from UNESCO trying to get into her knickers – just to see what it was like, a few months before they started demolishing it. Out of keeping with the image and the revenue they, the Brits, wanted, it had to go.

And, now, at last, so did she. She smiled.

She'd done her induction time in Chung King Mansions, one thousand nightmare-stained rooms lit pale and thin by flickering neon, redolent with despair and smelling like a tramp's crotch, but cheap enough to be permanently full. She left when police carried out an armed raid on a lanky, tattooed Austrian drug dealer on her floor, the echoes of shouts and gunshots chasing her across the water to Hong Kong Island. There, in Wanchai, sitting on the edge of her bed, she'd counted her money, gambled it all on a month's rent and hit the streets from bar to bar until she met Sophie.

A survivor herself, Sophie immediately recognised something in Kim's eyes, she told her later, something haunted in her too-big eyes, something tough and durable beneath the petite, coke-bottle figure. Her round, childlike face, framed by a Cleopatra wedge-cut of blue-black hair and punctuated by the thick Cupid-bow of her lips, gave the impression of almost perverse sexual parody, like a character in a Japanese manga comic. She thought her lips were her best asset – they certainly attracted plenty of attention – and accentuated them with whore-red lipstick. She'd read somewhere that enhanced lips excited men, subconsciously, the fools, because they were supposed to mirror a woman's vulva in oestrus. If this was true – and it always made her laugh, especially when she saw gaping-trout cosmetic casualties – she looked permanently on heat, permanently aroused. Not bee-stung so much as hornet-attacked, the term 'bruised' described her lips perfectly. Sometimes literally. Rather than tone them down in the interests of avoiding assholes, she tended to pout, leaving them slightly parted as if she had Chinese love-balls roiling around inside her and was *right* on the verge of orgasm (sometimes she did, sometimes she *was*). Besides, if she didn't attract the bad boys, how could the bad and worthless and dirty part of her that wanted to be punished be satisfied?

She and Sophie fast became friends, and Soph even put Kim up on the sofa of her tiny little flat until she got herself sorted. Never one to depend on others, she moved out after a couple of weeks and wound up joining the quasi-boho community on Lamma island, a small collection of scrubby hills and sandy beaches unwanted by the Chinese due to the feng shui-shafting power plant at one end, but with a thriving population of gweilo artists, musos, hippies and backpackers, a stack of cheap apartments and laid-back bars and a twenty-minute commute by ferry to the city.

She quickly worked her way up to manageress. Her no-bullshit attitude, numerical sagacity and punchy people skills gave a grateful Sophie more time with her child. Once she'd found her feet at Le Jardin, she quickly took over virtually all the responsibility for keeping the place full, which wasn't particularly difficult; keep the promotions fresh, the music funky and the food Mediterranean. Oh, and treat every customer, no matter how much of a twat, as if you're trying to decide whether to sleep with them or not. This was a trick she'd picked up hostessing in Bangkok; the insinuation, often no more than an averted glance down long black lashes, the slightest carrot-dangling possibility of something happening, was enough to keep men coming back for more. Pricks. Even though she played it deliberately cool, insultingly so, they kept on chasing the fluffy bunny round and round and round the track like the tongue flapping greyhounds down in Wanchai.

There was nothing fluffy about her though, as they quickly discovered if they tried it on in the bar – 'Get the fuck off, then get the fuck out' – or on the very rare occasions she actually did take one home for the night; like a lioness with a limp antelope in its jaws, she'd close the door and turn the latch with as much casual menace as she could muster, turn to where they were by now sitting on the sofa and, in her incongruous brogue, say something like, 'Right, boy, for the next four hours you're mine, solely, to do with as I want, when I want. Then I want you gone. D'y'understand?'

Gobsmacked at the sudden predatory change, few managed much in the way of resistance. Few could meet her down there, where the pretence was stripped bare, in the fierce reality of her damaged core and beaten past and get off on it with her. Few had what she needed: someone strong enough to take care of her, melt her steel in an unconditional fire, dominate her, *own* her, and in doing so guarantee everything would be okay. She doubted anyone could and it certainly never had been.

They always either submitted to her – the humiliation, pain and vengeance she visited upon their prostrate bodies – and she exalted in punishing them for their weakness, for their sex, or they reacted too violently, losing their tempers, smashing things, her. Either way, she'd leave them to dress, one or both of them spent and bloodied, and let themselves quietly out of the flat while she slept safe in the knowledge that no one would *ever* brag about a night with her to their mates.

No one had been up to it – satisfying her needs, meeting her demands. Understanding. Nowhere near.

Until Nikko.

He dropped by the bar often enough, usually with his banker buddies, usually Friday or Saturday evenings before sloshing onwards and downwards into the clubs until dawn. Together as a pack they seemed typical, par for the course – brash, loud and loaded, Big Swinging Dicks. He had been different from the outset though. Quieter, more controlled, never, as far as she'd seen, losing it completely and dropping his pants, hoofing coke off the tables and puking in the gutter – shit, waking up in the gutter – like the others. Reserved. Considered – a rare enough quality during these days of grotesque market spiking, million-dollar bonuses and champagne rivuletting down the streets like piss. That, and the way he looked at her, watched her – levelling, direct, with a light smile, so that the frenetic milling around him seemed to go into slow-motion, passing him like water – had immediately attracted her to him, flustered her, and that hardly ever happened.

The fact that he was obscenely minted and drop-dead gorgeous helped *a lot*. Obviously. Tight, curly brown hair slicked down flat, a sprig popping up now and then to be smoothed back into place, which was cute; gym-hammered body lean beneath expensive shirts; clean jaw, longish straight nose, sardonic eyebrows draw-bridged over amused eyes. But she'd seen him ass-cupping one of those impossibly flawless swans that appeared regularly on the island during school or university holidays: blonde, second-generation expat offspring whose taipan parents owned gaudy piles above Causeway Bay, junks moored in

Aberdeen Yacht Club and pied-à-terres in Chelsea. Out of her league, poor little Mick from County Kerry that she was.

He said so little it was almost a shock to discover he was Australian, though immediately his taciturnity made more sense. He was just playing the part of a Brit abroad, himself a colonial, not a colonist, not quite fitting into the role with the same smug arrogance of the English, especially the bankers, who pretended they were in the Golden Mile despite the stigma of Asia's second rate status.

Like her, he didn't fit in.

One evening, a weekday, relatively quiet in the post-rush hour, pre-dinner pause, he leaned on the counter waiting for her to acknowledge him. She ignored him.

'Hi, Kim.' Everyone knew her name; means nothing, she told herself.

'Hi,' she said, scarcely glancing up from the rota. 'What can I do for you?' That pause, the fizzing list he'd blatantly scrolled through in his mind, had made her blush. He smiled at her discomfort, not cruelly though, and ordered a round of cocktails. She busied herself with the order, cursing her weakness.

'Cheers, babe,' he said. Then, almost an aside, 'Hey, I've got the company junk for the weekend. Drinks, dancing. Be great if you could come.'

'You inviting everyone you meet? You must be desperate.'

'Not everyone,' he said, 'just people I'd like to get to know better.'

She was flattered, despite herself.

When she turned up at the quay on Saturday, self-consciously under-dressed and deliberately late, there was no one else there but him. She slapped him across the face, knocking his sunglasses off, and turned to leave.

'I never said there would be anyone else coming,' he protested, hands raised, laughing at her indignant flare-up. 'C'mon. It'll be fun, I promise.'

And it was. He laid it on big time. Not to impress her particularly, just because he wanted to, just because he could. A deep-throated roar out to Lantau for lunch at one of the local restaurants amid large, cacophonous Chinese families, then round the island to one of the remote bays where he cut the engine and tossed the anchor overboard. She didn't feel threatened or awkward for a second, and lay back on the front deck while he busied himself below.

He appeared with a grin and a bottle of '78 Hunter Valley Semillon, and they talked for hours, occasionally stopping to swim together in the clear, deep blue-green water. The connection was strong and immediate, soldered by their shared misfittery, crap-cutting directness and independence of spirit, and she listened while he told her about his great-grandfather who'd been shipped out, *transported*, from Ireland, where exactly he didn't know – 'With my luck we're probably related,' she said, not entirely joking – and making a go of it, setting up his family with a secure future, of growing up in Sydney, life on the beach, golden days of sun and surf, and how, as the only son, it had fallen on him to go off and make the family fortune when his dad got the bony-fingered tap of cancer, gone within six weeks of diagnosis. 'Sure takes the fear out of life,' he said gently, 'while adding a sense of urgency to it.'

Now, ten years later, he was earning a 'disgusting' amount of money as a derivatives forecaster.

'Which is what, in the name of God?' she asked. He laughed.

'Not entirely sure I know myself.' He thought for a minute. 'Imagine there's a river, okay? And there's a razor blade aligned to the flow of the water. If you turn the angle of the razor blade, even slightly, I predict the ripples.'

She, in turn, quickly found herself telling him things about herself she hadn't told anyone, things she barely peeked at herself. If he can't take it and it scares him off, she thought, might as well find out now.

So she told him everything: the rape, fleeing home, the grief of knowing she could never go back, that no one would believe her – a priest's word against hers – the abortion, the drugs, the barrel bottom in London and the clawed escape back out, working on cruise ships, seeing the world, wide and big and bad and beautiful, the escorting, the – sod it, tell him – hooking, Bangkok. Here. Him. He never said a word, and though his eyes momentarily welled he made no attempt to hide it.

By the time they made love on the mahogany double bed below deck – he easily held her down, overcoming her knee-jerk antagonism, pinning her beneath strong, kind arms, biting her neck hard as she climaxed, laughing as she nail-raked his back – she knew that she was falling completely, head over heels in love.

Simple as that. And it can be that simple, she told herself, she'd read about it, sure enough. Why the fuck not? She pinched herself nevertheless.

'Why me?' she asked, head on the small of his back as they lay back on deck in the afternoon sun.

'Because you can ask that question.'

'But you hardly know – knew – me.'

'Look,' he rolled onto his side, 'I know you don't fit here – shit, the *Cantonese* don't fit in here – but you know it and that's already interesting to me. I see how you handle yourself, I love how you handle yourself, how you move, what makes you laugh and what pisses you off, and I took a punt that it's the same shit as me. And I'm a very good judge of character. It was a hunch. Instinct. And now I know my hunch was right. Maybe that's why I'm so damn good at what I do, no?' he licked a finger and smoothed down an eyebrow in self-parody. 'I also don't believe in dicking about if you want something bad enough.' She savoured the implication that hung in the air. 'And don't even get me started on the accent. Christ babe, you could sell it.'

'What about the swan?' she asked.

'How do you know about that?' He looked sharply at her, surprised.

'I've seen you together –' she started.

'Oh, her!' and he laughed, loudly, head back. 'Long gone. Decorative. Shit babe, for a minute there I thought you meant –' he broke off, looked away for a moment, then turned back to her, 'C'mon. I want to show you something. Get the anchor, will you?'

Two hours and full throttle later they were in Macau. Nikko phoned ahead and a diminutive but stocky Chinese called Han met them at the twinkle-lit harbour where they were ushered promptly through cursory customs – no passport check – and into the back of an idling Merc, Han shutting the doors behind then with a solid thud. A darkened glass partition soundlessly slid up to separate them from the driver. Nikko leant across to kiss her, lazily spreading her legs with one hand as he did so, sliding a hand to her knickerless, clean-shaven pussy and quickly whipping her to a light clitoral lather before slapping in his two middle fingers to bring her off.

'Was that what you wanted to show me?' she asked, husky throated as she lifted herself back upright.

He laughed.

'No babe, tomorrow. I'm really running on instinct now,

gambling hard. I haven't taken a risk like this since the Barings float.' He wouldn't be drawn further. 'Patience, sweetheart. Enjoy the evening.'

By the time they'd slathered themselves in lobster, swigged expansively on some Grand Cru or other, skinny dipped in the pool and tumbled into their suite at the Marriot, giggling like school children and making elaborate demands of the sycophantic room service ('A set of police handcuffs and a truncheon, *m'goi*'), she'd stopped wondering why they'd come here in the first place, falling asleep amid the wreckage of the room, swathed in toga'd sheets and – *at last* – the safety of someone's – his – arms.

When she awoke, for a few seconds, she couldn't recall where the hell she was. Then, as she remembered, when reality turned out to be the dream – or was it vice versa? – she grinned sleepily and opened her eyes. He was propped on one elbow, smiling down at her.

'Morning,' he whispered, kissing her forehead.

'Morning yourself,' she said, pulling the sheet over her face with sudden self-consciousness as flashes from the night before flickered in.

'You okay?' he said gently. 'You were dreaming, thrashing about, shouting.'

'Fine, thank you. Welcome to my head.' She dimly recalled glimpses of the dream, of something being wrenched away from her, of reaching and reaching but never getting any closer to it.

'We've got an hour to get ready, of which I anticipate roughly half to be spent having sex. Or rather *gently* half.' Already his hand was on her, stroking. Her immediate conditioned response was to brush him off, but she caught herself in time – wait, he's being nice to me, loving – and kissed him back, then rolled onto her side to coquettishly thrust her still-slippery ass into his crotch with a soft purr and, for the first time in her life, Kimberley made love.

Afterwards, she burst into silent tears she couldn't explain. Nikko didn't ask her to. He simply stroked her head and held her to his chest.

An hour later, after coffee and a line of point-9 coke ('the only truly effective hangover cure and exactly what it was originally intended for,' he'd assured her) and wearing the tissue-wrapped linen skirt, olive T-shirt and espadrilles that had magically appeared in the hallway, they took the soundless elevator down to the foyer. Han was waiting for them. He greeted them with a curt nod of the head and led the way through the revolving door to the car. She wondered, briefly, how everything was being covered, since she'd seen no sign of any money changing hands, but found she could easily not worry too much about an answer.

They drove for half an hour through low-rise urbanisation and the occasional old Portuguese colonial façade, along the seafront past marinas with swaying forests of masts, until they pulled up at a dockyard surrounded by a high sheet-steel fence. Han hit the horn once and the gates opened. When he opened the door, she took his proffered hand, stepped out onto the gravel and looked around her.

Sleek, tapered yachts glistened in the sun, some unfinished, upturned like the cartilaginous remains of huge cuttlefish, others preened in their glorious perfection, masts chiming melodiously in the breeze.

'Hello, Mr Nikko, sir!' They turned to see a hefty-chested Chinaman bustling across the car park towards them. 'What pleasant surprise.'

'*Josan*, Qing, how are ya?' Nikko shook his hand, knowing

full well they'd been expected – it was a small island. 'This is my girlfriend Kim – a Chinese name but actually from Ireland.'

'Nice to meet you,' she basked in a post-nominal glow. Girlfriend. One word.

'You wanna see how she coming?' Qing asked.

'If it's no bother,' said Nikko.

'Ah, Mr Nikko. You some funny guy.' Qing grinned, gestured them to follow. 'I think you gonna like it.'

He led the way into the shade of one of the covered docks, Kim grateful for the cool escape, the air chemically sweet with the smell of fibreglass resin. Near the back of the hangar, propped up on padded bolsters, rested, *reclined*, with the complacency of a film star in a nightclub, a double-masted yacht with such a sleek smoothness of contour she immediately wanted to stroke it. So she did.

'This,' he said, 'is a Swan 55, probably the finest production yacht in the world, with which I intend to take to the high seas, wave goodbye to all this and sail all the way home.'

'She's lovely,' said Kim, trailing fingers along the slow grade of the hull. 'How –' She caught herself, nearly asking the question she had come to realise Nikko would find uncomfortable. Or not. Maybe not uncomfortable but distasteful, or unnecessary. In his world, she guessed, money became irrelevant. The question, the issue itself, would have seemed odd. No longer measured by how much you had, it left the much more pertinent means test – what you did with it – wide open. The true mark of wealth. She often took some solace in witnessing what rich people did with their money, the astonishing lack of imagination, crashing bad taste and downright insanity of it, like Trump's haircut, Dubai hotels in the desert, Jackson's Neverland or anything ever bought by a professional footballer. When people have enough money to create their own reality the results provided an insight into just how whacked the stuff actually was in its essence, in its core, and what monsters it created. She enjoyed reading stories of the rich imploding into overdoses, divorce and therapy with unabashed amusement. Darwinism gone mad, she thought, now that human evolution had lost any vestige of survival of the 'fittest'. From what she remembered of her Celtic mythology, leaders used to be hero figures: strong, intelligent, compassionate. Now it was survival of the greediest, sneakiest and most rapaciously dishonest. Politics had become Revenge of the Nerds, leadership and role model Triumph of the Cunt.

Today's standard bearers, trampling across a battlefield where no one was fighting, with deranged eyes and slavering grins, were all clearly gone in the head from the insidious corruption with which the slavish yearning for money infects people. Nikko, from what she'd seen so far, was without affectation, remarkably grounded and a refreshing blast of helium into the flaccid balloon of dream realisation.

'No one has ever seen her, except you. No one even knows about her,' he said. 'I assume your discretion is guaranteed?'

She smiled back at him.

'Course it is, you daft bugger. Where did you find her?'

'In Singapore, second hand, but she's good as new. Better. Twelve years old with one careful owner. Unfortunately – fortunately – he wasn't as careful with his investments as he was with his boat. Picked her up for a song, relatively, and my friend Mr Qing here is making a few minor adjustments for me.' Qing beamed proudly, gave a little bow and walked off. 'Shall we go aboard?'

He led the way up the gangplank. The teak deck flowed smoothly around the cockpit, tapering effortlessly to the prow.

'Come.' He held out his hand and led her below. Flawless veneer, modest fixtures, perfect space. She was impressed, and she didn't even know what she was looking at, not in nautical terms. All she saw was an object of great beauty, a balance between form and function rare among the ostentatious, top-end trappings of wealth.

'She's beautiful, so she is. What's she called?'

'Actually, you might be able to help with that. I've been trying to think of something appropriate. Something to do with getting out of the doldrums. 'Sea Change?' 'Wizard of Oz?' What about 'Calmer'?

'Karma?'

'No, calmer, as in, 'Now I am', but she's definitely part of my destiny so the pun's a good one. Or 'Escape Clause'? 'Serendipity'? Have a think, will you?'

As he looked down into her eyes, his arms around her shoulders, hers around his waist, she held his gaze, both losing themselves in the vitreous void of their pupils, past their own reflections, their faces blurring, locked together, complete, as one, and they momentarily lost track of where they were or who they were, just for a split second, like they had that morning wrapped around each other. He blinked, winked and broke it, as if he'd come to a decision.

'Give me a minute, will you?' He kissed her mouth, pinched her ass hard and went off to talk to Qing while she imagined being aboard, out at sea, the bow plunging through the water, the wind in her hair, Nikko at the helm. She smiled with anticipation.

Reclining in the pool, she lifted up her sunglasses and bounced sun-beams through the chipped-ice facets of the diamond that perched delicately on the gold \ around her third finger. It all seemed so long ago now. A lifetime, not six months. The dream was real, and she was wide awake. She laughed out loud, something she found herself doing quite often these days.

Within a month she'd quit her job. Sophie had understood, tears of vicarious happiness shining in her eyes – their favourite film was *Pretty Woman* – and the affirmation that fairytales can come true and that her turn would surely come.

Then she moved out of her flat on Lamma, packing up her mishmash possessions and stern-railing the ferry over to Central for the last time, waving goodbye to friends and her past, for the first time noticing how badly the harbour smelt and how the litter tide-marked the stony shore. He met her at the quayside, loaded her bags into the Porsche and whisked her up to his marble-cool duplex, floating in the air high above the teeming ant nest below.

Kept woman? Abso-fucking-lutely. If only her friends back home in the gossip-cobbled, tourist-clotted port of Dingle could see her now. They wouldn't even sodding remember her now, she reminded herself steely, stopping the tears, remembering the turned backs and flat eyes. Screw them! She'd been waiting for this moment since she left, when she'd make it on her own terms, find love, fortune, happiness – whatever that was – and peace, and had held onto a fantasy of returning home triumphant, to forgiveness, bunting and 'look at yous!' Now she had it, she could let the fantasy go.

Over the course of the following months, over numerous dinner parties on the terrace and coke-fuelled evenings in the clubs downtown, Nikko introduced her to his friends. Well, the people he hung out with anyway: arch corporate lawyers, self-satisfied financial journalists, stockbrokers and hedge fund analysts with whom he spent his working life, the small-pond-big-fish socialites and vapid PR girls who flittered and tittered around them. There was a slight coolness in their initial acceptance of her – who was she exactly, this *barmaid*? – but her Irish sense of humour, sharply defined sexuality and vampy-chic dress sense, a legacy of her fetishist tendencies, soon won the city boys ('She's a babe') and ice-queens ('Isn't she *funny*?') over. Not that he cared, quite the reverse. He loved the way she made them uncomfortable.

He helped her get a job organising the endless fund-raisers for various charities cashing in on fiscal guilt, social one-upmanship and tax concessions. Big, glitzy dos up on the Peak or in the plush, low-lit function rooms of various private clubs; she had natural nous for putting together guest lists, deciding set design and styling staff, especially when it meant she could indulge her predilection for latex and leather, essentially requiring the same people skills as running a bar, with the ability to make snap decisions thrown in.

They were good together, so they were. Despite her love for him, part of her that punished and blamed and scolded herself meant she hadn't had the same immediate intuition as he, the same certainty, unwavering as his hefty hard-on, until he proposed. Even though she'd secretly prayed for this, him, all her life, ironically it was she who had been the more cautious to begin with, always expecting it to fail, the bubble to burst, spinning out into another screaming emotional car crash. While she liked to believe that whatever you give your attention to, whether positive or negative, the Universe, in her infinite wisdom, does her utmost to deliver it with a genie-like, 'your wish is my command', and had often tried to harness this secret – that you get what you ask for – she'd always been a little too uncertain, lacking the conviction to pull it off. She always nurtured a kernel of doubt and that, she realised with wry cynicism, meant she never visualised anything clearly enough, left her impotently at the mercy of events, carried along in an uncertain direction, true, as ever, to the Principle. This time she caught herself when she entertained 'It's too good to be true', 'You don't deserve this' monkey-mind chatter, turning it, willing it, into 'You totally fucking deserve this, girl, and more, much more.'

Now, lo and behold, she was getting it and loving it.

He nurtured her tenderly like a flower, taking joy at the lavish character blooms that steadily grew stronger as she thrust out deeper, more trusting roots, revelling in her absolute yet un-submissive adoration, spoiling her like a little girl in the knowledge that later on at home or 'right now' in the back of a taxi, his reward would be tortuously orgasmic. As she calmed, like something wild slowly tamed, she began to loosen the grip of her masochism and begin to love, begin to trust; first him, then herself.

They named the boat *Nikkim*.

During a spectacular hurricane that thwacked bolts of pure, livid energy into the ground as it approached, they took their drinks out onto the balcony to watch. Beneath apocalyptic cloud and lancing rain they stripped naked, he bent her over the parapet, slamming into her as needles of rain stung her back, the drop yawning beneath her, and, screaming with exhilaration, she knew she trusted this man with her life.

Being with her created an inevitable schism between himself and his colleagues, which he enjoyed. Her indifference to etiquette, restaurant-silencing foul mouth and lack of inhibition set him apart from the honking Brits and their sneering, identikit arm candy.

She also knew how to give the impression that it was she who'd chosen him when they were in public, and he loved that. It was this – well-disguised – contempt he had for the bovine herd that ensured his escape. He knew of no one else, especially not any girl he'd met, that could have come with him – to chuck it all in and take to the sea didn't fit the prescribed route, the trodden path. Not the done thing. No one really got out, even if they maintained, loudly, that they were going to. Someday. No, they'd all stick it out to the Handover next year, hanging on by their braces while they whacked off panicky résumés back to London and the ensuing, inevitable crash loomed like a tsunami out to sea. She'd been bang up for it though. Said yes instantly, as if she'd already willed it, even before he explained how long it would take to get to Sydney, how dangerous, how many days out of sight of land.

The boat was his glass slipper, and it fitted Kim perfectly.

It was then that he proposed, on the last day of a week's diving in Micronesia, 30 metres down amid a kaleidoscopic, synchronised swirl of fish, in sign language (you – me – heart – together – forever – ring – yes?). He was a man of few words.

Over the last two months he'd taken her out on *Nikkim* almost every day. Going over the routines again and again until she got it right. She was a natural: quick to learn, balanced, strong, intuitive of the sea's infidelity, instinctively anticipating his orders before he called them, and now she was ready, physically tough enough. Mentally, she'd always been ready.

They were due to set sail next week – Tuesday or Wednesday, weather permitting – and it was looking pretty permissive.

'Hi, babe,' She heard him call and the front door slam.

'Out here,' she called back from the pool, undoing her bikini top and slipping off the g-string, reclining, supine.

'Listen, darl,' he said as he appeared on the terrace, took in her aquatic splendour with a lupine grin and began flicking off his cufflinks. 'I don't want you overdoing it, okay? I specifically told you to take it easy today and you have blatantly walked all the way from the bedroom to the kitchen and to the terrace since I left this morning. Possibly more than once.'

'Jeez, I'm sorry. I promise the most energetic thing I've done all day was asking Mai to cut some limes.'

'Good girl,' he said, stripping off his tie, shirt, trousers and boxers to join her in the water, his hardening cock swinging about as if sniffing her out. She sat him on a half-submerged step, slid back his velvety foreskin until the head strained and slurped him greedily like a kid with a lolly. When he could take no more, she straddled him, reached down to position him between the lips of her labia and, with a sigh of satisfaction, rammed her minty-lime tongue into his mouth as she sank forcefully down onto him. Ripples spread out across the pool's surface, gradually increasing in oscillation until wavelets slopped over the edge and seeped darkly into the sisal matting like blood.

'So. How was it?' Kim asked as they dried in the sun.

'Awesome, babe, as ever.'

'No, eejit,' she giggled. 'Your last day.'

'Also awesome. Though in a different way. Almost as satisfying, just without the gasping, moaning and shuddering.'

'Were they sad to see you go?'

'Nah. You should see what the bastards paid to see the back of me. Jealous though, for sure.' They leant on the rail in matching silk bathrobes, elbows touching, watching the first of a billion lights blink into life across the city.

'How many are coming tonight, exactly?'

'About fifty, I'd guess.'

'Fifty?' he said. 'That's a lot, Kim.'

'Only twenty for dinner, another thirty or so coming on later, depending on how many of your workmates fail to recognise the implied brush-off of 'You're welcome to come later for dancing.' Anyway, it takes two hundred to fill the place. And don't worry, there's only Jess, Jim, Alison, Jez and Gibsy on *Nikkim* tomorrow.'

'Cool.' He stared into the setting sun. 'I cannot *wait* to get the fuck out of here with you, my sexy souvenir, and watch you fall in love with Oz. To see how you bloom in a country where you can be whoever you want to be, no one gives a shit. Escape your past, reinvent yourself if you want to – they've been doing it for centuries down there.' He slid an arm round her waist and pulled her to him. 'I'm kinda hoping you won't change at all though 'coz I love you just the way you are. It'll be cool, just you wait 'til we get there.'

It was the most demonstrative she'd ever heard him.

'*If* we get there,' she said, biting the lobe of his ear. 'There's the small matter of four thousand nautical miles to negotiate first.'

They stood in silence, lost in thoughts that swirled away into the hum of the city, twilight shadows cast by the monolithic buildings throwing vast abysses of darkness up towards them, swallowing the streets. She shivered.

'Oh, I bought you something,' she said. 'A thank you present.'

'Thank you for what?'

'For being able to ask that question.' She winked at him and disappeared inside to return with a small lacquered box, twirled with delicate inlay. 'I found it in a little antique shop out in Stanley – tucked away off the main drag. Just sort of caught my eye. It's really old.'

'It's beautiful,' he said.

'Not the box, what's inside it. Open it, fool that you are.'

He prised open the lid. Inside lay a fountain pen, the black-blue shaft set perfectly amid the crimson satin lining of the box, the evening light caught in the nacreous translucence of the shaft so that, as he turned it this way and that, pelagic shapes seemed to move deep within its depths.

'Nice one, babe, it's lovely,' he said. 'Just what I need to sign off one chapter and begin a new one, starting with our marriage certificate tomorrow.' He slid it back in the box, snapped the lid shut and moved towards her. 'Come here, you.'

# Chapter 9

*Tuesday, 20th October, 1933*
*The Sinai Peninsula*

*My love,*
*I hope this finds you well,*

*Firstly; I must confess to a degree of disappointment – though God knows it's unreasonable of me – that there was nothing from you waiting for me in Alexandria. I'd built up such high hopes that I suppose the letdown was inevitable.*

*Please do send word if you can. You know my itinerary. Any of the post offices or embassies will hold your message, unread, until I arrive. Just one word from you would fill my sails and set my course the straighter.*

*While I remember; the evening with Jim in Alexandria proved most edifying. He led me deep into the heart of the medina, the fortified old town, filled with a throng to match that of daytime. Apparently much of the city's affairs are conducted after sunset for the simple reason that it's considerably cooler, therefore the mind is all the more rational. I ventured that it was also easier to carry out any clandestine business under cover of darkness, to which Jim simply smiled in that enigmatic way he does.*

*Firstly he led me to what he jokingly referred to as a Gentleman's Outfitters, of all places, or the equivalent out here – the goods on sale differed markedly to that of Mayhew's in St James – where, at his insistence, I was duly kitted out with a few things he deemed crucial to my continued survival: namely, a Panama hat to replace my fedora (I think the effect is quite rakish, darling, and feel certain you would approve). What else? – a canvas knapsack not dissimilar to his own; a knife called a Bowie, American; and lastly – don't be alarmed – a small, snub-nosed pistol, French make, a .25 'Le Sans Pareil', with a bone handle and a leather holster that fits snugly under the armpit, apparently vital for one's peace of mind. And, I hope, yours too. He expressed surprise that I hadn't already been issued one by the Company.*

*Thus 'armed' we moved on to an iniquitous den where they served wine and viscous, murky spirits, and where each low table featured a hookah – a water-pipe elaborately decorated with Arabic lettering – the fragrant smoke of which filled the dingy room. We took a table and played a few rounds of backgammon, the one game I am quite good at, though Jim knew set moves I've never encountered in games with you and Anna. I managed to hold my own, you'll be pleased to know, losing only two games in five. Some hours later, and buoyed by my minor victory, we returned to the hotel, slightly fuzzy from the rough wine and tobacco. I greatly envy Jim's sense of direction – I'd never in a month of Sundays been able to retrace my steps through the winding alleys in broad daylight, let alone the middle of the night.*

*We left quite early this morning just as dawn paled the eastern horizon, and I do not think I can, in this state, do this letter further justice.*

*Yours, ever,*

*R*

*Thursday, 22nd October, 1933*
*The Suez Canal*

*Dearest Lillian,*

*Currently you find me within the narrow confines of the famous Suez Canal.*

*We entered the neck of same not long after departing Alexandria, having rounded the Sinai Peninsula, a desolate expanse of desert as far as the eye could see to each side of us. What a difference it made though, to begin with, having land close to both port and starboard – it has made for very different sailing, the water completely smooth. We are now plagued by swarms of flies, however, so persistent that you must resign all hope of activity and devote oneself solely to keeping the buggers from eyes and mouth. I find the best way to keep them at bay involves swathing my head in muslin – over my Panama so the brim projects some space between face and cloth. At the expense of losing the breeze, mind.*

*We entered through Port Said, little more than a long, very busy quayside thick with ships of all shapes, sizes and nationalities, patiently awaiting entry to the canal itself. No sooner had we moored, taking a slot at the quay, than we were surrounded by dhows – triangular-sailed wooden dinghies, weighed down with all manner of fruits, nuts, dates, spices, and other tourist knick-knacks, the men aboard them demonstrating great skill in balancing baskets while they leapt about, courting business. Ingenious pulleys were swiftly rigged from the rails, and we had great fun hauling in our purchases, though you might have to wait a while for your present . . .*

*Buchanan must have particularly persuasive negotiating skills for we were moored scarcely an hour, with no shore leave permitted, before the British Vice Consul, Williams-Napier, came aboard and was led to the bridge. He departed briskly soon after and we were immediately ushered through – straight to the front of the queue, klaxon blaring. There are still some benefits to being a member of our foundering Empire, it would appear, though what business he had with the Apollonia I haven't the slightest idea.*

*We also acquired fresh blood, or as Jim dourly commented from our vantage point on the observation deck, 'new inmates to the asylum'. A couple, retired by the looks of them, and clearly well-to-do, they were accompanied aboard by Williams-Napier and introduced to Buchanan, who weathered the proceedings with a look of dutiful resignation. Maddox, source of all gossip, tells me they – the Hamiltons – are to join us as far as Aden, where he has a position as some sort of advisory attaché to the consulate there, a post that requires little or no active involvement – hence his recent sabbatical to the Great Pyramids – but is handsomely remunerated. I find it one of life's great paradoxes, my darling, that the more one gets paid the less one actually does. No doubt it's designed that way by those set to benefit most from the arrangement! Perhaps I should take it up with your father, who I know to be highly industrious, delegating little responsibility and working all the hours God gave him. On second thoughts, perhaps not; he'll assume I've become a Socialist.*

*The canal is rightly held as one of man's most accomplished engineering feats; over one hundred miles long and costing the lives of some 150,000 Egyptians and the blood and sweat of half a million more, it has revolutionised world trade. What matter that so many died, so long as the global economy thrives as a result! So much blood sacrifice at the altar of progress.*

*Control of the canal, currently neutral – though Jim is quick to point out that there is in reality no such thing, and that it would be better to look at it in terms of 'no one regarding it worth fighting over just at the moment' – represents control over all trade routes East. The region can look forward to considerable political and military 'attention' in the future, no doubt. Predictably, the most prominent naval presence is British; we are currently the 'defenders' of its neutrality, which must be convenient.*

*From the ship's rail we watched camel trains laden with swaddled bales and enormous baskets passing along the banks, caravans comprising some hundred animals or more, quite an odd sight, as the sight of us must have been to them – the slanting chimneys of the ship moving sedately through the desert. The merchants waved to us from their ungainly mounts as we passed, shouting what I hoped were greetings in their harsh-sounding tongue.*

*Jim and I had another boxing session, but my heart was not in it, and after the fourth painful clock to my jaw I lost my temper, took a wild swing at him and he caught my arms,*

*'What the hell's the matter with you?'*

*I explained the trip was beginning to get to me.*

*'Look, Ralph,' he said, holding my sore chin so I had to meet his eye. 'We're more than halfway there now, and you've done bloody well in my view to cope with it as well as you have. Not many men can simply up sticks and leave their lives behind without a few moments of doubt. Take heart, sonny, and keep your chin up!'*

*With that he pushed me back and feinted this way and that, ducking and sparring with invisible foes and looking so idiotic I had to laugh.*

*'That's more like it,' he said. 'Come round to mine after you've cleaned up and we'll christen a new one.' God bless him.*

*I retired soon after dinner –fish and potatoes – to find us back in open water, this time the Red Sea, when I woke. I berated Maddox for not waking me at Suez, where I had intended to get these letters off and had hope of a telegram from you. I couldn't bear the thought that you'd sent a message that I'd somehow missed, so perhaps it's better not to know. He tells me that no one was permitted ashore, yet I cannot help but feel angry with the man. I must remember that my situation is neither anyone's fault nor of anyone else's concern, and pull myself together. It's not as if he deliberately didn't tell me in an attempt to stymie my communication with you, after all.*

*Despite Jim's inspiriting, this voyage is beginning to wear me down. My morale is low, sweet angel, and I'll therefore write no more for now but will seek you out in my dreams, to sit with you beside some shady brook amid the green fields of home, so very far from this desiccated land.*

*Wait for me there,*
*Ralph*

*Sunday, 25th October, 1933*
*The Red Sea*

*My love,*
*A month already.*

*'Only eleven months to go now, lad,' Jim said with a laugh, clapping me soundly on the back and raising a glass. We do seem to be drinking rather a lot. It does help pass the time.*

*Also, my training has been intensifying – the fight's tomorrow. Jim's donned gloves and we're now making 'contact' from which he comes out markedly better than I. By God, I swear he's enjoying the pummelling he rains down on me each day. I am improving though, and managed to land a left (my left hand finally coming in useful) on him today that stunned him for a moment – and since the tournament is just round the corner, not a moment too soon. He suggested that it might be prudent to keep the left back, keep it in reserve as a surprise on the actual day. We don't go for long; even in the shade of the aft deck in this heat we're completely finished after half an hour.*

*I think I have a loose front tooth.*

*I must briefly update you vis-à-vis the Richards situation.*

*Symmonds, in an attempt to establish which of the two is the more deranged, and whether the entire fiasco is purely a figment of Claudia's imagination, instructed me yesterday evening, as we recovered from a session of unbridled pugilism, to proceed as follows. Since, he said, I have her confidence, I was the only man (you remember a boy, I'm sure!) for the job.*

*'What job, exactly?' I said, already alarmed.*

*'Well,' says he, 'first we need to work out whether this damned heat has got to her or whether she really is in mortal danger.'*

*'But you saw how the fellow behaved with us at the hotel – he's clearly a brute.'*

*'That's as may be, Ralph, but we can't very well go wading in there without some kind of evidence or we'll be put ashore before you can say "Oh, lack-a-day, my prospective father-in-law won't be very impressed by this at all', can we?"' He can put up quite a convincing argument, I'll give him that.*

*'So,' I said with a resigned sigh, knowing in advance that this will involve some risk on my behalf, if not to life and limb, then certainly of incurring the wrath of an allegedly homicidal maniac, 'what exactly do you have in mind?'*

*'Ah,' he says, 'very perceptive, for it is in exactly "in mind" that we have to put ourselves. Her mind, to be precise.' I clearly looked much as I do when you ask me which of two shawls looks more becoming, dearest, for he told me to close my mouth and try to pay attention.*

*'The mind is a powerful thing, my boy, quite capable of curing the body of many ailments, overthrowing the rationality of whole nations, and other more inexplicable feats that you'll have to remind me to tell you of' – I assured him I would make a point of it – 'since by their very nature they are seen by many to go against God's*

*law, and that can be a dangerous position to be in, as we now know'(the other night he enlightened me about the horrors of the Inquisition, the stuff you don't get taught at school, particularly the slaughter of women during that dark period).*

*'It sometimes seems to me,' he continued, 'that the leaders of all the world's religions regard the fairer sex as evil incarnate, and the act of procreation an abomination, an insult to God. Let's just think that through, shall we?' He was slightly squiffy at the time, and in tub-thumping mode, aboard one of his thought trains that are quite difficult to derail.*

*'The act of procreation, of Love Making, for the sake of a better word' – at this I had to glance around the mess to see who, if anyone, was within earshot, in particular any of the missionaries; a couple of course were – 'necessary for the future of humanity, and,' he said, stopping to eye me sceptically, 'as we both know full well, singularly the most pleasurable experience a man – or woman – can indulge in.' I was by now puce, my love, but he merely pushed it further: 'Repeat after me, Talbot, the most pleasurable experience etc.' – I repeated it quietly – 'is, in their view, a sin!' This continued in similar vein for some time and concluded with him muttering something about the lot of them 'either missing their mothers or batting for the wrong side', but I will regale you with it in its entirety another time.*

*Where was I?*

*Yes, Mrs Richards' mental state:*

*'What I propose is this,' he said. 'You present her with this medicine' – he covertly palmed me a small, stoppered phial of white powder – 'and persuade her to take it, telling her it's some remedy to counter the effects of poison. Say you picked up in Alexandria or something, even that you've taken me into your confidence, if that lends the tale more credibility.'*

*'What is it?' I asked, shaking the bottle.*

*'Nothing at all – bicarbonate of soda with a little sugar and flour – but that's precisely the point.' I must have been looking perplexed again. 'Look, if subsequently she shows a marked improvement it will be the placebo effect of the powder and therefore the poison can be assumed to be a figment of her imagination.'*

*I let it sink in. 'But if the mind is so powerful –' I began.*

*'Ailments, lad, it can cure, but immunity to some nerve agent or other, I doubt it. Ultimately, anything that might alleviate her suffering should be attempted, agreed?'*

*I agreed, though these past few days have not presented me with the opportunity to even say as much as good day to the poor woman.*

*I will keep you informed.*

*Wish me luck tomorrow!*

*With all love,*

*Ralph*

*P.S. Another nightmare – should I tell you?*

*I'm running through serpentine back alleys – Alexandria? – in the dark, trying to catch up with someone, not escape from anything; then, as I pass a side-street and glance down it I see you, fleetingly, your dress hitched in your hands, running away from me, or in the opposite direction anyways; I skid to a halt and hasten back but you've vanished, so I venture into the gloomy alley to where you last stood. But there's no other way out of what I sickeningly realise is a dead end; confounded I turn to leave, but the dark mouth of the alley is now blocked by the looming silhouettes of three indistinct hulking shapes, inhuman. I reach to my armpit for the pistol but the holster is empty, and they begin to advance as I frantically seek an exit. They are nearly upon me when I hear you call my name – there, from a low door I hadn't previously noticed, your hand beckoning me urgently. I reach it but it is too small, and on trying to squeeze through become trapped and you have gone on ahead and the men, beasts, are upon me, and I'm awake, pouring sweat.*

*Perhaps you are betrothed to a lunatic.*

*x*

*Monday, 26th October, 1933*
*Jeddah*
*Saudi Arabia*

*Lil,*

*You find me slightly battered!*

*The tournament began in the afternoon with much excitement as the draw was announced, what with the distinct probability of loss of face – though few passengers showed up. Luckily our weight was taken into account – I'm down to fight the only other chap my size, Peck, approximately my own age but quite a bit tougher by the look of him.*

*Thank God I didn't end up with Swaine; his bout with a Welsh fellow – Jonesy, well liked – was a vile spectacle though the crew bayed for blood, quite shocking, with neither man willing to succumb and both seemingly indestructible. Equally heavy set, they laid into each other for what must have been half an hour, broken down into six-minute rounds, and it quickly turned nasty with blood spattering their chests and cheeks. They pretty well just stood their ground and slogged it out; Jonesy took a hammering and had his nose broken – not for the first time, I'd guess – while Swaine, punch drunk for a change, had a vicious cut to his eye, and in the end it was declared a draw. Swaine wouldn't shake the man's hand for a few seconds – clearly had his ire up, and, to be honest, he gave more than he got – and there was an awkward moment before he complied, the spectators muttering. He doesn't make friends naturally, that one.*

*Another couple of matches – I forget the details since I was increasingly nervous and had Jim at my ear coaching me incessantly: hands up, head down, keep moving etc. – and our number was up.*

*'Keep it clean, no biting, gouging or holding,' said Maddox, who gave me a slap on the shoulder and said 'Good luck lad.'*

*With everyone shouting, Peck and I touched gloves, and before I knew it the sly bugger caught me with a right, knocking me backwards and following it up with two jabs to the ribs while I was off balance.*

*Winded, seeing stars, I thought this was going to be one of the shortest bouts in history, but he backed off rather than follow it up, letting me recover my breath. Over the yelling I could hear Jim shouting for me to keep my hands up. I shook my head to clear it and ducked back towards Peck, feinted to his left and jabbed at him with my right, catching him on the side of the head, not the chin, as intended.*

*He was too fast for me. After the third round, with swollen eyes, gasping for air like a gaffed fish and back in my corner, Jim splashed water over my face.*

*'Listen, lad,' he said, 'he's too good for you but I reckon his jaw's glass. I think now's the time for that little surprise we talked about. Let him come in close and try and land one with as hard a hook as you can manage.' I nodded and stood up shakily.*

*Peck came forward, smelling victory, and I went back, bluffing retreat. He leant into a right that whistled past my nose and threw him off balance, and I belted him with my left as he fell into it, right on the side of the jaw below his temple.*

*Knocked him out cold, Lil! Only for a few seconds, mind, but won the bout and some applause to boot, and Peck's grudging handshake once he'd recovered his feet. Jim was well pleased with his protégé, and plied me with brandy in his cabin later, re-enacting the fight like a proud father.*

*Having never in my life experienced anything close to paternal pride, I basked in his praise, darling, heart fit to bust.*

*Jeddah.*

*We put into port last night and only saw the lie of the land this morning (squinting somewhat through a socking shiner).*

*Flat sand stretches away in every direction, rising distantly to the east, shimmering liquidly in the heat, an endless expanse relieved only by the occasional cluster of palms. My initial reaction was amazement that people should chose to inhabit such a barren hell, so remote and exposed, but Jim soon put me straight.*

*Not only is it prosperous but sacred, due to the proximity of Makkah, the birthplace of Mohammed, not thirty miles southeast. It is to this shrine that all Moslims must, once in their lives, attempt to make pilgrimage, and this port serves the thousands who journey there from Northern Africa and the West.*

*I have now put a boot print on my third continent in as many weeks, an achievement not many of our friends can claim. I notch up these minor moments as punctuation in the trip, and that I might have something to brag about when I return!*

*Still no telegram.*

*Perhaps there'll be a bundle of them waiting for me in Mombasa, where at least you can be sure I'll receive them. That, at any rate, is my silent wish – one that will be answered in a week or so. Despite the going having been slow thus far, for one reason and another, Maddox assures me that the trade winds will help whisk us south once we clear the Gulf of Aden.*

*I'm now wholly adjusted to the five daily calls to prayer, the loud petitioning of Allah that seemed so haunting at first. The mosques' delicate minarets and the startling white of their central domes are quite beautiful, like the bulbs of ornate onions against the desert's rugged reds and ochres. Once ashore and revitalised by a splendid bath – a hammam, a tradition in the region – Jim asked permission for us to visit one this morning, something of an honour for us Infidels.*

*We were led through the town to the central mosque at a time when there would be no devotees to offend, and removed our shoes at the entrance. Walking in was like tiptoeing into another world; I never imagined such delicacy and elaboration behind the plain walls. Fine geometric tiling covered all the interior, weaving a dazzling texture of bright blues, greens, gold and silver throughout the vaulted hall, inspiring the same sense of wonder one feels on entering one of the C of E's cathedrals. I'm sure Allah is well pleased.*

*We couldn't stay long, and were not allowed to see the shrine itself, just enough to get a sense of quiet sanctity and to reinforce the suspicion that, to my mind at least, while these different faiths proclaim the exclusive existence of their own One True God, the similarity in doctrine and devotion points – surely – towards them being one and the same! Is it really possible that they sit up there, the Christian and Moslem deities, cursing each other sniffily like disgruntled neighbours who refuse to acknowledge each other in the street, competing for our groping souls as we fumble around in circles? I seriously doubt it.*

*I think it much more likely that though there may well be one God, one Creator, there are many different ways of placating Him, possibly as many as there are individuals alive, none of which particularly offend Him, so long as life is revered and it harm none. I'm quite sure He doesn't expect us to kill each other over nuances of ideology. Perhaps I'm being naïve – there are no doubt numerous political and economic incentives for the slaughter marking our progress down the centuries – but visiting that mosque induced a small epiphany in my questioning mind. Jim tells me the basic tenets of the Koran are identical to those of the Bible; essentially 'Don't kill anyone', 'Honour your parents', 'Do unto others as you would have them do unto you' and 'Try not to steal anything from anyone, whether their wife, land or food.' What could be simpler? As for killing in God's name? It just doesn't have a good ring to it, does it, angel? Allah, Yahweh, God; He – or She, if Jim has anything to do with it – is probably laughing his or her socks off at our idiocy.*

*Or crying.*

*Hopefully, after this so called Great War, we've learned a little more about each other and can look forward to a period of 'Great Peace' for a change, in which our children can flourish. insh'allah! as they say here – by God's will. Judging from the number of battleships I have seen since we left Portsmouth, like Buchanan I rather suspect we still have a great deal more to learn.*

*'Our children' – how that phrase makes me smile.*

*Yussuf, our guide, proved exceptionally genial to his charges for the day. After our visit to the mosque he insisted that we accompany him back to his home where we were treated like royalty, though it was clear he was not a wealthy man. His wife, hidden behind an elaborate burka so that even her eyes were veiled by a kind of gauze, brought us endless small dishes of spiced delicacies, lamb, fish and fruits, which we ate sitting cross-legged on elaborately decorated cushions in a cool, shady courtyard. When we finally boarded the ship I'm sure she ended up lower in the water.*

*Arriving on board I learned that Dr Richards was still ashore, endeavouring to stock up on supplies at the hospital. Seizing the moment, and having checked casually with Maddox that he'd be gone for some time, I went down to their cabin and gently knocked on their door. There was no answer. I knocked again, louder. The bolt was drawn back and Claudia's pale face peered out. It seemed to take her a second or two to recognise me – I had seen her only twice since Alex, and on both occasions she had ignored my greeting – but something registered and she let me in.*

*The cabin, though bigger than mine, was stale, close and dark, the porthole covered with a drape. I immediately started towards it to let some light in but she stopped me.*

*'Leave it be,' she said.*

*'Are you all right?' I asked, concerned by her appearance.*

*'What do you care?' she said sourly. 'I asked for your help and you crossed the road.' She eyed me suspiciously. 'Why are you here?'*

*'Well, I spoke with Colonel Symmonds and –'*

*'You did what?' she interrupted, her voice high and thin, slightly hysterical.*

*'It's quite all right,' I assured her, 'he's the paragon of discretion. He gave me something, look. To counter the effects of anything untoward you might have ingested. Quite a remarkable tonic, by all accounts.' I showed her the bottle, which she looked at dubiously. 'Just stir a little into your tea in the morning. It's perfectly safe.' Now that my eyes had adjusted to the gloom and I could see her properly I was a little shocked. Already slight, even in the short time since Alexandria she had lost weight, and her pallor was positively ashen. I had an idea.*

*'Can you show me what he gives you each night?' I asked.*

*She went to the washbasin set into an alcove and pulled out a small travelling bag from the cupboard beneath. She presented me with a tin, which I opened, and took out one of the small white pills inside, pocketed it and made to leave.*

*'Wait,' she said. 'Thank you.' Her shoulders seemed to slump.*

*'What on earth for?' I said.*

*'For believing me.' She smiled thinly.*

*'Think nothing of it. Let's just try to get to the bottom of the matter, shall we?' She seemed about to say more but I didn't want to hang around. I patted her on the arm.*

*'Try not to worry,' I said, trying to sound sage. 'He's not poisoning you, I'm sure of it. Either it's medicinal, as he says, or he's sedating you, as you suspect, which believe me, a lot of the time I quite envy.' And with that, I slipped out.*

*I've just come from bringing Jim up to speed re latest developments, sotto voce, in his cabin. He was, I think, quite impressed with my foresight.*

*'Well done, Ralph,' he said, handing me a now habitual pre-prandial Scotch. 'Let's have a look at the blighter.' I gave him the pill. 'Not much we can do here but –' He broke a piece of it off and put it in his mouth, 'Not poison, that much is clear. Bitter. My bet is lithium or codeine.' I looked blank. 'Sedatives, both quite harmless.'*

*'Well that's a relief,' I said.*

*'Yes, it is. But it still doesn't explain her behaviour. Let's see whether the placebo has any effect. I'm quite sure it will.' He raised his glass, somehow always able to find something to toast. 'To you, young Ralph, your keen sense of duty, courage in the face of danger and quick thinking. You'll make a fine emissary of his Majesty's realm.' Not entirely sure he wasn't mocking me, I raised my own in return.*

*I'll send further developments from Aden.*

*Please write to me! Any word. Just let me know you're all right; send it to Mombasa.*

*We sail within the hour.*

*Yours, ever,*

*Ralph*

*x*

# Chapter 10

*Kepulajawa, Indonesia. 1996.*

'It's time.'

Half asleep, Dirga Ikhwan registered the urgency in the voice and snapped instantly awake, 'It's time. Get up.' Someone jabbed him in the ribs. He stretched and scratched at the bites on his neck and face. He'd been dreaming – somewhere beautiful, reflections of a forest pool shining in her laughing eyes, the white of her teeth pure and clean against honey skin. But it was gone. Above him through the sifting, gently clattering palm leaves he could see the stars sparkling, as if dancing, and the sliver of a new moon.

Auspicious for some, he thought, not so much for others.

He swung his legs over the side of the canvas hammock, stretched and rubbed his eyes as his erection swiftly slackened. In the low light of the gas lamps he could see figures moving about with practiced efficiency. He heard the solid clunk of heavy metal over the thick resonance of cicada and tree frog, voices cursing at each other with jocular familiarity, forced bravado.

'Don't forget your nappy, baby *shishu*.'

'If you bring your mother, you won't need to stop sucking her tit.'

'I'm still sucking your sister's, *bai*.'

'*Ai benchod*!'

The same shit as usual. A year ago he'd have joined in – trading insults, strapping on inuring, desensitising, machismo armour, banishing soft thoughts of caresses in the dark and babies bounced on knees and replacing them with visions of viscera, the hunter-bonding, the dehumanising self-abasement that he realised must have gone on thousands of years, that must have existed all over the world, whipping up the killer instinct to hunt deer in the jungle. Or to slaughter the men, women and children in the next village. Now he didn't bother. Not that he was brave. He simply didn't care anymore.

Dropping silently to the sand, he retied his sarong, slung the machete across his chest so it hung at his waist and, without needing to look, reached for the pistol that gleamed at the end of his hammock, stuffing it into the waist-band at the small of his back, instantly conscious of the sense of cold invincibility its heavy presence gave him. He padded to the fire and poured out thick black coffee, popped out four amphetamine pills from a blister pack and washed them down, burning his throat in the process. He looked around. Down through the trees he could make out the orange glow of gaslight coming from the hut at the edge of the jungle, men crowded around the doorway.

Scattering scuttles of ghost crabs, he walked down the sandy path and, squatting on his haunches, leant back against the thatch wall, listening to the voices inside, the rhythmic ping of the radar and the hiss of the radio.

'About forty clicks out. No problem.'

'How big?'

'Don't know. Could be smugglers, they're moving fast.'

'Coast guard?'

'Not that fast.' Murmurs of excitement.

'Let's do it.'

He felt the energy inside the hut surge. Men spilt out onto the sand, down to the shoreline. He rose, sighed – here we go again, he thought – and followed.

He helped run the boat out, past the breakers that shone luminous with agitated algae, pushing and hauling on the fibreglass hull, everyone silent now, the shock of the water hitting him just as the chemical broke into his bloodstream, making his breath shorten so that he was hyperventilating slightly as he pulled himself aboard, shivering in the wind chill as the 250cc twin outboards hacked into life then bammed them out and away through the waves. They huddled down below the gunwale out of the spray. Here we go again, he thought.

He looked up at the stars, fingering on the string around his neck the brass amulet she'd given him, willing his chi to rise up and warm him like monks are trained to do, far away where the gods live high in the mountains. He'd heard about it on the Hindi radio station. The Holy Fire. Enabling them to live above the snow line – snow! – up in the mountains with nothing but a thin blanket, to thaw holes in frozen rivers by directing their body heat alone and to dry blankets dipped into the icy water by their master and draped around their shoulders until dawn. He tried to imagine temperatures so cold that the water became solid like rock. He'd heard some managed twenty blankets in one night, bone dry, and that this was possible with purity of spirit and intent, the man said. And other, more incredible things, in the name of God, in the service of Shiva. Anything was possible – even, he'd heard, the ability to be in two places simultaneously.

He closed his eyes and tried to imagine snow, then thought of her and imagined being with her, willing himself to be curled up in bed with her, warm, and gave a bitter laugh. *Possible*, maybe. With purity of spirit.

Not like this though, not here thumping out to sea, jaw clenched, knees to chin, pit-stomached, with dark intent. Now even the intent was wavering. He had lost something, some spark inside, the flickering candle flame of purpose that had always drawn him onwards had dimmed, possibly extinguished. Since that time, barely eight moons ago, when everything had changed. He looked across at his kid brother Domi, his grinning teeth clearly visible, gleaming in the dark. The psycho fucking loved it. Thought he was in some cheap American movie like in the badly copied DVDs they showed up the coast for the few tourists that ventured this far, with his headband and Marlboro and wraparound glasses pushed back and his teeth necklace. Human teeth. Gone mad on the speed and the rum and the blood. He remembered how he'd begged him not to do it, the look in Domi's eyes, the dead coldness of them, dull and black, glazed like a dead dog's, when he pulled the blade back across the old woman's age-slackened neck. How, like a chicken during the ceremonies, she had continued to blink her eyes and gape her mouth in surprise, unable to understand what had happened and trying to speak as the jet of blood pulsed slowly to a stop. His own brother – laughing, high and hysterical.

Thank God their mother hadn't lived to see that.

'You take care of him,' she'd whispered, not three years before. 'Take him to the city. To Jakarta. Promise me. Promise me!' Her dying words. How had he managed to mess it all up so badly? Was it his fault?

Yes.

He knew it, and one day, when this was all over, he'd face it. When he was ready. Perhaps, now the twins were grown up, he would go to the ashram in Pulau Bawean for a few years. He'd been distracted, lost for so long – since what, adolescence? They'd both grown up too quickly, missed out years of childhood where nothing should have mattered, where sunlight shone through splashed water and innocence ran through the forest laughing. But there had always been work to do and his father's calloused backhand to ensure it got done: watering, digging, mending nets, tending the animals. Taking endless beatings for his little brother. The stale, rancid reek of palm wine still reminded him of being young.

Then, when one of the boats was short of a crew member, his break had come and he'd jumped at it. He remembered the exhilaration of that first time, the sheer thrill of the chase, and the way it had tailed off over the years just like an amphetamine high, and how in its place had formed a tempered resolve, a risk-taking audacity that the others took for courage but was in reality just recklessness.

He'd been bewitched by the money, the slant glanced adoration from girls, the *respect* that came with his hard-earned reputation, the way the bar in the village went quiet when he walked in and the shy taps on the back door of his hut in the middle of the night. Of course Domi would follow him when the time came. He worshipped his infamous, dangerous big brother, would die for him.

That was long ago.

It was too late now.

This was the last time, he promised her, but she saw right through him. Always had done, ever since they first met. That's why he fell for her in the first place, why he'd given up on the others. He remembered the exact moment when he realised that she loved him; she was struggling with a sack of plantain that he'd shouldered easily to her home, receiving not a word of thanks but the briefest of eye contact as she turned away, and the slow spread of realisation up through his belly that he loved her too. If only he could earn her love, he thought, perhaps she could offer him salvation, some reprieve.

She never fell for the trappings of glamour his lifestyle had brought him: the watch, the sunglasses, the radio. That was one of the things that had drawn him to her – her aloof indifference to his status. She never looked when he tried to catch her eye at the well, never collapsed into shy laughter when he called out to her. He had been forced to follow the old traditions of courtship, dutifully approaching her father with gifts of strong nylon nets, a wild pig he trapped in the forest, honeycombs prised precariously from 30 metres high up in the trees. It had been weeks before he had even spoken to her, and even that had been under the watchful eye of a stern-faced aunt. Slowly she had thawed, almost as if she had resigned herself to him, his elementally handsome features – high cheekbones, prominent brow and jaw – good humour and roguish, piratical, swagger gradually wearing her down until she capitulated, with one proviso; that he never went out with the men at night again.

He promised.

The wedding had been one of the biggest the island – a dot in the Java Sea unnamed on maps that they called Kepulajawa – had seen in years partly as a result of three decades of political chaos, state-sponsored slaughter and the resulting poverty that squatted over the region like a thundercloud. But now he had money, was wealthy by island standards, and both his and Rani's families were respected, both having been held in some esteem before the civil war. The ceremony had been lavish, an outpouring of community celebration; people had come from miles around, from up the coast and high in the hills, citing tenuous family links.

Preparations were made for days beforehand, the women all vying to take the place of his mother – 'So sad she cannot be here to see it!', 'She is watching, even though we cannot see her, and she is proud of you, Dirga,' 'This is what she would have wanted,' – though no one mentioned his father. The garlands of flowers, the day of feasting, the gout of blood arcing from the neck of the water buffalo, its head succinctly sliced off with one machete stroke, the raucous dancing until dawn. It had been a night to remember, a beacon of hope in those dark days, and their songs had risen into the sky like spirits bearing dreams to the moon.

Slipping away with Rani when no one noticed – the exchange of vows now over, the guests were celebrating in earnest – he led her to his hut swamped in flowers and nervously undressed her, rendered as shy as she despite all his experience. Her soft body in the firelight, coconut-oiled and jasmine-scented, glowing like amber, the dark cascade of her hair – he'd been enchanted. Smitten. Would have moved the mountain an inch to the left had she wished it. He thought back to that day, the joy of it, so righteous and pure. It had seemed as if the whole island had pinned their dreams and hopes on them that day, and he had promised her the world.

Domi nudged him. 'Here, bro,' pressing a bunch of fibrous stalks into his hand. Qat. He preferred the speed pills to the rank bitterness of the plant but took it anyway, and a cube of gum to mask some of the taste, and started chewing.

To begin with everything *had* been perfect. He'd settled into married life, enduring the taunts of his friends, and returned to the land and the daily routine of coaxing enough to survive from it, content just to be with Rani. But the money soon ran out, gradually ebbing away just as the wedding ribbons faded to grey. He grew quiet, absent minded, lost in his thoughts. He never quite finished anything he started; the roof leaked in the monsoons, the chickens escaped and the charcoal burner filled the hut with smoke, and all the while the lure of his past fluttered before him like a velvet moth.

Then, one night after too much palm wine, he gave into temptation and rejoined the nocturnal 'fishing trips', as they called them – the old gang greeting him with smiles, 'told-you-so' nods and slaps on the back. They'd missed him, they told him, their luck had diminished without him, and he soon reverted to his unofficial role as their leader. But it wasn't the same as before. His broken promise stuck to him, stained him like the strange tar that washed up on the beach and clogged their nets, and each trip dragged him deeper into the morass, desperation clawing him down, the instant rewards for so little effort perpetuating the spiral.

Now, just as clearly as he recognised his culpability in Domi's derangement, he saw how he'd failed her, how the dream had splintered like a startled shoal of fish, how promises had hollowed, become dry and withered, how she knew when he lied. He could see it in her eyes, the warmth snuffed out like a doused flame and thc smile – her smile! – dying like sunset when he told her that first time. But they needed the money, he'd said.

'Why? What do we need that we don't have? What for?'

'For that,' he gestured to her swollen belly.

She didn't respond; she simply turned away, back to the fire, and refused to say another word.

Two doors had slammed shut when he walked out that night, but he'd make it up to her. She'd forgive him.

Then the twins, little Pura and Ori; dimpled, beautiful almond-eyed bundles, needed feeding, and he could never bring back enough.

'One more trip, I swear it,' he'd tell her. 'It's not so bad, is it? Look what I bring you. No one gets hurt – these people are so rich.' She said nothing. His words now meant nothing, he knew.

Until one night, a job had gone wrong, badly wrong – damn you, Domi! – and everything had changed. He realised it had been inevitable, that he'd expected it. Why hadn't they just given up when they could, when they knew they were beaten? But that white woman, she thought they wouldn't dare touch her, an elder, an *oma*, and had tried to radio the coast guard even as Domi strode over to her, snatching the receiver and ripping back her head by the hair, slitting her throat like a goat's in one swift motion – furious – simultaneously sealing the fate of the other three fat foreigners aboard with her. He knew it was his fault, that their blood was on his hands. His *karma*. The price for breaking his word.

Despite their vow of secrecy, rumours had got out, spreading like blood in water. People avoided his eye and no longer called out greetings to him in the market, no longer gave him gifts of salt fish or presents for the twins. The village seemed to shrink, tightened by their shared complicity, corrupted by their unspoken guilt. This was the last time, he'd sworn to her, but she hadn't listened.

He remembered what she said before, when he burst in drunk and wild, high on the haul; that she'd leave him if he went out again. But he knew she wouldn't. Where to go? She wouldn't leave the island, wouldn't move to the city. There were too many bad stories from people who'd tried; initial excitement, the goodbyes and good lucks, then some money, delivered to proud parents or crowing wives, then gradually less, then nothing at all until word filtered back of disease, drugs and occasionally – often – disappearance. Besides, he knew all he needed to know about the city. His father had taken him along as a wide-eyed kid to check out a possible business opportunity; the awesome noise and bright-as-day lights, the bewildering chaos of the roads, the shouting, the smell of too-dense life, the soaring glass buildings. He'd cried most of the time until his father became angry and brought him wordlessly home, another dream spiralling into the deep like the sharks they caught and hacked the fins from, just like the ones they'd hoped to sell to the Chinese dealers in the city. But the numbers of fins the dealers wanted had been too great, much more than his father could guarantee – 'You miss an order and we come looking' – even if the entire village had been involved, let alone just him on his own.

His father had given up after that, Dirga realised much later, too late, and one morning, after shouting and broken bottles, his father left and never came back. Dirga's mother, puff-eyed and bruised, forbade the mention of his name again and although Domi, Little Fish, had been too young to understand, he, Dirga, had – there are only a finite number of dreams a man can have, can put his heart and soul into and see fail, time after time, before something inside dies.

Beyond the reef the sea was calm, smooth as sleep, and they sped along in silence beneath the engine noise, under the stars, the stellar albedo a solid wash of light to the dark edge of the horizon where long, thin clouds shone like torn sails, the speedboat's wake pale, glowing with phosphorescence in the darkness behind them.

Gazing aloft, reverential, humbled, he sighed, then made his way back to the open wheelhouse where the screens of salvaged instruments blinked their neutral data.

'They still moving?' he shouted to Gunawan.

'Yes man, south-south-east at about eleven knots,' he shouted back, face pulsing eerie green as the radar arm swung around the screen. 'Twelve k's dead ahead. I'd say they're under sail.'

The others all heard that. A sailboat meant the possibility, the slightest chance, of rich pickings. Or just another fisherman running late and on his way home. Riches or fish. A throw of the dice, Dirga thought. 'We should reach them in about five minutes.'

Adrenalin, predictable as rain, spread coldly up through his thinning blood, contracting his throat and balls. He had hoped the boat was motoring – the engine noise would have covered their own, for a while anyway. Why were they moving at night though? Fishermen, surely. Or a yacht too scared to stay in these waters for longer than necessary, too afraid to drop anchor for the night. With good reason, *ai*.

South-south-east, he thought. Good. That meant they were heading into the wind and that we'll be down wind of them. Might just mean a few minutes more cover, an extra few seconds of surprise. He spat a stream of qat juice over the side.

'Get us in behind them,' he said. Perhaps, if they were lucky, they wouldn't hear them until the last minute. Yacht owners always carried a gun, even though it was illegal to do so.

Then he could see the pilot light, glowing red at the top of the mast, and the body of white beneath it. A big one. He pointed it out but they'd all seen it at the same time – their shared maritime ancestry, years of living with the sea, synchronising their senses. The tension stacked instantly, ratcheted further by the sound of guns being checked and rounds chambered. They all knew the drill.

They came in tight a kilometre behind her. She was still under sail, which Dirga thought odd for this time of night, just before dawn. There was a light on in the cockpit but no sign of life above deck. He had heard of automatic helm technology, autopilots, where you set the heading and the boat followed until otherwise instructed.

Or otherwise stopped.

At five hundred metres he was surprised they hadn't been discovered. They were coming in fast now and their engine pitch was high, certainly high enough to cut through any noise the yacht's progress through the water would make.

As if in response the cabin lights blinked on and a figure appeared at the stern. At two hundred metres whoever it was probably still couldn't see them, but they would have heard the engines now for sure. The figure disappeared below.

One hundred metres.

Dirga looked behind him, could make out Domi's fixed grin, Gunawan and the others staring ahead intently. He took control. As usual. It was never explicit before a run but inevitably it came down to him.

She was beautiful, expensive, state of the art. How could people spend so much money on an object, millions of dollars on a hobby, when so many in the world went hungry, when he had nothing? When he was reduced to doing this to fill his children's bellies?

'Give me the AK,' he said.

Someone passed it over. He snapped off the safety. As he expected, the figure reappeared in the cockpit and he heard a familiar popping noise.

'Down!' The odds of getting hit with a pistol at that range were down to pure bad luck but he'd had enough of that not to risk it.

He rested the gun barrel on the prow and let off a two-second spray above the figure's head, bracing himself against the recoil. I'm trying to save your life, he thought, take the hint. The figure ducked down out of sight. He heard the boat's engine cough into life. It's too late for that, whoever you are. We're upon you.

They came up parallel, still twenty metres out, and Dirga called out, in English:

'You! Stop the engine, no one die!'

Nothing. Okay, next step. He levelled the AK at the cockpit where he knew no one would be and, braced against the wheelhouse, let rip, bullets chewing up the woodwork in a ragged line, the noise terrifying enough on its own, or should have been.

Still nothing. This was going to be awkward, he thought – at least for somebody. Sairoma snapped on the spotlight and the whiteness of the boat was momentarily too bright to look at. He shielded his eyes with one hand.

'Last chance! You come out now!' he shouted, as they closed in.

He shot out the mainsail coupling, which flapped out, initially freed but then pulled down by the boom fixtures and into the water. The yacht listed heavily and began to arc around, pivoting on the sudden weight dragging on its port side. He gestured to Gunawan at the wheel to bring them in close behind, strafing the engine housing in the stern as they passed by. The engine faltered, revved wildly then died, and smoke began to sidle lazily out of the cockpit as she slewed to a dead stop. They circled once, predatorily, then cut their engines, the sudden silence broken only by the wavelet pattering on the hulls of the two boats.

'Now, motherfucker! Where you go to now? Nowhere!' he shouted, his voice overly loud, angry that it had to come to this. At least they could hear him now. No more excuses. 'You come out now and nobody die!' He was getting impatient, and they needed to be quick. Whoever was on board would have sent out a mayday by now for sure.

'Let me go on board,' said Domi.

'Don't be fucking stupid! You know they have a gun.' His brother was losing it. Now he looked hurt, like a child who'd been told off. Christ, what was this kid doing here? Let's get this over with, Dirga thought. Either set fire to it or board it – they couldn't steal it. Too recognisable. Too beautiful. If only he could take it, sail away on it with Rani. No, they'd be caught and they'd be hung. But they were going to get every damn fitting out of her first. Then he'd be done. Out. In the clear. Back to her, triumphant but not too cocky, with gifts, money. Yes! And promises that this time he'd keep.

'Last chance, friend!' He tried to sound reasonable; they must be terrified in there. 'You come now, I promise no one get hurt. We just want your money. Then we go.' Come on! He knew at least three of the guys were just as unpredictable as Domi, if not more so, and that keeping them off whoever was on board would be nigh on impossible once their fire was up, the fear and adrenaline-stoked blood flowing. And the longer they had to wait, the more the flames were fanned. Doused in petrol.

The cabin doors banged back.

'Okay! Okay! Don't shoot!' A man's voice. 'I'm coming out, like you asked. Okay?' A head appeared, tilted in the spotlight glare, then a torso, hands raised awkwardly through the narrow hatch, a revolver held by the barrel in one of them.

'Who else wi' you?' Dirga said as they bobbed closer, now five metres away.

'No one. Just me,' the man answered, shielding his eyes with one hand. He stood in the cockpit, only visible from the waist up, close enough that Dirga could see his watch face. 'I'm alone, sailing home to Australia. From Hong Kong. Don't shoot. You can –' He didn't finish. There was an explosion over Dirga's right shoulder, deafening him, and the side of the man's head seemed to vanish, like a mango bitten away by invisible jaws. The man spun around and fell out of sight.

Ears ringing, he turned to see his brother, wide eyed, his beloved Colt .45 pointing straight up from the recoil.

'What the fuck did you do that for?' he screamed, knocking away the gun and slamming Domi backwards onto the deck.

His brother just lay there looking up at him, an expression Dirga had seen before slackening his face, like a kid caught beating a donkey; guilty, but only because of getting caught, not because they regretted doing it. Shit. This was going bad. Calm it down.

'Okay. I'm going on. Gunawan, you come with me. Riyan, you cover us, okay? And don't let this little prick anywhere near the boat.' He snatched the Colt from his brother, unslung the machete and checked his old Browning in the back of his sarong.

'Let's go.'

Steadying himself with one hand on the base of the guardrail, he pulled himself aboard, up and over, feline, crouching low, the Colt aimed into the gaping hatch. The man, still spasming occasionally in violent twitches, had already pumped several litres into the well of the cockpit, forming a black pool. Riyan followed, staring at the body. He gestured for him to keep down.

'Whoever there, come out now!' he shouted.

Nothing. Cautiously, he crept down the blood-slickened steps, bare feet kiss-sucking the teak, into the cabin, gun held out in front of him, footprints bright on the thick white carpet. The interior was beautifully finished, all the trappings. His practised eye quickly took in anything of value. SatNav, radios, sonar, cupboards stacked with supplies. Beyond the galley he could see into the bedroom. He poked his head through and scanned quickly. Unmade bed – he'd been asleep, or resting, when they hit – books and charts, the litter of life at sea. Of solo life at sea.

'No one else here,' he called out. 'Let's take what we can and get the fuck out of here.'

He went back on deck where Riyan was already ripping out the instruments from their mountings. 'Domi, you prick, come and help. Find the safe, it's probably in the bedroom.'

His brother sprang over the rail, eager to regain some favour, and disappeared below.

How had this gone so wrong? he thought, staring up at the stars. Just for once it could have been easy, just this time. Something else was troubling him though. Down below. He tried to think. What was it? Something in the bedroom. The smell. Perfume.

A woman's perfume.

'Domi!' he shouted, turning.

There was an inhuman, high-pitched shriek from below. The hatch doors burst back and Dirga saw his brother stagger up the steps, clutching his face, screaming, shrill, like one of the black-bristled wild pigs they sometimes trapped in the jungle.

'Domi!' He jumped down to him and grabbed his shoulders. Blood pumped from a small puncture wound in his neck, pulsing arterial jets. But worse, something protruded from between his fingers. He pulled his hands back. 'Hold still!' From his brother's eye socket stuck a black blade of some sort, the eyeball lanced like a speared octopus.

He heard an abrupt shot from below, then another, hardly registering it as he forced his brother down onto the cushioned bench. Blood seeped like dark tears from between the clenched lids, grotesquely puckered around the weapon.

'Hold still, shit!' Domi writhed beneath his brother's weight. 'Someone help!' Riyan appeared from below, revolver in his hand.

'There was a girl hiding.' He said, matter-of-factly.

'Fuck that. Help me hold him.'

Riyan held Domi's jerking shoulders. Dirga put a hand on his forehead, grasped the shaft of the dart and pulled. It resisted for a second, skewered into the bone at the back of the orbital cavity, then popped free with a gush of blood and vitreous humour. Domi passed out. Dirga held it up to the light. The arrow head was cruelly sharp, gleaming gold in the darkness, with what looked like a heart shape in its centre, funnelling the poison along a channel to a viciously bevelled point.

# Chapter 11

*Tuesday, 27th October, 1933*
*The Red Sea*

*Dearest Lil,*

*Onwards to Aden.*

*We've been making good time, and clip along at a fair pace. The ocean of sand soon faded into a dusk smeared by smoke from the stacks, an inky signature that trailed away behind us into the distance, an entourage of gulls suspended in the air like kites fading with it, all bar one cocky fellow who remains with us, oddly, and appears to be hitching a ride.*

*As I write, he – I assume from his demeanour that it's male – is perched on the rail and fixing me with a beady stare. I took to feeding the bugger scraps smuggled from the table, more out of boredom than altruism, and believe he's come to regard me as a benefactor. I've named him Cedric and will be sad to see the back of him – which could happen any day now since the ship's cat, a mangy specimen called, without imagination, Tom, with no shred of affection for anyone aboard and little loved itself, has spotted him and stalks him ineffectually, much to my amusement and Cedric's contempt. I'm grateful for the diversion.*

*Meanwhile the heat mounts daily, and being hatless at midday is like being a blacksmith's anvil; a constant, relentless hammering on head and shoulders as within minutes one's pulse begins to ring in the ears, then vision starts to swim and giddiness follows (at this point I stopped my experiment).*

*There's nothing to be done during the day – even the crew retreat below, though our cabins are stifling. I stick to the shade on deck where at least there's a breeze, and have begun an inventory of the infinite textures, colours and contours of the sea as they appear to me, like the moods of the earth reflected.*

*At night I sleep under a single sheet, invariably thrown to the floor come morning. My sleeping habits have become curiously reversed; I sleep easily during the day but find it almost impossible to do so at night. When no amount of sheep-counting, Latin verb recital or remembering your father's political tirades will work, I'll often give up and walk the deck, maybe smoke a cigarette or two with the night watchman.*

*I have begun to appreciate how quickly, once flattered by the attention, people will bare their souls, particularly concerning their more 'amorous' adventures. This lot certainly meet the general preconceptions you might have of them – girl in every port etc. – and much of these late-night conversations are far too blue for me to recount. Jim is quite right when he asserts that 'Whatever you can imagine, someone, somewhere, has already done' and I've come to realise there's much about the world they fail to teach at school. This trip has already proven highly educational – I hardly recognise the youth who stepped aboard a month or so ago. Perhaps your father regarded me too green and this was his intention.*

*A full moon again last night, captivating out here with nothing but the water to reflect her light. I like to think that you gaze upon her too.*

*The ink is smudging before it dries so I'll call it a day.*
*You remain, as ever, foremost in my thoughts,*
*Ralph x*

*Wednesday, 28th October, 1933*
*S.S. Apollonia*

*Dearest,*

*Finally, a breakthrough viz. the Richards intrigue:*

*During last night's nocturnal prowling, some time after midnight, I'd been on deck stretching a leg in an attempt to induce sleep and was returning to my cabin when, upon swinging the heavy door carefully to prevent it slamming, I heard the oddest noise. A monotone hubbub that initially I thought to be coming from the engine room, a vagary of the pistons from deep below decks. (Maddox, after weeks of pestering, finally showed me around that Dantean hell hole just the other day; my complaints about conditions above deck were thrown into stark context by the overwhelming heat, noise and smell below. The air, thick with steam, oil and smoke and 140 degrees, was so dense as to feel almost solid. Conversation was impossible – the engineers, ears stopped with waxed cotton, have a system of sign language to communicate – and the source of the almost soothing thumping we've grown accustomed to is revealed in all its fearsome glory: the roaring inferno of the burners, scream of vented steam and incessant clanking of iron and steel – shocking in its intensity. Naked to the waist, glistening torsos slick with sweat and engine oil, the men – none of whom I even recognised – toiled with grim resolve, taking turns to feed the gaping maw of the boiler furnaces and monitoring the banks of dials relaying the pressure of the steam head. Slamming the inch-thick door on that bedlam was such sweet relief I vowed on the spot never to carp on about a heat rash ever again).*

*The noise had nothing to do with the engine.*

*As I neared the top of the central stairs from which four flights lead down to port and starboard, fore and aft, I realised it came up from my own corridor. I crept down the steps and along the darkened passage, passing my door, the empty room, to the Richards' cabin. The voice swung from a deep bass to the almost maniacally shrill, hysterical like a woman's, rising and falling in what sounded like religious chanting, like rapid Hail Marys or some other prayer, and unintelligible from where I stood. The Doctor.*

*I pressed my ear up to the wood to better make out the words; snatches of them rose like a ship cresting a heavy swell, though they made little sense – 'never, ever, ever', 'your damnable deception' (this shouted), and someone, a name, 'must be paid in full!' The 'ranting of a madman', Buchanan had said, but this sounded like the rantings of two, as if in furious discussion, and I realised, my blood chilling, that the pitches of the voice, one high, the other low, formed two halves of a conversation.*

*At that moment the ship rolled, only slightly, for the sea was quite calm, and I was forced to brace myself gently against the door. Not gently enough, for it gave the tiniest of creaks. The voice, or voices, stopped abruptly and I froze, my pulse surely audible. Before I could make a break for it I heard three striding steps and the door was thrown open.*

*Richards stood there dressed only in his rumpled nightshirt and bathed in a slight sweat, the interior lit hesitantly by a flickering lamp on the table. Our faces little more than a foot apart, I gaped back at him. I stammered something about not being able to sleep and whether everything was all right, but he did not respond, closing the door and turning the latch, allowing me the briefest of glimpses of his wife's sleeping form in the bed beyond. At the time I couldn't gauge his expression and it was only later that I realised what it was: he appeared not to recognise me at all.*

*I returned to my cabin – where you now find me – unable to sleep and slightly unnerved by the experience. Some relief though, that it is not I who am to blame as source of the commotion. Now I think of it, it's also a relief that Claudia's fears have been confirmed and that she is not suffering from delusions or heat-induced delirium at all. I will confer with Jim at the next opportunity, before we reach Aden.*

*Sorry to gabble away like this, my love; the process is cathartic, and just getting it down on paper is helpful, though I'd give anything to be able to talk to you directly.*

*Ever yours,*
*Ralph x*

*Thursday, 29th October, 1933*
*S.S. Apollonia*

*My love,*
*After breakfast and slightly bleary-eyed, I stopped by Jim's cabin and, while he shaved, asked him what action he thinks we should take, indeed if any. He remains adamant that we avoid direct involvement, though he was interested to learn the source of the disturbances. I also informed Maddox that the noises weren't from my cabin but another's – he intuited whose, the choice being limited along this corridor – and I had the feeling he already knew as much.*

*'My jinx appears to be lifted,' I said brightly.*

*'Ay, lad,' he replied, 'that it does. But that of the ship's remains in place.' Thanks for nothing, I thought.*

*The Richards' have taken to breakfasting in their cabin, if indeed they have any at all, and often have their lunch below decks too.*

*This can't be good for either of them, and though I have little sympathy for him, feel sure that their trip cannot possibly be anything but a failure. What on earth do they imagine they can salvage from their blighted relationship, I wonder? He needs some serious attention, professional help I shouldn't wonder, and I doubt he'll find it in the colonies.*

*I'm trying to distance myself from the entire affair though feel a degree of responsibility towards the woman, since it was I in whom she confided, me to whom she came for assistance. I'd feel better if I could speak to the Captain but Jim reckons he has more than enough to worry about without getting caught up with the 'marital difficulties' of his passengers.*

*'Slightly more than mere marital difficulties, don't you think?' I asked him.*

*'We'll see,' he said, gazing out to sea absently. 'We'll see.'*

*He can be infuriatingly aloof.*

*What more can I do? I've yet to clap eyes on Dr Death since our encounter last night. Perhaps in his 'agitated' state of mind he's forgotten the entire incident. I hope so.*

*Around mid morning I got chatting with the walrus-moustached Brigadier (retired) Hamilton and his wife, who joined me at my spot – specifically chosen to escape such 'intrusions'. Mrs H. shooed Cedric away with her parasol, making him caw indignantly. I suppose this nook is not exclusively mine; nevertheless it rankled.*

*A curious cove of the Old School mould, he fixes the world with such startling myopia that one can't help but feel sorry for him, leading as it must to an almost perpetual disappointment; puffs about as if he owned the ship – ordering G and Ts as if addressing servants – and so starched stiff with decorum that it is virtually impossible to communicate with him through blustering 'whats', 'old chaps' and 'ehs'. You would most definitely have had one of your giggling fits, my love, whose intensity I remember to be directly proportional to how inappropriate the situation. I nearly lost my own composure just picturing your shuddering shoulders. She meanwhile chirps in with the occasional 'absolutely' and 'rather' at almost timed intervals, like a duet, so that the thread of the conversation becomes quite lost. Once they had established, with almost visible disdain, which school I attended, run through the mental check-lists to see who they knew who might have been there and come up with not a single name, their interest in me waned tangibly, to my express relief.*

*He – Jim, that is – seems much preoccupied of late, and we have not had our once customary chats for some time. He spends much of the day in his cabin, mercifully cool compared to mine, or smoking his cigars and writing up on the observation deck. I asked him what was on his mind and he was dismissive, almost patronisingly so, saying 'Some people have better things to do than chat to seagulls.'*

*I've taken the hint and left him to his own devices.*

*Swaine and McAlister remain as garrulous as ever – blithely oblivious to social mores or careless of them, they seem to delight in upsetting the missionaries – and have become quite good company. Now that I can hold my own when the brandy is flowing they have adopted a more tolerant attitude towards me, regaling me late into the night with their hair-raising tales of wine, women and warfare.*

*Furtive glances tonight at dinner from Mrs Richards – whose appearance seems not to have deteriorated further – conveyed to me that she wishes to talk, though how she intends to achieve this I have no idea. The Doctor avoids my eye, unless it's my imagination, and seems not to recall our recent nocturnal encounter, confirming my suspicion that he failed to recognise me. The conversation is typically carried by the two huntsmen, anecdotes from the Brigadier once he loosens up a little after a shot or two of whiskey, and, I like to think, by my own contributions.*

*In the main though, my love, I'm become quite the recluse, keeping myself to myself and trying to gen up on my impending duties from the limited literature the Company provided me with. Please thank your father for his potted history of the cotton industry, about which I am now a font of information. Coming to appreciate just how the production of this invaluable fibre has shaped the world, sociologically, economically and politically, is truly fascinating; I am now eager to get stuck into the job and count the days 'til we arrive in Mombasa.*

*Ever yours,*

*R.*

*Saturday, 1st November, 1933*
*S.S. Apollonia*

*Dearest,*

*In haste.*

*I woke last night with a start. God knows what time it was but I felt dragged by my bootstraps from the depths of sleep (feeling all the worse for too much to drink), to a light tapping on my door. Stumbling to my feet and fortunately remembering to throw on my gown, I opened it to find Mrs R. trembling in the corridor, despite the excessively warm night.*

*'Come in,' I hissed. 'Quickly now!' Checking furtively down the corridor as she brushed past me.*

*She was in a right old state – wild-eyed, unkempt hair about her shoulders, and wearing only her nightdress, clearly having not paused long enough to consider her appearance or quite careless of it. I closed the door behind her.*

*'What in God's name are you playing at?' I said, quite irked, not only at being so roused but also, selfishly, concerned for my own neck. She responded by bursting into floods of tears. Thus chastised, I pulled out a chair.*

*'Come now,' I said, more gently, 'sit down.' Which she did while I fixed her a sharpener. 'Take your time and tell me what's the matter,' I said, perhaps a little cruelly since I'd a pretty good idea if not of the exact problem, at least of its nature.*

*'Where is your husband, exactly?*

*'I gave him a taste of his own medicine,' she said. 'Literally.' She gave a small, tight laugh. 'He won't bother us until morning.'*

*I was relieved to hear it, and thus reassured, lit us both cigarettes. Her hand shook slightly as she took small, hurried puffs.*

*'I need your help,' says she, laying on the charm a little with a touch of my forearm, 'and hopefully, dear Ralph, if everything goes according to plan, for the last time.'*

*'With what plan, exactly?' I asked her, requiring precise information at this juncture, believe me.*

*'Making good my escape, of course,' she replied, fixing me with a stare. 'There is, as I'm sure you realise, no point in my continuing further. If I do not run for my life, I will either lose it or take his instead.'*

*I knew she wasn't bluffing, and had written something not dissimilar to you in my previous letter. I nodded.*

*'Go on,' I said.*

*'Well, we're due in Aden tomorrow, are we not?' I nodded. 'There must be some way I can make a break for it before we – you – set sail for Mombasa, for I know that once there my fate is sealed.'*

*'What do you propose?'*

*'Oh, I don't know!' she said, too loudly for my liking. 'For the love of God help me think of something.'*

*The long and short of it is this, my love: once ashore in Aden I'm to find a sympathetic soul at the High Commission – this should be quite easily done with our new friends the Hamiltons on our side (though I shall be selective with what I tell them). They will prepare the equivalent to political asylum for marital refugees, and arrange to be at the harbour at the hour of our departure, at which point I am to cause a diversion – one long enough for Claudia to scarper and one that must occur on board, so that by the time the good Doctor realises his dear wife has fled the roost, it's too late for him to do anything about it.*

*What, I hear you ask, could possibly go wrong?*

*She rose to leave, thanked me, then stopped at the door.*

*'Ralph,' she said in a low, flat voice, her eyes unnaturally bright in the candlelight. 'If this does not work and I remain on the ship when it leaves port, I will not arrive in Mombasa, do you understand me?'*

*And with that she was gone, with dawn fast approaching – around five in the a.m. – and I lay down, abandoning any hope of sleep, to watch the disc of light slowly brighten through the porthole above the bed, pondering the conviction of her words.*

*I must have eventually nodded off for I was woken by yet more knocking on the door. Pounding, to be precise; Maddox's delicate way of suggesting I rouse myself. My breakfast porridge had long congealed outside my door, and he wanted to know if I would 'prefer all my meals similarly cooled?' I smiled with what I hoped was caustic sarcasm and took the pot of cold tea from the blighter as he turned to go.*

*'Maddox, wait,' I said, remembering the night's plotting. 'What time do we reach Aden?'*

*'Around noon, far as I know,' he said. Then, noticing my face, 'If that's all right with the young Master. Have any pressing engagements there, do we?'*

*I closed the door and leant back against it. I knew I couldn't count on Jim since this was expressly against his advice. I'd have to come up with a cover story for Hamilton, a Trojan Horse as it were, to gain entry, then try to find a sympathetic ear at the High Commission.*

*Ho bloody hum.*

*I have an hour to come up with something and, providing I am not clapped in irons, intend to update you further some time tomorrow.*

*And to think I was complaining of boredom.*

*All my love,*

*Ralph*

*x*

*Sunday, 2nd November, 1933*
*Aden*

*Lillian, my love,*

*Christ, what a day!*

*I write to you now from the relaxed environs of the Saba Hotel, a plan has been hatched, and tomorrow will reveal whether it succeeds or not. Either way, I will not be able to let you know until I can post this letter's conclusion from Mombasa. Pray for me. How odd to think that you will only hear the outcome weeks after the event (unless all is lost and I'm on my way home to you in custody – quite a tempting option).*

*The flanks of the Red Sea gradually closed in on each side of us, Cedric took his leave with a couple of vociferous loops around the chimneys, and we passed into the Gulf. I scarcely noticed his departure, my mind preoccupied with less frivolous matters.*

*Presently we drew into the old harbour, enclosed by a thin but protective isthmus of land and a perfect natural bay much coveted throughout its history, particularly by us Brits as a refuelling point since it lies almost equidistant between our various interests in Bombay, Zanzibar and Suez, – hence our visit. Although I was paying scant attention, Jim tells me that Noah is believed to have built the Ark here by those who treat the Old Testament as historically accurate and think the world was 'built' in seven days with the myriad life forms we now witness already in place, 4,000 years ago. ('One word for them to consider,' he said. 'Which would be?' I asked. 'Dinosaurs.' And we both burst into laughter – very welcome at the time.)*

*This morning, after my last log entry to you, I approached Hamilton and asked whether he knew anyone at the H.C. who might be able to help me file a report back to the Company. He naturally (duty to the Realm and all that) agreed to help in any way he could, and I followed him and his wife with their entourage of porters down the gangplank to their waiting motorcar, an enormous open-topped Austin. The trunks were duly packed, somewhat precariously, and we set off through busy markets up out of town to the grander colonial buildings beyond.*

*With much application of the horn we made our way through the bedlam to their official residence where I tried not to appear too impatient as tea and sandwiches were served – Wedgwood china and polished silverware, naturally! Hamilton huffed about, issuing orders, checking chores had been carried out and generally faffing. All the while the seconds ticked by interminably. I wanted to shout, seize him by the lapels and drag him to the Commission that instant, but successfully held my tongue.*

*Finally we strolled the short distance to the Embassy compound. There I was introduced to a junior attaché called Jennings: dapper, slight of build, not much older than myself, and for all I knew likewise bound by the diabolical demands of a prospective father-in-law back home. I thanked the Brigadier for his help, and Jennings led me through the cool corridors to his office, ushering me to a seat in a leather armchair while he sat down behind his desk, tugged his cufflinks and smoothed his hair.*

*'Now then,' he said, 'how can I be of assistance?' He steepled his fingers and regarded me across the desk. He knew nothing of my requirements, having been told only that 'This fellow needs a favour, old man. See what you can do, what?' by Hamilton. This at least meant I could approach the subject directly without seeming to have gained his ear under false pretences. I was grateful for the old goat's ambiguity.*

*I took a risk and told him everything, as much as I dared, anyway: Mrs Richards' desperation, her husband's erratic behaviour, the possibility he was a threat to her life and her rapidly deteriorating health – mental and physical. What did I have to lose? At worst he would take the matter higher or get the police involved, or he would help; either way some resolution might come of it.*

*He listened in silence, betraying no emotion whatsoever so that I was quite unable to judge how he was going to respond. When I had finished, he closed his eyes and remained silent for a minute, then opened them and said, 'I think we should go somewhere a little more private, don't you?' I nodded. 'Why not?' He stood, donned his hat and jacket and bade me follow him. He led us out of the building and down the sweeping drive, through the gates into the teeming streets, down an alley to an ancient tea house where old men were playing dice, sipping from delicate glasses and swishing at flies with horsehair switches.*

*We sat at a table back from the street. Jennings ordered a couple of mint teas and proffered a cigarette, which I accepted, as I did the silver lighter he struck for me with a practiced flourish.*

*'Now then,' he said, 'the obvious question is why haven't you taken this matter to the Captain?'*

*I explained, truthfully, that I feared being thrown ashore with the Richards', and my predicament vis-à-vis you, your father's conditions for our marriage and my contract with the Company. 'I would hate to do anything that might jeopardise the fulfilment of my obligations,' I said.*

*'I quite understand,' he said, 'but I'm sure you appreciate that this matter is completely beyond the remit of the Consulate. It is, is it not, a personal matter between a man and his wife, and any involvement on our behalf would be wholly inappropriate. There are various routes by which a marriage suffering difficulties can be dissolved or resolved, admittedly more easily pursued at home than here, but I fail to see what you expect me to do. Perhaps the lady in question could come here herself?'*

*I explained that this was impossible, that she was effectively under curfew and that were her husband to hear of my involvement, things could get considerably worse for us both. He paused, looked me in the eye and said,*

*'Mr Talbot, are you quite sure you are telling me everything?' I said that I was, to my knowledge, as far as the facts of the matter appeared to me.*

*'Are you sure,' he asked, 'there are no, ah, personal motives for your involvement?' I suddenly realised what he was implying.*

*'Nothing of the sort!' I replied, quite indignant. 'She's a friend, nothing more, and clearly in some distress. What man wouldn't try to help?'*

*He clearly didn't believe me, so I decided to tell him about her suspicions regarding the death of her lover, the sedatives, her suicide threat and the nocturnal diatribes emanating from their cabin, his eyebrows arching incrementally as I did so. He thought for a moment, stirring the sweet amber tea, then seemed to reach some internal decision, placing the teaspoon carefully on the saucer.*

*'Very well,' he said finally, 'I'll help where I can but with one proviso.'*

*'Name it,' I said, much relieved.*

*'That my involvement is strictly between the two of us. On no account can the Consulate, nor myself, be seen to be involved in any of this – not until she is within the Embassy doors when it becomes an official matter for the Ambassador himself, do you understand?'*

*'Of course,' I said. 'What do you propose?'*

*'Well, clearly we need to get her from the ship to the Consulate without her husband suspecting a thing, and time it so that by the time he does the bird has fled the coop, so to speak.'*

*'My thoughts exactly,' I said, and told him my idea for creating some kind of diversion that would involve the Doctor long enough for her to make good her escape.*

*'Very well,' he said, when he had heard me through. 'I can certainly arrange to have a motorcar at the quayside at the time of your departure. At noon, you say? From there I will have her brought straight to the Consulate and she will be in the hands of the proper authority – we do have a procedure for this sort of thing, you know. Cogs will turn and will, I imagine, finally result in her repatriation to Blighty. As for how she gets off the ship, and whether he ends up pursuing her – I leave that entirely to you, and I wish to know as little about it as possible. No, make that 'absolutely nothing about it'. Is that clear?'*

*'As crystal,' I said, shaking his hand firmly. 'Thank you for your time.'*

*'We are human too,' he said, as we stood to leave, smiling thinly for the first time, and looking anything but. 'Contrary to what you*

*might think. Just make sure she's off the boat in time.' He turned to go, checking his watch. 'Oh, by the way . . .'*

*'Yes?' I said, half expecting him to change his mind.*

*'Good luck.'*

*The plan's afoot, my love, and I have a crucial role to play in its fruitful outcome.*

*I have just had dinner with Jim, telling him nothing despite every instinct urging me to do so. He knew something was amiss, however, and twice asked if everything was all right. It's late. I have no further plans for today other than to try and get some sleep; I must be up early to get back to the ship and attempt to communicate tomorrow's plan to Claudia. And come up with a suitable diversion.*

*Goodnight, my love, I'll get this off first thing.*

*Yours ever,*

*Ralph*

*x*

# Chapter 12

*Sumatra, Indonesia. 1997.*

Irregular tapping on Lazaro Molina's shoulder woke him.

Opening his eyes, the darkness was so complete he momentarily forgot where he was; whorls of colour chased themselves across his retinas in lieu of any information for them to relay. It was deathly quiet, unusual for the rainforest with its beetling, chewing, clicking, grunting biodiversity. He brushed off his shoulder – Cain flailing about in his sleep again no doubt – and the tapping, intermittent as it was, stopped. Not even bothering to swat a mosquito greedily sucking at his cheek, he drifted back to sleep. There were still a few hours before dawn filtered down through the canopy and he'd need all his energy for the long trek ahead – up into the mountains to deliver much-needed medicines to a remote village beyond the falls, inoculate the inhabitants for yellow fever, typhoid and cholera, and carry out a quick census of who was up there.

Almost instantly he was awake again. The same flicking tap on his shoulder.

'Cain,' he whispered, then louder 'Cain!'

Cain moaned in his sleep.

'Stop it, *basta, hombre* –' He broke off abruptly when he heard the rustling of something in the food bag behind their heads.

Something big.

Slowly, heart surging, he reached for the Maglite beside him and twisted it on, aiming the beam behind them in the same movement. Suddenly spotlit, the massive, orange-and-black head and headlight-yellow eyes of the tiger turned to face them. The light hit it, a brief snapshot of narrowing irises, exposed four-inch yellow fangs and halo of dense white fur around the ears, then all hell broke loose.

It let out a deafening, guttural roar, snapped out its forearms sinking claws into the earth, haunches bunched with musculature, and leapt away, scattering the contents of the backpack, crossing the stream with a single bounding splash and disappearing in a receding rush of undergrowth.

It happened so quickly neither man had time to react; they sat there, bolt upright with their mouths hanging open for several seconds after it had vanished.

'*Dios mio*,' Lazaro eventually managed, 'a tiger!' He realised he'd been holding his breath.

Cain was shaking visibly. Lazaro reached out and patted his arm. 'It's okay, brother. It won't be back. This is a good omen, *amigo*, a good sign for your quest. Come, let's get up. I for one will not sleep again tonight.'

Their guide, Kuwat, a sinewy hunter from the town on the river – once totally cut off from the world, the ramshackle community had recently been thrust into the twentieth century with the arrival of the road – disagreed and muttered fast incantations to himself nervously. In the light of their torches they peered at the tracks the creature had left, following its movements as it padded around their recumbent bodies, pausing to sniff their sleeping forms, skirting the now cold embers of the fire – 'We should have piled it higher, no?' – before it found their supplies for the trip hanging from the branches of a tree above the bank. The Gore-Tex was shredded like paper.

'Bad luck,' Kuwat keened in a high voice, whistling through a gap in his teeth and making complicated hand gestures to ward off the evil spirits, 'we go back.'

'We cannot,' said Lazaro flatly, 'these people need us.'

He looked around.

'Where is your son?' Lazaro asked, thinking the boy had gone off to find them some food for breakfast.

'He has gone.'

'Gone? Where?'

'He has gone,' Kuwat shrugged and pointed back the way they had come. He must have fled in the opposite direction to the tiger.

He quickly assessed their situation; not great.

Their food had been decimated and now they'd be hard pressed to carry the remaining bags between the three of them. It would take them two days to reach the village. He squatted down and sifted through the torn bag, discarding anything that was either ruined or extraneous to their immediate requirements. They would have to live from the jungle around them; eat what they could either pick or catch. They'd be fine. At least, he thought, you wouldn't die of thirst in a rain forest. It was still only early morning, the sun yet to set the vegetation steaming, yet the humidity was oppressive and his shirt was already soaked with sweat.

Kuwat took some persuading, but the offer of double pay and Lazaro's waterproof watch soon dispelled any superstitious qualms. Around them the first daylight was beginning to solidify the night's soundscape into a monochrome wash of layered vegetation. Vast tree trunks soared up into the gloom, smothered in thick moss and trailing long, knobbly-elbowed lianas, reminding Lazaro, as they always did, of a cathedral's vaulted pillars. This was his church. One in which he truly felt the presence of the Lord and one he'd long suspected Catholic architecture subconsciously attempted to emulate.

He stood there, head back, hands on his hips, breathing in the sweet, slightly foetid air, occasional drops of condensation from far above exploding deliciously on his upturned face.

Here he felt a peace he had never managed to find at home in Andalusia, though God knows he'd tried. The youngest of four brothers, his die had been cast at his birth and he had duly entered – been entered into – the priesthood on his fourteenth birthday. The abbey in Ronda was one of the best, one of the wealthiest and most beautiful, though the austerity of the buildings hadn't much impressed him at the time. He had been too young and too apprehensive of what lay in store for him there. He promised his father to be good, to do his best. But the confines, physical and spiritual, of the seminary, had soon proven too stifling. High in the old town, he could look out to the wide views from the vestry windows, out over the spectacular gorge with its high-arched Roman bridge from which Franco had made dissenters jump, to the rolling plains, the golden fields of wheat, the cork and pine forests and the terraces of vines and olives in the distance – where she was – and this only made it worse. He yearned to be out in the hills with his brothers, running free in the rugged limestone mountains that surrounded their village, chasing wild boar through the woods and, when the day became too hot, swimming like otters in the icy springs that seeped from deep in the earth.

Each night he could hear the melodious clonk of the goat bells as they returned from the high pastures and the soft hoots of owls that called to him, 'Come back, come back.'

Then there was Gabriella.

Light limbed and grey-green eyed – a genetic legacy from her Moroccan grandmother – she was very different to the sturdy, swarthy *campesina* girls of the village. They'd become friends through their similar ages and the friendship that existed between their mothers. When Gabriella's mother had died, his own, Pilar, had taken on much of the role. His brothers, the nearest five years older, took little interest in her and, unchallenged, they had gradually fallen in love, a natural extension of the shared secrets of growing up together, and became lovers just before he was sent away to Ronda. The memories of those sweet afternoons amid the waist-deep meadows full of flowers, laughter and light tormented him more than anything else. The more they drummed into him the necessity for chastity, the more entrenched became his conviction that something so pure and wonderful could not possibly be a sin. When he confessed his thoughts he was punished. And when he tried to recreate her touch, late at night when the other boys were asleep, they told him that too was a sin.

He began to resent the God that had taken this love away from him, sullying her memory, nailing his youthful joy and feral liberty to a cross of shame and guilt. The cloisters became a prison, and he became more surly, disobedient and angry with each passing season. His rebellion in turn brought more punitive castigation down upon him in a perpetuating cycle: his sabbaticals were often cancelled – opportunities to slip back and see her – and his hours of confinement often extended, until he could take no more.

One night after vespers when the moon was full, bathing the quiet town in her pale light, he left, sliding back the heavy bolts, especially olive-oiled earlier, flitting through the shadows of the immaculate, sweat-tended gardens and over the high wall above the ancient cobbled streets.

As he dropped from the wall he caught his left armpit on an old, rusty nail and, suspended for a second by his body weight, ripped a deep gash up through to his shoulder before falling to the ground. Stifling the pain, he staunched the blood in the village fountain, tied a strip of his shirt around his shoulder in a tight tourniquet, and set off for home.

He was eighteen.

The shame his flight would bring on his family meant he could never return to Grazelema, the pueblo of his childhood perched high in the hills, not to stay, but he walked briskly through the night towards the familiar peaks, every step filling his soul with the fresh air of his liberty, expelling any of the doubts he might have had about the wisdom of his actions, and stripping away his melancholy.

Arriving just before dawn, he gazed across the valley at the sleeping village, listening to cock-crowed salutations, a smile upon his face. All was as he'd left it. His mother would just be rising, chiding his father lovingly. His brothers, all married off and with their own children to look after, would be looking for excuses to meet in the bar before work, already full of garrulous old men, cigarette smoke and the steam of coffee. There Tio Paco would be demanding his first *aguardiente*. Pablo, his old friend, would be leading the goats up to summer pastures studded with ancient, hollow-trunked oaks in which they had often played as kids. He smiled at the thought of old widow Valentina, who, driven *loca* by grief when her husband was murdered by the Fascists, now hoiked up her skirts to passing men and demanded 'satisfaction'. The smell of fresh bread would be drifting through the narrow cobbled streets. And Gabi would be waking.

He knew her routine, that she would soon emerge to feed the horses her father kept on a small plot behind their thick-walled cottage on the edge of the village, and he hastened through the dewy fields and over the dry-stone wall to await her in the barn, reassuring the stamping horses with the palm of his hand beneath their flared, steamy nostrils.

Presently the door swung open and there she was, the first light silhouetting her body exquisitely through her dress. Though he had seen her on a few occasions, on brief exeats, they had been strictly chaperoned, unable to speak to each other, exchanging furtive glances when no one was looking. Now, he was struck by how she had bloomed, filling out into a beautiful woman, and he watched her breathlessly for a minute, unseen as she went about her chores.

When he stepped from the shadows to speak her name she cried out, dropping the pail, before running into his arms, making him wince with the impact to his shoulder, and he silenced her questions with kisses, savouring the familiar taste of her breath and the smell of the sleep-musked skin at the nape of her neck.

She pulled back to look at him. He looked tired from the walk, and stubble shadowed his face, but she could see that he too had changed; he was leaner, paler from two years shut away behind the high walls of the abbey. Older. But when hers met his, she could see the same intensity shone in his eyes, the same love light.

'What happened to your arm?' she asked.

'I fell,' he said. 'It's fine.' But she unbound the cloth to find it inflamed, red with the beginnings of infection.

'Wait for me here,' she said, tipping the remaining oats and beans into the feeding troughs, then disappearing through the door. He heard her talking with her father. When she returned a few minutes later she dressed the cut with iodine and a fresh bandage while he gazed at her, enraptured by the little frown of concentration, the mole on her cheek, the way she tucked her hair behind her ear. Once she was satisfied with the dressing, they bolted out of the back door and ran up into the hills through the silvery olive groves up behind the village, each tree and rock part of the story of their time together, part of their interwoven tapestry, and collapsed breathless and laughing in the dawn-damp grass. Safe from other eyes and ears, he listened patiently to her stories of the last few years, the changes in the village, the gossip, who had run off with whom and scandalous rumours of ambiguous paternity, laughing at her levity, delighting in the simple, clean purity of the life that he'd missed. Then, when she had finished, he told her what he'd done, and her face clouded as she realised the implication.

He searched her eyes for a solution.

'You could come with me,' he said.

'Lazaro, *cariño*,' she said sadly, her eyes welling, 'I cannot.' His stomach hollowed.

'There's someone else,' he said, 'I knew it –' But she cut him off with her lips upon his, pushed him back and straddled him, looking down at him, his face framed by her long amber hair.

'There is no one else, idiot.' she said. 'It's Papa, he –' She paused, glanced away, 'he is not well – all those *puta* cigarettes – and cannot do half of the things he could. There's no one else to help, no one to look after him.'

'I'm sorry,' he said, kissing her hands, her arms. 'I had no idea.'

He pulled her close and kissed her mouth, tracing light circles on her cheeks with his fingertips. He stopped and held her face, seeing himself reflected in her eyes, and sadness flowed between them, the weight of the long years apart and the impossibility of their predicament. Then, all words spoken, they fell upon each other, their love lust surging, fiery and fierce. Propped above her now, her legs wide, knees back, he held off for a moment, rested himself against her pungent lips, looked deep into her eyes, breathing hard, before sinking all the way into her, rippling through her ribbed muscles and making her gasp. They rocked together, entwined, clutching, wracked with emotion, sobbing and panting, laughing and crying, making love and fucking simultaneously until they collapsed back in the morning sun, the energy dispelling into the air around them like honey stirred into tea. As their breathing calmed they watched the vigilant spiral of two eagles far above them.

'What will we do?' she said, dangling her ripped panties at him with mock reproach. 'My Lazaro. Back from the dead. I can't bear the idea of losing you again, just when I have you back in my arms.'

'Now we're finally together, you cannot leave and I cannot stay,' he said with a dry laugh. 'I always knew He had a sense of humour.'

'Oye *corazon*,' she said, startled by the bitterness in his voice, 'shhh! We'll work something out. If our love is strong. If we both believe in it.' She stroked his hair until his face softened again.

'I don't know what I believe in anymore,' he said, turning his head to look at her sex-flushed face, brushing away a strand of hair that had stuck to her cheek. 'Except you. Everything they taught me at the seminary was a lie – it just cannot be right, nothing made any sense to me – that by denying the physical body we in some way purify the spirit? It just doesn't ring true, my love. But I do believe that God is here, all around us, in everything,' he gestured at the view, bright and clear under the cloudless azure sky. 'Particularly here!' She squeaked as he shot out a hand and tweaked her dew-dropped mons. He wrapped his arms around her and held her and looked at her directly. 'To have remained there would have been lying to myself and made a lie of how I feel for you. An insult to love, an affront to nature and therefore surely to God as well. That is all I know.'

That was what, twelve years ago?

He sighed and wiped the water from his face with both hands. Too long ago, certainly, to entertain such memories, to regret the errors of his past. Not errors. He'd been forced to make decisions, to take control of his life. Who but God knew whether what one chose was right or wrong? No one, not for sure. Any regret he felt now was no more than a lament for lost youth; his soul seeking meaning. Look at the life he had led, the adventures he'd had, the places he'd been. Would he really swap all of it for life back in the village, even if it meant being with her? Again, the question itself was irrelevant. Back then, without ever questioning it, maybe they could have been happy. But he was rattling cages, looking under stones, even then – demanding from his tutors how the world was made in a week, why evil was 'necessary' to test us, how Adam's rib sprang Eve, how did they know, for sure, there was a Heaven and a Hell – and knowing what he knew now, he realised he would never have been able to survive the parochial, plodding pace of life, the banality of the bar-room banter and the insularity of the village chattering for all the beauty of the land, for all Gabi's beauty; the difference would be as profound, as irreconcilable, as it had been between the village and the seminary. It was, he smiled, all relative.

He walked down to the stream bank, took off his shirt and squatted by the tawny, sweet water. Cupping both hands he splashed his face, neck and thickly haired chest. As the ripples settled, he looked down at the stocky man reflected back at him

– the shoulder-length black hair hanging bedraggled in the humidity, his beard, the beginnings of a stomach over his belt – and absent-mindedly touched the scar on his shoulder.

It had taken a long time to heal, and when it had it formed a livid raised weal the shape of a ragged cross that always itched, even now.

His mark.

He was different now, unrecognisably so. And Gabi? She'd be long gone, certainly to him, anyway. She would have waited for him for a little longer, perhaps, for word from Granada where he'd gone to earn enough for them to leave, bidding her follow when the time came. But her father had held on longer than the doctor, anyone, expected – years longer, despite being reduced to a death-rattling, bed-ridden skeleton – and gradually the impetus of their love, the life spark vitality, had dimmed. The letters he sent her, despite her illiteracy, had faltered, their ink drying up over time. By now she would have surely married someone from the village – Pablo perhaps – borne him children and cut her hair. He liked to think she occasionally thought of him, but doubted it; sometimes it's easier to forget.

In Granada he'd met his first foreigners – *guiris*. Hippies, students, writers, drifters, they spent hours at the bars he worked in, swapping stories and tales of faraway countries and, as he began to understand English, he became increasingly intrigued by the lands beyond the Sierra, drawn again and again to the sunrise each morning, gazing east. And when he had a thick brick of pesetas he left, hitching up the shimmering coast to Barcelona. He loved the vitality of the city, of a different culture, language and people, yet recognisably related to his own, and he could have stayed forever, but his soul was restless, leading him on.

On into France, following the gilded coast up to Nice, cutting up into the meadow-mantled Alps that dwarfed the mountains of Grazelema. Amongst the hills he felt more content, at home amid the goat bells, ancient drystone walls, whispering pines and simple pace of life.

But he travelled on, down into Italy, through Turin, shunning Milan and heading south rapidly, partly due to a foot-to-floor lift from a contessa with a red Ferrari and a nymphomaniac streak who ran him straight to Bari and into her apartment. Two weeks later, feeling spent and light, standing on the quay amid the reek of sardines, he watched a fishing trawler being towed into port, crammed with hundreds of dehydrated, half-starved Albanians fleeing their blighted country; gaunt, expressionless faces hung from the rails and pressed at the portholes like scenes from a gulag. The police sirens had driven him away but he heard the gunshots – a popping noise in the distance – as he reached the edge of town. From Brindisi he jumped a ferry to Athens where he worked for a few months before moving on, through Thessaloniki, and crossed the Bosphorus into Istanbul, leaving Europe behind.

He found work easily, and followed the tourist route along the Aegean coast, labouring on building sites or painting the endless villa complexes that smothered the beaches with egg-box uniformity. Near Olu Deniz he found sanctuary for a while: Butterfly Valley, a beautiful bay only accessible by boat that lay between a steep 'V' of cliffs like the spread thighs of the goddess. He stopped for a summer, helping out with maintaining the scattering of beach huts run like a commune, gardening and digging irrigation channels, exchanging his sweat for food and shelter. Nestled at the head of the bay lay a uterine cave in which thousands upon thousands of bright orange butterflies lived, mated and died, exploding in thick clouds around anyone who disturbed them.

He loved listening to the travellers' stories and guitar music that coiled into the night with the sparks of the fire, and joined in with his own tales of the road. He fell in love, so he thought, with a frisky-spirited Canadian called Amy and, after six weeks of sex, swimming and soul-serenading tranquillity, would have stayed with her had she decided to stay with him. But she went home to start college, and he followed suit a few days later, in the opposite direction, waving farewell to his friends till the boat rounded the headland. He took with him a love of the sea he never lost.

At the ancient walled city of Antalya he took a fishing boat across to Cyprus, the Taurus Mountains already capped with snow, stretching off east and lit pink by the sunset. The island, flat and dry, with pebbly beaches and vast, inescapable skies, made him uncomfortable, and he caught a ferry to Lebanon, resigned to the call of the Holy Land. Something in his heart whispered it, and his scar became more itchy than ever.

Eighteen months after leaving Granada he arrived in Jerusalem. He stood on the Sacred Mount with a hot wind slitting his eyes, looking back at the setting sun and the way he'd come, his pilgrimage complete and his wanderlust – for now at least – sated. With his long hair, beard and simple clothes, people told him he looked like a holy man. Had they looked closer they would have seen it was more demeanour than appearance; quiet and reserved, he had achieved a sense of calm not wholly due to the asceticism of his journey, for though he readily fell for pleasures of the flesh, he never lost control when drinking and neither smoked nor accepted any of the various drugs he had been offered along the way. When he spoke, people listened, for he chose his words carefully.

Keen to stay, and having existed successfully for so long on a wing and a prayer, on faith, now hard up against the realisation of his debt to others, he took a job with CAFOD distributing aid in Palestine and Gaza – the perfect balance between his peculiar, self-tailored creed and his desire to express his reverence outdoors – and finally hit his *métier*. With a good head on his shoulders, self-effacing, apolitical views and a genuine sense of altruism, after a few years he was managing the projects themselves, taking on more and more responsibility for logistics, finances and staffing until, one day, he realised he'd been trapped again, this time by desk, office and computer. Not that he couldn't do it or didn't believe in it – he just couldn't shake off a heartbeat hankering for nature, for more. He felt the familiar sense of suffocation from the abbey a decade earlier, spoke to the Regional Director and took a field posting to Sumatra.

He felt no guilt for his long sojourn, all these years in the wilderness. After all, his family had once tried to get rid of him, though he bore them no grudge, forgave them unconditionally and of course understood their reasons; the oldest in the book – poverty and praxis. They had done what they thought best, and through their actions he had found his calling. The subtle shift of rhyme and reason behind seemingly arbitrary twists and turns of fate sprang his step, imbued him with a sense of peace, especially here in the jungle.

And now, for the first time since he'd left, he was due to return. He'd recently received word through the organisation that his mother was dying. He always sent at least one letter home every year keeping them informed of his location – physically, spiritually, mentally – long, rambling narratives that he knew were written more for their cathartic justification of his own life – his confessional – than for the peace of mind of their recipients.

Right now though, they needed to get going.

They packed their bedrolls and kicked over the fire. With his machete, Lazaro cut a six-foot length of bamboo. He and Cain then slung the two backpacks of medical supplies over it, struggled into their own already damp packs, and hoisted it onto their shoulders so that it sagged and bounced between them. Kuwat, much stronger than Lazaro despite his leaner build, effortlessly lifted his own load and what was left of the food, and led the way, padding along barefoot and silent on the leafy path that threaded between enormous boles.

The dank jungle, now alive with the chatter and caw of the bird and mammal day shift as they took over from the night watch of crickets and frogs, drew quiet as they approached. Shafts of steamy sunlight occasionally pierced the canopy high above, and Lazaro felt many eyes upon them. Now and then they heard the sudden crash of unseen animals careening away through the undergrowth. He knew they could pass within ten feet of a rhino, rare though they were now, and not see it. The humidity was so thick that butterflies seemed to labour under it, their wings flapping slowly as if under water.

Bringing up the rear, sweat streaming down his face, chest and legs, the weight of the bamboo pole bearing heavily on his shoulder, he nevertheless felt his soul soar. As the rhythm of the pole-bounce synched with his and Cain's steps, Lazaro began to sing; an old shepherd's ballad from his childhood, lamenting the end of summer and the loss of love, confident in the return of both.

Having spent a fortnight with him on a previous trip, he had complete trust in Kuwat's sense of direction. In the two years since he'd set up the office in Banda Aceh he'd learnt some of the Indonesian language, though Kuwat's dialect was difficult, and had grown to love the directness, openness and dependability of the Sumatrans. As with all the world's poorer nations, this left them wide open for exploitation by the insatiable demands of the West. Even in the short time he'd been here vast tracts of what remained of the rainforest had been plundered outrageously and the region languished in poverty, despite a multi-billion dollar natural gas industry. He kept his senses tweaked. A ragtag militia, the Free Aceh Movement, had attracted the attention of government forces in the area, who had a shoot-first policy, not bothering with questions at all.

He was overjoyed to have seen a tiger. They were almost extinct.

In front of him Cain plodded on expressionlessly with his head down. Lazaro knew that if he didn't call a halt he would walk forever. He hoped his idea would work. Life was too short to spend in perdition, especially if it was self-imposed penance. The Anglican priest in Aceh, Mike Jameson, an Australian who shared broadly the same vision of benevolence towards humanity and love of the country and who had become a good friend over the last couple of years, had come to him six months previously completely at a loss about what to do with the man. Mike had found him crouching on the porch steps of the wooden-walled, tin-roofed church, half naked, skeletally thin, with no possessions but for a small leather bag he wouldn't let go of, and could get nothing out of him. Not a word. He would neither enter the church nor leave it. Nor would he eat or drink unless at the brink of unconsciousness. What had most concerned Lazaro had not been his physical condition but the look in his eyes; as if he were already dead. Glazed, dark ringed, they'd looked straight through him.

Together he and Mike had tried everything. Cajoling, bribery, jokes; nothing registered, although, having tried Thai and Malay, they established from a giveaway flicker of idiomatic recognition that he was at least Indonesian. At this, in desperation, they found someone who was willing to read to him, in the hope that it might snap him out of his stupor. He would have none of it unless it was from the Holy Bible. This seemed to appease him somewhat, and he would close his eyes as if in the peaceful embrace of death.

One day, Jaya, the young refugee from East Timor given the task of reading out loud to this lost soul, came running into the vestry where Mike was working, in a state of great excitement. The man with no name had spoken. One sentence. Once. When Jaya had begun reading from Genesis,

'I,' he said, in an unusual dialect that the boy didn't recognise, 'am Cain.'

And that was it.

Lazaro and Mike guessed that he had killed his brother, and that this must be the reason for the hell he now inhabited. Lazaro, in a flash of inspiration, had an idea. Quickly he explained it to Mike, and together they rigged up the church's battered television and video player so that, from the porch he had made his home, Cain could see it. Then, with Jaya translating as best he could, he pushed in an old cassette of *The Mission* – Roland Joffé's film about the catastrophic clash between Portuguese and Spanish colonial politics in South America, and the indigenous tribesmen who pay the price – and hit 'play'.

To begin with he refused to watch, but as the dialogue developed and the story revealed its relevance, he began to pay attention and was soon engrossed. At the scene where, as penance, the fratricidal slaver, Mendoza, drags his conquistador armour up and up and up into the mountains to the village where he had once hunted for slaves, Cain broke down and cried.

Now here they were, trudging through a not dissimilar jungle, on a not dissimilar quest and though Cain – whatever his real name was – had yet to speak, Lazaro detected in his steps and body language a lightening of spirit. He wasn't sure what, exactly – a decisiveness that hadn't been there before. His lassitude seemed lessened. The jungle will do that, he thought, taking in the verdant density and richness of colours, the infinite greens, that surrounded them. He was happy here, and with the realisation his own load lightened. Just as it did so, it seemed the path steepened slightly. Lazaro smiled. He loved the subtle irony with which life had taught him the lessons he had learned, the humour and perfect balance of the universe all around him – if you allow yourself to see it, he thought.

They were approaching the falls and were planning to reach the top of them before nightfall.

That evening, exhausted, they pitched camp at the first sign of dusk on the bank of the river, out in the open near the edge where the solid sheet of the river disappeared silently over the precipice, darkness falling an hour later up here than in the dark forest below.

From their spectacular vantage point they watched the sun set, an infernal collapse into the sweaty vapours of the jungle that carpeted out before them as far as they could see, an undulating vegetal shroud mantling the earth, softening and smoothing the rocky contours beneath. Below them the water smashed thunderously into the ground, throwing fine mist out over liana-draped trees.

Each was moved in their different ways. Kuwat cast a swiftly whittled stick into the current, chanting gently under his breath. Lazaro, who always prayed with his eyes open, smiled as he received his spiritual manna.

And Cain spoke.

He told his story, in Indonesian, gazing out as the light faded while Kuwat built up the fire. Lazaro didn't move, expressionless, occasionally closing his eyes until the tale drew itself to its tragic conclusion. And when it had, he sat there in silence still, then reached out and gently laid his hand upon Cain's shoulder.

'It was not your fault, brother,' he said. 'Domi made his own choices, as you made yours and your wife made hers. You can regret those decisions, of course, since it is our nature to make mistakes in order that we might learn from them. That's life. But no one is entirely accountable for the mistakes of others, and dwelling on them, watering them with tears, allowing them to grow and curse the rest of your life, is not God's will. Providing you truly feel contrite, absolution is possible, freedom from the weight is possible.'

Cain said nothing for a few minutes as the last rinse of vermillion faded from the satin, star-strewn sky, then reached into his shirt and pulled out the leather pouch, snapping the thong on which it hung, and stood up. Walking to the edge of the precipice he made as if to throw it into the darkness, but stopped, walked back and handed it to Lazaro.

'I no longer need this,' he said. 'You keep it. Maybe you can sell it, raise some money for more medicines.' The Spaniard opened the bag and took out a thin tube of bamboo five inches long, turning it over slowly in his hands, unsure what to make of it. One end was corked with bark. He prised out the *tapón* and shook the cotton-wrapped contents into his palm. Unravelling it, he was astonished to find a black fountain pen that seemed to shimmer and shine with incorporeal depth as he turned it in the firelight, the nib giving off a dull gleam.

# Chapter 13

*Tuesday, 4th November, 1933*
*S.S. Apollonia*
*The Arabian Sea*

*Dearest Lil,*

*I'm still alive, at least, though there have been moments I wished I were not.*

*Having seen my previous letters safely dispatched, I shot back to the ship in order to try and communicate the plan as drawn up with Jennings to Mrs Richards. Having made a few casual enquiries to ensure her husband was not yet on board, I slipped down below and knocked lightly on her door. She answered and, deeming the chances of his returning and catching me in their cabin too great, I suggested she meet me on deck at my usual spot where we could be relatively sure of neither disturbance nor eavesdrop. This presently she did, and I ran her through my intentions.*

*She listened avidly without interruption, she even smiled when she thanked me for everything I was doing for her; the first time I have seen her do so, and what a difference it made. She actually looked rather pretty – despite her pale, pinched complexion – eliciting further sympathy for her plight. But I digress.*

*Once she'd been thoroughly briefed, she left to go and pack a small bag. (I told her to keep it strictly to a minimum – no more than her most important documents and a change of clothes; she would have to sacrifice some, if not all, of her possessions for her liberty.)*

*'Dear Ralph,' she said, 'isn't this thrilling!' clapping her hands, for all the world like a child playing a game, gave a queer little laugh – which, with the benefit of hindsight, should have alarmed me – and off she went.*

*I then set about trying to figure out how to create a suitable diversion – and quickly. I considered cutting the thick pulley ropes securing one of the lifeboats to its gantry but decided against such a drastic move: too easily seen, almost impossible to ensure the timing accurately, and the subsequent investigation would no doubt match my knife to the scene of the crime. The drop would also have risked damaging the small vessel, one of two designed to ensure safe escape of some thirty odd souls if she went down.*

*The clock was ticking, and my desperation mounting. Our departure nearly upon us, I elected for one course of action over which I had control;*

*I informed Maddox that I was feeling terrible, having eaten something bad the night before (quite possible, I assure you), and generally laid it on thick that I felt like death warmed up, etc. Then, muttering something about needing a breath of fresh air, took to the deck where the company had gathered to wave off the Arabian mainland and her good people. Dr Richards was there, chatting to Swaine, so too were some of the Dutch contingent, somehow enduring the heat despite their heavy robes, and a few new faces I assumed must have joined us for the last leg of the journey. The crew were busy preparing to cast off; the engine, already idling, was fired up, sooty emissions belching from the stacks, and the excitement that always seems to greet or bid farewell to ships was stoked further by the deafening klaxon.*

*I checked my pocket watch; five to twelve – it was now or never. Without thinking further I distanced myself from the people at the rail (making sure my complaints of feeling faint were heard by at least some of those gathered), removed my jacket and tottered across to the other side of the deck, unoccupied by passenger and crew alike, made as if to stagger slightly for effect, stumbled against the chain that closes off the gap in the rail, and with a shout went over the side.*

*It was more of a drop than I'd anticipated. I fell through twenty feet of air, sea-ship-sky-sea-ship-sky, and hit the water with an almighty smack which very nearly knocked me out; the air was driven from my lungs, and for a split second I had a flash of my own imminent demise – ingloriously drowned; in a harbour, of my own volition – and of how I'd explain myself to St Peter.*

*I struggled up through the water to the surface, my boots dead weights, and broke it with a ragged gasp. Above me, to my considerable relief, a head appeared over the rail, promptly withdrawing again, and I heard the shouted words my life depended on, 'Man overboard!' Then one of the ship's orange life rings sailed out through the air to land fifteen feet or so away from where I splashed about.*

*Now that I was sure of my survival, and with an audience already gathered above, I made great show of my attempts to reach the life ring, floundering in the water as if I had never swum before in my life – not entirely acting, what with the weight of my boots and clothing, but certainly dragging the moment out for a minute more, vital if the plan was going to work.*

*A dinghy appeared around the stern of the ship and began making its way towards me while I hung onto the life ring, puffing and blowing for the benefit of the crowd above.*

*There were shouts. I looked up and tried to give a gesture of heroic fortitude signifying that I was all right, that they needn't worry further. Someone shouted something, pointing out to the harbour beyond me. I turned to where they were looking but could see nothing. I looked to the dinghy, which appeared to have picked up its pace, the two crewmen at the oars straining in unison, glancing over their shoulders between strokes.*

*I turned again, and this time saw what was causing consternation; cutting steadily towards me in a thrusting zigzag was a ragged, triangular fin. A shark. A big one. I had seen a few from the safety of the rail – no more than a glimpse of swift shadow in the water – and knew that what approached was no dolphin. I had also heard enough from Maddox to know exactly what would befall me if I didn't move, sharpish.*

*I reached the dinghy in approximately five seconds.*

*There I was seized under my arms and hauled over the gunwale just in time to see the beast glide past beneath my quickly retracted boots, ten feet from snub snout to tail if it was an inch, with mottled grey-green skin and an awful lazy sinuosity.*

*I lay there panting while Jake, between grunting strokes of the oar, explained how sharks, ever opportunistic, often loiter around ships in port for whatever scraps as might be thrown over the side.*

*'Bugger probably thought all its Christmases had come at once,' he said, and they both began laughing. I did not laugh with them.*

*Five minutes later, back in my cabin, dried off, changed, resting on my bunk with a medicinal hot toddy to steady my nerves, I listened to the familiar sounds of our departure and prayed that she – Claudia, that is – had managed to get away. To delay her absence being discovered, I was about to call Maddox and get him to summon the Doctor so I might distract him awhile further, when the man himself knocked and entered before I could respond, quickly taking in the room with a sweep of his cold eyes.*

*My heart rate doubled for the second time in an hour, adding convincingly to my pallor. I tried to smile.*

*'That was quite a show,' he said humourlessly, fixing me with a long stare. Did he know of my complicity? Had we been discovered? I surreptitiously checked my pistol was within reach – it neither was nor would I have known how to use it had it been. He placed his case on the table. 'Maddox tells me you were feeling off colour before you fainted – something you ate, perhaps? – so I thought I'd drop in on you and make sure you're all right,' he said, snapping the latches of his case. He took my temperature and felt my brow, pressed around my abdomen, asked my symptoms and what I'd eaten in the last twenty-four hours, then withdrew a bottle of pills from the case and shook out a dozen or so into a fold of paper, telling me to take five now and one every hour from then on until I felt better.*

*'What are they?' I asked, poking the grey-black pastilles dubiously.*

*'Charcoal,' he said. 'It absorbs any toxins you might have ingested. I'll get Maddox to bring you a tonic for the dehydration, minerals and salts, and we'll see how you feel later on.' He stood to leave. At the door he paused. 'Listen, Talbot, I know you are, ahem, a friend of Claudia's' – my stomach lurched – 'she has often mentioned you as being her only real chum aboard,' he hesitated, searching for the right words. 'I just wondered if she had spoken to you about what she expected to find in Mombasa.' He looked uncomfortable, and sweat shone on his brow, 'Whether, I don't know, whether she has given any indication of not being entirely happy?' He examined the handle of his case, unable to meet my eye.*

*He clearly had not discovered her missing; was it possible he still suspected nothing?*

*His act did not fool me in the slightest.*

*I replied that as far as she had intimated to me – not very far, it must be said, I assured him – she felt a little homesick but was looking forward to her new life overseas. He looked at me, and I had the impression of a young boy filled with the expectation of promised sweets, so eager was his look, like – forgive the simile – a drowning man just thrown a lifeline. Most confounding. Is the depth of his delusion such that he cannot see what he's done to her, how the prospect of a life with him had driven her to the edge of madness, the brink of suicide?*

*He continued, though I wished he would leave me be.*

*'As I'm sure you know, her illness has been pronounced these last few weeks. I fear her constitution may not be up to the strain the African Continent can exert upon a girl unless she can somehow change her outlook. She tends to always expect the worst – as is common for people with her condition. Be a good chap and try to keep her spirits up a bit over the next few days, will you? Try and instil some hope in her? I'd be most grateful.' And with that he left.*

*I lay back, resisting the urge to shout out that I had saved her from him, the monster, and confident that though he himself might not realise it, I had already done as he wished. Exhausted, I fell asleep, only to wake to some commotion in the corridor outside – doors slamming – but it faded and I drifted off once more.*

*Later on, after supper taken in my cabin, I had the pleasure of a visit from the skipper, though he didn't stay long, making sure I was recovered as well as possible – uncommonly civil of him, I thought – and I took the opportunity to apologise for all the fuss I had caused.*

*'Not at all, lad,' he said. 'Though it appears in the confusion we seem to have left without the full complement of passengers.'*

*I did my best to look surprised.*

*'Why?' says I, all innocent. 'What on earth happened?'*

*'It seems Mrs Richards disembarked at the last minute, when you had your, ah, accident.' He tugged at his beard thoughtfully, gazing through the porthole; distracted, fortunately, for I'm sure he would have noticed both the relief and guilt in my expression.*

*'Damnedest thing,' he said. 'Dr Richards is quite distraught' – oh really, I thought – 'says she left him a letter saying their marriage was a sham, that she never loved him, poor chap. Between you and me, I think these young girls wholly unsuited to the colonies, let alone highly strung fillies with a history of mental illness such as hers. And, what's worse, she took off with all his savings. Completely fleeced the poor fellow. Ah well, nothing to be done now. We're too far out to turn back. Let's hope she is not in any danger, either to herself or to anyone else.' I was about to enquire what he meant by his reference to 'mental illness' but he seemed to catch himself, as if surprised to find himself speaking aloud.*

*'Well, I must be going,' he said, standing up. 'I've said far too much and I assume I can count on your diplomacy in the matter.' I nodded.*

*'Absolutely, sir,' I said, and with that he bade me goodnight and left.*

*My final visitor was Maddox. He has just left me in peace, the oaf, though I'm not sure peace is the right word. I have the terrible feeling that something's rotten in the state of Denmark, dearest, a sense of foreboding I hope is due to the day's events and not the premonition of something dreadful. He – Maddox – has clearly relished what happened earlier; with a sense of humour like his, Armageddon itself would probably induce paroxysms.*

*'Evening, sir,' he said. 'Had a good day, did we?' And I noticed his shoulders were shaking, though he kept his back to me as he busied himself around the cabin.*

*'I gather you nearly caught a whopper on your fishing trip, though*

*apparently you weren't using quite the right bait,' he said, and burst into laughter. 'Never in all my days ...' He wiped his eyes.*

*'Look, Maddox,' I said, trying to keep my cool. 'It's been a bloody long day, I was nearly eaten alive and I gather Mrs Richards has jumped ship. It's not funny, damn you.'*

*'All right, all right, keep your shirt on. No harm done,' he says. Then, as he's leaving, 'Don't go overboard,' and I hear him trail off in peals down the corridor.*

*Well my love, peace at last; I can now catch up with events and try to give you some idea of just what I've let myself in for with this Quest (you are my Grail, naturally). An asylum, indeed! May we arrive in Mombasa as quickly as possible so I can acquit myself of this voyage.*

*With all my love,*

*Ralph*

*Wednesday, 5th November, 1933*

*Lillian,*

*What have I done?*

*Symmonds came to my cabin first thing. God help me, I can barely write the words.*

*'Ralph,' he said, 'I need to talk to you.' My heart flipped at the severity of his tone.*

*'Of course,' I said, buttoning my shirt, trepidation chasing sleep from my brain as the sun burns away morning mist. 'Whatever is the matter?'*

*'That depends,' he said.*

*'On what, dear chap?'*

*'On what exactly happened yesterday.'*

*'My stupid tumble over the side, you mean? Well I must have –'*

*'Ralph,' he said, 'before you incriminate yourself further by lying to me, consider the following. What are the odds of you "falling" overboard at exactly – exactly, mind – twelve o'clock? Who would remove their jacket beforehand, as if anticipating said fall?' At this he produced my jacket, which until then I had completely forgotten about, left where I'd dropped it by the rail. 'And how on earth would Mrs Richards coincidentally be well enough prepared – packed, with her travel documents – to flee at that precise moment?'*

*'Well, I –' I began.*

*'Do not take me for a fool, lad,' he said quietly, visibly trying to keep his temper in check. 'I hope you know me better than that by now.'*

*I elected to come clean.*

*'Look, Jim,' I said. 'I know you thought it best not to help, but I had to. You knew how her situation was desperate, how miserable she was, how he was treating her. For God's sake, he was trying to murder her, for all we knew! I felt I must do something. As a gentleman.'*

*'Ha!' he exclaimed.*

*'So I spoke to someone at the Embassy in Aden – Jennings – and he agreed to help, to take her in and give her refuge. All I had to do was ensure she made it off the ship safely.'*

*'You stupid, arrogant, gullible, meddling fool. Do you know what you've done, you blithering cretin?'*

*And he told me.*

*At Jeddah he had wired an 'associate' in London with connections in the Yard and who owed him a favour, asking him to dig up what he could on the Richards'.*

*'The reply I received in Aden makes quite fascinating reading. Would you like to hear what it says?'*

*I knew at once that I did not.*

*He read out loud:*

*'dr richards stop david calum stop born bristol eighteen ninety eight stop trained exeter college medicine stop distinction phd psychology and neurology stop meteoric career culminating as special consultant st marys london correctional institute for criminally insane stop struck off med register after personal involvement with patient claudia jane walters stop persuaded jury same mentally unfit to stand trial for murder of fiancee robert lund nineteen thirty one stop walters acquitted stop married richards august nineteen thirty three stop article in lancet to effect med sci not ready for his work greeted with ridicule by sci community stop message ends'*

*Given even more weight by the disembodied language of the telegraph, the implications of the words hung in the air as if sculpted. Sculpted from the ice that slowly froze across my heart. My vision tunnelled and the pounding of the ship's engine seemed to merge with the blood thudding through my temples. I collapsed heavily on the bed, my head in my hands.*

*'But I saw him,' I whispered, 'that night. It was him, ranting like a lunatic.'*

*'No, Ralph. It was her. The disturbances at night, all her. He was trying to protect her.'*

*'Why in God's name didn't he say anything?'*

*'After the treatment they'd received back home, would you? They were trying to escape it!' He sighed. 'He spoke to me about that night. That you had come to the door during one of her episodes. Do you know what he asked me, Ralph?' I shook my head miserably. 'Whether he could, in my opinion, rely on your absolute discretion.*

*I vouched for you and replied that I was sure of it. Christ Almighty, I'd like to know what your idea of indiscretion is.'*

*'The poison?'*

*'Sleeping tablets. Sedatives, Ralph – lithium, as I told you.'*

*'Why didn't you stop me?'*

*'Because we both agreed not to do anything rash – so help me God – or at least I thought we had. By the time I discovered your jacket and realised what you were up to it was too late, she had gone and the ship pulled anchor. I decided then and there that it would cause more harm than good for there to be a huge scene, turning her about, et cetera, and that you, laddie, would undoubtedly lose your job, passage and fiancée were news of your intervention ever to get out.' He walked to the desk and picked up my Mabie Todd, turning it over in his hands, lost in thought.*

*'Besides, they'll keep her at the Embassy once they find out exactly who she is. If what you tell me is true and the full extent of your deception – and it bloody better be everything, sonny boy – then Richards will be somewhat relieved. He is on the ship-to-shore radio to the Embassy as we speak, attempting to track her down and, if she's there, will be able to give them some instruction as to how best handle her. Hopefully – hopefully – he'll be able to pick up the pieces next week when he returns.' He placed the pen carefully back on the desk.*

*'So he doesn't know . . .' I stammered, 'about me, I mean?'*

*'You're testing my patience now, boy,' he said, the same quiet anger in the quaver of his voice. 'Try to stop thinking of yourself and try to understand the amount of damage you've caused. And don't for a second think that I misunderstand your intentions. You might try and dress them up as honourable but we both know they were at best bloody idiotic and at worst vainglorious. This is the real world, sunshine. Not one of your childhood adventure stories.'*

*He turned to go.*

*'I'm sorry I let you down, Jim,' I said. He stopped and turned around, his face softened slightly.*

*'As am I, Ralph, as am I,' he said. 'Just try to learn from it, pray that they manage to pull together whatever it was that they had between them again, and pray even harder that Richards doesn't put two and two together and figure out that you were involved. Not until he gets it from her, at least. By then he might forgive you. As might I.' Before he closed the door, he said, 'Oh, by the way. Nice swimming. Haven't seen anyone move that quickly since the detonator tripped on a landmine in Gallipoli.'*

*I am too wretched, embarrassed and ashamed to write any more just at the moment, my love, and only hope that you can forgive me also. I hope my candour in relating everything to you goes some way towards helping the process.*

*Yours ever,*
*Ralph*
*x*

*Thursday, 6th November, 1933*
*The Indian Ocean*

*Dear Lillian,*
*The final leg of the voyage continues, the atmosphere aboard subdued and, certainly as far as I am concerned, laden with apprehension, not least due to events in Aden.*

*I have learnt nothing.*

*And to think how full of myself I had become. It makes me wince at the memory. I try to 'learn from the experience and move onwards' but nevertheless, whenever I encounter Richards it is all I can do not to flee the room, let alone meet his eye. For his part, he bears his heartache and the worry he must be feeling with admirable stoicism. I can only assume that since he can do nothing to relieve the situation while stuck out here in the middle of nowhere, he has resigned himself to whatever cards fate deals him; indeed, temporarily freed of the burden of his charge, he has become considerably more demonstrative – further deepening the pit of my own culpability. Unfettered by his responsibility, and with my eyes descaled, as it were, it is clear that he is a gentle, kind, honourable man, his previous reticence a defensive veneer.*

*He still suspects nothing of my involvement in his wife's flight, and though a part of me wants to confess, I know this won't help matters. I am keeping a low profile and busy myself in my books, preparing myself as best I can for the months ahead, though at the moment I feel wholly out of my depth.*

*We have, apparently (and for all I care at the moment), left the Arabian Sea and entered the Indian Ocean, though the undulating silk of the water looks no different, and are blessed with a following wind so the ship labours less and the going is good. To starboard, little more than a hint on the horizon, lies Somaliland and the African continent. To port, far to the east, India. And here, crawling along the surface of this vast expanse of water, we continue.*

*It's disconcerting to have the sun change its aspect so dramatically; now we sail south west, it's as if one has picked up one's house, turned it forty-five degrees and set it down again. We have covered half the angles of the compass in our side-winding zigzag of a voyage; setting off south west, turning east across the Med, then south through the Red Sea and now back south west once more. My sense of direction is spinning wildly, like a magnet run around a compass.*

*Jim appears to have forgiven me, and has taken me back under his tutelage, continually joshing me to snap me out of my self-recriminations because he 'needs to get me up to speed' before we arrive; his words, not mine.*

*'Get off the cross,' he said. 'We need the wood.'*

*This instils me with a rising sense of foreboding; what am I to expect? I hardly know anymore what it is I am here to do, it's been so long on board this bloody boat. I am so familiar with her every groan, moan, rivet, rust stain and knot that I could probably recreate her to the last detail, given the right materials. How these men survive for periods of time much longer than this aboard without going mad I have no idea (perhaps everyone is a little doolally, I can no longer tell). At least my claustrophobia seems to have been cured; my cabin now seems positively spacious – perhaps I have exchanged it for agoraphobia instead. Out with one, in with another.*

*The voyage nears its end, and what have I to show for it? – a markedly improved game of chess, intimate knowledge of several card games, a beard and a profound sense of my own impetuosity.*

*I know we agreed we would not, but I intend to try the telegraph in Mombasa – to get word to you that I am arrived safe and sound.*

*See you in our dreams. You'll recognise me by the donkey's ears.*

*Ralph*

*x*

*Friday, 7th November, 1933*
*The Equator*

*My angel,*

*This morning, as I rose in slightly better spirits and took a stroll around the deck, I could see we are closer to land – a grey-green streak, virtually devoid of feature, that marks our progress. Knowing my destination, Jim was able to point the Lamu archipelago out as we passed, though it appeared no different to any other part of the coast so far.*

*The port itself is apparently tucked away behind the headland, thus invisible from the ocean. Why they cannot just put me ashore now I don't know – I will have to make my way back up the coast overland from Mombasa. I could see numerous dhows upon the water, their white sails flecks against the land.*

*Soon thereafter we crossed the Equator and, though I didn't know it then, I was soon to wish they had made me swim ashore.*

*Unbeknownst to me, this marks quite a moment for the nautical fraternity, representing as it does passage from one hemisphere to another, denoting another world – the unknown. Anyway, I was quite ignorant of this. I say 'was' with emphasis; I am now a qualified 'shellback', as those who have 'crossed the line' are known.*

*What happened was as follows –*

*We were all invited to the viewing deck around mid morning. I should have known something was up from Maddox's incessant winking, so much so I thought he'd developed a twitch. 'Reckon you'll enjoy this, lad,' he said – from where we could see over the fo'c's'le, the open deck at the bow, with some protection from the sun.*

*On deck were assembled the entire crew – some twenty men, all in high spirits, some dressed lewdly, in grotesque parodies of women – and a raised stage with two armchairs set on it had been placed at the prow.*

*Once we fifteen or so were gathered, a conch was blown and Buchanan appeared, dressed, hilariously, as King Neptune in flowing green robes, festooned in seaweed, wearing a crown of shells with a gaffe in one hand and a fishing net in the other. On his arm walked a beautiful 'woman', regally done out in a fetching blue dress, with a conch and a green glass ball, a net buoy. (This was Queen*

*Amphitrite, I was duly informed – though this is, if I remember rightly, confusing Greek and Roman mythology somewhat; Jim told me not to be such a pedant.) The Queen, camping it up something rotten, turned out to be Johnson, the First Mate, though I scarcely recognised him under his long blonde wig. Buchanan on the other hand, with his white beard and craggy face, actually looked more truly himself than usual.*

*They duly took their 'thrones', and the ceremony began.*

*The two 'Pollywogs', young Peck – my partner in pugilism – and Porter, initiates for whom the Equator was hitherto uncharted territory, were led out before these gods of the deep, stripped to the waist and bound by the wrists. The quartermaster, a Dane called Redelius, called out, 'Be there any here amongst us yet Pollywog?' To which the crew shouted 'Ay!'*

*'Who might they be?' And the crew chorused the unfortunate's names. 'No more?' he asked. There was a pause; all present fell silent as if waiting for someone to speak up.*

*Then someone did.*

*Jim, the blighter, shouted 'Ay, one more!' and before I could react, called out my name.*

*After that, proceedings become a bit of a blur.*

*Much to the delight of the others, I was seized and taken to the deck, my shirt removed and hands bound, then forced to kneel before the throne with the others. He then read our charges, slanders against our characters that I'm quite sure sent the missionaries scurrying back to their cabins. The crew fell about.*

*My turn came. 'Ralph Talbot, you are accused of excessive toffiness, righteousness, seasickness, aloofness, ingenuousness, cluelessness, reclusiveness, absentmindedness and general immaturity; of hiding a sneaky left fist, of cruelly baiting the beasts of the deep, of which the shark is Lord Neptune's favourite, of regularly drinking enough liquor for two men, and of driving Able Seaman Maddox to distraction.' Everyone cheered loudly between each charge. Then Neptune thundered, 'How do you plead, Pollywog?'*

*Following the lead of the other two, I cried 'Guilty!' An error, in hindsight.*

*'Then let justice be seen done this day,' he replied with gravitas.*

*We were then pulled to our feet, dragged to the rail and tied over it so we were looking down at the water below, our posteriors pointing to the heavens. Then what I had so far taken to be good-natured larking about was promptly turned on its head; before I knew it rough hands had wrenched down my trousers and those of my fellow victims, and we were bare-arsed to all the world. Before I could protest I heard yelps of pain and craned my head to see what was happening – two fiendish 'women' were scouring Peck's backside with deck scrubbers, stiff-bristled brushes. He yowled in agony, then the same treatment was meted out to Porter next to me, with the same yells of pain, and then it was my turn.*

*Most definitely no laughing matter, dearest! With a few violent scrubs, the bastards took the skin off my behind while I strained at the ropes and cursed every one of them to Hell. Thus humiliated, I demanded that I be untied, red faced with embarrassment and rage.*

*But it was far from over yet – Peck was untied and, with everyone following singing shanties, dragged off – where to I couldn't see; I hoped that he had been released, but soon heard a great cheer from the other side of the boat. My terror was mounting. Then it was the turn of young Porter next to me to be led away, and a great cheer went up a few minutes later. Finally it was my turn – untied and borne off fighting and struggling like a landed eel, but the hands that restrained me were too strong. I stopped struggling when I saw what was in store for me; I was tied by my ankles to the gantry and hoisted up into the air, the arm was swung out over the side, the waves charging past beneath – and the rope released.*

*I plummeted headfirst into the sea – bear in mind we were moving at the time, though slowed to five knots or so. The sudden slam of the water momentarily took my mind off my nudity, but not for long, and any pain, humiliation and anger I felt was quickly replaced by fear since the shock had emptied my lungs.*

*Dragged underwater, backwards and drowning, what felt like minutes must in retrospect have been seconds, thirty or so; the noise and chaos of churning water filled my ears, exploded into my nose and lungs, and I remember thinking that they must be trying to kill me.*

*Had my crimes been found out and had I been summarily sentenced to die?*

*Then, just when I thought all was lost and I'd never see you again, like the hand of God – Neptune? – reaching down to save me, I felt tension return to the rope and I surfaced feet first into bright blue sky, choking and spluttering – literally at the end of my tether – eyes streaming, unable to see, up into the air, swung back over the side and was dumped unceremoniously onto the deck where I lay coughing like a coalminer with emphysema.*

Recovering my senses, I tried to cover myself; the infernal crew, leering grotesques in their costumes – demons and harlequins, women and animals – like some diabolic clown show, were all gathered round close, laughing at the three of us as if it was the most hilarious diversion of their lives. Finally my ropes were cut and I sat up, wiping the hair from my eyes, cursing my tormentors vociferously between lungfuls of air.

*Livid, but grateful to be alive, I snatched the proffered blanket and wrapped it around what remained of my modesty, put my head between my knees and prayed Hell would open and take the lot of them, tears of humiliation and pain mercifully hidden by the seawater and my bowed head, while they danced and capered around us like a carousel of whirling dervishes.*

*There was a tap on my shoulder, and I looked up to inform whoever it might be precisely what they could do to themselves and their loved ones; it was Jim, presenting a mug of rum to me.*

*'Well done lad!' he laughed. I knocked the cup from his hands and got to my feet with every intention of hitting him, my anger red and tight.*

*'You bastard,' I said, 'of all the –'*

*He looked into my eyes, his twinkling with good humour, and gestured with his eyebrows behind me. I turned around and there was the whole company – Richards, Swaine, McAlister, Buchanan, Maddox, my two fellow sufferers, Peck and Porter, the crew – turned towards me, mugs raised, broad grins upon their faces;*

*'Hail, Shellback, son of Neptune!' they toasted me unison.*

*I turned back, uncertain of how to react, caught off guard by the good will and camaraderie. Jim had refilled my mug.*

*'Hail, Shellback,' he said, 'Son of Neptune,' offering the cup, which I took a gulp from, grateful for the oily burn of the liquor.*

*I coughed heavily, and Jim clapped me resoundingly on the back. Everyone laughed, and then I did too. And then we laughed more, and an accordion struck up. My two Shellback brothers clapped their arms round my shoulders and we compared wounds, and then I was dancing around, flapping my blanket like wings, whooping and shouting with the others, quite careless of my nakedness until Maddox, with a polite cough, brought me my clothes.*

*'Better cover up, sir,' he said. 'Don't want you adding sunburn to the list.' I pulled on trousers and shirt and collapsed in the lee*

*of the superstructure, quite out of breath yet at the same time exhilarated, while the others continued their revelry.*

*Richards approached.*

*'If you drop by my cabin I might have something for that,' he said, genially.*

*'Thank you, Doctor,' I replied, meeting his eye for the first time in days, wanting to tell him everything. But I didn't. Not then.*

*Later, the light beginning to fade in a wash of pale blues and crimson pinks and the last of the brandy long drunk, I stopped at his door.*

*'Come in.' I entered and he presented me with a pot of foul-smelling ointment.*

*'This should help,' he said.*

*'Doctor,' I said, 'I need to tell you something –' But he raised a hand, cutting me off.*

*'No, Ralph,' he said, 'you do not.' He gave me a look I cannot accurately explain, dearest; one of understanding, forgiveness and sorrow all wrapped up together with a slight smile. There was no need for words. I shook his hand, thanked him with all my heart and retired here to my cabin, more elated, more sorrowful, more clear-headed, more confused and more moved than I think I have ever been. And more exhausted! I must sleep, or wake with my head upon this table.*

*We arrive tomorrow – at long last – and I cannot wait to get ashore and get going, yet at the same time I know I shall miss all those aboard and the time spent among them.*

*I think I may have learnt something after all.*

*All my love,*

*Ralph*

*x*

*Sunday, 9th November, 1933*
*Mombasa, Kenya*

*My Love,*

*Finally, after six weeks at sea, we have arrived.*

*Before we reached port – quite stunning, with long white reaches of sand to the north and south, scudded with a fringe of palms that give way to seeming endless mangroves – Jim gave me what I suppose was some kind of debriefing; he sent a message for me to join him in his cabin after lunch – itself quite a jolly affair, with Buchanan and the first mate Johnson joining us; toasts made to a successful trip and many a back-slapping 'bon voyage' between passengers. This I duly did, already slightly the worse for wear (the yard arm seems to have been somewhat raised recently). I knocked and he bade me enter.*

*'Well, lad,' he said, sitting back with a cheroot. 'It's been quite an adventure. I hope you're as ready as you can be for what lies ahead – testing times, I have no doubt. You've a good head, my boy – just always try to use it, and think before acting. Take a few seconds before making your move, simply taking a breath or two can make all the difference to the outcome of any situation. And you'll be in good hands. I don't know this Cotton Charlie chap personally but have heard he's a good egg, I'm sure you'll be fine.'*

*'Thank you. For everything.'*

*'Mm.' he looked at me seriously. 'You know, this country is entirely what you make of it. Full of opportunity, extraordinarily warm and hospitable people. My only further advice is to treat her and them with respect. Too often we whites plough in here and cudgel what we want from the land and often as not her inhabitants. Walk gently and she'll give you everything you want, and more.' He reached into his pocket and pulled out a small package wrapped in cotton. 'Here,' he said. 'For luck.'*

*I unwrapped it to discover a brass disk on a leather thong. Turning the disk over revealed an engraving – two overlaid triangles forming a six-pointed star within a circle, with strange symbols and glyphs etched into each delineated section of the hexagon I recognised from the box on his desk. I looked up at him quizzically.*

*'The Star of David? Are you Jewish? I didn't realise.'*

*'Star of David to some. Solomon's Seal to others. It's a good luck charm, a talisman from Ethiopia in the north. I was given it by a very powerful man and it's stood me in good stead so far.' He tapped the fleck of white hair at his temple. 'Perhaps it will do the same for you.'*

*'You no longer need it, then?' I asked, half joking, since I had no idea what importance, if any, he attached to the thing.*

*'Not as much as you,' he replied with a dry smile. 'You should keep it on you at all times. I wore it round my neck. Here, turn round.' I did so and he tied it so that it hung beneath my shirt. Since it caused me no discomfort I humoured him, said thank you and left it where it was.*

*'So,' I said, feeling awkward and wanting to change the subject, 'we're due in pretty soon. I had better go and get ready. See you ashore.' And left him to his thoughts.*

*Slowly I packed my valise and knapsack, and cast a last look around the cabin that had been home to me these last seven weeks. On the table I left a note thanking Maddox for his patience and for looking after me (he had made himself scarce as we approached land – busy with other duties no doubt – and I wasn't to see him again) together with a ten-shilling tip for his trouble.*

*We drew under the intimidating battlements of Fort Jesus and into port around eleven, the heat of the day already sweltering despite the breeze, the ship's klaxon heralding our arrival, to be greeted by great numbers of locals of all shades; from almost blue-black, ebony Africans to fairer-skinned Arabs, all clamouring for work unloading the cargo. I took one final tour of the Apollonia, rather fancying I could make out where my feet had worn a path in her teak deck, stood one more time at 'my spot' and trailed a hand along her rails, suddenly filled with nostalgia for the old girl. She is a fine ship, and I shall follow her fortunes and that of her crew for as long as she floats.*

*The gangplank was lowered and we clanked ashore, Buchanan, back in uniform, shaking hands with one and all and wishing us well. I turned to give what crew were gathered a final wave, which they returned, several giving mock salutes. The two hunters were taking the recently completed railway to Nairobi, the newly established Kenyan capital, and from there heading up into the highlands where the game could be found in greatest numbers. We shook hands and they wished me luck, as I did them (secretly wishing the animals the same) and Swaine even gave me his hipflask, which was very decent of him. I watched them load up their guns and equipment and disappear into the crowd, already yammering away at each other in their good-natured, abrasive banter. The Dutch, similarly taking the Nairobi train but heading further afterwards, all the way into Uganda, from where they would disperse to their various postings across central eastern Africa, also bade me farewell; I wonder whether their faith will be enough to keep them safe in what I gather is dangerous territory.*

*As for Richards – he immediately set off for the harbour master's offices to try and secure the next possible passage back to Aden. I never did get an opportunity to apologise to him properly but suspect it is taken as read.*

*Jim, having invited me to stay at his club, commandeered a couple of chaps with a donkey and cart and we followed them on foot, out of the port and along the dusty road into the old town, the sun-bleached Portuguese colonial architecture oddly incongruous amid the coconut palms and the chaos of street vendors, labourers, mule drivers, burka-shrouded women with only their eyes visible, and children tearing about. The hot air was filled with the smell of food cooking in dingy, fly-blown shacks and the spices – cinnamon, pepper, nutmeg, cardamom, clove – and coffee that, along with those of the nearby island of Zanzibar, make this region so desirable for trade.*

*The Kalifi Club is straight out of Pall Mall, Lil, you would have found it most amusing (had you been allowed through the door); deep leather armchairs, clouds of cigar smoke, clipped King's English and all the vestiges of Old Establishment – single malts at the bar, photographs of the old man, lithographs of the City,* even framed cases of neck ties of every institution, college and school, donated by those who have passed through these doors before me. There already existed one from Rugby which, though I bear little affection for the place, nevertheless triggered a rise in my emotional tide; a link with my past. *Were it not for the attendant staff, ceiling fans and rictus-grinned animal trophies (lion, kudu – an enormous member of the antelope family with lethal-looking, javelin-like horns – cheetah, leopard etc.) on the walls, I'd have thought us still in London.*

*The club itself has begun to show signs of anachronism, a sign of declining fortunes, perhaps, or dilapidation setting in since the administrative HQ decamped to Nairobi, some 250 miles inland. After the voyage, though, it seemed like heaven; we had a fine dinner of rump steak washed down with a bloody claret, then watched the sunset from the terrace – a spectacular gradation of yellows, oranges and blue giving the sky tremendous depth – while brightly feathered birds chattered to their roost and cicada swelled their ragged chorus. We spoke little beyond occasional reflection on the journey.*

I write beneath the gauzy mosquito net that surrounds my bed in an air-deadening shroud. The choice seems to be this: either try and cool yourself in whatever breeze there might be but expose yourself to the persistent attacks of the insect horde, or seek refuge behind this muslin and sweat your heart out. Since the risk of malaria is extremely high here, the choice is already made. Apologies if the ink is a little smudged.

*Another milestone, my love, and still early days though it feels as if the year has already passed.*

*Yours,*

*Ralph*

*x*

# Chapter 14

*Marrakesh, Morocco. 1998.*

Turning over the old thuya box, Tomas Morales marvelled at the intricacy of the knotted veins and ghosted stains that dappled the grain like mould in blue cheese, abstract faces and animals and landscapes forming readily out of the rich, lustrous browns and dark ochres. He had heard of the fabled trees – highly valued by the ancient Greeks and Romans for their carvable density and the heavy-scented oil within the wood – that once covered this region of the Atlas mountains and this region alone, long before the slash and burn of progress.

The store owner bobbed expectantly at his elbow.

'This very nice piece,' he whined, narrowing the chance of Tomas buying it with every syllable. Honestly, he thought, these guys are supposed to be the best salesmen on earth. 'Owner was princess in Rabat. Maybe still jewels inside.'

The jewellery box had hidden compartments that the man said he would reveal only if he bought it. He gave it a shake. Nothing in there, he thought. That said, he couldn't see the joins for any drawers, any chinks or deviations in the flow of the variegated grain. The workmanship was impressive. He handed it back. He was supposed to be looking for silver. Maybe he could get it for her though. She'd love it. He'd try and come back later.

'No thanks, amigo,' he said. The man's wide, yellow-toothed smile didn't falter.

'Maybe you like rare pieces? Special.' The oleaginous way he rolled his r's made Tomas queasy.

'No, merci,' he said, but the guy pulled out a tray of black velvet bags from beneath the counter as Tomas turned to go, keeping his attention like a pro. Taking the lead, he opened the drawstring of the first bag and tipped out a silver pendant wrought thick and dense, laced with intricate geometrical engraving. Tomas picked it up. It was heavy. The silver had a glow to it, a pink lustre that Tomas knew to be particular to the area. Tuareg silver. He masked his interest. If this was the guy's opening gambit, Christ knows what else he's got in there, he thought. He turned to the rectangle of light, past the rich tapestries and carpets that lined the shop walls that led out onto the street.

Gabriella. His Ella.

He should tell her he was going to be a while longer. This was why they were here, after all, and he had trailed around the market after her all day. Where had she gone?

'I'll be back, mon ami,' he said, 'just give me a minute.' He walked out into the midday glare and the chaos of the souk, and was instantly hit on by three hawkers, selling what, he neither noticed nor cared. He looked over their heads left and right, shading his eyes with one hand. He couldn't see her. *Come on, babe. Where the hell are you?* She'd been just behind him – he'd been talking to her over his shoulder – as they walked through the bustling bazaar. What had he been saying? He'd been relaying his theory on how not to get fleeced: always pay fifty percent less than what you think it's worth, whatever it is. That way everyone wins. The vendor will think it's his birthday, guaranteed, and you'll think you've got a bargain. He personally didn't have the patience for haggling, though he could manage the requisite poker face, start low and then go through the courtship motions – coy, teasing, brusque, final – all the way up to the point of walking off if necessary, but he preferred just to look the fuckers in the eye and hit them with one price, fifty percent below what he thought it was worth, and leave it to them to work out whether he was bluffing or not, whether they could get any more out of him. Whether they could be bothered to try. It usually worked. He had the sneaking suspicion that, although it was their equivalent to going to the office and cold-calling housewives from nine to five who don't-want-anything-thank-you, they appreciated his no-nonsense approach. More likely, they didn't give a fuck.

She'd replied, he remembered. Something about enjoying the whole charade. Must be a girl thing, he'd said. And then he'd ducked in here, into this shop, assuming she was right behind him.

But she wasn't.

Later he thought back to that moment. The brief vestige of how his life had been before. How simple and easy it had been, how happy. Then he played through the rest of the day. How he went back in and told the guy he'd come back later, how he went back out to the alley and retraced their steps, peering into all the dingy, incense-hazed shops she might have been distracted by, might have slipped into without telling him. Without telling him. Did she think he'd follow her? How could he? He'd been in front of her. How could he have seen where she went? So he walked up and down the alley. Back, back, back. Retracing it all. Then up and down the ones that crossed it and the ones that ran parallel to it. Then the ones parallel to them until he became quite lost, unable even to find the original alley where he'd last seen her.

The last time he saw her.

So he made his way out into the main square where acrobatic kids were tumbling to shallow drums and the high pitch of flutes coaxed flaccid-hooded cobras from their baskets. He'd spot her when she came out, a head taller than the Moroccan men and distinctive in her turquoise shawl. Distinctive in anything, he thought; she stood out in a crowd. He knew from continually having to stamp his ownership like an alpha chimp marking his territory how she was always attracting attention. It was exhausting, though he loved her indifferent lack of guile. Not obvious, like the Americans, with their shorts, tank tops and blonde hair ensuring they'd get hassled and then moan about it when they returned to picket-fenced mundanity and holiday snap sessions, reaffirming the stereotypes of the wild world beyond America's borders. If it put a few of the assholes off ever leaving home, then so much the better, he thought. At least with her colouring and blood she could pass for a local, albeit a rich one. It was her demeanour, her posture, her saunter – casual and detached – that made even him crave her attention, let alone other men. And her green eyes – the way they seemed to draw light towards her. Bending it in on herself.

He bought two cups of orange juice, freshly squeezed in front of him, and waited with a clear view of the main entrance. Of course there were other exits, countless ways in and out, but she would come out the same way they had gone in, surely. She had lost him too, he reminded himself. She would be going through the same process as him, backtracking, fighting the mounting panic, telling herself to be calm, to think it through, think logically and come here. Any second now and she would tap him on the shoulder, pretending she had been there all along and they would laugh and hug and walk off back to the hotel hand in hand.

But she didn't tap him on the shoulder.

After half an hour he gave up. She'd be back at the hotel. She'd have given up sooner than him, he thought. She'd be there, lying on the bed or reading on the balcony in the fading light of the afternoon, frowning like she did when she was concentrating. She'd look up when he walked in and say 'You took your time' and they'd laugh and he'd jump on her and tickle her and they'd make love.

But she wasn't back at the hotel.

He knew even before he tried the door, finding it locked. He opened it. The room was empty, her hairbrush clogged with hairs on the bedside table, her book face down on the bed, the empty coffee cups by the sofa from breakfast, her knickers on the bathroom floor where she'd left them after their bath the night before.

He slammed the door behind him and swore. '*For fuck's sake*!' He walked to the balcony and looked down the alley. Then he trotted down the cool stairs and across the tiled courtyard with its tall palm straining for the square of sky above, to the reception desk where the bored man sat reading a cheap pornographic magazine.

No, he hadn't seen her. Yes, he remembered what she looked like. *Très belle, oui*? No, he hadn't seen her come back and go out again.

It got dark.

He lay on the bed but he couldn't sleep. What was he supposed to do? He leant on the terrace ledge, looking down the shadowy alley that led to the street that led to the square that led to the souk, willing her to come swinging along, bags of shopping over a slender shoulder. Nothing. She'd arrive back in the morning. She'd have – what? Gone out all night? He drank the bottle of vodka they'd sneaked in with them, the second of the two they had brought with them from Spain, and finally drifted off in the chair by the French window to the terrace, facing the door to the room, fully clothed, and dreamt of running down alleys, darker and darker and narrower, of everyone going the other way, of struggling against the tide of blank-faced, dark-robed Moroccans until he could go no further.

Of shouting her name.

He woke when the sun hit his face, his head thudding with a dry, dull ache. For a second he wondered why she hadn't called him to bed. Why had she let him sleep in the chair? Then he remembered and rushed into the bedroom, to the unmade bed still rumpled from their first night there. Together. He fell on the bed and buried his face in the pillow that still smelt of her, of her skin and hair, and he shouted her name into the pillow.

The gendarme had the same infuriating, heavy-eyed placidity as the man at the hotel. The questions were stated, not really questions at all. Name. Nationality. Passport number. Description. Distinguishing marks. Clothes she was wearing when last seen. Had there been any dispute. Any disagreement that day. *Happens all the time.* You'd be surprised.

At that he lost his temper, and the policeman withdrew his humanity, what little sympathy he had, like a hermit crab until his eyes died.

'We'll do our best,' he said. Finality.

'What is that, exactly, your best? Will you call your men and issue a description and send them out to find her?'

'We cannot do that. I suggest you go to your embassy and tell them. Maybe she is already there. People get completely lost all the time. People disappear all the time. Couples break up all the time.'

'But she is here and the embassy is in Rabat!' he shouted and stormed out of the police station leaving shrugs and raised eyebrows in his wake.

When he saw his haggard reflection – two-day growth, bloodshot eyes, dishevelled, even for him – he smashed the mirror in the bathroom, cutting his knuckles and dulling his frustration briefly. The receptionist heard the commotion and told the manager and the manager asked him to leave.

'I cannot leave. My girlf– – my *wife* – is missing and I have to be here when she returns.' The manager looked sceptical. 'Please, I'll pay extra.'

The manager let him stay.

He sat on the bed and put his head in his hands.

Falling.

'How did it go, babe?' Tomas asked, casually throwing back the thick black coffee in one synchronised toss of his wrist and head. As she sat down and poured sugar into her coffee he watched her carefully while trying not to, fully aware of how important today – the meeting – had been for her, and despite the unsparing honesty he loved and feared in her in equal measure, he was only human, only male, and small serpents of jealousy slithered in his mental undergrowth.

'The funeral?' Ella said, reading him easily, slightly piqued that all he was concerned with was his delicate ego. Pilau Maria Delgado had been like a mother to her, had effectively been her mother for half her life, but he had ducked the ceremony on the grounds that he'd never met her, and wanted to catch up with a few of his Argentinean hermanos in Gaucin. 'How do you think it went?'

It actually had been fun, and the first time she had been back to her hometown in years. A fiesta *peceña*, as is the way in Latino countries, where death is celebrated.

Her grey-green eyes, inherited from a Moroccan grandmother, watched him demurely over the rim of her *café con leche*, playing with him. She knew exactly what was going through his mind and, although not quite like a cat fucks with a mouse, she was definitely toying with his head, just a little bit. He had meant her reunion with him, with Lazaro.

'Oh,' he said, 'yeah, the funeral. Good turnout, was there?' He back-pedalled.

'Of course. She was well loved. The whole village was there. I caught up with everyone from the old days – quite weird, going back, seeing them all again with their kids and their bellies. Nothing changes, really, as if it's outside time, stuck up here in the mountains, unspoilt. Probably why the property prices are going through the roof. You know, no one from the village can afford to buy there now, and those that have any land are sitting tight waiting for it to go higher. I almost wish I hadn't sold when Papa died. Almost.' He's going to ask, she thought, as she wittered on, deliberately evasive, playing him. He has to. She could see the question bubbling up like magma. 'And it was the first time their whole family has been together for years.' Now.

'And, ah, was he there?'

'Who?'

'You know who,' he said, starting to get riled. 'Your childhood sweetheart, the amazing resurrected Lazaro.'

'Naturally he was there,' she said. 'I told you he would be.'

'And how was that?'

'How was what?'

'Seeing him after all these years!'

'Fine,' she said, arching an eyebrow and gazing nonchalantly out of the window. Tomas realised she'd bounced him like a yo-yo.

'Gabriella,' he said, with mock severity, 'either you tell me how it went, word for word, or I'll –'

'You'll what?' she said, putting down the cup and leaning forward, pouting provocatively. He glanced around the busy café to make sure no one could hear, then told her.

'Okay, okay, *bas*,' she laughed. 'Although that does sound wonderful.' She paused, old memories clouded her eyes. 'Seriously, it was fine. Really. After so long – Jesus – how could it not be? I would have preferred to have caught him before the service, alone, so we could have said hello outside the scrutiny of the entire village but, hey, *que sera*.' She sighed. 'He's very different now, we both are, physically – he's like a bear! – and mentally. You should have seen his face when he saw me, *ostia*! I had to tell him to close his mouth. We were both so young then, it seems like another life. It *was* another life. I don't think I was quite how he expected me to be, though.' She laughed, covering her mouth with the back of one hand. 'He was totally amazed that I can write at all, let alone that I'm a journalist. I suppose it's him I have to thank for it, in a way, since it was his letters all those years ago that got me reading in the first place, made me want to peek beyond the head of the valley.'

She took a sip of coffee.

'When I told him he gave me this, look,' she reached into the inside pocket of her black linen jacket and produced a beautiful, blue-black fountain pen. She handed it across the table to Tomas, who turned it over in his hands, unscrewing the lid to read the imprint on the nib.

'He genuinely expected me to still be the illiterate mountain girl he left behind, though, I could tell; tending goats and pressing olives with eight children and bad teeth. I think part of him, deep down, still expected me to be waiting for him too, though he hid it well and would never have admitted it.'

'Mabie Todd & Co., Blackbird, 1933,' he read out loud. 'Made in England. 18-carat gold nib. It's beautiful. I wonder who 'RJT' was.'

'No idea. I don't know where he got it, he wouldn't say, only 'to make up for all the words I never managed to write to you'.' She thought for a minute. 'Ja ja ja, if he hadn't disappeared, I'd probably still be there, a good little wife, and I'd have never met you. I didn't think of that.'

'It's lovely – must be old, probably worth quite a bit,' he said, handing the pen back to her. 'You told him about me?'

'Of course,' she said, sighing. 'It was the first thing he asked: Are you getting laid? No, but he did ask if I was married and I said that I was not, but that I was deeply in love with an amazing, gentle, handsome, well-endowed man' – Tomas rolled his eyes – 'who had no immediate plans to go away and leave me for twelve years. He wants to meet you. But that's not going to happen, is it? Since you're so "busy".'

'Since *we're* so busy *cariño*,' he said, checking his watch. 'I said we'd be back in town by five and it's four already. We should hit the road.'

He stood and walked to the counter to pay for their coffees.

The bar, La Fuente, was filling up with all sorts escaping the afternoon heat, pink tourists and post-siesta locals alike. The mid-season inundation of visitors the village attracted meant it stayed open all day, which, judging from a table of drunken English outside, not only he had been grateful for.

Gaucin, impossibly quaint with its flower baskets, steep winding alleys and gasp-inducing views over Gibraltar into Morocco, was firmly on the *pueblo blanco* trail that led over the mountains to Seville and Cadiz. Although he'd only visited a few times, he knew the small enclave of fellow Argentineans who lived here via mutual friends on the coast. They all knew each other through friends of friends and family back home anyway; one fortune-seeking emigré sending overblown reports back of the money to be made triggering a steady tide of more hoping to escape the five hundred per cent inflation ravaging Buenos Aires, incrementally reversing the emigration two hundred years earlier.

He'd been luckier than most, many of whom ended up labouring on the cheap and competing with wetback Moroccans. He'd come out here skilled; his apprenticeship as a silversmith had ended a few years earlier, just as the silver market – along with everything else back home – collapsed like a pithead. She told him an Argentinean silversmith was a little too predictable, a cliché, she called him, the day she'd insinuated her way around the studio-cum-shop he shared with a clinically insane Swedish painter called Oscar in the heart of Tarifa's old town. On impulse, he'd given her an ingot-heavy bracelet set with a tiger's eye, right then and there. The amber refractions of the semi-precious stone perfectly matched the disc of chestnut that orbited each jungle-pool iris, while the weight of the silver emphasised the delicacy of her wrists. He reminded her, smiling, that the reason the Land of Silver had none left was because the Spanish had looted the lot, stripping the mountains bare of it.

She'd accepted the bracelet, turning the burnished stone in

the sunlight, and then accepted the offer of lunch, immediately struck by what she took to be impulsive romanticism (actually nervousness) and the impression of smouldering intensity in his eyes (actually short-sightedness from hours bent over his mounted magnifying glass). He only had a proper look at her at lunch, after his Latino vanity hurdle had been jumped and he'd slipped on his glasses. When they met, he told her as they lay breathless and post-coitally confessional a month later, she had been little more than a slim blur, her face – no, her eyes – had been the first thing that had come into focus, as if surfacing through water, when she approached his work table.

Although she hadn't travelled halfway round the world to get there, and his family were from a once wealthy barrio in La Plata (which had made her choke on her gazpacho; 'A silversmith from silver town in silver land? It just gets better!'), they both shared the urge to bolt from the small, claustrophobic communities in which they'd grown up. Over hummus, pittas, soup and a bottle of wine, they quickly slid into a state of ease in each other's company that, despite the giddy swirl of mutual hormonal attraction, neither initially expected. His hands, normally steady, had shaken imperceptibly to begin with, while she had laughed a little too loudly at his self-deprecating humour, but by the time the bill arrived they'd both relaxed, mocking the tourists wandering past the restaurant with the smug authority that residents of beautiful places tend to have.

She was in Tarifa on a job, researching a story on the numerous illegal building permissions issued within the Parque Nacional for *Viva Andaluz!* magazine, and had to get back to Malaga to file it. When she left he returned to the studio, where he spent the afternoon trying, unsuccessfully as it turned out, to persuade Oscar not to destroy two months' worth of Munch-inspired anguish on canvas with a blow-torch. He'd meant to call her, keeping her card in his wallet but, through shyness and the absent-mindedness peculiar to artists, became lost in his work, and never did. He was convinced someone as light, as delicate, as her couldn't possibly be interested in someone as dense and earthy as he thought himself.

One month later, the mercury seeping into the forties, the surf shops booming and the incessant Levanter making the dogs bark mindlessly, he looked up from a tightly spiralled ear-ring he was working on to see her clearly, already within focus, standing at his work bench...

'Hey,' he said, putting down slender-nosed rosary pliers and reaching for his glasses.

'Hi.' She bent down to kiss him on both cheeks. 'You busy?' She wore a semi-transparent white muslin dress – simple, yet incredibly exotic on her – and the air conditioning had stiffened her nipples to bullets, distracting them both equally.

'Flat out – they buy the stuff faster than I can make it so I've quadrupled the prices, but that only seems to make them want even more. 'Perceived value or something.' He shrugged.

'So if I told you I'd been commissioned to do a piece on the Argentinian ex-pat community in Andalusia and needed some inside information, you wouldn't be able to take an hour or two off to answer a few questions over an expenses-paid lunch at the best restaurant in town?' He turned off the solder, flipped the sign on the door and followed her out into the blanching light.

In the lush, frangipani-scented gardens of the Hurricane Hotel he answered her questions, neither of them able to concentrate, the sexual tension between them sitting there like a fidgety, impatient guest.

'Is that necessary for the article then?' he asked.

'Is what necessary?'

'That question, whether or not I find Andaluz girls as beautiful as the ones back home.'

'Oh,' she said, 'all just part of building up background colour, you know, giving the piece a personal feel.'

'Okay then. The answer is no. But there's so much mixed blood in Argentina that you can't generalise; there is no Argentinean "type". Some are like the girls here – cute when they're young, then when they hit twenty-five they grow beards and their tits hit the floor. Others are slender, elegant, honey-skinned, green-eyed, with moles on their left cheeks and a Moroccan ancestry. These ones,' he paused for effect, 'I love.'

She looked up from her pad and he leant over and kissed her.

Her surprise caused a momentary stiffening of her lips, but then, like the sigh of summer, she melted, slow and languid, their shared breath ripened with rosé. An Englishman on the next table with a frosted, rarely laid wife muttered 'Get a room.' Ella overheard and thought this was an excellent idea, so they did.

The next morning when they checked out, her expense account having been thoroughly spanked and her ass more lightly so, they walked back to town hand-in-hand through the wind-bent pine woods that paced the beach, cutting down to the sand where the trees petered out, watching the straining surf-kites that littered the sky and the zipping, leaping figures that pulled them down to the sea's whipped surface.

That had been eleven months, three weeks and three days ago.

He worked it out as he sat there in the maddening dark of the room.

She had immediately quit *Viva!* and turned freelance, something she had been meaning to do for a while, and moved down the coast from her tiny flat in a utilitarian concrete block in Marbella to join him, cluttering up his small apartment with the chaotic composition of her life. He adjusted to pink disposable razors in the shower, tampons under the basin and an extra toothbrush in the glass easily, happily. He loved waking up to find her there, loved tiptoeing off to make coffee for her, loved the way she sashayed around the place naked, sunning herself like a cat where the sunbeam slowly crossed the room in the afternoon. She set up her laptop in the sitting room next to the sun-blistered shutters that opened out to the old Moorish fort and the flashing sea, and having her there made him realise how solitary his life had been before he met her.

Her latest story, a travel piece they'd collaborated on in order to crowbar in a holiday at the same time, was to be on the legendary silversmiths of Tiznit, way down the Moroccan coast south from Essaouira. Not only was it somewhere he had often thought to visit – to gain some insight into the techniques they kept so secretively, to get some inspiration for his designs – but she wanted to track down her ancestral home, Ourgane, where her grandmother had lived before she came to Spain in the twenties; a remote village up in the High Atlas above Marrakesh. There might even be some family still living there, and though she'd always felt the urge, Ella had never set foot on the continent, despite being able to see it when the air was clear and the shroud of clouds dispersed. She appointed him her photographer, just so it looked kosher when she put in the receipts. At least he had a camera.

She just had this funeral to attend first, before they could leave. She told him everything about her childhood in Grazelema, and about Lazaro and how he'd deserted her, and he listened with the easy patience of a confident new king, but then he hadn't expected him to reappear, to burst back into her life so soon. He'd been a mythical figure. A dream. Not someone of flesh and bone and cock and heart, and a possible threat. He hadn't been ready for that. Neither had she. He'd seen her reaction when Lazaro's elder brother, Diego, called about the funeral and mentioned that Lazaro was expected to be there; slumping slightly and turning away from him, though she quickly recovered herself. Christ, he thought, after twelve years it wasn't surprising she was shocked. Anyway, he'd said, what kind of idiot would leave her in the first place?

In his mind he retraced their steps, barely a week ago. They'd paid and left Gaucin, past the splashing fountain and the pissed Brits, down the hill to where her old Lada was parked in the shade of a eucalyptus. The drive down the mountains required some concentration, the tight, precipitous hairpins made all the harder by the distraction of her warm hand on his thigh. They were home by five-thirty, packed quickly, and caught the eight o'clock ferry over to Tangier. From there it was a quick taxi dash to the station and onto the sleeper they'd – she'd – booked the previous day. Overnight in their own slow, romantically rhythmed couchette to Marrakesh, the rock of the clacketty carriage alone had brought them to a gentle, tongue-locked climax as he slid in and out of her, pivoting on her hips.

'I thought you said it was a sleeper,' he murmured.

Disembarking to the clear fresh sky of the early morning and the sharp smell of the orange trees lining the station, they checked into a guest house called Dar Zelda, sumptuous to the point of kitsch but near the medina. They hired a Fiat Uno from a cowboy outfit called Horse Car Rentals. Tomas: 'Is this car okay off road?' Fayed: 'Oh yes, sir, *c'est la souris du desert*!' Tomas: 'We'll take it.' Fayed clearly wouldn't notice a scratch or two or mind if he did, and they set off early the following morning, arriving mid-afternoon at the city walls of the improbably picturesque fishing village of Essaouira.

They dumped the car outside the medina, found a nondescript but functional self-catering apartment for a few days, and went for a long walk around the old harbour walls where the Atlantic stretched out to the setting sun and throaty hawkers hassled them without much conviction. At a café on the main square they sat in contented silence as the sun lowered itself gently into the sea.

They needed to make some inroads for the story, and for that they needed to enlist some local knowledge. Of all the lacklustre attempts at hitting on them, one guy in particular had made an impression, not least because of his American accent; a diminutive figure, four foot five at the most, Saadi claimed to have fought in Vietnam as a GI, but when his Illinoisan wife snapped out of the Sixties like waking from a coma and left him high and dry, taking the kids, he was forced to return to Morocco, to here, his home town, disillusioned, junked and defeated. The bridge of his nose had collapsed from too much cocaine, the occupational hazard, he told them, of his illustrious career smuggling drugs to the Spanish mainland.

'Whatever you need, you tell me,' he'd said with a smile. Tomas and Ella went along with it, just so long as he could show them the inside track to the silver trade in town.

'No fucking problem, man,' he said through teeth that looked as if each one had come from a different corpse. 'You meet me here first thing tomorrow and I'll take you where you want to go.'

'Great,' said Tomas. 'We'll be here at nine.'

'As a sign of good faith, maybe you could let me have something as a guarantee you're not wasting my time,' he said, eyeing Tomas' wallet on the table between them. Tomas flicked out a ten-dollar bill.

'Ah, a greenback,' he said nostalgically, folding it away with practiced sleight of hand. 'See you tomorrow.' And he shuffled off, his ill-fitting clothes making him look like a child from behind, not the fifty-year old wreck that he was. It was only then that they realised that it should have been Saadi convincing them of his integrity, not the other way round. He was good.

And good to his word. Not only was he there at the appointed time but he really did know where to take them, or so it seemed, confidently winding this way and that through the maze of alleys until they needed him just to find their way out again, knocking twice on a low, nondescript door flaking with blue paint, and ushering them inside into the gloom when it was opened. An incurious boy led them down a dingy corridor that opened into a courtyard where they were introduced to Abdul, a fez-wearing silver merchant in a gold-trimmed djellaba and flamboyantly curled slippers. Once introduced, he clapped twice for mint tea which when produced he served to them in small engraved glasses.

An hour later they re-emerged into the sunshine armed with a dozen contacts and precise addresses of where to find them in Tiznit. Now firm friends, while the dollars lasted anyway, they accepted Saadi's suggestion they all go to an underground bar he knew of – low lit, reeking sweetly of opium and seedy enough for Ella to hold back the pee she desperately needed – and there they toasted their success and planned the next stage over several bottles of sickly saccharine wine that they regretted, deeply, in the morning.

Sipping his coffee and wincing, Tomas suggested they become Muslim to avoid feeling like this ever again.

'But these guys *are* Muslim – Saadi, the rest of them,' Ella said.

'Not bothered about taking the Koran too literally, clearly,' he said. 'And as for the attention you attracted all night . . .' Despite her modest attire, she'd been leered at, stared at, propositioned and goosed with predictable regularity. '*Joder*, no wonder the girls wear burkas,' she said.

Still, you couldn't fault their taste, and perhaps not being covered up implied availability – especially in that dive, just being in there probably meant you were selling your ass – though how anyone could think that ramming your flat hand up between a girl's thighs would work as a chat-up line he had no idea. Just something to whack off to later, he guessed. He watched her as she dressed, overlaying cotton slacks and a long-sleeved T-shirt with a shawl that covered her arms and her lean, hip-bracketed belly, hiding the navel piercing he'd made her. She moved with an insouciant, economy of energy that drove him gently crazy. His pulse rose and his headache increased.

'Ready?' She asked, catching his look and smiling shyly.

'Ready.'

From Essaouira they took the coast road south, winding through the red, low, scrub-smothered hills to Agadir, where they stopped at the kasbah above the city for some falafel and pitta overlooking the long curved beach, the horn-honking streets and cluttered port below, happy in each other's company and saying little. Then they drove on down until they reached Tiznit.

It had all gone so well, he thought, as he wound back through the days they'd spent there. They'd successfully tracked down two of Abdul's leads, dealers who brought together antiques from the surrounding chicken-pecked, sand-blown satellite villages – tribal jewellery with heavy, age-cracked amber and veinous turquoise, and contemporary silver work by Berber tribesmen and silversmiths from outside town – and sold them on to Marrakech, Fez and Rabat. She had her story, and he left with a freshly buffed insight into the methodology behind the ornate, almost baroque workmanship, interwoven geometry and status symbolism that defined the style of the region.

They drove back to Marrakesh in high spirits, intent on making the most of their last few days at Dar Zelda before heading up into the mountains, to Ourgane and what remained, if anything, of her blood relatives. One last trip to the souk, she pleaded.

Now, sitting here on the bed, it still made no sense.

There was nothing, no possible logic to her disappearance, no chink of light to illuminate the dark cave in which he now found himself. His thought process began to loop, round and round, unable to break out of the cycle of events and questions, inevitably returning him to the beginning. Would she have gone without him? If so, why? And where? But to leave all her things in the room? She had her passport with her; the hotel had only needed the numbers. She'd need a change of fucking clothes by now, for Christ's sake. He hoped she had, impossibly, decided to go home without telling him, but he knew it was ridiculous. He knew she had not left him of her own volition. He knew that she was in danger somewhere, the empty pit in his stomach told him that something terrible had happened; she had been taken, kidnapped, abducted by someone and he didn't know what to do. He had no choice but to keep asking, keep going through it again and again.

The loop began to make him mad.

He rocked back and forth on the bed; hours slid past like snakes, waiting, jumping up at every footfall in the courtyard outside as, every few hours, the amplified wailing from the minarets marked time, placating the heavens until the sun dropped. When he rose and returned to the market, lit garishly at night – a blur of neon and ornate table lamps and brightly lit spice stalls and noise and smells – the whirl of activity was overwhelming. He walked through the souk as if time-lapsed by the director of his nightmare, people flowing around him, the mania in his reddened eyes parting the crowd like the prow of a boat parting water. At the shop where he'd lost her he stood and screamed out her name over and over and over until two policemen were called and led him back to the hotel, held – gripped – firmly by his elbows.

The next morning, unslept and having not eaten for two days, he packed both their bags, muttering, meticulously folding her clothes, sniffing her out in the material, imagining the lashes that the mascara brush had painted, touching hair caught in her brush. He loaded up the car, left a note for her at the desk saying he'd be back, to wait for him here, and drove out of the irrigated plains up into the mountains to Ourgane. As he pulled up, map on the empty seat next to him, rickety doors slammed shut before he'd turned off the engine. In broken French he asked an old man sitting beneath a fig tree that knobbled expansively out of the cobbled square whether he'd seen a foreign girl recently, tall, with green eyes and brown hair, but the man looked blank, one eye milked with cataract, and he realised he didn't even know the name of Ella's grandmother. No one had been here, he knew it. There was nothing of interest to tourists here, and any stranger would surely have been noticed. His intuition told him in a gentle, insistent whisper that she was lost to him.

So he drove on, up into the purple, snow-capped mountains, to Ait Ben Hadou, whose mud-walled medina and crumbling fort perched high on the hill had been used in so many films it now looked like a set, styrofoam Roman pillars and biblical colonnades strange against the impoverished mediaeval reality of the village below. Then on to Ouarzazate, cruising the long, incongruously modern high street slowly, then on, down now, back in time through wide, fertile valleys of date palms and old Berber kasbahs, across scorched plains of basalt and boulders where kids sold split geodes that they glinted in the sunlight to attract drivers' attention, to Zagora, an oasis on the shore of the Sahara, the first stop for the old camel trains that used to cross the desert from Timbuktu, two thousand kilometres out east across the sand.

And on he drove, on over the huge granite escarpments that rippled like petrified tidal waves before disappearing into the sand, out into the desert, the dead straight road pointing east, and on until the petrol ran out and the car coasted to a halt and silence enveloped him, ringing in his ears. After a while, he got out of the car and started walking, his shadow lengthening further and further out before him until the sun faded, on towards the stars and the blue night sky until the road too slowly submerged into the sand. Slightly delirious now, he walked on as the chill night temperatures dropped, the heat of the day evaporating swiftly from the sand. He walked for hours, on and on, up the steep crests of the dunes and down into their troughs until eventually he stumbled and fell and rolled over and over, and lay still in the darkness while the stars turned slowly above him.

He lost consciousness with her name upon his cracked lips.

He woke when the water choked him. Opening his eyes to look straight into the black, kohl-rimmed gaze of a Tuareg, silhouetted against the mid-morning sun, the rich midnight blue of his turban allowing only a slit for his eyes. The man said nothing, but he could hear voices nearby. He opened his mouth when the man lifted the goat skein flask, squirting another jet of water into his throat. He croaked unintelligible thanks through his wrecked lips. The man nodded.

He was surrounded by sand, gently sculpted undulations as far as he could see. Sitting up with the man's help he saw three camels to his right, two other blue-robed men squatting patiently in their shade. They called out in their staccato tongue and the man beside him called back, standing as he did so and rearranging his turban, then gesturing for Tomas to follow. He stood up slowly, leaning heavily on the man's iron-strong arm, and they brought a complaining camel to its knees so he could straddle the high-pommelled saddle. Aching and stiff, he swung himself onto its back.

They walked for an hour through dunes that looked identical to him until, in the lee of an enormous bank of sand fifty metres high, he saw their camp: two low-ridged tents that shimmered like mirages through the heat haze. When they unwound their turbans, they revealed aquiline profiles, black beards and flashing smiles – brothers, he guessed, from the facial similarities and their familiar, easy banter. They fed him fragrant, melt-in-the-mouth lamb with squash, raisins, dates and almonds from a tagine while he, acting out scenes and drawing in the sand floor of the tent with his finger, briefly explained what had happened. He slept straight through the night under thick rugs, the stars visible through the coarse weave of the camel-hair tent.

When he woke, the eldest, Ali – the man who had given him water – asked for the keys to the car and some money – 'Gasol, gasol', he said – then set off into the dunes on foot. Five hours later Tomas heard the sound of a car, and the Uno appeared in the distance, bouncing through the sand like a ship tossed on the sea, trailing a cloud of dust behind it like smoke.

He spent a week in their gentle, patient, unquestioning company, grateful for the peace and tranquillity of the desert and the opportunity to recover his grip, restore his sanity and corral his thoughts, doing nothing but thinking, scarcely noticing the wheel of the sun. There was no sound but an almost imperceptible hiss of the sand shifting in the breeze, like static, the occasional bleat of a sheep and spectacular flatulence of the camels. He felt as if he had stepped off the planet, as if Gabriella had been a dream, his whole life before rendered irrelevant, erased. As if smothered by sand.

He would go back to Marrakesh, though he knew nothing would come of it, make a statement at the embassy in Rabat, fill out the missing persons paperwork and go home. Not to Tarifa. Home, to Argentina. It would take a while to raise the money but he knew he couldn't stay in Spain. Not now.

Finally, he opened the boot, took out her bags and returned to the tent. He went through them, slowly, methodically, partly looking for a clue, partly for the nostalgia and partly – he knew, deep down – partly saying goodbye.

He found her diary stashed in a small pocket in the inside lining of her leather shoulder bag, together with the pen that Lazaro had given her. Reading it, he broke down into silent, lung-wrenching sobs; she had never been happier, she wrote, never loved anyone more, and when he read that she thought she was pregnant, how, secretly, she'd hoped he would propose before they returned home, the tears coursed down his cheeks in salty rivulets, dripping from his nose to blur the black ink in small wet explosions.

# Chapter 15

*Tuesday, 11th November 1933*
*The Kalifi Club, Mombasa*

*Lillian,*
*I sent the latest batch to you this morning, and was disappointed to find nothing from you.*

*Lil, still no word. I probably shouldn't ask – unfounded fears and all – but in the interests of honesty feel that I must: Is there something wrong, is anything the matter, is there anything that I should know? Not that I for one second doubt your love for me, but this silence is, as they say, deafening. Please try to get some message to me, for the love of God. Whatever it is, to know would be infinitely preferable than this state of uncertainty. I have been suffering the most dreadful nightmares, the details of which I will spare you, but I wake with an unshakeable fear that you are lost to me, an unnameable dread that takes the morning to wear off.*

*You must have received some, if not most, of my correspondence by now – the mail ships are so much faster than the Apollonia – in which case you must appreciate how dearly I long to hear from you.*

*My hope is that it is due to some quirk of yours; the medium of the telegram too crude, too impersonal for you to express yourself adequately and that, as I write, there are ships laden with envelopes bearing my name steaming towards me, that the skies are full of planes made heavy with your correspondence.*

*Christ, imagine if just one was to get lost en route. A casual, unintentional error, an oversight on behalf of some crescent-rimmed clerk in a sorting office yet with such dire repercussions. Best not to think of it – besides I have much to distract me, which I shall relate later.*

*I gather they are trying to open up an air-mail service, a continuation of the existing one to Cairo, and will endeavour to find out more. If so, you might well get subsequent letters long before their older cousins. Extraordinary to think how quickly the boundaries that define the world are shrinking.*

*I remain at the club for as long as Jim's hospitality lasts.*

*Yours, ever,*

*Ralph*

*x*

*Thursday, 13th November, 1933*
*The Kalifi Club, Mombasa*

*Dear Lillian,*

*My departure north looms, my darling, and I find myself caught between the two pillars of wanting to crack on and trepidation of what lies in store for me when I arrive. The last few days have been a wonderful respite from my responsibilities; indeed I have done little but eat, sleep and read. Admittedly the reading matter has been relevant; I feel sure that little remains of all there is to know about the riveting details of managing a cotton ginnery. Here I feel in touch with the world and, therefore, you.*

*Once I head north alone I know the full weight of my exile will hit me.*

*At the same time the various duffers at the club, while endeavouring to do their best to 'welcome me into the fold', succeed only in scaring me witless, providing as they do a mirror of what I might become; pompous buffoons, one and all.*

*Perhaps I do them an injustice; the pressures and strains of holding it together out here must be considerable, and it's no surprise that they should cling to the vestiges of home as a drowning man clutches at straws. I have promised myself that I will immerse myself in the culture of these so-called 'savages' up north; Jim assures me, during the interludes between members' jingoistic diatribes, that I shall find the people 'infinitely better company than those present'. Bless him. He is doing his best to ensure my peace of mind. My debt to him is mounting.*

*Today we took a tour of the fort – Fort Jesus, which so impressed me on arrival. Now a prison, I fail to see how it could ever have been otherwise; the idea of being stationed there 'shivered me timbers'. One enters up a long rampart, through squat, thirty-foot thick walls, the plan of which apparently represents a recumbent human form, into a central courtyard (the torso?) utterly devoid of character; looming walls close in around one and it seems as if even the cry of birds is muted. Built by the Portuguese in the late sixteenth century, it has been assailed by numerous foes; impenetrable from the sea, they lost it to the Arabs a century later following a nine-month siege from which a mere thirteen people survived, only to be put promptly to the sword. God only knows the number that have died upon its walls, or within them, since it became a point of transition, a holding bay, for Arabic and subsequently British slavers – I swear the cries still echo in the dank corridors. It now serves as penitentiary for those who dare disobey the strictures of the King.*

*The point of our visit was not, it transpired, purely touristic.*

*Jim asked to see the Governor – a bull-necked brute with a scar punctuating one eyebrow, who emerged hastily buttoning his tunic – and bade him give us access to one Lieutenant Murdoch.*

*I do wish he'd warned me of his intentions in advance.*

*We were duly led down narrowing corridors, then tunnels – I was reminded momentarily of the crypts of Malta, though I reined in the urge to bolt – through heavily hinged wrought-iron gates until, in the very bowels of hell, it seemed, we were ushered into a room the size of your dressing room lit by a flickering lamp.*

*'Call when you're done,' the Adjutant told us, 'and don't take your eyes off him, not for a second, mind.' He left us with a heavy clank of the turning lock. I thought us alone, but from the gloom there came a wracking cough.*

*'Martin,' calls Jim, 'are you there?', lifting the torch so it cast its light further.*

*'Ah, the indefatigable Colonel Symmonds,' came a stentorian voice laden with malice. 'To what, may I enquire, do I owe the pleasure?'*

*Jim beckoned me close and whispered, 'Right, lad, keep your wits about you, answer directly, and whatever you do keep your distance.' Thus briefed, I followed him into the recesses of the chamber.*

*In the fickle light there was a man, manacled by wrists and ankles to the iron bed on which he sat, hollow-cheeked, stick-thin, dressed in filthy trousers and shirt stained with God knows what, his beard and hair matted with grime. As I drew closer, covering my mouth and nose at the stench of the fellow, I was immediately struck by the gleam of his eyes; clear, preternaturally bright, unblinking.*

*'How are you, Jim?' he said, turning from Jim to look at me, cocking his head like a bird.*

*'Very well, thank you,' Jim said, 'You, by contrast, appear not to be so fortunate.'*

*'You know how it is, Jim,' he says, all cordial, 'one day blue skies, the next day rain,' never taking his eyes off me for a second, nor blinking once either. 'Aren't you going to introduce me to your young friend?'*

*'Lieutenant Colonel Martin Murdoch, Ralph Talbot.'*

*'Ex-Lieutenant Colonel, Jim. They relieved me of my duties, as I'm sure you've heard,' he said sarcastically, jangling his fetters.*

*'Of course,' Jim said. 'How are they treating you?'*

*'Well enough,' he replied, 'considering. Though what I wouldn't give for some human company –' It was the way he said 'company' that chilled me.*

*'Well, I'm here,' said Jim, his voice hardening. 'Tell me what you need and I'll see what can be done. I owe you that much.'*

*'Really? How uncommonly civil of you, old man. But then you always were able to rise above the throng, weren't you Jim, always the one to step forward and do the right thing. Once more into the breach. For "King and Country" and all that. Pick your favourite platitude – I'm sure you have them all down pat – and educate this handsome young man, since that is presumably why you brought him here. Am I a cautionary exhibit?'*

*'Just thought I'd come and see what I might do to help, Martin, that's all.'*

*'Come now, friend,' he said, massaging his wrists. 'You're as transparent as ever. Surely you don't need me in order to salve your conscience, to absolve your guilt, to somehow put into a more palatable context all those lost lives you've been responsible for. Colonel, Colonel, Colonel,' he said, shaking his head. 'No matter what was asked of you, you have never once shirked from your duty, have you, never staked out your honour in the midday sun and left it for the ants. Never once questioned anything, did you Jim, no matter what the cost?'*

*'Never had the luxury, my friend,' said Jim quietly.*

*'You think it a luxury to think clearly, for yourself, to question orders? I think it our responsibility, in the eyes of the Lord our Maker' – he spat the phrase – 'since ultimately it is to Him alone we are accountable.'*

*'And you believe your actions reflect that accountability?*

*'I did what I had to do in the circumstances, and I defy you or any other to question it! You were not there, no one was. You don't know what happened. There was no one to counsel, no one with any idea, any understanding of what was really happening on the ground. You know what's going on, Jim, behind the political rhetoric. Oh yes, Colonel Symmonds, you know the true nature of our darker purpose here in Africa, feeding the Empire's insatiable greed, so don't you dare come in here all high and mighty, my "friend"!' He was becoming agitated, testing the chains. He slumped back. 'Besides, I fulfilled my mission.'*

*'You rewrote your own, man!'*

*'Nonsense. The implications were crystal clear, as clear as if the Cabinet had issued them directly. I simply read between the lines. Used my initiative.' He looked at me again, I felt paralysed by his dark stare, as if he gauged my soul. 'But I've been through this a hundred times, and see no need to revisit the subject with you. Perhaps you'll enjoy the court-martial? I shall request front-row seats for you both.' He smiled. 'Until then, leave me be.'*

*'As you wish,' said Jim, gesturing for us to leave.*

*Before the door slammed behind us, he called out,*

*'Jim, there is one thing.' His voice lacked the malevolence it had been steeped in until then. 'Tell Angela the truth of what happened to me, what happens to people out here. Spare her nothing. I should hate for her to spend her days mourning me for what I was not. They will dress up events to suit their ends – whatever lies,*

*embellishment and propaganda they'll feed her to soften the blow and maintain the deception. I'd much rather she knew the truth, that she should make up her own mind and forget about me all the sooner.' Jim listened, not turning around. 'You do know the truth, don't you Jim?' The guard shut the door with a heavy clang but we could still hear him shouting as we walked away.*

*'The truth, Jim! Tell her the truth!'*

*I was relieved to reach the sunlight of the courtyard. Jim said nothing, ignoring my questions until we had left the Fort altogether. It was the first time I'd seen him rattled.*

*'What in God's name happened to him?' I asked him again when we settled into a bar on the harbour front. Jim paused,*

*'About a year ago it started. He was in command of an exploratory mission into the Congo – strictly off record and ostensibly reconnaissance only. The orders were, in principle, no more than to reconnoitre the extent of Belgian penetration of the area. He and his men disappeared, went completely off the chart for six months. Not long afterwards reports began coming in. Disturbing reports. It seems he became caught up in a localised tribal conflict, one to which he should have paid no heed. He . . .' – Jim put his head back and sighed – 'he indoctrinated, armed and trained the warriors of one tribe, ignoring all recalls, indeed even coercing one young officer sent to bring him back into joining his cause, then launched a massive offensive against their enemies. Things got . . . out of hand. There were questionable acts, rumours of massacres, wholesale torture and mass decapitations – entire communities butchered. Hundreds died. It was the Belgians who finally caught him, at considerable collateral expense, not to mention the political ramifications. It nearly sparked an international incident and it's all very hush-hush at the moment while they try to decide what on earth to do with him. Seems he was running the place as his own personal fiefdom.'*

*'Man's a bloody lunatic,' I said, looking out at the clamour and bustle of the harbour market.*

*'He's no lunatic,' says Jim, 'at least he wasn't. He's one of the most intelligent men I have ever met and was a good friend. What he did anyone could have done given the right situation, with the right pressure exerted upon them. We all have our breaking point,' he said. 'He was right about one thing though – why I took you there.'*

*'Which was?'*

*'To impress upon you that this continent requires – demands – our respect. As I said before, tread lightly, and though you shouldn't throw away your preconceptions – they're a valuable moral plumb-line against which to gauge your experiences – certainly be prepared to have them shattered. Don't hammer the country to fit your will, rather let your will be tempered by her. Find your balance, boy. Though this is what Martin aspired to do, in the process he lost sight of his own humanity, his compassion, submitted to his, ah, baser inclinations and, with the power to implement them, made them reality. In short, lad, whatever ye sow, so shall ye reap.' He gave me one of his indefinable, piercing looks. 'We're capable of such wonderful dreams, Ralph, but we're just as capable of the most terrible nightmares.'*

*Thus 'enthused' I returned to the club to conclude this missive. While I'm sure he deems it necessary – part of my tuition – to unsettle me so, personally I believe that my posting will prove relatively plain sailing. It's not as if I'm either fighting an enemy or embroiled in clandestine activity that's to the detriment of any third party. He does tend towards the melodramatic, does our Colonel Symmonds, and I determined not to be caught up with his sudden pessimism.*

*The evening sky, clouds daubed with reds and oranges like smudged watercolours, is a wonder to behold, my love, and I was reminded of something Jim said to me as we leant on the rail and watched the sun set on one of our many days at sea; 'Without clouds, sunsets would not be nearly so beautiful.' I rather think he was summing up his attitude to life.*

*I should retreat indoors – the whine of mosquitoes heralds another nocturnal campaign against the flesh.*

*Good night, my love.*

*Ralph*

*x*

*Friday, 14th November, 1933*
*The Kalifi Club*

*Dear Lillian,*

*I have to wrench myself away from the epicurean pleasures of the club and head up north. I freely admit the transition will prove a challenge but, as Murdoch says, duty calls.' Besides, I'm chomping at the bit. To stay longer would mark the beginnings of a descent into sloth and hebetude as evidenced by these stuffed shirts around me; all barking mad, quite as mad as Murdoch anyway, or so immersed in the clouds of their cigar smoke they seem to think themselves still in Blighty. I trust the Empire is in better hands than these (though it might go some way to explaining its decay were it not).*

*Food's damned good though – fresh fish straight from the dhows, and fruit the like of which I have never seen: pineapples galore; strange paw-paws, or papayas, vaguely pulpy in flesh and taste; star fruit, a kind of cross between an apple and a grape; bread fruit, more vegetable, fibrous and starchy than its relative the jack fruit; and the small, yellow marula, on which elephants get completely sloshed, apparently. Drunken elephants, my love! Now that's something I'd like to see. From a distance, mind.*

*There's beef and mutton from the highlands of the interior, goat stews which incline towards the stringy but are edible enough, and various varieties of bush game such as impala, gazelle and buffalo. All types of cereal thrive inland, and the kitchen gardens in Mombasa have soil so rich that one has simply to drop a seed for it to spring vigorously from the earth like Jack's beanstalk.*

*It is surely a land of plenty, Lil, an Eden.*

*A brief word on the wonders of the coconut, the uses of which seem endless; for sustenance, it is unparalleled, the milk has such a clear, fresh taste – apparently you can take the stuff intravenously in the event of blood loss or dehydration. The pure white flesh can be eaten and makes a fragrant oil used for cooking; the husks of the nuts are used to make rope, matting, boat caulking and compost; the trunks for canoes, construction and drums; the leaves for roofing and woven baskets, all in all extraordinary versatility.*

*When I added that the shells are also ideal for imitating horses, Jim told me not to be so fatuous. Ho hum.*

*I have been taking long walks along the spectacular beaches that stretch off south; wide aprons of fine white sand quite blinding on the eye. The shore is littered with beautiful shells of all sizes and colours – delicate pinks and beige and purples – my pockets are permanently full with the fragile carapaces of molluscs, long thin razor clams, the spiralling geometry of nautili, spiny cones, conches with delicate pink interiors, clams, cuttlefish and the cowries that were once used as currency. I shall send them back to you to decorate our first home.*

*The Apollonia left for England today.*

*Jim and I strolled down to the port to send her off. There was something poignant about her hefty bulk disappearing out to sea, returning to you without me. Another door closing, and all that. The sound of the klaxon, so familiar, heavy with the loneliness of the open ocean, echoed twice and she was gone.*

*Well, my love, I should leave you now and track down Jim, who I've arranged to meet at the bar. He wants to introduce me to someone he knows who's familiar with Lamu.*

*With all my love,*

*Ralph.*

*x*

*Saturday, 15th November, 1933*
*The Kalifi Club*

*Dear Lillian,*

*At last. I leave tomorrow morning. At the advice of Toby Deacon, the chap Jim introduced me to last night, I've decided to commandeer a small dhow for the journey north. The cargo boat is, he tells me, a long voyage, indirect and slow since she pulls in at all the villages en route. The small thirty-footers, by contrast, can complete the same trip in thirty-six hours, and providing the sea remains calm and the winds favourable, comparatively painlessly. This means I'll arrive two days before I'm expected, which should stand me in good stead with my employer, displaying, I hope, both ingenuity and enthusiasm and benefiting me also.*

*Toby seemed a friendly chap; around thirty years of age and with the same twinkle to his eye and dry sense of humour that I've noticed in Symmonds. Must be something in the water. He's been working for the Government as a surveyor cum cartographer – I think he studied in Durham – conducting an arduous, twelve-month tour of the coast from Somaliland to German East Africa in the south. Fascinating what he discovered in terms of natural resources, and one hell of an adventure – as well as amassing some personal wealth as he went, all quite legally and above board.*

*'In what field?' I asked.*

*He produced an unimpressive piece of what I initially took to be pumice stone or the like, but no. The coalesced sputum – mucous, my love, of a whale – the elusive and much sought after ambergris, more valued weight for weight than gold. They use it for scent, and no perfume is considered decent without it. I'm not sure which is the stranger, the musk from the rectal glands of stags or the intestinal effluence of whales. He had collected enough to retire on, so he said, and urged me to keep an eye peeled for any I might discover for myself when walking on the beaches.*

*The length of his tour of duty was what caught my attention, and I asked him what advice, if any, he could give me. He was most reassuring, and told me that it would pass in a flash. Not only that, but he reckons that Lamu is so beautiful I am sure to want to extend my contract further. I offered to get your photograph and he could judge which, you or the archipelago, was the more lovely . . .*

*He had one word of caution. It seems a group called the 'Freelanders' – idealistic reprobates and leisured aristocrats by the sounds of it, profligates originally from Hamburg, Britain and France – still have a few members kicking around. Their central tenet, as you may ascertain from their name, is that the world should be free of such arbitrary concepts as sovereignty, borders or nationality; a utopian playground for men to occupy as and where and how they wish. They arrived in the nineties and have left rather a bad impression, to say the least. Their plans fell apart almost immediately, the whole dissolute lot of them descending into a spiralling mess of drink, drugs and debauchery, taking local girls as wives and generally wreaking havoc, much to the displeasure of the local – Arabic – populace, who are, it seems, extremely conservative and pious. One even drowned swimming ashore!*

*Some never left, either through death, disease, or choice, and he tells me a few, and their illegitimate offspring, survive to this day. He suggests I give them a wide berth; 'Local colour', he calls them. I'm intrigued.*

*Otherwise he assures me the DC, John Clive, is amiable enough, industrious and fastidious, with the respect of those he governs. Also, valuably, since any insight into what I can expect up there is gold dust, he tells me that the chap I am to assist, Charles Whitson – aka Cotton Charlie – can be hard work initially but once you get to know him is perfectly decent. He's somewhat the recluse, by all accounts, and has a dependable and reliable manager to whom he delegates much of the running of the place (reassuring news). Can be a little prickly, though. After five years completely off the beaten track, with the fortunes of the area in decline since Mombasa came to the fore and the slaving trade collapsed, it's hardly surprising the man's a little unused to the finer social norms.*

*I am now as prepared as I'll ever be.*

*Sweet girl, before I leave you there's one thing more I need to get off my chest. Forgive me if it comes across a little muddled, for I am writing as it comes to me and by the very nature of what I am attempting to express, it remains a work in progress: I feel changed somehow, altered.*

*Since we arrived or, more accurately, since we crossed the Equator, I have begun to see things in a somewhat different light. By things I mean 'us'. I am suddenly aware, acutely so, that my approach to this entire venture has so far been that of the mooning adolescent, and that I've been overplaying the role of exiled lover somewhat. Not 'overplaying' exactly, for my emotions have been genuine, but it's as if I have created for myself a character to play in some second-rate theatre in the West End, complete with two-dimensional sets and an improbable script. It's as if the person*

*I was is struggling to resist being usurped by the person I feel I am now becoming and, like a steamer that takes half a mile to stop, the transformation has a lag time to it. I find myself writing words that seem misplaced, out of sorts and out of keeping with the man writing them.*

*Since I've been here the full reality of my position has made itself apparent to me in all its vivid verisimilitude. It's as if the voyage was already a dream and – please don't take this the wrong way – England and my life before now even more so. Of course you remain the most dear thing to me in the world and the reason for my presence here, but I believe that I must adapt and change to match this setting if I am to make the most of it – indeed survive at all, if Jim's darker pronouncements are to be believed (some eighty percent of Europeans who come out here never return. Did you know this? Did your father?).*

*I must, to coin a phrase, 'pick up my game', toughen up and slough off the various mantles of 'boy', of 'fiancé' and of 'prospective son-in-law'. I must look forward, not back. I must put my immediate environment first, my present situation and immediate future, and dwell less on what I have left behind. I must, in short, devote less of my day dreaming of you. I am here to do a job. If I maintain this mind-set of trying to get through the year, I won't make it. I must become my own man. Perhaps this is why twenty-one is such an important age? Perhaps this is what all men go through in the last months of their twentieth year?*

*For whatever reason, I feel a sea change swell in my heart and look to the eastern horizon with clear eyes, hope in my heart and a strength of purpose I have not until recently truly recognised or acknowledged, though might have spoken of often.*

*I will write at the next opportunity.*

*Wish me luck.*

*I love you with a fierce joy, clarity of will and purity of intent that will bring me back to you, of that have no doubt.*

*Yours, ever,*

*Ralph.*

*x*

# Chapter 16

*St Josep, Ibiza. 1999.*

'How much do you want for it, sweetie?'

Nina Lytton held out her hand at arm's length, turning the chunky ring – silver with a coconut inlay and a nugget of jet-black onyx in the centre – where it sat on her middle finger, regarding it with head-cocked appraisal. Without moving her head, she eyed the bespectacled stallholder sitting behind the trestle-table through the riot of blonde ringlets that corkscrewed to her shoulders. Bloody hell, she thought, he's cute. Just the sort of intense-looking Latin type she went for.

'Thirty-five euros, *cariño*,' he said, then paused. 'For you, thirty.' He pushed his glasses back on his nose and put the book he'd been reading, one of Louis de Bernière's South American trilogy, face down on his crossed knee.

'You're too kind. You made all of these?' She gestured at the spread of silver rings, necklaces, pendants, buckles and bracelets with their eye-catching kaleidoscope of stones that shone against the black velvet.

'Of course,' he said, feigning offence. 'And sourced all the silver also.'

'What a lovely way to spend your time,' she said, 'and a great excuse to travel, I imagine.'

'It can be,' he said. She thought she noticed something tighten in his voice, a retraction like a prodded sea anemone. Ah, well. He is a little young for you, old girl, she thought. At forty-one she still turned heads, giving off a salacious sexuality that had unfailingly got her into trouble all over the world. Men couldn't help themselves; moths to a fucking flame. She put it down to the vulnerability that her slight, girlish frame gave her that appealed to their paternal instinct, her big, pale blue eyes and the way she always seemed to be smiling, a levity of spirit. Also, even though they quickly discovered a steel core, she was goddam fun to be around, so young at heart, so free, they always remained enamoured, friends, even when that very liberty, her independence and refusal to commit, drove them away.

The kids kept her young too. She'd been twenty-three when she had Zak, twenty-five when she had Kai, and felt little or no age gap now they were in their teens. They were friends; mates or buddies, depending whether she was feeling like the Brit she was born as or the Yank she grew up as. Where the hell were they? she thought, as she scanned the busy market. Causing trouble, no doubt, though she had no idea where their propensity for it came from. Their bloody father, that's where. Damn musicians.

She turned back to the silversmith, catching his quick appraisal of her figure. As he bloody well should, she thought! Except for the smile lines, 'laughing-my-fucking-ass-off-lines' as she referred to them, and the stretch marks – yeah, she could bluff it out half her age. A dancer's body – hell, she'd been a dancer, so it wasn't that surprising – slim hips, no bust to speak of, brazen nipples though, clearly visible and ridging the front of her T-shirt. And obviously knickerless – she knew men could tell, she'd been told often enough – beneath her mint-green pedal-pushers. She'd spent enough time in communes in Boulder, Big Sur and Mexico when she was young, naked half the time, sharing food, beds and partners, not to give a damn what she looked like frankly; she loved her body.

He did though, give a damn, she thought, as she caught his eye; *busted*, poor dear. She smiled at his embarrassment. Gotcha.

'Hey,' she laughed, 'I saw that. I bet all this is just an excuse to sit here all day and check out the chicks that come by, isn't it? Well reel it in, sunshine, and pick on someone your own age.'

'I – but – er –' He fluffed it, pushing his glasses up his nose again.

'Look,' she said, 'I gotta find my kids. Save it for me – the ring I mean – and I'll try and come back after lunch, okay?' She started to go, 'By the way, I love your work.' She smiled at him and lilted away, so light on her feet it almost seemed like she was skipping.

'No problem,' he called after her, flustered at himself for getting fazed, getting caught out by her casual openness.

Once in the crowd she switched on her maternal radar, scanning left-right-left like the Terminator until she got a match. There. She spotted Zak's bobbing mop over by a stall selling kick-ass techno, R'n'B, rap, trance, house, everything. He had headphones on, ducking his head to something death-metallic, Nina guessed, judging by the neck-dislocating twitches. She had 'dug' every known type of music she'd encountered; hell, she lived for music, but thrash metal – *Jesus*, she thought, give me a fucking break. Where's the joy? What's the point? Discordant bullshit. No wonder kids are shooting up schools with Uzis if that's the shit they're listening to. 'Maybe I'm getting old,' she muttered out loud as she reached him, able to hear the roaring, incoherent rage coming from the padded head-set from five feet away. They'll grow out of it, I hope, she thought, or all those piano, guitar and God-knows-what-else lessons were a total waste of frigging money. She tapped him on the shoulder, having to reach up to do it, marvelling as she always did, that this beautiful boy had come from her womb. This huge, beautiful boy. Their father's fault; useless, lovable giant, with his straight-to-bed guitar slides and smothering, you-better-go-on-top girth.

He grinned at her, and her heart skipped.

'Hey, Ma!' he yelled, way too loud. 'Check this out. Totally awesome!'

'Yes, sweetie,' she said, 'I and everyone within a fifty-metre radius can hear that it's awesome, it comes through clearly in the lyrics.'

'What?' he bellowed. She snatched the headphones off him. The shaven headed DJ running the stall, his arms serpent-slithered with tribal tattoos, grinned a thumbs-up at her. Yeah, yeah, she mouthed back.

'Where's your brother? I told you to keep an eye on him. And pull your pants up.' How they stayed halfway down his ass without hitting the floor remained one of a list of questions she had for the next physicist she met.

'Aw c'mon, Ma,' he said, and she melted.

'Where the hell is he?'

'Over there, where he was when I last saw him. What's the problem? He knows where the car is.' They both looked where he pointed, but there was no sign of Kai's peroxide shock of vertical hair.

'Well he's not there now,' she said testily. 'Tell you what, why don't you go and find him and I'll wait at the café, how about that?'

'Sure Ma, whatever,' he shrugged, gave a devil-horn, evil-eye warder-offer or whatever it was supposed to be to the DJ, and loped off.

At a cluttered table under a canvas sun umbrella, with a glass of chilled Viña Sol in one hand, she people-watched contentedly while she waited for them. Was it just her imagination or did everyone look implausibly beautiful? Did they have some sort of aesthetic screening at the airport, or what? 'Is your face symmetrical? Okay, madam, thank you sir, welcome to Ibiza.' There were beautiful people everywhere; willowy blondes in white kaftans; feral pagans in richly coloured earthy hues; psychedelic trance loons with dreads, fractal-print latex and Rajasthani waistcoats; over-tanned longevity freaks from Europe and the States – she knew *that* scene well enough from Boulder – sipping wheatgrass and spirulina juice; born and bred off-road hippy kids whose parents moved here in the sixties and never left; ravers still spaced from the night before, muscle-bound poofters. Jesus, even the wrinkled smackies and the wild-eyed pissheads looked good.

Her eye was caught by two hammered English wastrels, one of whom, a chaos of dreadlocks and reeling bonhomie, was diligently buying all the handmade sheepskin slippers from a bemused stall owner and handing them out as well-done-you presents to any pretty girl that passed by. His T-shirt read: 'Who's in charge?' Who indeed.

Music – congas and flutes, ambient chimes and the thud of dance tracks – wove through the honeysuckle-heavy air from several different sources. Bright, clean sunlight dappled through the branches of the trees above. A bus-load of tourists from San

Antonio disgorged itself of fat, waddling Brits with socks under their sandals and cameras to snap the weirdoes, and she smiled; ah, she thought, *there* they are. The signs of the times. She personally resisted the overheard café complaints lamenting the 'good old days', when Las Dalias was the hippy Mecca on the island's weekend activity list, before mega clubs and traffic jams, vomit on the beach and the drug-dealer cartels that followed the money. She didn't mind; the market still thrived as a slice of how it had been, still run on old community-based managerial principles, everyone mucking in, exchanged services instead of cash. You scratch my back, I'll give you Reiki.

Although it was getting a bit crowded, the vibe was still upbeat, fresh, happy; the hippy dream still scampered through the throng, twirling ribbons and dispensing love, albeit conditional nowadays, like fairy dust. Same for most of the island, she thought, though kids these days kicked off big-time with the drugs, much more than they ever had. More to escape, she supposed.

She did her utmost to come out here for at least a month or two every summer, well, every summer since she'd lived in Barcelona, an overnight ferry ride away. Eighteen years now, *mas o menos*, enough to see the change, and though her priorities had changed somewhat over time too, what with the kids and all – no more outdoor full-moon parties in the pine forests above San Juan, no living naked on the beach for days on end – she still had enough friends tucked away on self-sufficient *fincas* in the hills up north not to mind the annual expansion of the villages and towns, not to be affected by the interminable development, ever more hotels and apartment blocks, clubs that could turn around twenty thousand people in a weekend. If you knew where to look, there were still small enclaves way off the well-flogged track where nothing had changed for decades, centuries; little bays that hardly anyone ever went to with pebbled beaches strewn with bleached driftwood and upturned fishing boats and crystal-clear water where fish darted like splintered mirrors in the shallows.

The boys loved their summer holidays, even if they were now getting to the age where fingering girls and getting wasted were higher on the agenda than snorkelling or hanging out with their mother. They were becoming more studiously disaffected, cynical and apathetic, that hormonal simmering and melatonin melange that made her laugh and worry in equal measure. She knew it was an act, an adopted attitude they had to go through, masking the helplessness and insecurity that came with a realisation of how big the world was, how crazy and uncertain life could be, but she hoped it wouldn't go on for long; life was too damn short to waste moping about.

She had taught them about love, life and respect for themselves and others as best she could. Now they were becoming men, she could only hope they'd be sensible and sensitive, kind and strong; the kind of men she herself had wanted to meet, not the ones she seemed to end up with. She had been mother and father to them, by necessity since their father had turned out to be – what was the word? – 'troubled', messed up, sinking into a spiral of alcohol and drugs as one big break after another never materialised and his dream of making it as a musician faded with the years. Eventually she had been forced to leave for all their sakes. Of course she still loved him, and their relationship, despite being long distance, had remained strong, relatively undamaged. Mike took the boys for a couple of months each Christmas, spoiling them rotten so that they returned with the latest GameBoy or DiscMan, starry eyed from the States and on fructose-highs from the junk food.

After so long, having long resigned herself to their separation, his letter had been a bit of a shock. She knew she was taking a huge risk by giving him another chance, stepping off the cliff edge again. What else could she do? She loved him. She would always be there – if he could prove her love to be justified. Safe.

He'd managed to stay sober for a year – one of her stipulations – and had finally dumped the vampiric bitch who'd driven him further into his morass, dragging him down and turning him against her. He'd sounded strong again in the letter, full of hope and dreams, like the man she once knew, and told her he'd begun to write about his experiences; a cathartic, no-holds-barred, roller-coaster journey down to the depths of sobbing, red-eyed hell and the slow one-rung-at-a-time climb back out again. He even had a publisher interested, so he said, one of the small independent outfits in Boulder knocking out self-help and lay-spiritual guides for the inner Zen in everyone that deserved to be healthy, wealthy and happy.

She heard it in his voice, too, on the phone during their recent tentative communications; unable to see the other's face so a little guarded, each, bit by bit, exposing their damaged hearts a little more, retracting at the slightest hint of danger, coaxing each other out. He had lost some of the defensive, apologetic edge to his voice and the deep, resonant timbre was coming back again; she knew she owed it to all four of them to give it another try. Besides, she'd given Barcelona her best shot, as good a shot as she had the energy for, and it never quite worked out; she was always just breaking even, just making the school fees and the rent for their top floor *apartamento* in El Borne. Importing batiks from Bali, bedspreads from India, furniture from Morocco – she'd tried it all. She was, finally, tired, and she wanted a break from it, she *deserved* a break from it. Goddamit, she'd done her share, raising the boys, and now hoped Mike would take up the slack.

She'd miss Barcelona. The food and the bars, the mountains and the beach. The way the cobbled alleys, full of glitzy boutiques by day, turned into seedy rat runs sheltering seedier absinthe bars and dimly lit tapas joints at night; the noise of the densely packed buildings where everyone heard everything you did and everyone knew your name; the creative vibrancy, the endless fiestas and concerts, how there was always something going on somewhere; the *correfoc*, the fire festival that, with typically Catalan disregard for health and safety, unleashed ear-numbing pyrotechnics upon the crowd, often igniting small children in the process; the stamping sexuality of *sardañas* on stages erected in the tree-lined plazas; the huge Sonar music weekend that filled the streets with raving revellers; the towering, breath-baited acrobatics of the *castellers*; the Sundays in Parc de la Ciutadella, where drummers gathered in groups of thirty or more to send a tribal heartbeat out over the barrios; the poi-twirlers and fire-jugglers who jiggled like rhythmic marionettes on strings; the lithe capoeira dancers who turned and spun on finely muscled arms; the jewellery, lungi and mojito vendors on the beach; the way everyone she knew was either an artist, musician, film-maker, sculptor or poet. It all reminded her of San Francisco in the seventies, where her own parents had briefly, nearly, worked it all out. Now, she prayed, she had an opportunity to break the pattern, snap out of the inherited dysfunctional behaviour loop.

Ultimately her work, freelance interior design, had proven too hit-and-miss and too unpredictable for her to ever completely relax, even with the erratic maintenance cheques from Boulder. It was time to move on. And if Mike was serious, if the big old bear really had got his shit together, she felt – when she meditated on it, going deep down the winding passages of her conscious mind to where her intuition shone like a diamond – she knew they had a chance.

After all these years, with all the commune craziness of their time together behind them, when she'd been little more than a girl, twelve years his junior, maybe it could still be the beautiful dream, the fairytale she knew existed, how it should have been then. The free love hadn't been quite so free, she thought wryly, though *damn*, the orgies had been fun. 'No strings' had turned into a tight knot. Now they were older, possibly wiser, with all the breathless humping of their youth behind them, maybe this was a chance to rediscover some of the purity, like closing the shutters during a storm only to open them much later and find clear blue sky, blinding sunlight.

'Hey, Mom,' Kai said, snapping her from her thoughts. He collapsed into the chair to one side of her and put his unlaced Vans on the table, and Zak slumped into the other. 'Wassup?'

'Oh, nothing,' she said, smiling brightly. 'Just thinking about your father – take your goddam feet off the table – how it might have been all these years if we'd stuck together.' She'd always been as frank as possible with them both, telling them everything, even when Mike had gone into rehab for six months, the first time, years ago; even when her boyfriends – Tio Paolo, Uncle Jamie, Tio Luis – left for good, sometimes too angry and hurt to even say goodbye to the boys. Even without Mike the three of them were a tight unit, and she took it as testament to the boys' maturity that they usually understood, or did their best to, especially Kai; he'd frown while he thought it over, then nod, give her a hug and come out with something so wise for a kid it always surprised her: 'Don't worry, Ma, all good things come to an end,' or 'Plenty more fish in the sea, mom' or 'You've still got us, Ma.' He gave one of those little frowns now.

'No point in dwelling on the past, Ma,' he said. 'Let's just see what happens when we get there, take it slowly, one day at a time, yeah?'

She put an arm round each of their shoulders – like a rugby hooker between two enormous props – and pulled them close to kiss their cheeks.

'I love you guys,' she said.

'Cut it out, Ma,' they both said in unison, wiping their cheeks with tatty sleeves and looking around to make sure no chicks – shock horror – were watching.

Kai, a year and a half younger than his brother, was the more introverted of the two, much quieter, and she worried about whether the move Stateside would unsettle him, the change of schools and friends. His grades weren't great as it was. If she was honest, she worried he might have some of Mike's demons, their sly-fingered beckoning when anything went wrong, their promise of temporary escape, though at least she knew it couldn't be genetic: What really worried her, what woke her up sweating in the middle of the humid nights, was what would happen when they hit Boulder and when, as part of the new start, the *entente cordiale*, she was going to tell a few truths, they were both going to come clean, put it all behind them, and how Mike would react to discovering he wasn't Kai's father.

And, more unpredictably, how Kai would.

She ruffled his gel-spiked hair and he pulled his head away.

'Seen anything you like?'

'Sure, Ma. There's a smokin' babe at the crystal store,' Zak said. Both boys laughed and high-fived over her head.

'Oh yeah?' she said. 'I was thinking more along the lines of something practical, like a belt.' Zak made a 'blah, blah' gesture with one hand, rolling his eyes.

'Well at least get something to eat while we're here.' She gave them both menus. 'Then I thought we could go to the beach? We've only got a couple more days so let's make the most of them. God knows when we'll next be back here, and Boulder's a long way from the sea.'

They half-heartedly glanced through the list of veggie offerings, and she knew they'd rather have burgers. Christ, she thought, I hope it wasn't all wasted on them. She understood that kids rail against their upbringing, a Newtonian recoil from their parents like two magnets being forced together; she just hoped that, having tried out the alternatives and realised the integrity, the truth, if such a thing existed, of what she'd tried to instil in them, they'd come round eventually. They'd probably end up as investment bankers, keep me in style, she thought, though she doubted it.

'Order what you like. I'm going to try and find your father a present.' She finished her glass of wine and left them gassing about whatever the hell it was they talked about. She swore she didn't understand half their argot-encoded bilingual banter, a baffling blend of Spanish, Catalan, English and MTV-ese.

Wandering through the stalls, not really concentrating, she used a crowd-cutting trick she'd been taught by a white witch sister, of not looking at people directly but focussing on the gaps between them, so that she never once had to stop to let someone past, do that strange 'after you' dance, but glided serenely through the throng with her hands lightly clasped behind her back.

'Hey, you came back.' The silversmith smiled at her, self-consciously tucking a strand of hair that had escaped his ponytail behind his ears. 'I kept it for you.' He produced the ring she had tried on earlier.

'That's sweet of you, hon,' she said, 'but I actually need something for my ex-husband' – she added on the prefix almost without realising – 'and he's not too big on jewellery.'

She cast an eye over the stall, more out of politeness than anything else, distracted by his gaze, the wine and heat stirring snakes in her abdomen, the idea of an afternoon in bed with this boy sending quick tremors to her belly and instantly lubing her pussy. Right, that's enough, she told herself. Concentrate! Jeez. She needed to rein it in one of these days, and had hoped that the imminent reconciliation would go some way to keeping her flirtatiousness in check. Evidently not. She had a dull, wanton ache; her libido craved sex like a junkie craves a hit.

'Never mind, babe, I'll take it anyway,' she said. '*Gracias*.' He reached under the table for a small, velvet drawstring bag into which he dropped the ring, pulling it tight.

'And say,' she said, indicating the blue-black fountain pen that lay next to his notebook on the table, 'that's beautiful.' In the afternoon light it glowed with unusual luminescence, a lustrous opacity that, even from where she stood, gave the impression of strange depth to the casing. 'It looks like an antique. May I have look?'

He hesitated for a second then handed it to her. Unscrewing the lid she noticed the nib had a heart-shaped reservoir that channelled ink to the point. 'I don't suppose you'd be interested in selling this, would you, sweetie?' she murmured, entranced. 'It's exactly the sort of thing he'd love.' She recognised a talismanic quality in the pen that Mike, with his aspirations towards the occult, magick with a 'k', would find appealing.

'*Lo siento*, no,' he said, extending his hand for it. 'It has too much sentimental value. Besides, I have no idea what it is worth.' He slid the pen into his shirt pocket with finality.

'Three hundred euros?' she said, not entirely sure what made her say it.

That got his attention. He looked at her intently over his glasses then shook his head.

'Sorry, I cannot.'

'Oh well, *no pasa nada*.' she said lightly, looking around, 'there's bound to be something here somewhere. Spoilt for choice really.' She thanked him for the ring and walked away, conscious of his eyes following her. She threaded her way towards the restaurant where, hopefully, by now the boys would be eating something.

There was a tap on her shoulder.

'*Oye*.' he was slightly breathless. 'Four hundred, *vale*? I need to get back home, quickly, to Argentina, and this would make it possible, if you're serious. Otherwise I have to sit at this stall for the rest of the summer.' He gave a what-to-do shrug.

'I've already given you thirty,' she said, with a lascivious smile. 'Look, tell you what, let's not haggle here. Meet me later at Anita's up the road and we can battle it out over dinner. When do you close up shop?'

They agreed to meet at eight.

You are naughty, she scolded herself with an impish smile, waving to the boys when they spotted her. They still had time to go to Agua Blanca, the old freak beach nearby scattered with pink Germans with bald heads and waxed scrotums. The boys could have a swim, play some bat-n-ball and then she could zip home to change. She knew *just* which dress to wear, and that the boys would be out for the night as per usual, and she was technically still single – and hell, she was on holiday after all.

# Chapter 17

*Sunday, 23rd November, 1933*
*Lamu Archipelago*

*My love,*
*I've made it, safe and sound.*

*Sorry not to have written sooner but I have been much occupied since my arrival, settling in and also on, and have scarce had time to sit down, let alone indulge myself in these letters. Besides, having still heard nothing from you, my enthusiasm for them is beginning to wane. They serve a confessional purpose perhaps, or something similarly cathartic.*

*I left that morning with mixed emotions, due in the main to leaving Jim. He has, from the moment this escapade began, been a supportive rock upon which I have relied. The elder brother I never had – hell, the father I never had. He walked with me down to the port and gave me a warm handshake and back-slapping embrace.*

*'Thank you, my friend,' I said. 'I'll be forever indebted to you – I don't know what I'd have done without your guidance.'*

*'Don't mention it, dear boy. Besides, it's I who should be thanking you.'*

*'What on earth for?' I asked.*

*'For reminding me that the world ain't quite so dark and*

*hopeless as I had grown to suspect, for your youthful optimism, foolhardiness, good humour and refreshing idealism. Since losing Josephina I had thought part of me died with her, that's how it felt. Your romantic adventure has rekindled some of the fire I once had for life, some hope for humanity – perhaps we are not as irredeemably buggered as I'd thought.' With that he shook my hand and gave me a squeeze of the shoulder and strolled off out of sight, not turning back once.*

*It was the only time he ever mentioned his wife in all the long hours we spent together.*

*I hope our paths are destined to cross at some point in the future.*

*So my second voyage began.*

*The sail up the coast was blissfully calm, wholly different to the Apollonia – lacking engine noise or other clanking of metal and clanging of bulkheads; the most that one could class as a disturbance was the gentle creak of the boom, the flap of canvas and the slap of the sea upon the hull; melodious sounds all. These dhows are the most lovely craft; simple yet perfect, the result of thousands of years' invention, so well honed as to need no further improvement or modernisation. The rudder was steered with nimble-toed precision by Omar, my broad-smiled skipper, who reclined in the stern with an enigmatic look of contentment on his face that I never once saw change, while his first mate, Femi, leapt about as and when he needed to, admittedly not that often; hauling the sail around the front of the mast when we changed tack or clambering up along the out-rigger – a plank inserted into the side of the boat that affords the extra ballast of a man's weight at its end. I even had a go myself, mid morning, when we were zipping along at quite a clip; most exhilarating, ten foot above the sea's surface, fifteen feet out, 'on a limb', the wind in my hair. Wonderful. Then with one sly turn of the rudder, Omar brought me to within inches of a dunking in the water, soaking me in bow spray. From their laughter I knew it was deliberate but found it impossible to be riled.*

*We stopped for lunch – fish grilled on an open fire – on a sandy spar, after which Omar produced a calabash of some foul-smelling liquid, mnazi, which, through the usual process of point-and-nod – at which I am becoming daily more fluent – finger-drawing in the sand and aided by a well-thumbed Swahili dictionary I acquired at the club, he explained to me to be the juice of the palm tree. It begins to ferment immediately upon contact with air, so when taken fresh, has approximately the potency of beer, by day two that of wine, and by the fourth can strip the enamel from a cup. This must have been a day or two old for I fell soundly asleep for an hour or two, waking to what felt like being gently but firmly tapped on the head with an iron bar. Pokey stuff.*

*A quick dunk of the head over the side helped no end – nice for it to be of my own volition on this occasion – and we resumed our voyage.*

*Lil, I saw my first elephants. Large, half submerged shapes at the water's edge, which I initially took to be boulders, on closer inspection turned out to be a herd of around fifty carrying out their afternoon ablutions. Omar, at my request, took us in closer for a better look – they were definitely playing, even the adults; spraying each other from their trunks, flapping their enormous raggedy ears as if shaking out rugs and generally floundering about; it struck me that there must be little on earth more pleasurable for them than taking their weight off in salt water and simultaneously escaping the heat. Their strange vibrational 'conversation', for that is how it sounded, carried clearly across the water to us; a most lovely noise, like purring. One surged further out until it had completely submerged, just the tip of his trunk visible above the surface. They eventually stopped what they were doing and plodded off into the trees like so many baggy-trousered gents, following a large female (even at a distance you can spot the enormous-tusked, well-endowed males); the matriarch of the herd, I assume.*

*Later, with dusk dimming the celestial house lights, Omar whistled to Femi and gestured out to a flock of what looked like gannets hovering in the sky above a patch of agitated water, the silver flash of innumerable fish on the surface visible from where we were. They poised above their targets with great precision, heads hung down and fixed still with concentration, quite oblivious to us. Once aimed, they folded their wings, becoming pointed darts, and disappeared into the water with neat, concise splashes, emerging triumphant often as not, a silver sardine or some other fish struggling in their beaks. Every so often the surface would churn, as if boiling, and some of the fish would clear the water, huge skipjack following hard upon them.*

*We passed over the shoal – so dense the water teemed thick with life – and cast out lines behind us. Within minutes we were joined aboard by several of the sardine-like blighters and three huge skipjack, which thumped about in the bilges until coshed still by Omar's deftly swung priest. Their lidless eyes and gaping mouths seemed to convey final, mute supplication.*

*We sailed right through the night – both my companions knew the coast well enough and there was still vestige of a moon. I for my part enjoyed one of the most refreshing and restorative night's sleep for a long time; no mosquitoes, no net, no oppressive, stifling heat and no nightmares. Perhaps I am now wholly attuned to the rhythm of the sea and should join the merchant navy?*

*Not long after dawn – as captivating as dusk but clearer, fresher, as if untainted by the day to come and rinsed clean of the day before – we rounded the headland and trailed a long, curved, dune-backed beach some ten miles long. At its end we tacked into a broad channel past a small white village, little more than a mosque and a scattering of thatched Arabic-style houses; Shela. To starboard, a low mass of mangroves and vast baobab trees standing like silent sentinels along the shore – Manda Island, apparently.*

*After Shela a long wall appeared to port – my first sight of the ginnery – with a jetty for loading the boats and yielding little more than a quick glimpse of outbuildings around a courtyard through the open gate.*

*At last Lamu itself came into view; a fleet of dhows with furled sails, a motley collection of flat-roofed or thatched buildings along the walled seafront, a jetty thrusting out into the channel and, behind and above it all, an impressive fort, all set prettily against the palms that swayed around the town as if in greeting.*

*The now familiar cry of 'Muzungu!' went up as we approached, and a crowd of villagers gathered along the jetty to see the 'white man' arrive; handsome, Arabic looking men in wide-sleeved white djellabas and muscular Africans in shirts and kikois – a length of coloured material cleverly wrapped about the waist as a long 'skirt' in the evening, or worn higher during the day or when working (clever because somehow modesty is always maintained).*

*Luggage borne ahead of me, I stepped ashore, conscious that this was to be my home for the next nine months.*

*There was no one from the Company to meet me – unsurprisingly, since I was a day or so early. I thanked Omar and Femi for their time, and paid them what they asked without bothering to question it – the journey had been worth every penny – and retreated from the midday sun's heat beneath the colonnades of a merchant's offices, happy just to watch the activities of the port.*

*I was beginning to wonder who on earth I should ask to start the process of finding Whitson when I heard a polite cough behind me. I turned to find a young man grinning broadly, his hand extended.*

*'Mister Talbot Sahib,' he said, not asked – I suppose there can't have been many other contenders for the name. 'Karibu sana. Welcome to Lamu. I am most pleased to make your acquaintance, bwana.' He continued to pump my hand with great vigour, grinning all the while. He must possess some Arabic blood for his features were sharper, his nose narrower, than the local tribesmen, yet not as aquiline as the pure-blooded Moslems.*

*'Asante sana,' I replied. 'And who might you be?'*

*'My name is Kamau, bwana. I came as soon as I heard of your arrival. We did not expect you until tomorrow but you are here, Allah be praised!' He clapped his hands with a laugh. He had an engaging smile that shone in his eyes, was around my height and I'd guess about my age, similarly lean, but by the way he slung my valise easily onto one shoulder, clearly stronger in the way that wiry men sometimes are.*

*'This way,' he said. 'Come! Let me show you to your lodgings.' And, leaving instruction for my trunk to follow, strode off ahead of me. He led me along the quay and past a group of donkeys that stood about swishing their tails with the impassive resignation of those destined to a life of toil. We cut through one alley onto a broader lane that took us towards the fort, channels on each side of the street funnelling effluent to the sea. We crossed the courtyard before the fort's imposing gates, a wizened acacia in its centre, and followed an exceptionally narrow alley, too close for even a cart to pass along it, one side of which was the outer wall of the fort; any present attempt to breach the walls could be easily achieved from the top floors of the facing houses.*

*We took a left and a right – of that much I am certain, after that I must admit defeat – through the busy lanes, passers-by paying me scant heed, and arrived here – my home! – where you now find me, reclined on a divan in the shade of the roof terrace of my splendid quarters.*

*Intricately carved, seven-foot-high double doors, complete with foot-long iron spikes (an Arabic tradition to deter battering war elephants) and a sliding grill so that one can vet one's visitors before admitting them, give onto a small hallway, delightfully cool after the heat outside, at the end of which is a cobbled courtyard open to the sky. I was introduced to two men – the older, Charro, my cook, greying at the temples and from one of the local tribes judging from his condensed, negroid features, and whose faltering greeting told me I must improve my Swahili immediately. The younger, Salim, is my house boy, a slight Moslem perhaps seventeen years old, in white kaftan and kofia, the small embroidered pillbox hats popular here amongst the Arabs. He greeted me with 'Salaam Halikum', touching his heart with his right hand as he did so, and they whisked my trunk upstairs while Kamau showed me around.*

*In the middle of the courtyard is a tall coconut palm, cut with notches that I assume enable someone more agile than I to climb it, the swaying fronds all but blocking out the blue sky beyond; the open roof creates a constant up-draught through the building, while the foliage provides shade below. To the left of the courtyard, high columns with trefoil arches lead onto an open living area with low, carved tables between raised benches, and a tiled pool six feet or so deep and ten long. Beyond are the staff quarters, kitchen, etc.*

*From the courtyard runs an open flight of stairs, its banister woven with violet-flowered bougainvillea, that take one to the main bedroom. While Salim unpacked my few belongings I took a look around; high ceiling, a vast four-poster and swathe of netting tied back during the day. Shuttered double doors open onto a veranda with a view over the roofs and across the estuary to the stilted mangroves of Manda.*

*Along the corridor, open on one side to the courtyard below, is an office with the same view as that of the bedroom. Beyond that, on the third side of the courtyard, another smaller bedroom. The stairs then run up another flight to the roof, to my mind the best feature of this magnificent building; an open-sided thatched area covers one end, a large stone cistern at the other. The view, all three hundred and sixty degrees of it, gives a great impression of the town; in the distance, the open ocean.*

*I felt instantly at home, much to Kamau's evident satisfaction. He told me the building is over two hundred years old, and showed me a section of decorative brickwork in the master bedroom that overlooked the courtyard, perforated with gaps that I had taken for ventilation but which in fact enable one to observe whomsoever is below without being seen oneself; a sort of architectural burka. Curiously, when I asked further about its history his smile wavered for the first time since I'd met him. I changed tack and asked him about himself – always good policy when unsure of the thickness of the ice.*

*He's exactly my age, it transpires, and hails from Malindi. His father is something of a name in the exportation game, one of the few Africans to have established his credentials under the auspice of Arabic slavers in the 1880s. Kamau, neither ready nor willing to follow the family tradition just yet, and with a good command of English, managed to get a job as a runner with the Company, swiftly working his way up to becoming Whitson's personal assistant. He remains single, he says, until 'kissed by a princess'. When I asked whether he thought himself a frog he looked at me as if I was mad.*

*He left me to it. I liked him immediately, and hope he'll prove a good friend and useful ally in the months ahead.*

*Due to report at Whitson's office the following morning first thing, I resolved to get an early night. Supper – fish with rice and 'kachumbari': chilli peppers, eye-wateringly strong, with tomatoes and coriander as a kind of coarse sauce – was delicious and accompanied by gin and plenty of tonic water, which we are advised to drink as much of as possible for the quinine it contains. Might well be an excuse, though.*

*Afterwards I commandeered Salim so as not to get lost, and took a stroll through the town, down to the seafront and along the shore to where the buildings stopped and the pale sand gleamed under the palm trees. Crickets and cicada hailed us with their racket, and the bray of donkeys echoed from the now empty streets. I sat a while on the sea wall gazing out across the water in contemplative silence until the mosquitoes discovered me and we were forced home. Salim respected my privacy, answering the few questions I asked with none of his own. His English is passable – though my attempts to get him to drop the 'Sahib' he uses like commas failed.*

*The following day, 24th November:*

*Slept well and deep, waking to the five a.m. calls to prayers from the mosque nearby, then at five-thirty by a cacophony of cockerels and finally at six-thirty by a light tap on the door and the mouth-watering smell of fresh coffee. Charro brought it to my room – service, Lil! – and, after a mug of the black stuff I took a bracing douse with a bucket to clear my head. Kamau was waiting patiently downstairs so, foregoing breakfast, we headed for the Company offices, located not far from the merchants' warehouses on the port where I'd yesterday loitered.*

*Odd that, since Whitson surely must have seen me arrive here yesterday from his window. Perhaps that explains Kamau's sudden appearance. I was led through the marbled reception, up a flight of wooden stairs and along a gloomy hallway to a door with Whitson's name on it, all the while aware of sidelong glances from the clerks, front office and flunkeys making themselves look busy, perhaps for my benefit.*

*'Come in,' a voice said when I knocked.*

*I took a deep breath and entered.*

*Portly, with reddened cheeks and a polished pate, 'Cotton' Charlie Whitson sat behind a large desk dressed in an immaculately pressed white linen suit. A pith helmet, a panama not unlike my own and a pair of binoculars hung on a hat stand inside the door. Two chairs faced the desk at which he sat and from which he did not look up. I stood there awkwardly for half a minute, then ahem-ed. He seemed not to have registered my presence, and appeared surprised to find me there when he stopped his writing – filling in some ledger.*

*'Yes,' he said, 'what can I do for you?'*

*'Ah, Talbot, sir. Ralph Talbot,' I said, a little taken aback. 'I've been sent from Head Office. The project manager position.' Surely he was expecting me. I handed over my letters of introduction.*

*'Have you, indeed?' he said, ignoring the papers and screwing a monocle into his right eye socket (instantly giving him the impression of having one eye much larger than the other) to inspect me. His browless eyes were a peculiar pale blue, wan and insipid, and he had the curious habit of blinking them often, a nervous twitch, so that I felt scrutinised like a bug under a magnifying glass.*

*'Yes,' he said, casting a slow look at his diary. 'I see you arrived earlier than we expected, mm, didn't you?' I hadn't expected my avidity to be taken badly, yet felt somehow it had.*

*'Yes, I hoped to get here a little ahead of schedule in order to acclimatise all the sooner. I hope that didn't interfere with your plans –' I left it hanging.*

*'No, no, think nothing of it. Glad you made it safe and sound.*

*Pleasant trip?' I could tell my response was surplus to requirements as, the possibility struck me, might I myself be; perhaps there are currents of political schemings at work here that I am unaware of. I must play my cards close to my chest, my love, until I ascertain what exactly is going on out here (the alternative conclusion, and the one I left the room with, is that the man's slightly mad).*

*'Fine, thanks,' I replied – where to start, otherwise? – 'most pleasant.' I stood there like a plum for another minute or so.*

*'Do take a seat, old boy,' he said, at last, resuming scribbling in his ledger. 'So, how are your lodgings? Everything to your liking? Mm?' The high pitched hums with which he punctuates his sentences were at this point new to me; as if he's on the verge of either breaking into song or coughing up catarrh.*

*'Splendid, thanks,' I said. 'Much more than I had expected, and after so long a journey, quite luxurious.'*

*'Good, good. And Kamau has been showing you around, mm?' His hands fluttered to his bald pate now and then as if checking for new growth.*

*'Yes, in what little time I have had to date. I should like to borrow him, if I may, for a tour of the operation. If you are too preoccupied, that is.' Whether or not he noticed the insinuation in my voice he made no sign.*

*'Naturally,' he said, looking up briefly. 'Why don't you go and have a reconnoitre and come back to me this afternoon with any questions you might have?'*

*And that was that.*

*The brief meeting was most bizarre, and left me feeling rather unwelcome. At the time I supposed the man had other, more pressing things, on his mind but now, a couple of days later, I realise that this is his manner; unless there's something vitally important to the fate of the Company, he simply isn't interested.*

*I left, donning my hat as I emerged into the sharp sunlight with Kamau.*

*The fellow is, by contrast, a breath of fresh air. Chatting away amiably, we walked down to the ginnery – ten minutes along the dusty coast path then cutting inland through the palms, round to the main entrance comprising a high set of double gates with a sign proclaiming 'Lamu Ginnery' in bold blue letters and the Company name beneath. Two 'askari' – guards – snapped to attention as we approached and took our names with a flourish of efficiency.*

*He led me to the main office and introduced me to Mohammed, the manager, a slight, industrious looking fellow with small round glasses, a trim beard and white kaftan who greeted me politely and took me through the order of the day, neatly displayed on a large blackboard screwed to the rear wall: lists and tables that I shall familiarise myself with in due course. Fortunately for me he seems competent and reliable and worthy of all my delegation skills!*

*Arranged around a wide yard and surrounded by low warehouses on three sides, the compound has two entrances: the main one and, in the wall facing the entrance, a gate leading to the jetty – the one I passed aboard Faisal – through which the raw cotton arrives and the processed cotton leaves. Arranged logically enough for the process involved, the building immediately to the right of the seaward gate receives the raw cotton from the jetty in hand-propelled wagons on rails running around the edge of the yard. From there the buckets are pushed inside on rollers where they are upturned and the contents fed via rollers into the machine that strips the cotton from the plant (the seed is separated and compressed into 'cotton cake' for animal feed); several men were feeding the huge gin machines with mounds of white fibrous clumps.*

*Picking up one ball I couldn't help wonder what all the fuss was about, that this tuft is what wars are waged for and for which many men had died.*

*In its raw state it looks quite unprepossessing; little more than a tangled mass around a seed-like central pod. Once separated it is then washed and sterilised with chlorine, then reloaded back into the wagons and onto the second building housing the enormous, clattering looms that weave it into a coarse fabric amid tremendous racket. Then out once more and onto the final stage for baling and storage ready to ship out.*

*Sounds simple, doesn't it, my love? But the noise, especially in the loom building, is deafening – the poor souls slaving away in there scarcely looked up when we walked in – and the work dangerous; one lapse of concentration and you'll lose a limb (this has happened several times, before you ask, though not for the last six months or so).*

*The generator, housed some distance away but audible nevertheless, runs solidly from dawn 'til dusk – the duration of working hours out here. Wages are competitive, easily enough to support one's family, but nevertheless extremely low; around a shilling per day. I suppose it could be worse. At least there's the guarantee of work for the fifty or so employees and, though they might not appreciate it, it's not the harshest place on earth, at least to my eyes. Perhaps they would exchange it all for the bustle of London, the throng of Oxford Street, the freezing, dismal weather and the choking smog – but I doubt it. Indeed, they seem a content enough lot – always ready with a smile and a wave. All in all far cheerier than your average Londoner (I hope that doesn't sound patronising; it's not meant to be. We Brits are a dour breed, are we not?).*

*Re what I said about guaranteed work; it transpires that this might not necessarily be the case for much longer. Mohammed tells me the cotton crops have taken a terrible hammering for the last two years – unexpectedly bad droughts to the north west, combined with the general downturn in world demand due to market undercutting from the Americas; the picture in general isn't rosy – I suspect my role might well be wrapping up the operation. We'll see.*

*I spent a couple of hours with Mohammed going over the past year's figures, production levels etc. and asked him to be as candid with me as possible, to tell me everything. He seems to regard the workers with mild disdain, if not worse – I saw him haul two men over the coals on separate occasions for trivial matters while I was there. Can't engender much loyalty, can it? Surely respect is a two-way street. Maybe my managerial skills have simply yet to be tested in the crucible of real life.*

*Kamau translating, I also took a moment to speak to the brawny, oil-smeared foreman, Kijana, asking him whether the workers were well treated and what, if anything, he would like to see improved. Whether due to Kamau's presence, my foreign-ness or Kijana's plain lack of trust in authority, I could get nothing out of him except that everything was 'sawa kabisa' – very well.*

*I came away from my Q and A session with the monosyllabic Whitson later that afternoon even more disquieted; I tried to keep it formal and to the point, discerning that that's how he wants it. I asked him nothing of his time here, his experiences or any advice he might care to give me other than the purely objective and work related. What a dullard. Honestly, you'd think he hadn't spoken to another Englishman for years (dear God – perhaps he hasn't!). The rest I shall discover for myself. If he chooses to show me no amicability then I can accept it. If, however, he wants to meet me halfway then so much the better. It would certainly make my life a little easier. Maybe in the future we will become at least acquaintances, possibly friends, but for the moment it seems as if we are to be no more than colleagues. He is a curious fellow, humming away all the while, quirky in the extreme; I find myself intrigued as to what makes him tick. Why was Toby so effusive about the man? Perhaps I had read too much into his words. What had he said? That he was a 'good man once you got to know him'. Something like that. Yet I have seen nothing to give the impression of anything but thinly veiled hostility. No, not hostility per se, but a kind of apathy, as if I matter not a jot to him, my presence neither here nor there.*

*Perhaps, my dear, I am treading on his professional toes and something of a threat to the man's future. As far as I am aware from the briefing I received in London, my role is purely a supportive one. I rather gathered that the operation was in desperate need of more hands on deck. Now that I am here it seems that this is not the case; production is down, not due to lack of adequate management or infrastructure but because the harvest is itself in trouble. And there's little I can do about that.*

*He also had me up about my chat with the foreman.*

*'I gather you – ah – had a word with Kijana, mm,' he said rhetorically. 'Let me remind you that things have been done here in a certain way for a very long time indeed and we – ah – don't need anyone upsetting the applecart.' I assured him I had no intention of any such thing and that it was part of my acclimatisation to the new position to try and get as good a picture of how it all worked as possible. It does rather beg the question of how he found out. Perhaps Kamau is not the open book he at first appeared. Then again, perhaps he simply and truthfully relayed everything that happened and all that was said. Either way, I might have to watch myself around him in future.*

*Listen to me ranting away. It is my first day and already I suspect the boss dislikes me! Surely anyone who has ever started a new job has thought the same thing. I shall dispel all preconceptions of the chap and play his game at his pace, which I assume to be more in step with our present environment than the one from which I've come.*

*I returned to the house after my first day at work in good spirits, delighting in the capering monkeys that followed me loudly through the palm groves until the outskirts of town and the parakeets that cawed above. I did my best to greet every stare with a 'Salaam' or a 'Habari' and smile, touching my hat to women and men alike.*

*Once home I treated myself to a dip in the pool – sloughing off the grime and sweat of the day – and capping it off with a stiff G and T on the roof, from where, between long spells of gazing into the milky distance, I now write to you.*

*Dinner is served, and after that I think an early night is called for, my love, so I bid you adieu.*

*Yours,*
*Ralph*

*Monday, 1st December 1933*
*Lamu Archipelago*

*My love,*
*What to report?*

*Not a great deal, it must be said. I have settled into something resembling a routine, which goes thus:*

*Up at dawn. Not because I have to but in order to catch the sunrise, which is quite exquisite; a tentative lightening on the horizon that gradually intensifies before the sun erupts from the mangroves like a phoenix, accompanied by the sounds and smells of the town beginning its day; chapattis cooking, cockerels crowing, donkeys braying, dogs barking and the mullah's plaintive wailing.*

*Breakfast comprises coffee and fruit – I can rarely contemplate more for some reason, especially odd if you remember how I'd pack away anything I was offered when you knew me. Perhaps in this climate one requires less fuel. Shower and shave (my beard is now quite well established but requires a degree of maintenance), dressing (the colonial uniform of khaki shirt and trousers seems to be de rigueur) and out of the house by eight having first conferred with Charro or Salim re the evening meal. They have both come to realise my requirements are minimal, and seem pleased by it. What they do during the day is their affair, and I certainly don't expect them to confine themselves indoors needlessly. That said, they appear able to do nothing at all with a kind of studious languor; sleeping whenever the opportunity arises and – especially Charro – never quite shaking off a kind of sluggishness I assume is due to the heat. Salim, to be fair, is relatively full of beans when I'm around.*

*And so to work.*

*My commute is one I had never in my wildest dreams expected; a stroll down through the market to the seafront – all kinds of vegetables and fruits I don't recognise, chickens in wickerwork baskets, monkeys on chains, open air, fly-blown halal butchers – stopping briefly at the office to find out what, if any, special duties the day holds for me, then to the ginnery where I have an office adjacent to Mohammed. I was given the choice of basing myself here or in town and chose the former; it affords me some privacy, is removed from Whitson, and despite muted noise from the ginnery, has a degree of tranquillity I find invigorating. I can also slip out to the ginnery jetty whenever I feel the urge for a breath of salty air and dangle my feet above shoals of darting fish.*

*Viz. my duties; I have to tell you Lil, I really don't see why they need me here at all. I had expected to be run off my feet with the workload, nose to the grindstone etc. I find myself instead off my feet with boredom. I have to actively try to find things to do. Don't tell your Pa, whatever you do – might not be what he had in mind. Please try to give the impression that I am slaving away, that my role is critical to British interests in Eastern Africa and that no other could possibly get the job done. Hell, that the Empire itself is at stake.*

*In truth, a child could manage quite well; I make sure the deliveries match the orders and the stocks match the invoices, that the processing is done with such efficiency as can be expected and that the resultant bales fit the figures. Other than that I am thumb-twiddling, day dreaming of my time on the Apollonia, of you and home, of Jim and what he might be up to up country, writing a journal of what I remember (I have decided these letters are not enough, and I need something for my own purposes) and often away with the fairies. Quite happily so – don't get me wrong. The year will whip past at this rate.*

*Mohammed, via Kijana, deals with any mechanical or supply issues, and all the shipping details are taken care of at the office. Were you to turn up at the door on any given day, you would likely as not catch me with my feet upon the desk, a fly-whisk dangling from one hand and a book or my pen in the other. Obviously my surprise at seeing you might mean I was subsequently sprawled unconscious on the floor, but you get my meaning.*

*My time spent outside working hours is proving engaging. Most evenings I take long walks along the beach that stretches south; one could go for hours and not reach its end. Other forays into the archipelago have revealed little of interest, though it is undeniably beautiful – tropical and lush – and last weekend a tour of the whole island itself, just to know the extent of my world and to ensure that it had no sudden edge.*

*I enlisted Salim as a guide, packed a few provisions in my knapsack, strapped my knife to my belt, jammed on my hat and we set off. This took all of both Saturday and Sunday, perhaps walking for eight hours each day – some thirty-five to forty miles in total I'd guess – over dunes and fording creeks, hacking through thorny bush where necessary and breaking whenever we felt like it. I slung a canvas hammock between palms for the one night we spent out, while Salim slept on the sand wrapped in a blanket. A fire kept at bay the chill of the night while rice and smoked fish dealt with the wolves at the door. Well supplied with water, and never far from a coconut if we ran low, it was the happiest I have been for a long while, just sitting by the fire, stargazing and smoking contentedly.*

*To the south there is a network of sandbars and tributaries that separate us from the mainland with less emphasis than the deep channel to the north, and where big game – lions, buffalo and elephant – have been known to cross, driven by hunger in times of drought. The landward side of the island is harder going, and we were often forced to cut inland along the dunes when the mangroves proved too impenetrable.*

*Although quite at ease with the silence, and utterly accustomed, now, to solitude, Salim kept me entertained with his version of the region's history, riddled with myth though it might be. What is certain is that it is predictably violent and complicated, quite in keeping with that of the rest of the world. I have ceased to be surprised.*

*It seems the archipelago has been of great strategic importance for around two thousand years, used and abused variously by the usual culprits: Persian, Roman, Hindu, Jewish, Arabian, Phoenician, Chinese, Portuguese, German and, most recently, we Brits. The descendants of the Syrian inhabitants of Pate island, to the north, held sway for decades until disputes with the Persians of Manda over precious drinking water – of which there is scant supply even now – culminated in an all-out war (the bleached bones of the slaughtered beneath the dunes are occasionally revealed after a particularly heavy storm, Salim tells me).*

*They were subsequently routed and fled across the channel to Shela, the small village on the headland. When the wells promptly ran dry in Manda, the port of Lamu – until then little more than a trading point for Arabs seeking gold, ivory, slaves etc. in exchange for silk, porcelain and glass – took its place, Shela having no deep anchorage.*

*I did my best to keep up with him, and shall attempt to learn more from my dinner with the DC, John Horace Clive, arranged for next Monday. Kamau says the man is putting together a potted history of the district, partly, no doubt, to keep him from going stark raving mad with boredom. What must the poor bugger have done to end up with a posting such as this? Though undeniably an earthly paradise, it can hardly bode well for one's career if this is where they send you. Perhaps this goes some way to explaining Whitson's curious disposition . . . I'll not comment on what reflection that casts on my own presence here.*

*I'll leave you for now. Sounds strange, doesn't it? How much more leave of you could I possibly take than being here, at the other end of the world from you, where the constellations appear flipped like an egg-timer, the climate inconceivably strange compared to the one I left behind, and I, though foreigner in a foreign land, already feel closer to it than to that of my upbringing and past.*

*If truth be known I never felt 'at home' in England, knocked from pillar to post, from foster home to school. Here I can forge a new identity, unencumbered by the stigma of my fostered childhood and murky pedigree.*

*Here I am who I am, not the construct of my past.*

*My memories of England – you aside – not exactly the happiest, already start to fade, lost like tears in the rain, washing gently away as if clearing space for new ones. I am a vessel ready to be filled.*

*Yours as ever,*

*Ralph*

*x*

*P.S. After a persistent campaign of following me around and loitering outside the house, I appear to have acquired a companion, a dog – mangy cur, to be charitable – with dun-coloured fur, solidly built and good humoured, if a little gruff; have named him Maddox. Until someone claims him, I shall attempt to nurse him to better health. I have set him up in the courtyard, and although Charro is disapproving I've caught him slipping the mutt scraps when he thinks I'm not looking.*

*21st December, 1933*
*Lamu*

*Lillian,*

*How long since I last wrote? I neither know nor care.*

*I am now twenty-one years of age.*

*No longer a boy, but a Man. Master of my own Destiny and answerable to no one but God. Old enough to seek the identity of my own parents! Who could ask for more?*

*Ha! Forgive my cynicism.*

*My birthday was unremarkable, spent, as it was, alone and uncelebrated. That said, it will remain the most memorable to date, and I suspect for the rest of my life. I told no one of the day and received no mail. Who would send any?*

*Not you, it would seem.*

*It fell on a Friday, as it transpired, and, not wishing to spend this 'most important day' engaged in the mind-numbing futility of inaction that has become my employment, I decided to skive off work for the first time since I started. Citing fever, a credible enough excuse here where the ravages of stomach upset, dengue and malaria are never far from sight, I sneaked out of the house around noon with a picnic and a flask of coconut wine – mnazi – and made for the dunes with Maddox, cock-eared and now much recovered (virtually unrecognisable – wet of nose and shiny of coat) scouting ahead in the way he does when he knows I'm watching; regularly checking I'm paying attention to his brave endeavours as he charges about this way and that, snuffling and puffing with great self-importance, chasing imaginary game, convinced he is in fact leading me.*

*There is a gnarled baobab, its trunk ten feet in diameter and hundreds of years old, on top of the highest dune above Shela that provides both shade and seclusion with a clear view in all directions, and I like to think the spot mine. Certainly I have never encountered anyone else on the many salutary excursions I have made there. Once ensconced beneath its elephantine limbs I happily fritter away hours at a time; simply staring out to sea often as not, smoking and reading, or writing – an occupation increasingly filling my time. On this occasion I just sat there, thoroughly depressed, floating with the clouds, Maddox at my side pretending not to notice my lunch.*

*Before me the island was laid out beautifully. Facing east with the mainland behind me I had an uninterrupted view out over the lesser dunes to the cobalt sea where occasional dhows cut across my line of sight, tacking out to where the best fishing can be found. To my right, south, the long arc of the beach rolls away into the distance, hazy with mist from the crashing surf, before curving around to the peninsula. I became swiftly entranced, as I often was aboard the Apollonia.*

*Ah, Lil. What's to become of us?*

*The wine made me maudlin, and I hit low ebb like a ship settling slowly into mud. The ridiculousness of my situation, Lil. Here, utterly without purpose as far as the Company is concerned, simply to prove a point to your bloody snob of a father.*

*It all came crashing in on me. I should be with friends, with you, doing something worthwhile, something to further myself and set the course of my future. I know, I know; that is what I am doing. Technically. On paper.*

*But then, there, in this, the real world, the practicalities of the situation seemed abruptly quite different, as if waking from a nightmare to find reality worse.*

*Proof of my existence seemed suddenly reduced to little more than these endless lines and lines of ink, sent off into the blue with no sign you're reading them. For all the world as pointless as putting messages in bottles.*

*Should I tell you? I think I will. I actually pulled out the pistol from my bag, Lil, hefting it in my hand. Cocking it, captivated by the slick, neat mechanism, the innocuous dull snout of the bullet, the way that the slightest movement could alter everything, irrevocably.*

*I flicked off the safety catch.*

*Lil, I thought about ending it then and there, but it seems I am too much a coward and threw the gun away in disgust.*

*Proud of me yet, Lil?*

*I broke down, cried long and hard.*

*I cried for a father I never knew, a mother who gave me up, who never knew me, for the love I never had until I met you and for having that same love snatched away from me so abruptly. For the damned injustice of it all, for this endless rejection.*

*What can I have done to deserve it?*

*Am I self-absorbed? Perhaps. But I felt a whole lot better for it afterwards, for the sense of catharsis, much as I felt after crossing the Equator.*

*Like the air feels after a storm.*

*Lillian, I believe your dear Pa to be wrong. Grossly, criminally, morally wrong. Moreover, I have begun to resent both him for this imposition, your mother for her acquiescence and, dare I say it, you for toeing the line. Is 'resent' too strong a word?*

*Again, perhaps. I care not.*

*I'll not write as often as I have from now on. To do so only keeps emotions in flame when they should be subdued as embers that they might last the night.*

*Who do I write to? Are you even there? I sometimes wonder whether you even exist.*

*I was relieved of my mood by Maddox, the lovable fool, sensing my distress, perhaps, and demanding attention. I laughed, pushing him off me, to which he boldly retaliated, rollicking about like a loon, thus prompting a no-holds-barred wrestle, sand covering all, until I was breathless.*

*As we sat together, with the sun dipping to the west, a strange elation filled me, fiery and strong, and I smiled. More of an idiotic grin, in all likelihood, but to hell with it – I felt good.*

*I perceived the fey humour and merciless lack of compassion with which fate, God, whatever you want to call it, marks our lives. I appreciated, in a Damascene flash, that the minutiae of our pathetic little existences, the vanity of our puny endeavours and our fumbling attempts at ascribing meaning to the world matter not and come to naught. Things are as they are – often as not of our own volition, since we make our own choices, do we not? – and regret for what might have been is the profoundest indulgence, a futile waste of what little precious time we have on this earth, this frail promontory.*

*To hell with your father! I'm here for myself, of MY own volition, mine and mine alone.*

*My righteous indignation was interrupted by a low, serious rumble from Maddox, whose hackles were raised and ears cocked; I followed the line of his fixed stare, away to my right where the dune palms began, immediately reaching for the pistol in case a lion was nearby, but I could see nothing, and he ceased soon enough. Presently I decided to make a move for home.*

*As I stood to leave, I saw something that rooted me to the spot, dumbfounded:*

*Neatly carved into the trunk, to the side of the bole in which I'd just been sitting, were my initials:*

*R.J.T.*

*And carved recently by the look of it.*

*I looked about, my blood chilling, and struck by the thought that whoever had done it might still be watching me, and might have witnessed my moment of weakness. Whoever the joker was they were well hidden. Shaken up, I collected my belongings and scrambled down the dunes back to town.*

*Who on earth could have done it? I have told no one of my occasional sojourns there. Perhaps I myself did it in some state of daydream? I even inspected the blade of my knife for signs of recent use, but could not say for certain that this sap stain or that wood fragment could have been from this tree. Madness loomed momentarily, flashes of the accusations at sea returning. I took strength from that; I would be vindicated now as I was then. I calmed my breathing, rationalised my thoughts.*

*Since whoever did it anticipated my going there in advance, as soon as I reached the house I interrogated Salim, but no, he said he'd never been up there, though he knew of the tree I referred to (it is quite unmistakable; some consolation that, as a natural point of focus it is conceivable others might have the same inclination as I). Bloody odd. Disquieting in the extreme.*

*However I must be on good form for drinks tomorrow with the DC and for now push it from my mind.*

*Yours,*

*Ralph*

*P.S. I have managed somehow to lose the talisman given to me by Jim – possibly while ragging with Maddox. Damn it all. I feel somehow naked without it.*

*Christmas Eve, 1933*
*Lamu*

*Dearest Lillian,*

*Happy Christmas.*

*Utterly impossible to imagine the festive season – the pomp, ceremony, jollity, snow and darkening evenings – from here, where the unremitting heat, sights, smells and sounds and the echoes of the muezzin shatter any attempt to think of home as a pebble shatters reflections in a millpond.*

*I have been asked over to the DC – Clives' place – for Christmas lunch tomorrow – very kind of them, I'm sure, but I remain sceptical about these attempts to recreate the trappings of home wherever we go; wholly ludicrous if you ask me. Obviously I shall attend the service in the rather shabby Anglican chapel towards the back of the village (I ain't gone completely heathen yet), where we will no doubt swelter under the tin roof and raise our few voices to heaven, but the idea of sitting down to mince pies and the like seems an anathema. Hopefully – and if the other night was anything to go by, in all likelihood – he will lay on enough drink to distract me from my nostalgia. (On reflection, nostalgia is the wrong word since I was never particularly happy in England in the first place. From my apostasy then. My melancholia.)*

*The drinks were enjoyable, and not just because as my first social engagement in over a month Christ knows anything would have been. I met some interesting people. Sorry – an interesting person.*

*I arrived at the DC's residence – a sprawling bungalow amid extensive gardens further along the shore from the ginnery towards Shela – bang on seven, spit'n'polished, hair slicked and necktie closing around my throat like a constrictor (it has been a while), the sun, duty performed for another day, dragging the night behind it as it retreated off stage to the applause of cicada and the drop of a cerulean curtain.*

*The door was opened by an immaculately liveried houseboy in a white tunic and a neat red fez who led me through the hall and out to a veranda where half a dozen whites, an Arabic gent and a couple of Africans stood around chatting. I was met by Clive, a head shorter than I with a clipped manner that suggested the brisk mores of a disciplinarian. I was glad I'd bothered with the tie. He made a few polite enquiries after my health, how I was settling in etc. then introduced me to the assembled guests: Mr and Mrs Owen, sturdy, red-faced Welsh cattle ranchers from the highlands here for some r and r – well-earned by the sounds of it; Revd. Nyeri, whose thankless task it is to spread God's word amongst the local populace; Tim Barton, vacationing up from Mombasa where he is employed in a similar capacity to mine but in the coffee trade; Captain Stewart and his first officer Briggs, ashore from the Bristol-registered steamer that came into port a couple of days ago.*

*From the Owens I gleaned news of Jim; apparently the 'natives are restless' up country, and Jim has been called upon to 'help muffle the drums.' I'm quite sure he's up to whatever diplomatic task he's given.*

*From Stewart, news of the Apollonia; safely returned home for a refit.*

*I was comparing notes with Barton – a good egg, we've much in common – when Mrs Clive joined us; prim and pinched, with a fixed smile that didn't quite reach her eyes and a way of cocking her head when listening to me that belied her interest in what I was saying, she seemed perfectly pleasant, but I could tell she was monitoring all the conversations taking place simultaneously, a trick that women seem to manage but of which I am incapable. She asked me whether I found a beard uncomfortable in this heat in a way I knew meant she disapproved.*

*I was just replying that I found it provided some protection from the equatorial sun on my face when a man's voice spoke behind me, resonant and heavily accented in what I took to be French:*

*'The negligible impracticalities of maintaining the things notwithstanding, Mrs Clive,' he said, 'I find our Moslem brothers markedly more congenial to those of us sporting them. Do you not agree, Monsieur Talbot?'*

*I turned to meet the steady gaze of the man I had taken to be Arabic; in his fifties, I guessed, smiling at me and extending a hand.*

*'Ralph Talbot,' said Mrs Clive, 'may I introduce Monsieur Maurice Foules, our resident Bohemian' – she pronounced the word with audible distaste – 'and longest-serving Lamu adoptee.'*

*Dressed splendidly in a long, loose-sleeved burgundy kaftan trimmed with gold and sashed at the waist, pantaloons and kofia, he shook my hand firmly, his cool hand strong. Most striking of all was his neatly combed grey beard, which reached his sternum. Tanned and weathered, with a strong Roman nose, were it not for his eyes, a sharp blue, he could have easily passed for a Moslem.*

*'Wrong on both counts, Madam,' he smiled. 'Bohemian? Such a misemployed term,' – he gave a soft laugh – 'usually by those who feel confined by the restrictions of their own ideology' – I felt her bristle beside me – 'or threatened by those of others. As neither originating from Bohemia nor born a bohemian gypsy, despite my parents' humble origins in Geneva, I tend to prefer the term Epicurean, if I am to be classified beyond mere homo sapiens, and as such am delighted by your hospitality.' He raised his glass to his now flustered hostess who gave a little tight-lipped twitch of her head, pretended to catch someone else's attention and moved away.*

*'And on the other?' I asked.*

*'Ah, adoptee? Well, I'm being deliberately pedantic, but perhaps "refugee" is more apt.'*

*I twigged who he was suddenly. Foules; I'd heard about him. The only surviving member of the Freelanders, of whom Toby had spoken. He gazed out across the darkened sea, as did I, then – he must have been regarding me sidelong – said, '1894.' He paused, 'In answer to your next question.'*

*Momentarily baffled, I realised I had been about to ask him when he first arrived here. I laughed. Was it arrogant of him to assume I would have heard about him, or simple logic that in such a small community the antics of the Freelanders would have gone down in local history?*

*'You take all the fun out of conversation,' I said. 'Whatever shall I ask you next?'*

*'If I were you,' he said with a sly smile, 'I'd ask why the movement failed, why I stayed on and how I lasted so long here without going stark raving mad. Come,' he said, bidding me follow him to the edge of the veranda. Glad of the opportunity to escape the rest of the company, and already intrigued, I walked with him. The sky was now a luminous indigo at the horizon, graded to black above*

*us, and the waves flattened themselves up the beach below in long exhalations. We sat on the low wall, looking out to where stars met water.*

*'Beautiful, n'est ce pas?'*

*'Very. Please continue,' I said.*

*'Let's see. Briefly? I don't know what you have heard, though I can imagine. The movement failed for a variety of reasons, primarily bad planning – or the total absence of it. We were all so young, hopelessly idealistic – deliberately so; since Utopian philosophy must by definition be based upon the pursuit of the untenable – and we thought ourselves immortal, immutable, beyond the restraints and conventions of society. However, society develops rules for a reason, for its survival and propagation. Without rules, in a state of pure anarchy, the outcome becomes difficult to foresee. Then again, perhaps it didn't fail. I am still here, after all.' I could see his eyes gleaming in the house lights.*

*'What of the others?' I asked. 'If you don't mind talking about it.'*

*'Not at all. They all quit, whether life here or life itself. Pouf! Some returned to Europe, some established themselves in the Italian Alps, so I hear, where the challenges are less, ah, gruelling, and where they are flourishing by all accounts in a principality called Damanhur. Some are still here, at peace amongst the dunes, where their memories live on in the stories you have no doubt heard something of. For a brief moment it nearly worked. It did work. We were happy, fulfilled, close in a way no family ever could be. Liberated from guilt, from regret, from doubt, from blame. We were God's children seeking to return to Eden, and we found it, or so we thought, momentarily. But we had forgotten why He threw us out in the first place! Soon enough we were reminded, soon enough the cracks began appearing in the veneer. Do you know what*

*the single most destructive emotion, the most dangerous state of mind that human beings are capable of, is?'*

*'Hatred?' I volunteered.*

*'Non,' he wagged a finger at me. 'Jealousy. One man's envy of what another has. Envy is the fuel, the kerosene, for hatred. Beyond the actions of a drunkard, beyond the lunacy of madness and drugs, at the source of all torment and anguish on earth and the cause of all wars, lies envy, green eyes glittering in the caves of our souls. Most of the seven deadly sins you can get by with – they're an intrinsic part of any society – and we had more than our fair share of lust, lethargy, gluttony and pride, believe you me.' He laughed. 'But as soon as envy entered the equation our fate was sealed. It bred the anger.'*

*'In what way were you different?' I asked, slightly impetuously.*

*'Ha!' He laughed. 'Three things. Firstly and most importantly,' he raised an eyebrow – I shrugged, 'Luck, of course! Second. I never really wanted anything. I mean really wanted, craved for, hungered after something. So, alors, I envied no one for what they had, even though I was not from nearly as privileged a background as many of them. Perhaps because of it. My expectations were lower – all these blue-blooded madmen, it must be something to do with the small genetic pool from which they spring!' That laugh. Infectious.*

*'If you do mix together money, women, guns and alcohol, for God's sake don't then deliberately rewrite the moral rulebook. Say what you like about religious and political dogma, for all its flaws doctrine can provide an effective moral plumbline, a code of behaviour, even if its most vehement proponents often ignore it.'*

*'I had less to lose and, for me at least it was never anything more than an adventure. A very big adventure. Third, what really, how do you say, clinched it, was that I fell in love. Yes!' he almost shouted, clapping his hands as he said it in ecstasy – I saw a couple of people*

*turn our way. 'Love saved me, without doubt.' He was grinning from ear to ear.*

*'With someone from your group?' I said.*

*'No, you fool,' he said, bursting into a fit of giggles, 'With Lamu, with Lamu!' This time he did shout and, raising his hands in the air, tipping back his head and saluting the night, he did a little jig with his hands.*

*The man's off his rocker, Lil, of that I have no doubt, but there was something about him, a kind of childish playfulness, a happiness that drew me to him like the moths that spiralled around the veranda candles. He doesn't care a fig what anyone thinks, which is a refreshing trait out here, let me tell you.*

*'Ah,' he sighed contentedly. 'I was well clear by the end. Saw it coming a mile off. By that time there had already been a few, erm, incidents. Despite our attempts at egalitarianism, that anyone was free to do as they wished so long as no one was harmed in any way, emotionally or physically, the reality of the situation was that we were in someone else's country, a country where the rules are strict. Islam is not the most liberal of religions, and Allah demands a degree of abstemiousness, modesty and restraint we fell spectacularly short of. Mon Dieu! We were crazy – drunk on liberty, unchecked, at play in the fields of the Lord!' He shook his head in wonder.*

*'At first we were treated with respect, given some land and left to our own devices. This was good. For a while. But the levels of egotism among some of the group, ay, ay, ay.' He shook his head again. 'Triggered by envy, don't misunderstand me, but, inevitably, pride followed and schisms developed. Not content with the few fine women we had amongst us and whom we held as equals, whom some of us revered, "forays" were made into the immediate community. Certain members' – he paused at his own pun – 'required the expression of their sexual domination, their virility,*

*which can be a problem when the only available women are sexually equal and willing to give it. The chasseur, the hunter, is made impotent, n'est-ce pas?'*

*'There were unfortunate repercussions. The duels became something of a spectator event out in the dunes, there were a couple of fatalities among the locals, and eventually the community had enough. Citing alcohol as the precipitating reason, things came to – how do you say it? – a head.' He sighed.*

*'But enough! I am keeping you from meeting other guests, all more interesting than I.' I swear he winked at me, though it was difficult to be sure in the dim light. 'Let's rejoin our hosts. If you're not yet bored, please feel free to visit me whenever you like and we can continue our little chat.' With that he clapped an arm around my shoulder and we walked back to the vapid small talk on offer, pleasantries passed around like stale canapés.*

*What I find remarkable, Lil, is that, for someone who has had such a spectacularly colourful past he seems utterly lacking in conceit. Indeed the opposite; down to earth, honest and frank, if barking mad at a superficial level. Would I emerge from such a scenario, where 'anything goes' and anything clearly went, as composed, mentally, as he? As compos mentis? I seriously doubt it. I am having enough trouble hanging onto the precepts of all I was taught to be right and good and true, all of which seems completely irrelevant out here. I suspect his approach bears more validity. Total immersion. Rejection of the rules of law intended to serve a foreign, distant society, a different world; adoption of those with which you find yourself surrounded. If one has the strength of mind to adapt to your immediate environment, to wholly take it on as Foules appears to have done, then might not life's oyster split open before you to reveal – perhaps – a pearl of contentment?*

*Later, on my way home through the clattering palms, I realised what it was that had so struck me about him: he's happy. I assumed him off kilter simply because in my limited time on this ravaged earth, amongst its shell-shocked cast, I have yet to encounter anyone so content and failed to recognise it. Now that I have, I see that Whitson, Clive et al are by contrast not so blessed; futilely hammering the round-pegged reality of being here into the decidedly square hole of what they have left behind. Jim, despite his inner restlessness, possesses a similar jocularity and, though too scarred by the war to be what I could call joyful, has a phlegmatic serenity, a tranquil acceptance of things as they are.*

*I left with a smile, my concerns about you for once allayed. Be happy for me, for although you are temporarily relegated in my thoughts, for the briefest of moments I feel a soar of spirits, freedom from the weight of my responsibilities, that the worst is over, positive in outlook and with a swelling heart that we will be reunited in due course.*

*I hope you have (had?) a truly lovely Christmas,*

*Ralph*

*x*

*P.S. Yesterday I returned to the baobab in search of Jim's pendant, somewhat nervous of what else I might find etched into its trunk (there was nothing more). I did not find the charm, despite Maddox's vigorous digging and the quizzical looks he gives me, head tipped to one side, as if it is I who requires a leash.*

# Chapter 18

*Chichén Itzá, Mexico. 2003.*

The guide, a young Mexican dude with a ponytail and wrap-around sunglasses, continued with the tired, well-rehearsed drawl of a school teacher, his monotone somehow rendering riveting information dull:

'The Mayans succeeded in an almost impossible mission with the completion of their structures at Chichén Itzá. Built around AD 800, the Pyramid of Kukulkan is a poetic combination of form, style, function, religion, philosophy, mathematics and geometry; a true union of all of their intelligence and art in one location.'

'By far the most impressive aspect of the Pyramid is its relationship with the sun and how it reflects the equinoxes and solstices of our solar year with astonishing accuracy.' He paused, making sure a blonde chick in a tight pink tank top was paying attention. 'Before one can fully understand the workings of the Shadow of the Equinox, a few basics on astronomy need to be reviewed. An equinox occurs twice each year when the length of the daylight and evening hours is equal. The spring equinox occurs on March 21st. Today, *señores y señoras*.'

Murmurs stirred the crowd like wind on corn.

'Six months later, on September 22nd, we have the fall equinox. The summer solstice occurs on June 21st. On this day, earth sees the longest duration of daylight. Six months later is the winter solstice on December 22nd, when we see the shortest daylight and the longest night of the year. On these days the sun almost seems to pause in its orbit, directly above the temple, before resuming its course, which is why the word solstice is based on the Latin *sol*, for "sun", and *sistere*, "to cause to stand". This cycle then repeats itself as the Earth continues to rotate around the sun. It is interesting to note that there are exactly 91 days between each of these events, and 92 days between the June 21st summer solstice and the September 21st equinox. This adds up to the 365-day solar year, first developed by the Mayans, with the 91 days between each event matching the 91 steps to each side of the pyramid. There are four staircases of 91 steps, which makes 364 steps in total. Add the top platform and you have 365.'

He waited, checked his watch. It was nearly time.

'Coincidence? No. For the Mayans there were no coincidences, as what you are about to see demonstrates. Now, if you would all care to watch El Castillo carefully, you will witness the annual rebirth of the Mayan god, Quetzalcoatl, or Plumed Serpent.'

Aidan Tanner moved away from the group, out of range of the guide, to where the ground rose slightly and he had a clear view of the ancient pyramid of Kukulkan where it squatted massive and time worn against the forest, and he could see over the crowd of tourists already snapping away before it. The new devotees, he thought; hands raised towards the temple much as the original architects must have done centuries ago, just with cameras instead of offerings. A group of New Age types formed a circle and struck up with drums and didgeridoos, the deep reverberations undertowing their chanting and clapping, white robes and long hair blowing gently in the breeze.

From where he stood, some fifty metres off the north-western corner, he had a perfect view of the western face, brightly lit by the afternoon sun, and that of the north, currently deep in shadow.

A gasp rippled through the gathered crowd, a collective sigh, as a sliver of sunlight spilt over the western face to illuminate the top of the north-facing staircase, the stepped edge of the pyramid casting the light as a triangle. Then another, and another, down the steps until an undulating diagonal of serrated light reached all the way from top to bottom. Finally, in a spectacular denouement, the sun hit the huge stone snakehead – gape-mouthed and fierce-eyed with a collar of flowing feathers – at the foot of the stairs, and the writhing serpent of light was complete.

The chanting reached a crescendo, camera auto-winds whirred, people cheered and clapped. The echoes of handclaps off the Pyramid – he had heard the guide explain earlier – precisely imitates the clipped chirp of the Quetzal, a brightly feathered bird revered for its plumage and regarded as the emissary of the gods. Were the steps any other dimension, any other depth, the acoustics would be completely different. Coincidence again? Aidan felt goose-bumps ripple across his forearms.

The effect lasted only a few minutes and, still jittery from the mild panic attack he'd suffered in the close, airless inner chamber half an hour earlier, he found himself keen to escape the claustrophobia of the crowd. Still running through the calming techniques he himself once used on his patients – concentrating on his breathing, focusing on the beauty around him, disassociating from thoughts as if they were carried in and out by waves on a beach – he angled off around the complex, impressed at how such ostensibly simple use of space could belie such extraordinary subtlety in their architectural alignments to the heavens. They'd understood the precision of the universe and the movement of the heavens in a way until recently lost to modern man, and much of their knowledge remained obscure. While the masons of the Middle Ages certainly achieved superlative heights with their cathedrals, encompassing similar sacred geometric principles, their architectural engineering was understood, their construction explicable. The megalithic blocks of masonry that made up the monumental Meso-American architecture were by contrast often impossibly heavy, far too heavy for any conceivable lifting technology at the time.

Even with the most up-to-date modern engineering technology, attempts to recreate some of the structures had failed. As with their Egyptian cousins; the 1,000-ton Stone of the South at Baalbek in Lebanon; the dead-straight, eight-mile lines in the Nazca desert; Stonehenge in Britain; the submerged pyramids off Japan's coast in Yonagunino – the list, he knew, went on – no one had yet come up with a plausible explanation of how any of it might have been done. Unlike the rectangular blocks in Egypt which at least were clearly cut, there were Mayan structures with 100-ton blocks that were organic in shape, irregular, with not a straight line or cutting-tool mark in sight, yet perfectly fitted together so perfectly you couldn't slide a razor between them.

As if *moulded.*

Obliquely southwest from the pyramid rose the Warrior Temple, at the summit of which reclined the leering figure of Chac Mool, a grotesque altar on whose belly the still beating hearts of sacrificial victims were laid. He cast only a cursory glance over it, as he did El Gran Juego de Pelota, the Great

Ballcourt where contestants had to – somehow – knock balls through concrete hoops twenty feet up on the court's sidewalls without using their hands or feet. The incentive to win must have been compelling, since members of the losing team were decapitated. He tried to imagine the half-time pep talk.

Feeling inexplicably nauseous and seeking refuge from the tourist mill, he made his way down the ceremonial causeway to the Sacred Cenote, a deep, fifty-metre diameter limestone sinkhole with sheer-sided cliffs and thick, algae-jaded water below, long a place of pilgrimage in the Yucatán. Finding a shady spot off the path, he sat on the lip of the precipice and gazed down into the green water between his dangled feet, the ripple-less surface creating an imperfect mirror-world below, murky and Hadean.

His travel plans and itinerary, drawn up hastily over half a bottle of Jameson, had already begun to show signs of not fitting the bill, whatever that was. The requirement at the time – only a few weeks ago, though it felt much longer – had been straightforward enough: to provide some purpose, some direction to the extended break he was taking, distraction from everything that had happened. A 'sabbatical' – he could see the quotes hanging around the word like the raised eyebrows in the staff room – he'd been told, in no uncertain terms, he *had* to take. Dr Griffiths, one of the senior partners at the clinic, had called him into his office, sat him down and peered at him over half-moon specs and steepled hands.

'Aidan, I'll get to the point. I and a few of the others here are worried that your, ah . . .' he searched for the right word, 'professionalism, your judgement, may have been somewhat clouded – *compromised* – by what happened with young, ah, what was his name?'

'Kai.' Detached sonofabitch, he thought. Griffiths wasn't

someone to get emotionally involved, his professionalism wouldn't ever – couldn't ever – be compromised. To him, every patient was just another specimen in a bell jar, to be dissected, prodded and poked – observed, just as he's observing me now.

Aidan resisted a sudden urge to turn the desk upside-down, straddle the bastard, seize two pencils and drive them hard into those beady, blinking eyes, and tried to stop his left knee from bouncing by staring at it, willing it steady. His knee slowed to an indiscernible tremor.

'Yes, Kai. Most unfortunate. But we can't let these things get to us or we'd lose our objectivity, the perspective that enables us to appreciate all the psyche's many facets in the first place, mm? You see what I'm saying?' Stabbing pencils. 'Aidan, are you listening to me?'

He did see, of course he did. A cool, objective part of him knew he was losing it, the rational part that knew he'd done his best for the kid and understood that luck happens. Luck happens all the time. It was the central tenet for much of his positive psychology approach; that life hurts much of the time, that if it doesn't, you're not living. Deal with it, learn from it, detach and move on. That the victimisation, responsibility-deferral, entitlement and blame-apportioning that comes with Freudian and almost all clinical psychology, by endlessly focussing on the cause of the problem not the solution, entraps people in their mental prison of suffering while maintaining a steady income for the therapists. That life can also be miraculous and wonderful, if you choose to see it as such. That it's all just a matter of perception. He also knew that psychotherapy, of whatever discipline, was demonstrably catalytic, at best, and that the single most effective solution to a patient's problems lay within themselves.

'Sounds like you've got a problem, kiddo.' He'd said, after listening to Kai's litany of grievance.

'Damn straight, Doc. Mom's a slut and Dad, well, he ain't Dad.'

'No. It sounds like *you've* got a problem.' He needed to shake the kid up a bit, think of something to snap him out of his self-pity. Kai had thought about that one for a while, letting the implication settle, chewing his bottom lip in silence.

He broke it.

'Do you think they don't love you, Kai?'

'No. I know they love me, in their own way.'

'Good. Then you need to understand one thing immediately – beyond the nature and nurture of your upbringing, the biochemistry of your brain and the sociology of your environment, there is a *you* in you that no one put there, one that makes choices every second of every day. At the moment, you're making the choice to hate them, because the frightened part of you wants to feel aggrieved, wants to lash out, wants to blame someone or something for everything that's wrong in your life. You can just as easily shift that perspective, choose to understand why they did what they did, forgive them, and get on with writing your own story. Everyone has flaws, everyone makes mistakes and everyone deserves to be forgiven for them. Do you understand?'

They had made some progress that day.

Not enough, though.

However, the irrational, emotional – *human* – part of him that couldn't accept what had happened kept on gnawing its fist, picking off the scab, cycling through how it might have been different if this or that had been said or done, if he'd listened with his heart instead of his head, if he'd been there when the call came through; endless 'what ifs' that stalked the edge of his sanity.

Although he couldn't yet bring himself to look in the mirror, he knew from people's expressions that he looked like shit – unshaven, sallow skinned, shadow-ringed eyes – and that he probably stank of stale Scotch. Not fit for duty, that much was clear. The irony of being a sick physician hadn't escaped him either. He began to understand some of what his patients went through. Perhaps this would make him a better consultant, he thought wryly. Other than the Scotch, he needed to get off the Xanax as quickly as possible. Shit, he knew the side effects of neuro-pharmacology better than most. Griffiths was still talking:

'I – we all – think it would be a good idea if you took some time off. Take as long as you like, recharge the batteries, take a step back from it all.' He breathed laboriously – Aidan willed him to reach for his Ventolin – as he wiped his misty glasses slowly. 'What do you say?'

He'd agreed readily. Not that he'd had a choice but because he was so sick of it all, of Boulder's smug, corduroy-jacketed liberalism, the hypocrisy of left-leaning environmentalism and SUV yuppiedom, the manicured tulip beds of Pearl Street, the 'My Karma ran over your Dogma' and 'Are you Sirius?' bumper stickers, the slightly forced attitude everyone had that implied that if we all discussed our problems in a sensible, open and honest way, everything would miraculously turn out all right, or the let-it-all-out, heart-on-sleeve primal whimpering that rewarded mental implosion with a 'There, there, feeling a little better now?' and a cup of green tea, as if all psychosis was just the result of itsy-bitsy repressions needing expression. Well, he thought grimly, Kai had certainly fucking expressed it. And he,

Dr Aidan Tanner, star in the ascendant, had failed, scorched through the atmosphere and burned up.

Frazzled.

Ignoring the commiserations of his colleagues, he'd cleared his desk and walked out into the crystalline morning, his breath hanging in the still air, the winter-stiffened grass rimed in ice, brittle and precise, and crunched to his car. As the engine warmed up he watched the fern-like spirals of frost on the windscreen unravel, the delicate centres slowly unfurling like fractal formation in reverse. He drove out of town, parked and walked up the trail through the naked forest, crossing oily streams with sharp, splintered collars, stalactitic icicles and waterfalls frozen solid as if time had been momentarily stopped while he walked past, lost in the creak and squeak of the ground underfoot.

Climbing all the while, he emerged at a rocky outcrop high above the town and sat down, out of breath, on the edge of a precipitous drop. Sure it crossed his mind, but only in the way it does everyone who's been pulled, entranced, to the edge; *hypothetically*. Picturing the funeral. Self-indulgently, he thought.

From where he sat he could make out the skyscrapers of Denver on the gently taut, pastel-tinted horizon, the glint of sunlight off glass. Below him Boulder went about its day, oblivious. His hands began to stiffen and he stuffed them under his armpits. He sat there long after his body began to freeze, welcoming the numbing sensation and the implied creep of death. He turned his head to his left. Fifty yards away a large buck watched him with unblinking, liquid eyes. They stared at each other for minutes, hours, seconds, his vision telescoping down until the deer was all he could see, framed by a halo of wintery light and panted breath. Then, with a derisive snort, it was gone. He needed to leave too. Creaking stiffly to his feet he nearly toppled over the edge. Imagining the headlines and common-room commentary made him laugh out loud.

He'd already been treating Kai's father – well, father figure, Mike – who, teetering towards the end of the Twelve Steps, needed as much help as he could to get through the often shocking reintroduction to iron-cold reality. Without the embalming anaesthetic of alcohol, he'd found it difficult distilling the stark vividness of day-to-day mundanity, the disappointment of life, down into manageable sips. Usually he'd reach for a bottle when things went well, or badly, or for a first thing in the morning hair-of-the-dog, or to get psyched up before a gig, or if it was cold or because it was summer, or, on those rare occasions having made it through the morning without finding an excuse, when the clock hit twelve. Or eleven.

For Mike, a big part of moving on involved letting go of his dream, the all-or-nothing dream of making it big-time as a musician, while at the same time not denying his gift. The step-change down to accepting the odd session, the odd gig in The Tavern once a month, teaching recalcitrant, untalented kids, had been a difficult pill to swallow, and Aidan had done his best to help him honey the teaspoon. The guy had been under the gun a little at the time, probably a good thing; the long-awaited reconciliation with his estranged wife and two boys looming and his desperation to make it work sure had been good motivation.

Then the shit had hit the fan.

Turned out only the eldest was his, though why she – the wife – had to drop that particular bombshell just at the moment Mike was pulling himself out over the brink of the pit he couldn't figure. Kicked him *right* back into it. He shook his head; was there ever a 'right time'? Probably not, but the fallout had been spectacular; Mike, after a week-long bender that hospitalised him, took it none too bad. Perhaps he had a genetic inkling, some intuition that his paternal blueprints didn't quite map the territory accurately enough, but, after a week or so systematically taking the wheels off the wagon, he'd turned up at the clinic of his own volition, checked in and pulled himself back from the edge all over again, all of them getting together for a few tearful but purgative family group sessions.

All of them except Kai, that is.

He refused to come, point blank. He hadn't taken it well at all, poor kid, turning it into an excuse to derail comprehensively. Christ, who wouldn't find it tough? He tried to imagine how he'd handle it, but couldn't. His home birth, boho upbringing in Baja in a tight community with endless support mechanisms had he needed them, open armed, hug-aholic folks and wide open country precluded any childhood trauma scapegoats. No excuses.

In session – a bail condition – Kai maintained an impressively resilient silence for weeks; he'd sit there, staring at his feet, bleached hair more severely cut each time, clothing darkening by shades each week as his shadow grew, the rage tangible, until the hour was up. Beyond the confines of the clinic he'd torched the world. The touch-paper had always been there, from what Aidan could gather, but this had provided the match he then struck, grinning at the phosphorous glow, and flicked. Fights at school, drink, dope-dealing, vandalism to begin with; then once he'd been kicked out, upgrading to Benzedrine, and God help us, Ritalin – which, like twenty-five percent of the nation's youth, he'd been prescribed. Aidan marvelled at a society that slaps a kid exhibiting the slightest behavioural quirk, usually a result of boredom, on an addictive amphetamine. Then meth, aggravated assault, auto theft, possession with intent; the charge sheet had lengthened over the months. He was rapidly running out of time; once he hit sixteen and was no longer classified as a minor, the odds on him staying out of jail shortened spectacularly.

'Aidan, I'm terrified that if this doesn't work, nothing will. Please – please, will you . . .' The plea went unfinished; there were no words to express her fear. His mom, Nina – pretty, very pretty, despite the worry lines – sobbed then sniffed, straightened and pulled herself together, her voice hardening, impressing Aidan with her strength.

'He's been given his last warning by the Sheriff's department,' she said. Thank God they had a good lawyer.

'You've made the first step bringing him here.' They both looked through the blinds of his office to where Kai sat, impassive, blank, his full lips and slightly heavy features lending themselves to a natural petulance.

'It's exactly why we're here, exactly what we're here for. We deal with cases just like Kai's all the time. For a start we'll get him off the drink and drugs. After that, with a bit of luck and patience, everything else should follow. In the meantime try not to worry, he's perfectly safe here, in good hands, and I'll make him my personal responsibility.' He tried to smile reassuringly; some premonition had prevented it reaching his eyes, though, even then. She hadn't noticed; straw-clutching, praying, seeing only glimmers of hope.

He reached into his daypack and pulled out the envelope, withdrew the letter and tipped the pen into his hand, rolling it in the dappled light. The writing was almost scored into the paper,

*Where the hell are you, Doc? And your cell's off. Gone fishing for the weekend? Well, here's one that got away. Tell Mom what you like, tell her everything I told you if you want. I sure don't give a fuck about confidentiality anymore, wouldn't you say?*

*Thanks for your time and effort.*
*Sorry to let you down.*
*Fuck you.*
*Kai*

*ps. here's the pen I told you about, the one she screwed that guy for in Ibiza – the time I walked in on them – then gave to 'Dad' for his birthday. Sure gotta hand it to her. Maybe you can use it for those endless fucking notes you take.*

Afterwards, he'd been so shocked, so freaked out by events and what he took as his professional dereliction, he'd neglected to mention either the note or the pen to Nina. Or at the inquest. More than enough to get him struck off.

At first a trip around the region's numerous beauty spots and monuments had seemed an ideal option. Starting in Mexico, daily baptism in the turquoise ocean, immersion in the mystery and magic, the hocus-pocus strangeness of an ancient culture, all should have been the perfect distraction from the constraints of his profession, the cold logic of the tried and tested formulae with which he was supposed to crack open his patient's heads. He hoped that some insight into how these enigmatic people achieved such feats of astrological perspicacity, architectural genius and societal advancement when Europe was emerging, blinking, from the Dark Ages might rekindle some sense of wonder in his soul, currently stifled by his bleak realisation that therapy was increasingly just a matter of keeping a lid on a boiling pot; that the values presented as sane, normal and acceptable – violence is fun to watch, cheat on your spouse, pretend you are wealthy, compete with your neighbours, follow fashion obsessively, material wealth equals self esteem, show obedience to authority over screaming common sense – are themselves symptoms of psychosis.

That the side effects of the anti-depressants he prescribed included, amongst other things, 'suicidal thoughts and behaviour'.

That the world's poor were starving while the rest, trying to look thin, were obese and taking drugs to lose weight.

That fifty percent of Americans, who are perceived as possessing all they could want, everything they could possibly desire, were on anti-depressants or painkillers or some form of psychoactive medication.

That the country with the most nukes had the highest incidence of mental illness, murder, judicial execution and state incarceration.

That the world had gone mad.

What he had discovered so far, however, was that while they – the Olmecs, Mayans and Toltecs in particular, Aztecs to a lesser degree – were indeed exceptionally 'out there', with their claimed Pleiadian stellar genealogy, their incredibly precise calendar, and their ultimate inexplicable disappearance as if anticipating the arrival of the Spanish, in the end as far as he could make out, they were simply a mirror of what he was trying to escape.

Slaves to gods gone mad, they appeared to have lost sight of what was beautiful and pure in the world and, ripping themselves apart trying to rediscover it, had unleashed hell. Or rather, he thought, through the indolence, hedonism and profligacy of evolutionary 'success', they had enslaved their gods, corrupted their doctrine and exploited their religion in order to secure their dominance, justify their murderous barbarity; the path skipped down merrily by every civilisation the long-suffering world has endured. Then the Spanish had arrived and fucked them off the edge of the planet.

*Unfit* to survive, after all.

Whatever the cause, the end result was their destruction; a pattern repeated, according to their mythology, five times. What really screwed with his head was the imminence of the next predicted Fall, the date when, apparently, the Mayan Calendar comes to an end – what they called End Time: 21st December 2012.

He could easily, if not believe it, at least consider it possible just from reading the papers or watching CNN's grotesque platforming of the latest round of weapons testing; or the crusading mayhem and slaughter in the Middle East; or from the world weather report – the firestorms, floods, droughts and famines. It made sense. It felt possible; there was a tangible quickening of events, as if the world's spin was picking up, matched by an exponential increase in ecological destruction. He could feel sociological debasement happening around him – hell, he was on the front line of it, witnessing a growing obsession with the corporeal, the carnal, the base, the sullying of purity and innocence; he could see it in the parade of walking dead at rush hour, on TV. He could see it in the faces of people he passed on the street, like their features had been scratched out. Everyone looked misshapen, freakish, ugly, unnatural. All he could see were bloated pig people stuffing the world into their gaping maws, a spreading herd of mindless consumers, eating, belching, fucking and shitting. Wallowing in their own mire.

He slotted another Xanax.

He'd hung out on the coast at first but, unable to lie on a

beach longer than a few minutes without finger-drumming at the best of times, had soon headed inland. Listening to the hippy hokum and pseudo-scientific theories that pin-balled around the cafés and *chiringitos* of Cancun had deepened his despondency. He knew the territory from some of the New Age lectures and seminars back in Colorado, which, although dressed up in more semantic formality, covered similar ground. So what if the 'end' might not be terminal but 'transformational', a shift in humanity's group consciousness? So what if it was purely a matter of Gaia rebalancing herself, rapping our rapacious knuckles and carrying out a little pruning? He didn't want to hear it. While he appreciated the seductive trivialising quality these apocalyptic predictions had on the implied absolution of personal responsibility, how one's own problems conveniently paled to insignificance, just at the moment it was the last thing he needed. He'd seen too much, had become too cynical and needed his faith in humanity restored, not his despair in its future or his revulsion at its acquiescence reinforced. Whether or not it meant 'issue denial', he didn't care. He needed to get further afield, he needed to find beauty, peace, escape. Flowers. Central America still smelt faintly coppery, still had a hint of blood on the air, and his past still trailed behind him unshakably like a whining dog.

He wanted to run, flee, to outrun his demons. Besides, he figured half of running away from something is by definition running towards something else, whatever it might be. Something else. Journey-not-destination theory.

There was a deeper malaise. One he similarly shrank from. Extended insight and overexposure to the damage that people wrought upon those they loved most, including themselves, had honed his cynicism down to a fine blade with which he dissected his own relationships. An occupational hazard. Like gynaecologists who, unable to associate pussy with anything other than disease, go off sex, he found himself incapable of genuine emotional expression. Terrified of exposing himself to the lachrymose pain he witnessed daily, he never returned post-date calls, cited work as a reason to go home immediately after perfunctory coital interaction, and resisted attempts by the few close friends he had to set him up with women.

Whether the girls he met really didn't meet his expectations – he seriously doubted that any of them would have shown interest were he not so 'successful'; hey, maybe now he'd fucked it all up he'd actually meet someone who saw him for what he was, he thought darkly – or whether he projected his own preconceptions onto them, deliberately sabotaging, seeking out flaws, recoiling at the way they sipped coffee, answered their cells or smacked their freshly sticked lips, the end result was the same. He was alone.

Swinging his feet back from the drop, he spun on his ass and stood up to leave. Hearing a high keen, he squinted up until he at last made out a condor, turning effortlessly on unseen thermals far above, a speck against the clear blue sky.

To his surprise, when he looked down again, retinas slightly seared, there was a withered Indian standing in front of him, indeterminately old, wrinkled and creased, gnarly with age but with a bright shine in recessed eyes shadowed by the brim of a beaten-up straw hat. He wore a thin cotton shirt and trousers, well-worn sandals and a leather bag over one shoulder.

'You have something for me, *señor*,' he said, more statement than request. The man extended a bony hand.

'Yeah, sure.' he sighed and looked around, wondering why the old bastard had decided to hit on him and not any of the genetically ingenuous, gum-chewing, Nike-wearing, squat-souled waddlers with fanny packs and maps. He had, naively evidently, thought himself distinct from the herd, that his old chinos, linen shirt, scuffed boots and stubble protected him from tour touts, hotel reps and hawkers, that he was unnoticeable, as insubstantial as he felt in this heat. He sure as hell didn't *feel* approachable, and anyone looking him in the eyes would have backed off immediately. As far as this guy was concerned he was obviously just another gringo with cash. He fingered his pocket for his wallet then stopped, on a whim pulling out the pen from his shouldered bag and placing it in the old man's palm.

'*Aqui amigo*. For you.'

The man turned it over in his fingers, admiring the light playing upon it, small reflected beams dancing in his eyes and on the underside of the brim of his hat. He seemed to narrow his eyes as if in concentration and his lips began to move, though Aidan couldn't hear what he was saying. Aidan's vision narrowed, his nausea rose and sweat broke out across his brow. Stood up too quickly, he thought. He felt like he might faint.

'*Gracias señor*,' the old man said after a minute or so, placing the pen firmly back in his still outstretched hand, 'but you keep this. You need it.' Then he turned and walked away into the forest.

Aidan watched him go, perplexed, then shrugged and made his way back to the main temple complex to find some shade. As he wandered towards the car park and its attendant taxi mafia, he spotted a low timber visitor centre and ducked inside, mainly to get out of the cloying humidity and buy a soda.

Browsing the local information display – brochures and leaflets, well-thumbed books on the region and others to buy in plastic covers on the shelves – he came to the UNESCO section.

Chichén Itzá had, it transpired, been awarded World Heritage status in '98 and there were copies of the latest reports available for anyone interested. There was also a section on the aims of the organisation: 'to encourage the identification, protection and preservation of cultural and natural heritage around the world considered to be of outstanding value to humanity', with a list of the 830 locations currently deemed by the committee to be of 'universal value'.

He smiled. He had his new itinerary. With this list, eyes closed and a pin, he'd cast himself into fate's turbulent charge.

# Chapter 19

*1st February, 1934*

*Lamu*

*Happy New Year, Lil, belated though the sentiment may be.*

*What is it? Three months already? It feels so much longer. And I no longer count the weeks, let alone the days. I even begin to wish it were longer. Sorry, angel – why, again, must I feel guilty? – but I'm starting to like it here. No, more than that; to love it.*

*Imagine. The irony. I have at last begun to feel at home.*

*Lillian, I tire of this, the futile correspondence, I mean. To whom do I write? I keep sending these damned letters off, but why?*

*I have set aside the entire day to try and recap the last six weeks but remain unconvinced as to the motive.*

*I can write anything I like, can I not, since you are not there, not real, not even reading this, in all likelihood. A dream! Without the 'proof', such as it is, of your photograph, I would easily assume you are a phantom and England a myth. A dream of companionship, of moments shared, of laughter stifled in low-lit sitting rooms, of the crackle of fire and the chink of teaspoons against porcelain. Of sunlight filtered through pale green beech, of rustling squirrels stashing nuts in autumn, of the brittle splinter of frosted ruts underfoot, of steamy cows beyond the ha-ha, of sunrise glancing through spider-webbed dawn dew, of crocuses and snowdrops and the velvet carpet of bluebells in oak woods vivid against the green, of cuckoos calling, the bleat of lost lambs, of thrusting foxgloves, of kicking through leaves, of point-to-points and gaping trout, of crows in the horse chestnuts and smoky pubs and Maypole ribbons. Of harvest festivals and gypsy fayres, cakes baked in the afternoon, of the love we made amongst the meadow grass, of your foot against mine beneath the dining table . . .*

*Of elsewhere. A dream.*

*Meanwhile, I am here, awake, swathed in this steamy tropical heat.*

*Wide awake.*

*Alive.*

*They hanged Kamau from the Company gates, a month ago now.*

*I don't care what he did – the allegations against him notwithstanding; petty theft. A trifle, even if true. The evidence was at best circumstantial, at worst the conjecture of the manager Mohammed, with whom he'd never seen eye to eye.*

*His body turned slowly as I entered beneath, as we all entered. His bloated, fly-blown face, the rictus grin of his split lips a grotesque parody of the smile he gave so freely while living, will haunt me to the end of my days.*

*Turning slowly around and around and around in the breeze.*

*Business as bloody usual.*

*Whitson stood there, switch in hand, and I, in this Noble Role I have assumed, was supposed to stand there with him, bolster his position, kow-tow. Christ help us. I can write no more. I retched, as I do now upon recalling the sight. My pathetic attempts at mustering some defence, some mercy for the poor man fell on deaf ears: 'Examples must be made!' the bastard said, blinking at me as if measuring my distress.*

*An example.*

*Well that at least was achieved. All else pales. I have avoided work and Whitson since. Several of the workers have deserted us, and the atmosphere is tangibly tense, ugly. Hell manifest, forged by man amid this paradise.*

*Well.*

*I should tell you about Christmas lunch at the Clive's, for it changed my outlook; lengthy, intolerably tedious, I had difficulty stifling my boredom, counting the seconds. Is that ungracious of me? I had hoped Maurice would be there but was disappointed. Whitson was, however, and I was disappointed further. He and I have had, what, five encounters in as many weeks, all work-based, brief and to the point; usually a point so pedantic that I suspected he was pulling my leg. He was not. The man is lost. Holding him up to Foules makes it clear as day; one alive, open-hearted and full of joie de vivre, the other clammed shut, beyond reach, dead of soul. I have nothing further to say about him or my position.*

*Tell your father what you like, I am beyond caring. If me turning out like Whitson or Clive is what your dear Pa is hoping for, I think he might be in for a surprise.*

*As might you be, my betrothed, my beloved, my dear.*

*I was angry then, a month ago. Deep down I could see it writhing like a serpent; an inner resentment at all of this, coiling and turning, blindly seeking respite from the offence of my situation, an outlet. But I became aware of it, recognised it and therefore could turn it, nudging it towards escape from an echoing well of expectation. And it was only the expectations of others – yours, your father's, the Company's – that created my conflict.*

*I can tell you now; I shall not meet them.*

*The job had become a sham; I felt no sense of duty nor patriotism*

*– quite the reverse. I had begun to despise the bloody Empire and anyone or anything to do with it. Ha! Treason!*

*But – and here's the rub – beyond the walls of that office, I had, even then, already felt the first signs of serenity here. Out in the dunes, walking on the beach, canoeing through the mangroved channels with Salim, swimming through the waves or wasting hours on the roof at home. That was my salvation. Looking around the gathered company that Christmas, twittering, insincere, actors in a drab play or some bizarre pantomime, I felt profoundly out of place, claustrophobic. I wanted to scream, shake them from their tennis and 'Pass the salt, would you, dear boy?' script. My vision narrowed and I heard a rushing in my ears –*

*'You all right, old chap?' asked Clive. 'You look a little peaky.' I was immediately grateful to him for providing me with my chance to escape. Everyone momentarily hauled their slobbering chops from the trough to look on.*

*'Bit of a headache,' I lied. 'Too much rich food. Would you please excuse me?' I folded my napkin and headed home, already having missed the morning service, and frankly careless of our Saviour's birth, breathing in the fresh air, my anxiety fading with each step.*

*The following few days were miserable. I sat in my room, shutters closed, scarcely eating, oblivious to Salim, my thoughts spinning around and around like a dog maddened by confinement.*

*In a moment of clarity I appreciated that I needed help, guidance, that I was going under and needed a life ring, and that there was only one person I could think of who could throw it.*

*I think this might have been the moment my life changed forever.*

*I took action, and greeted the New Year with Maurice, taking him up on his offer to drop by whenever I wished (I had wished it days before, truth be told) on the afternoon of the last day of 1933.*

*His house, along the shore to Shela, is at the back of the quiet, sandy alleys of the white-washed village, with excellent views in all directions except south since there the sand rises up behind the village – rampant, full of bones. Salim, having shown me the way, took his leave promptly, as if keen to get away from the djinn I imagine buried there.*

*He opened the door as I raised my hand to knock upon it.*

*'Ah, Ralph,' he said, fixing me with his merry Mediterranean eyes, 'I've been expecting you. Come in, come in.' Perhaps he had seen me coming. He bent to scratch Maddox behind the ears, who closed his eyes in pleasure, tail thumping against my legs. 'This fellow might have to wait here, though, if he doesn't mind. I have a rather protective cat who wouldn't hesitate to leave her mark on him.'*

*Barefoot and bare-headed – whether shaved or bald, I could not tell – he wore a blue-black kaftan embroidered at the neck and sleeve, and with his long beard and heavy gold rings seemed nothing less than a Magi disturbed from his alchemical bubblings. The smell of amber wafted past me into the street as I followed him inside.*

*There was no evidence of staff, no cook, no houseboy, no one – or so I thought that first day. Maintaining a steady monologue he led me through the house, not dissimilar to my own in plan but larger and cluttered – festooned – with artefacts; all manner of antiques, pottery, paintings and handcrafts – a veritable museum, though full of colour and life and not in the slightest bit musty. Enormous narrow-necked demijohns squatted in the cobbled courtyard under jasmine trees that wound thickly around the pillars and through which butterflies jigged in the filtered sunlight. In the centre, a small fountain the shape of an open lotus splashed and tinkled, filling the air with a light laughter and scattering rainbows across the white walls. A dining room doubled as a gallery – paintings and prints covering every inch of available space and every artistic movement of the last five hundred years appeared to be represented.*

*Off to one side, the sitting room-cum-library was similarly chaotic; bookshelves crammed with arcane, leather-bound tomes lined every wall, and the desk that faced the open French windows was deep in papers, open books, glass paperweights and a human skull that leered up at me, its grin fixed in perpetuity. Certainly I'll not want for reading matter. Maps lined the pillared passage walls around the courtyard, and an open stone staircase led up to the first floor where the bedrooms lay. Another ran on up to the roof garden.*

*He showed me around, pointing out various objects and regaling me with the stories of their provenance. I listened, captivated, as the record of his time here unfolded, as each item offered up its memories. We talked long – though I mainly listened – and continued through the afternoon, eventually retiring to the roof to watch the sunset and the chapter of the year come to a close.*

*We chatted lightly over G and Ts, poking fun at the various characters we both knew, discussing the future this country could look forward to under its incumbent rulers, the pompous folly of triumphalism, the inescapable ramifications of hubris and the myopia of greed.*

*I laughed for the first time in weeks.*

*Disappearing for a few minutes, he returned looking pleased with himself and brandishing a bottle of Château Lafite, 1899. What a treat, Lil, and what a setting. The pop of the cork had me salivating like one of Pavlov's dogs. Maurice smelled it approvingly.*

*'Santé.' He raised his glass to me and we sipped simultaneously, the rich flavour spreading thickly across my palate. 'From the tail end of a momentous millennium,' he said, admiring the lowering sun through the glass, savouring each mouthful slowly.*

*'Back then no one suspected the project would be anything but*

*a success. No one but me, that is. I distanced myself from the Movement not long afterwards, a few years into this century. I could see things were starting to get out of control – perhaps I was not as wrapped up in the idealism as they, not as steeped in the progressivism, which became as overly determining as that which we had hoped to escape – and something happened that occupied my whole attention, that gave me necessary objectivity, the perspective I needed that none of us had, so wrapped up in ourselves had we become. The means of my redemption.'*

*'You mentioned before that you fell in love with Lamu?'*

*He looked at me seriously for a moment.*

*'In a way, yes, I did. I already loved the island and the people, perhaps more than anyone among us. But –' he broke off. 'I was not entirely honest with you the other night, nor entirely dishonest neither. Come, bring your glass –' And he led me down to the first floor, along the corridor to a dressing room, where everything was neatly arranged; a commode on which lay the accoutrements of a lady's boudoir – glass, hairbrush, jewellery box etc. – long unused yet evidently cleaned and dusted.*

*On one wall was a large, unframed oil painting of a woman.*

*Of Arabic blood, she was strikingly beautiful; with high cheekbones and wide, grey eyes the shape of almonds, ringed thick with kohl. The composition was simple – she was sitting at the very commode in this very room, I realised – turned to face the artist, a slightly questioning lift to her eyebrows and a light smile upon her full lips. The silk robe she wore, ornately patterned in cream and gold, hung loose, offering a tantalising glimpse of her body beneath, and her jet-black hair cascaded down over one shoulder to her waist, gleaming in the sunlight that streamed through the open window. Despite the simplicity of the room she seemed every bit a Persian princess. I was dumbstruck. Spellbound.*

*'Ralph,' he said, with the slightest hesitation, 'meet Fazir, as beautiful now as the day I first met her,' he raised his glass to the painting, as did I.*

*'How do you do,' I said, unsure of how to play out the scene.*

*He continued, 'I must have been your age, just twenty-one, correct?' (I had a flash of the engraving in the tree.) 'She was a couple of years younger, impulsive, wild. She ran away to be with me, turning her back on so much – her faith, her family – and never once looked back, never once complained. Despite the ostracism, the contempt she endured within the community even when we moved here to Shela and away from the insults and the spitting in the streets of Lamu, she stayed with me. Oh, I suffered too, make no mistake. The others – not so utopian after all! – they couldn't or wouldn't understand why I was forsaking them and the dream, and became resentful, though towards the end a few of them began to see – too late, mind you, much too late. In a way we both became outcasts for a while, martyrs to a much grander cause than that of the Freelanders. To love, Ralph. What grander cause is there? The most irrational, the most compulsive, the most wonderful emotion of all. One should never resist it, no matter what price Aphrodite demands in exchange. Life itself, if necessary.' He was silent for a while. 'But let's not mourn the past for too long. She certainly wouldn't want it.' He took another sip, reached up and touched her lips, then ushered me out of the room. We made our way back up to the terrace where the sun was now half submerged in the sea. He stood, gazing out to sea.*

*'She had a difficult pregnancy and then, when it really mattered, no one would come to help. I remember that terrible night, running through the town, begging for help on my knees in the rain, but the shutters remained closed, the doors never opened. I will never forgive them for that, though in time I have come to understand why. As*

*she rejected them, so she in turn was spurned. A valuable lesson in life, Ralph, though I'm sure one you don't need to be taught, eh?' Swig, pause. Before I could ask what he meant: 'She died in my arms, amid all the blood, after so much pain, but peacefully in the end.' He poured us both fresh glasses and we sat in silence for a while, each adrift in our thoughts, both I suspect, quietly lamenting lost love.*

*Feeling the time right, and in an attempt to show solicitude for the man, I began to tell him a little about myself – although there's not a great deal to the story, I felt I could at least understand and empathise with his loss. Are these letters to you not a similar invocation to the spirit world as his addresses to the painting, as his maintenance of a shrine to her memory? He listened without interruption, though I had the feeling he already knew much of what I told him, if only the gist. His intuition is strong, his ability to read my thoughts positively unnerving, and his empathy slaked something deep inside me.*

*When, upon railing against your Pa, I became a little too impassioned, he reached out and touched my arm, stopping me.*

*'Ralph,' he said, 'he was not wrong.' At the time I thought he meant simply that the wish of a father to protect his daughter cannot be misguided. Since then, and it is some weeks now, I have begun to think he meant something quite different. That, perhaps, your father realised I would fail this test, that we are not intended to be together, that it is not written. Before I could enquire further:*

*'To 1933,' he said, as the last glimmer disappeared, 'and the past. Adieu.'*

*Something else sank out of sight at that moment, Lil, beneath the waves, behind this vast celestial body of rock. Something I can't yet put into words, all these weeks later, since it's still not clear to me, even now. It sits in the peripheral vision of my mind's eye, and when I try to turn to see it more clearly, it disappears. I have my suspicions and assume my soul recognises it, yet keeps it out of sight until the time is right. For this reason it makes me ill at ease.*

*But I speak now with the benefit of hindsight; the luxury that enables us to right wrongs, rewrite our past and – insh'allah! – move forward.*

*We sat up the rest of the night, he and I, utterly at ease in each other's company (at least I in his), for my own part speaking little, listening to his stories of growing up in the Alps of Switzerland, of his tutelage as a painter in Genève and his consequent travels through Europe; of living hand-to-mouth from his prodigious talent. (Many of the more recent works in the dining room are his, it transpires, including the painting of Fazir; rich, colourful abstract landscapes and portraits radiating the character of their subject.) He took commissions where possible until, aged just twenty, he ended up in Munich with the artisans, poets, radicals, sybarites and aristocratic malcontents who made up the Utopian movement.*

*Quite a tale. I asked whether he had written it down, since his story would make wonderful reading. He said he had not, that his abilities lay on canvas, not vellum. 'Perhaps you might care to record it for me, though. I understand you are something of a writer.' How he knew this I could only wonder. My household is clearly not as watertight as I had assumed.*

*'Merely for myself, and the letters I've been sending home. But I should love to try, if for no other reason than to hear it all first hand.'*

*And so, that fine morning of the New Year, it was agreed. For two days a week I make my excuses to Mohammed (at the ginnery – not in heaven) and slip happily away along the sand to Shela like a schoolboy playing truant, persuade Maddox to take his position at the front door and enter into what I am beginning to think of as Wonderland; one reason for not having written to you over the last month.*

*Though that is not the whole story, Lillian, as I shall – and must – explain.*

*Since the New Year there have been several events that have thrown me into a state of confusion – if that is the right word. Perhaps turmoil is more accurate – that's only now beginning to resolve, much like the fogs we encountered at sea, revealing a clear view of the horizon and clarity of purpose to my actions. Please bear with me.*

*Firstly (I hope you are seated):*

*I have resigned from the Company. Weeks ago, in fact.*

*Now, I can well imagine your reaction. Should justification be necessary after what they (we! God help me) did to Kamau, then let me keep it brief; as I've said, my role was to all intents and purposes superfluous. They will not miss me. More importantly, I detested it. As Maurice once remarked; 'Life is too short to spend it engaged in activity that one does not enjoy or, if tolerated for some long-term aim, one is not wholly convinced to be worthwhile.' The 'end' – gaining your father's favour – has long since failed to justify the means. But, before you run wailing to your room, I would not have renounced my intentions towards you on something so whimsical as my own short-term happiness - heaven forbid! - had I not established some other means.*

*(Maurice elaborated on the matter, while I remember, and I believe his words relevant; 'The central tenet of existence, insofar as it pleases the gods and enables us to find a clear path down which we may stroll, appreciating the view, not distracted by the obstacles in our way, is that of affirmative action; simply this, if what you are doing feels good, makes you happy and harms no one – including yourself – and here he tapped his wine glass and smiled – 'continue*

*to do it, for it is what you are supposed to be doing. If it does not make you happy, try something else. This does require appreciation of the importance of moderation, since one can easily forget the harmful attributes of some of the more seductive vices, but otherwise it stands up to cross examination in the Higher Court. It also comes with a proviso, that if you continue to do something you know to be wrong – the definition of evil, incidentally – you accept responsibility for your actions and can claim neither ignorance nor innocence. Once you apply this principle to your life, everything else falls into place, for this is the will of the Creator, the Universal Law, which will conspire to provide you with whatever you ask for. This, Ralph, is the secret of life!')*

*But back to the other means.*

*I was wandering around his house one day as I am wont to do, discovering, with childlike wonder, new delights in this treasure trove, this Aladdin's cave, with each perusal, when I chanced upon an object I could not for the life of me identify. It appeared at first glance to be an unremarkable, mottled grey rock, about the size of a man's head, but weighing less. Rough to the eye but waxy to the touch, it was the texture of what I imagined elephant hide to be and, when held to the light, slightly opaque. Naturally curious, at the next opportunity I asked Maurice what it might be.*

*Ambergris.*

*With a jolt I recalled the conversation with Toby in Mombasa and the piece he had shown me – one tenth of the size of the one I now held. Maurice put me straight; it is not a whale's sputum but an intestinal secretion produced solely by male sperm whales, probably to help them consume the indigestion-inducing beaks of the giant squid with which he wrestles in the Deep. (Whalers have found beaks six inches long embedded in the centre of ambergris bolii, and sucker marks the size of dinner plates scored into the whales' skin. To provide some sense of scale, squid here two feet long have suckers an inch in diameter.) Imagine these Leviathans locked in mortal combat, a mile below the surface!*

*They are doubly damned, the sperm whales, since specimens clearly capable of yielding negligible oil are still greeted with a warm welcome and a ready lance by opportunistic blubber-hunters. But they do excrete this resin naturally, like a cat its fur-ball, and it is often found floating far out to sea where, Maurice reckons, the odour might impart some form of communication, a beacon, if you will, of amorous intent to other whales in the region. Indeed, its value lies in the demand for its mythical fertility and aphrodisiacal properties, as well as its redolent scent. He tells me it is also washed ashore along this coast, though rarely.*

*The quality depends on the colour; with grey representing the best, the oldest, and black the worst. Or rather the least good, I should say. The colour subsequently depends on how long at sea it has bobbed and therefore how 'refined' the smell. While fresh, the smell is by all accounts overpowering, but the scent issuing forth from well-steeped 'floating gold' Maurice describes as the equivalent of 'catnip to humans'. Taking a knife, he cut a little from the block, warmed it in his hand awhile then held it under my nose. Strong, pungent, earthy, yet simultaneously marine and musky, and shocking somehow to the senses, almost illicit.*

*The long and short of it Lil, is this (you'll think me taken leave of my senses, if you do not already): since the first week of January and with my mentor's help, I've successfully trained Maddox to track down the stuff like an Italian truffle hound.*

*After a frustrating process of coaxing, cajoling, threats and bribery, most of our attempts at which he regarded with disdain, it turns out that nose of his is actually quite well-tuned, and over the course of the last few weeks we have dug up a little – a nugget here and there – just from the seaward beaches of Lamu and Manda. There are many hundreds of miles yet to cover, and if the current demand for it is in any way near what it was five years ago, the pittance I was paid by the Company will soon seem rather short change.*

*Add an extra petition to your prayers; for Maddox's nose.*

*Last week:*

*My diligent recording of Maurice's life fills my days.*

*Even the most unaccomplished scribe could not fail to compose a riveting account, so fascinating is the tale. He and I take to the roof and begin whenever we feel like it, usually with a recap of the previous entry.*

*He often closes his eyes when he speaks, casting himself back in time, recalling in extraordinary detail the names, conversations, sights, even smells, on occasion, of the event in question. In truth I'm little more than stenographer, though he seems pleased with my embellishments.*

*He was deeply struck by your fountain pen – most captivated, entranced by the play of light along its shaft. Perhaps, between the fine yarn of his memories and the well-crafted loom of the pen, the final tapestry might belie the failings of its weaver.*

*I take notes, then attempt to coalesce them around the core of what I know of the man, through the eyes of someone assessing his life, seeking to find the tributaries of purpose – destiny? – that have contributed to their river's course, and in turn led them here, to the ocean.*

*On Wednesday, as I was leaving to head home, he stopped me at the door.*

*'Yours, I believe,' he said, and, to my astonishment, handed me the talisman given to me by Jim.*

*'Where on earth did you find it?' I said, dumbfounded.*

*'It was passed on to me by, ah, by a mutual friend. They came across it up in the dunes, near the tree you often visit, but they*

*thought it bad juju, bad luck, and thus assumed it must have once belonged to one of my old associates, and gave it to me. If it had done, believe me, I would definitely have known.' With a quick movement he reached under his beard and from beneath his shirt pulled out an identical disc.*

*'May I enquire where you obtained yours?' he asked.*

*'A friend from the voyage here,' I said, stupefied, 'though I had until now taken its loss as a sign I might not see him again. I'm greatly indebted, Maurice.' I replaced it around my neck and immediately felt subtly reassured, as when circles are closed or jigsaw pieces fit – an omen that my decision to quit the job was the correct one, that I was 'on track', and that I might someday run into my friend once more.*

*'How on earth do you have one like it? Have you been to Ethiopia?'*

*'No,' he laughed. 'I'll tell you all about it in due course.'*

*It wasn't until I reached the house that it struck me as odd that he knew of my spot beneath the baobab.*

*The following day I returned as planned.*

*Knocking on the door I received no response but had the curious sensation of eyes upon me. Looking up I noticed that he had the same latticed brickwork above his front door as I above my courtyard, through which one might spy unobserved, and thought I detected some movement behind it, a shift in the shadows. There was someone at home, of that I was certain. I called out his name but received no reply. After a minute I gave up, assuming he was otherwise occupied – though why he wouldn't come and tell me himself, I couldn't guess. Putting it down to one of his many caprices – idiosyncrasies in his behaviour which are prone to change with the weather – I shrugged, and headed off.*

*As I strolled back down through the village, who should I bump into but Maurice, hastening to the house in the opposite direction.*

*'Ah, there you are! I was worried I might have missed you. Come. Let us continue with our labours.' I said nothing about the flitting shadow I had seen nor the presence I'd felt, and we were soon immersed back in the last century. The sun's slow arc slid by until, late in the afternoon, we called it a day. I closed my book and gently screwed the lid back on my pen.*

*'I confess to looking forward immensely to these gentle meanders down memory lane,' he said, 'and would like to thank you for indulging the follies of an old man.' I replied that it was my pleasure.*

*'But I should nevertheless like to show you my appreciation, Ralph.' His eyes were intent upon mine. 'I realise things have not been easy for you here, that you have had deep misgivings about your future and that you are often given to a sense of failure. Perceived failure, I should emphasise. Failure to have lived up to your obligations back home, to honour your agreement.' He raised his eyebrows. 'Am I right?'*

*I told him he was, that he knew the reasons for it, and that it was, to a degree, thanks to him that I'd begun to shake off some of the shackles that these obligations had placed me under. That his was a story to inspire. That each day I understood more of my own mind from the insight he gave me into his, and of my gratitude for it.*

*'Then I hope you take this advice as it is intended, with sincerity and warmth and, if you'll forgive me the presumption, as a father would advise his son.' He sat back, studying me. I glanced at him but could not meet his eye and stared out to sea.*

*'Ever since we met I have tried to impress upon you the value of freedom, of trusting your intuition and recognising the signs along the road. "Tried" is not the word, for it is effortless, the simple result of my own small endeavours to answer similar, if not the exact same questions.' He paused. 'Follow your heart, Ralph. I recognise*

*the torment in you and how it has increased since you left your employment. It was a brave thing to do, and shows the courage of wisdom, namely to never get too stuck in too fixed, inflexible, a perspective; it limits your view. And yours was a logical step in the right direction. Now you need the courage to take another. Torment often arises from indecision and doubt. Yet I believe you have made your decision already; perhaps you intuitively realise this to be true in your heart but have yet to recognise it with your head. The next step is to commit to it.'*

*'Decision concerning what, exactly?' I asked, frustrated by his riddles.*

*'You know the answer to that, Ralph.'*

*'Do go on,' I said, slightly peeved, defensively. I felt a rising panic, as if being forced to look at something I would rather not.*

*He was about to answer when a small bell chimed, light and high-pitched, somewhere below us in the house.*

*'Excuse me for a moment,' he said, and disappeared downstairs. I heard the low tone of his voice, indistinct, engaged in conversation. I must emphasise that in all the time I had visited him here I had never heard any bell ring, nor had anyone ever visited or knocked on the door. And now I think of it, though I had never seen him cook, there was always food prepared when we needed it, the place always spick and span, the flowers always freshly cut.*

*He returned a few minutes later, and suggested we reconvene the following Monday to continue with our discussion. He thanked me again, but had withdrawn, retreated like the mangrove crabs at low tide, all of a sudden elsewhere in his thoughts. I felt a little chagrined, I must say, as if cheated of a revelation the second before the conjuror lifts his cloak, but promised to return, and took my leave, leaving him standing there, hands clasped behind his back, gazing to the horizon.*

*Descending the stairs, I crossed the courtyard to the hall and retrieved my hat. As I put it on, I turned, why I know not, and glanced up to the first-floor balcony.*

*To my surprise, there was a woman standing there, beside one of the pillars, half hidden in the afternoon shade and wearing a burka, a black shadow in the half light, so concealed that I did a double take. For a moment, a split second, through the arcing droplets of the fountain, our eyes met, hers large and clear, framed by the letterbox slit of her headdress, then she turned and vanished like a ghost into the room behind her. The dressing room. I stood where I was for a minute, rooted to the ground by my surprise, then pulled myself together and let myself out.*

*The imprint of those eyes has stayed with me since. Quite striking, Lil, I must say, full of compassion, though to whom they might belong is utterly perplexing. Why would Maurice not tell me of a servant or mistress? Why had I not seen her before? All very mysterious. And those eyes; though of course I cannot be entirely sure from such a distance, they seemed to be smiling.*

*Later:*

*I arrived at his house at the specified time and upon knocking found the front door ajar. Receiving no response I let myself in, calling Maurice's name once. Still nothing, so I made my way up to the roof to await his arrival.*

*He often has the habit of disappearing for an hour or so at a time, requesting that I do not disturb him. Once, when I asked whether he slept during these retirements he replied that no, it was not sleeping exactly, but a form of waking sleep, or 'sleeping wakefulness', that was what he called it, 'rather like prayer'. He promised me he would enlighten me further over the 'next few years'. Startled by this unusual slip of the tongue – he usually chooses his words with great care – I said, 'Months, you mean. I'm nearing the halfway mark, according to the scratch marks on my prison wall.' At this he gave me the most curious look, penetrating and deadly serious, almost one of anger, so that I felt as if I'd said something to upset him, and he dismissed me rather abruptly soon after.*

*Anyway, as I was making my way up the stairs I heard a sound from one of the rooms to the left of the staircase. Since Maurice's quarters are to the right, and remembering the strange apparition of the previous Saturday, I decided to investigate further. I could always claim to have wanted to sneak a peek at the portrait again should I run into him. I tiptoed to the dressing room door and, my breath unaccountably tight in my chest, turned the handle.*

*I suppose half of me was already prepared for Maurice to tell me, quite matter-of-factly, that the ghost of his beloved Fazir, somehow, through sheer force of love, or ritually invoked from the grave as a spectral companion until he could join her in the hereafter, lived here with him – I would have believed it – but I was nevertheless unprepared for what I saw.*

*It was her, Fazir. Sitting at the commode. When she heard the door open, she turned, in precisely the same pose as in the painting, to look at me; the same slight lift to the eyebrow, the same arch smile, the same cascade of hair, the same mesmeric eyes, which now calmly held mine.*

*'Hello, Ralph,' she said clearly. 'Please, don't look so alarmed. I know all about you, and I hope that soon you will get to know me.'*

*God knows how long it took me to splutter out a coherent word. I think I ran through most of the vowels before managing, 'So sorry to disturb you, please forgive me,' and closed the door again, my hands shaking and thoroughly spooked.*

*Wholly willing to accept the presence of her ghost, I made my way upstairs. Maurice was waiting for me, arms folded, wearing the blue-lensed pince-nez he sports when in the sun, smiling.*

*'I was wondering where you had got to. You're late.'*

*'I, er, I . . .,' grey matter still reeling.*

*'You look as if you've seen a ghost, dear boy. Sit down before you fall down.' I took his advice. He turned away from me, and I knew he was waiting, playing with me, which piqued me a little. When I had recovered my breath:*

*'Look, Maurice, I know I shouldn't have, you know, poked about, but I saw someone the last time and heard a noise and I, well . . .'*

*'My daughter,' he said flatly, without turning round. 'My beloved daughter, Soraya. It was inevitable the two of you should meet eventually but I had wanted to postpone the moment a while longer.' He turned, came over to where I sat under the pergola, and sat down opposite. I was expecting him to be angry, but he was not.*

*'She, like you, is at a crossroads in her life. She doesn't know whether to stay here, where her heart lies, where her father lives and where her mother is buried but where the opportunities for a woman are limited, or whether to leave. With my peripatetic background, I am not in the most qualified position to tell her to stay, which naturally, if selfishly, is what I want. I didn't want your, ah, confusion to affect her. Fortunately, beyond these walls she is protected by the anonymity of her burka, which, unconstrained by the tenets of Islam as she is, she hates wearing though it does have its uses; she has often seen you around the town while remaining invisible herself. While you are here I request that she confines herself to her room.' He sighed, and smiled. 'Furious at my imposition, she let you see her the other day as an act of rebellion, and against my wishes. She is her mother's daughter, after all. Now I shall have to introduce you.' He thought for a moment. 'Why don't you come for dinner next week?*

*While slightly stunned by the deception, I'm also relieved I've not lost my wits altogether. I thought I'd seen all the works of art within these walls, and it transpires there is one, living, that I had not.*

*Enough. That's all for now.*

*It is late, my Mirage, I'm tired and my fingers are ink-stained and grooved from where the pen rests between them. I seem to spend most of my time with it in my hand, when not out beachcombing with the mutt Maddox. I have had to resort to using a local squid sepia derivative, the Quink having long run dry, and find it curious that both current occupational activities, the ambergris and my writing, have become somehow dependent upon this strange cephalopod.*

*Yours,*

*Ralph*

*P.S. Cotton Charlie Whitson got his comeuppance. Clive had him arrested and sent to Mombasa for the murder of Kamau, though he'll probably get off on a plea of insanity; he has apparently been slipping off the rails for a while – locking himself in his house etc. – perhaps why I was sent here in the first place. Had this been made explicit from the beginning I might have been better placed to do something about it.*

*Too late. For Kamau, but not for me.*

*Perhaps Whitson will meet Murdoch in Mombasa gaol. They should have much to talk about.*

*10th February, 1934*
*Lamu*

*Lillian,*

*Extraordinary news.*

*My endeavours in securing an income have proven rather more successful than I had believed possible.*

*While my, or rather our – credit where credit's due, Maddox and my – findings have been pitiful in comparison to the massive 102lb item possessed by my friend (pieces of which we tutored the mutt with, that, if nothing else about his character, at least his nose for the grey amber might be refined), we have nevertheless had considerable luck.*

*To date:*

*One 3lb 10oz;*

*One 16lb 3oz;*

*And, last, but by no means least, another, larger: 36lb 7oz.*

*A total of 56lb 8oz, discovered in the space of a fortnight.*

*If this continues I shall soon be rich. I mean to say, extremely rich.*

*Lil, ambergris currently sells in Paris for 80 shillings per ounce.*

*Which means, give or take a few pounds according to the quirks of the market, I have made a clean 3,700 quid, earned in a fortnight.*

*Not so loopy after all, wouldn't you agree?*

*Forgive me for allowing myself a little smugness, but the relief is enormous. I was in a bit of a quandary as to what would befall me if the plan did not work; return to England, tail between my legs? I think not.*

*Maurice, as pleased with my good fortune as I, has been good enough to loan me capital against the value of the booty, enabling me to retain my lodgings for the time being. With this security, Lil, much of my melancholia has lifted; truly, I have never been happier. I trust this will find you equally buoyant of spirit and rude of health.*

*Meanwhile he and I continue with our literary labours. Also, he has asked me to instruct his delightful, if enigmatic, daughter Soraya in English, which, if I have the time, I agreed to do, since*

*I am greatly in the man's debt and wish to make it up to him any in way possible.*

*Go well, dear girl.*

*Yours,*

*Ralph*

*15th March, 1934*
*Lamu*

*Dear Lillian,*

*The ides of March.*

*I don't know whether you'll ever read this, nor whether you have received any of the countless letters I have sent you. Short of your death, I cannot for the life of me understand why you have made no attempt to contact me these six months past.*

*No matter. What is done, is done.*

*I should have written sooner but could not. To begin with I didn't know what to say and, once I did, lacked the courage to say it.*

*Lillian, I've tried my utmost to do this by the book only to realise that there isn't one.*

*I shall not come back to you, nor return to England.*

*I love you, and perhaps always will, but I have come to realise that there is some purpose, some reason for my being here after all, beyond proving my 'worth' to your Pa or proving the mettle of my love for you. Our fragile flame has burned brightly for so long, Lil, and its light has guided me and given me comfort when I've needed it most, but it has finally burned down to the wick, sputtered and gone out, only for me to realise the sun had already risen.*

*It seems to me now as if everything, my whole life, has led me here.*

*Your father was right after all, it seems – I have failed the test. Happily so. Please thank him for me, for us both. If my discovering this for myself was what he intended, then he is far more astute than either of us – than I, certainly – ever gave him credit for.*

*Lillian, I should also tell you that I, like Maurice, have fallen in love with Lamu, its beauty, its wild nature. Its complex past, haunted present and hopes for the future – and with the people who live here.*

*With someone who lives here.*

*Dearest Lil, I give you the greatest gift anyone can give another – I set you free.*

*I return the writing case and all its contents, since to keep it would be to retain ties with someone I no longer recognise: myself.*

*Forgive and forget me, sweet girl.*

*Ralph J. Talbot*

# Chapter 20

*Luang Prabang, Laos. 2003.*

At the first sign of dawn, little more than a wan diffusion of light beneath the high cliffs of surrounding limestone mountains but enthusiastically broadcast by the demented cockerels that strutted the town's back yards, she swung her legs over the edge of the bed and stretched.

Lifting the gauze of the net and taking care not to wake the sleeping form beside her, she crossed the room to the bathroom, feet slapping on the time-sheened, dark teak floor, experiencing as she did every morning an inbuilt tweak of guilt that, despite a career dedicated to conservation, she lived in a house built entirely from an endangered hardwood. It was simply what they used then, she told herself, and is the reason why it's still standing a hundred and fifty years later, which in turn was why the rent is cheap. 'So thank you, O noble tree', she intoned, palms clasped with a nod. She had always talked to herself, ever since she was a kid, not always out loud necessarily, but there was an internal narrative that prattled alongside her day, keeping time, holding pace.

She stood in front of the cold shower, took a breath, braced herself and spun the tap on full. The cold water made her skin fizz and sent endorphins careering through her bloodstream like eight-year-olds on a big dipper. She gasped with shock and delight.

Hoiking on tight jeans, T-shirt, ex-army jacket and a deep green silk shawl shot with silver thread, she gently opened the screen door, padded round the intricately carved balcony and down the stairs to pull on her desert boots. The morning air already carried a hint of incense wafting down from the many *wats* – the monasteries and temples passively punctuating Luang Prabang's colonial gridwork of streets like so many spinning tops scattered by the Buddha himself.

The monks were preparing for their daily dawn alms collection, a slow procession along the main street where the charitable, the curious and the penitent gathered to give them food.

This was her favourite time of day, a personal act of pilgrimage she tried to make every morning, cutting up from the slow, cappuccino spread of the Mekong, through bougainvillea-bedecked alleys to the middle of town, through Wat Pa Houk where young, orange-swathed monks laughed and shouted during their ablutions, then up the three hundred and fifty-five steep steps to the Phu Si stupa, a white teat perched on the thickly forested hill that rose like a swelling breast from the town's centre. Here she would watch the day begin, undisturbed as often as not, since all but the most enthusiastic tourists preferred the more convenient timing of dusk to take their obligatory pictures.

Below her the long-shadowed town spread postcard-perfect along the river, smoke from the first fires caught beneath the chilled morning air and mixing with the mist, giving the water an ethereal insubstantiality. The sun, already risen beyond the mountains, would take a few minutes more before it broke over her, and longer still to reach the streets below.

She turned east in anticipation, sharing the infectious

excitement of the birds around her, their flittery twitter building with each moment, their rapture unfailing, pure and delightful, as it was every morning.

As the light hit her as if a blind had been raised, she closed her eyes, shivering as her body released its chill clench, absorbing the delicious warmth, her chi opening like a lotus, lighting up her caramel skin and gleaming in her long dark hair. She smiled, her lips a wide cupid bow.

Her year-long posting was nearly up, and she knew it would be a wrench to leave. She couldn't believe how quickly the time had gone, slipping silently past like the river below her, and she was going to miss the peace and tranquillity of both the country and the Laotians themselves. She hoped they would hang onto what they had, though deep down she knew it was unlikely; despite the government's attempts to preserve the diverse cultural identities of the various tribal groups that made up the land-locked, river-beribboned country, ultimately the dollar would win. It always did.

What was it Aidan had said?

'Anything not economically viable, whether cultural, zoological or ecological, is called history.'

Already work had begun on another bridge over from Thailand, and construction of a road joining Singapore to China had been given the green light; a road cutting straight through the untouched forests of the north, and one destined to bring all the myriad ills of the West to a population too innocent to see, to even look, behind the curtain.

For now, though, despite being the most bombed people on earth, with a legacy of unexploded American ordnance that littered the forests, they were the loveliest, most hospitable and gentle people she had ever met. Like the Thais must have been thirty years ago, before drugs, AIDS, sex tourism and rapacious, unchecked development had punched the smiles from their faces and left Bangkok one of the most morally and physically toxic places on the planet.

Even in the year she'd been here she'd seen the visitor numbers double. Word spread along the backpacker bush telegraph that there still existed a paradise, a forgotten backwater where you could leave your room unlocked, the police wouldn't set you up and *USA Today* wasn't yet on sale. The parochial laws making it illegal to sleep with the exquisite, sloe-eyed local girls and the 11 p.m., politely enforced curfew wouldn't keep the wolves from the door for long. UNESCO status had put it on the map; there were direct flights from France, chic teak and bamboo hotels, lip-smacking restaurants and silk-shimmered boutiques selling antique Buddhas stripped from temples and Paris-priced jewellery. Thank God for the French, she thought. At least in countries they colonised you could count on beautiful architecture, relative bonhomie from the populace, good coffee, proper croissants and the occasional bottle of Saint-Émilion.

Had anyone asked her she would have fixed them with her grey eyes, let loose one of her shy smiles and told them she had never been happier in her life. The first four months had been pure privilege – she knew the post had been much sought after – and she had immersed herself in the various projects, educational programmes and report compiling with the enthusiasm of an intern. Fluent in English, Arabic, Swahili, Giryama and French, she had picked up the singsong, ping-pong complexities of conversational Lao relatively quickly, though the written word remained elusive, and her close group of easy-going colleagues, once they got used to her appearance – she could have been anything; Middle Eastern, Native American, her genealogy was complicated – all respected and liked her.

She hadn't noticed when he first walked into the centre – people were in and out all day – but looked up when she heard his voice, something in the measured American timbre catching her ear. He was leaning on the counter, slightly weathered in an unkempt, Timberland ad way, asking Wah where was good to visit, when had Luang Prabang been made a Heritage Site, and whether the magnificent, magical Plain of Jars in Eastern Laos, was ever going to be Heritage shortlisted.

He'd caught her look, blinked like a fish and lost his train of thought, coming out with something comically unintelligible which made her turn back to her work, stifling her laughter. He pulled himself together, grabbed a street map from the counter, and beat a retreat. She heard his boots thump down the wooden stairs, and thought no more of it. It wasn't the first time guys had fluffed it in front of her and lost her cool, though to her credit she never really understood what the fuss was about.

'He was cute,' Wah teased. 'For an American.'

'Was he? He moved so quickly I didn't get a good look at him.'

'Sure you did. Just your type, sister. Rugged but vulnerable.'

'And that's "my type", is it?'

'You know it is.'

'Oh do I?'

'Yep.'

The next morning, sitting where she now stood, eyes similarly closed, she had opened them to find him standing there, at the other end of the iron rail, watching her. It was her turn to feel self-conscious, and he smiled, slightly relishing having the advantage of surprise, she could tell.

'Hey there,' he said. 'Sorry to disturb your meditations.'

'Not at all. It's not my private hill.' She was a little rankled though, irrationally, at the invasion of what she secretly thought of as her space. He was very cute, though – Wah was right – if a little sad looking, something mournful to the eyes.

'Quite a view,' he said, continuing to look pointedly at her, a slight smile on his lips, and she felt herself flush. Kids stuff, she thought, annoyed with herself, playing it straight.

'Isn't it? Stunning.' She stood and joined him at the rail. 'Never seem to get bored of it. The way the light catches the gold of the palace differently each day, the gradated hills like a Japanese watercolour. Every day there's something else I notice. Like today. See the buffalo on its own down there on the bank?' He looked where she pointed, leaning ever so slightly too close. 'All its friends are in the other bit but it still won't cross the footbridge over the ditch to be with them. I guess it could be worse, it might be lonely during the day but at least it gets the whole paddock to itself, unlimited river access.'

'A very discerning buffalo, clearly,' he said. 'Maybe it's a philosopher, needs the space to ruminate.' She laughed. 'Perhaps it sees itself as an outsider, a sociopath, and uses the excuse of the footbridge to avoid the others, escape the herd.'

'Maybe it knows the grass isn't always greener.'

'What's your excuse?'

'Excuse me?'

'You're obviously not from here, though I can't for the life of me begin to guess what your nationality is. You're not married' – he nodded to her ring finger – 'and clearly academic, so I'm wondering what brought you here?'

'You need to ask?' She gestured at the vista, the sun now clear of the mountaintops, and plumes of wood smoke rising from the leafy town below them. 'And what makes you think I'm academic?'

'It was the glasses you had on earlier, made you look like a distractingly beautiful librarian. Seriously – I assume you speak Lao, which is no mean feat from what I've heard of the language, you're obviously working for UNESCO, who I happen to know are quite – what's the word? – "picky". They can afford to be, I know. I applied for voluntary fieldwork in Peru, Sri Lanka, Mongolia and Cambodia, but with no experience whatsoever I was dead in the water, and to have been sent here means you're troubleshooting; I'm guessing a consultant logistics role. How am I doing so far?'

'Way off. I worked for them for years back home in Nairobi, ever since I left college, but after ten years I needed a break. I loved the job, don't get me wrong, and didn't want to quit, so my boss suggested I took a posting somewhere. They have an exchange programme for long-term employees; a kind of working holiday, really. The stuff they give me to do is pretty mundane but the location more than makes up for it, no? Jesus, I'd stamp envelopes all day if it meant being able to live here. So not quite the whizz-kid you thought, huh?'

'Well put your glasses back on, okay.' They were now both leaning on the rail gazing out across the valley, already so relaxed in each other's company they hadn't even registered it yet.

'What about you?'

'Mm.' He turned to look at her, assessing, eyes smiling. 'Long story. I'll tell you over dinner.' She feigned shock, then checked her watch, and swore.

'I'm late,' she said, already leaving. 'Your fault.'

'Wait. What about dinner?' But she was gone.

She hadn't expected to see him again, another of life's brief encounters, souls passing each other like ships at sea, though she hoped that she might, and it was only when she reached the bottom of the steps and threaded her way through the chaos of the morning market – orchids, jasmine and frangipani everywhere she looked; tiny birds in baskets; moiling snakes in sacks; racks of dried fish; bicycle bells and tuk-tuks honking for space; olfactory overload of spices and flowers and musty undertones – that she realised she was as ignorant of his name as he was of hers. She smiled. It hadn't seemed important, as if there would be plenty of time for such minor details later.

The world smiled back.

He came by the office that afternoon, shifting awkwardly within Wah's earshot, and told her he'd booked a table at L'Eléphant for that evening and that he'd be deeply honoured if she would join him. The best restaurant in town, even though you still had to try hard to blow more than a hundred bucks between two. She dragged it out, playing to Wah, sucking on the arm of her glasses ingenuously – um-ing and ah-ing, was there something else she had to do tonight? She couldn't remember – but nevertheless, inevitably, accepted. Besides, she reasoned, she'd never been to L'Eléphant before.

Arriving a few minutes late, she threaded her way between the tables to join him at the bar. He hadn't changed, maybe a fresh shirt, she couldn't tell, but she didn't mind, appreciating the lack of pretence. She had, however. She wore a low-key but low-cut, sassy dress handmade from raw, pale turquoise local silk that set off her own mulatto colouring perfectly.

'You made it.' He stood to kiss her on the cheek, unconsciously enveloped in her delicate cocktail smell of jojoba oiled skin.

'But of course,' she said. 'Did you think I wouldn't?'

'It did cross my mind,' he said. 'I mean, this is a little random, and I'm rusty as hell at this.'

'Small town, middle of the jungle, Friday night, what's a girl to do?' she said as she sat down. 'Besides, rusty at what exactly?'

'Dating. Asking a girl out. Especially exquisitely beautiful ones.' She was flattered, incrementally, despite the cliché. It wasn't a line, she realised. The waiter appeared, and offered to show them to their table on the terrace overlooking the river's broad reach.

'Please,' he took her arm, pulling out her chair for her and gently pushing it in as she sat down. Slick, she thought, or just well brought up.

'So,' she said, once they'd ordered a couple of stiff vodka and tonics, 'you were going to tell me something. And make it interesting.'

He had quite a story as it turned out, and though he tried to make light of it – 'This is the first time in six months I've been able to talk about it without people shooting themselves' – the first half-hour of their date had been heavy enough to prevent either of them from ordering.

'And the killer is that even this conversation is a self-indulgent luxury, one that ninety percent of the world's population cannot even imagine, don't have time for and cannot pause long enough for because they're too busy trying to feed their family.' He lit a cigarette and exhaled slowly. 'We talk about happiness endlessly in the West, but I'm no longer sure it's something to strive for. That it even exists as something discoverable. I think we've been sold it as a concept, a will-o'-the-wisp to keep us reaching for the unattainable.'

'This lot' – she gestured to a couple of passing monks – 'are hot on that, the whole "You can only achieve enlightenment when you stop trying" Buddhist paradox. I kinda like it.'

'You know what I find fascinating? That people with nothing – I mean nothing, poverty-line people on less than the dollar a day, who don't know each morning where the food for the day will come from or where they'll end up sleeping the night – they have the biggest, widest, most open smiles in the world. People back home with everything, who ostensibly want for nothing, can't meet your eye, spend more on therapy, weight loss and cosmetics than Chad's GDP and still look miserable. If I could work out why that is, my entire profession would be redundant. I'd probably make a fortune from an anti-possession, non-consumerist self-help book at the same time; except you wouldn't be able to sell the book. I'll call it *The Emperor's New Therapy*.' They laughed.

'Lack of expectation? I mean if you don't want stuff, you'll never be disappointed.'

'Yeah, that's definitely part of it, forming the flip side to our sense of entitlement, blame culture gone mad, that the world owes us; and for sure it's to do with having nothing to lose and having no alternative but to live each day as it comes, in the moment, and making the most of each second, but it's more than that. It extends further. Take their generosity, for example. The same people will often as not take you in and give you a meal, even if it means they themselves go hungry. That simply wouldn't happen in the West. And it's not because we have any reason to be less trusting of strangers; these guys have been fucked by everyone going since the Middle Ages' – he gestured around vaguely – 'and they're still smiling. You wouldn't get past the front door without getting shot back home – "It's mine, get your own" mentality, fences, property, guns, litigation. And with so much to give. Makes me physically sick.'

He had a lot to get off his chest. He would flare up, not in anger but impassioned, righteous indignation, and launch off on long diatribes against what he called 'Them': the pharma, arms, oil and banking conglomerates, the mega corps that ran the world. After working for the UN for ten years, she could, and did, sympathise. The bureaucratic behemoth, convoluted to the verge of impotency, a self-perpetuating monster consuming more finances than a small country, often got things very, very wrong, distributing aid ad hoc regardless of the local economy and destroying any chance of autonomy to the billions of unaccountable dollars that evaporated into thin air annually.

'Better to do something than nothing, no?'

'Not always,' he said. 'I was trying to help Kai, remember.' He looked away.

'It wasn't your fault. You know that, don't you?'

'I know, I did it by the book only to discover there isn't one. It's the system that insists on one normal manifestation of self-expression, which is impossible, and leads the other aspects of self to build up and up until they explode, but I'm only now starting to believe it. It's taken six months of running, six months of not looking at it, and focussing on the sunrises, the flowers and the smiles. Now I'm tired of running and I can rein in the frustration – though I've yet to test it in a big city – and want to stop. I guess I've been waiting for the right –' he paused – 'place.' He looked around. 'Could be worse, like you said.' They held each other's eyes for a moment. 'C'mon, let's order.'

As he scanned the menu she sneaked quick glances at him, the frown lines deeply etched into his forehead, the vaguely dishevelled appearance despite the clean shirt, barely resisting an urge to give him a hug. When he looked up and caught her, his whole face changed: broad grin, intricate crinkling around the eyes, guileless, honest, utterly unreserved. It had been that smile that had started it, she thought later, the germination point, as if half of her, her romantic, instinctual self, had decided right then and there and immediately begun negotiating with its pragmatic twin.

The remainder of the evening was simply a matter of her id convincing her ego to give in, and for the deal to diffuse through her body in a viscous, lusty cocktail of amino acids, hormones and enzymes.

And she in turn had told him her story of growing up, utterly unselfconsciously. Of growing up by the Indian Ocean, barefoot and wild, the sound of the breakers she would always miss, at one with the sea; diving for lobsters and netting crabs in the mangroves, catching post-natal leatherbacks and riding them into the surf, swimming with dolphins as they spiralled around her or rushed past in a blur of fin and muscle, or drifting with the dugong, the placid sea cows and origin of the mermaid myth.

'My grandfather says they were once young and beautiful,' she told him, 'hundreds of years ago when they looked after the whales, singing to them, teaching them. But the whales moved far away to escape man, to where the dugong could not follow, so they became silent, sad and wrinkly, never moving far, always listening out for the songs of the whales returning.'

She told him about guiltily watching – it seemed so sacred, so secret – copulating octopi make undulating love, intertwining around and around and around each other in an erotic ballet, flashing iridescent colours like lightning ('How do you know they were making love?' he asked. 'Trust me, they *definitely* weren't fighting'), of a childhood steeped in folklore and fable, magic and myth.

How her father, Marco, had grown up just as she did, free to chase the waves of his dreams, smashed into the surf on occasion, borne triumphant upon the crests on others, the youngest of four, and unencumbered by the parental expectations the other three felt, with no one to answer to. And of her mother, Kirimira, the daughter of a Giryama chieftain, her blood ringing with nobility and her eyes shining with light reflected off the sea.

Then later, in the mid-eighties, in her teens, there came the sudden shock of moving to Nairobi when her father's marine environmental project – mangrove-planting, beach-clearing, turtle-monitoring, lecturing at local schools – became an established NGO and went national, then continental, and finally became part of the worldwide conservation charity, Terra Firma.

The chaos of the city, the mayhem of the fume-choked roads, the huge, million-strong slums of Kibera and Mathare, the grinding poverty beneath the tall towers of glimmering glass, the wealth stashed beyond the bougainvillea-garlanded, guarded gates of the private estates. Of being different at school – the only one with eyes *that* colour – and how the holidays back in Lamu were never enough, the wrench of having to leave, the yearning ache to be back by the sea.

Then, a woman, the environmental science degree from Canterbury in England, fees covered by her grandfather. Always home for the holidays; the token boyfriends, Nairobi rich kids, an Australian photographer, no one she'd let in, suspecting they were more impressed by her family wealth than by any depth of regard for her; her dedication to her work – though she didn't need to – starting at the bottom and, to her grandfather's quiet pride, working up through the ranks through her own endeavour.

And behind it all her grandfather's unfailing devotion. Perhaps it was because she looked so much like her grandmother, for although he loved all his many offspring equally, it was she he indulged the most; it was to her he retold his stories most often, over and over until she could recite them herself; to her he taught his principle of trusting your instincts; in her he instilled a reverence for nature and faith in the universe, that life hurt sometimes, and that if it didn't you weren't living it properly. That whatever you focussed your energy on, the universe would do its best to provide.

And the secret of life; that if you enjoy doing something, and it harms no one, keep on doing it. If you don't, stop.

Aidan was captivated. Mesmerised.

Magick was at work, seeping up through the earth, summoned by their souls and the drumbeat of their hearts, seeking their bodies to possess, tangible, quickening their pulses and flashing in their eyes, intoxicating and heady, sparkling in the air between them, helped along by *foie gras* with red fruits washed down with oily, sweet Gewürztraminer, shrimp-stuffed sole, seeping Camembert and a dense Bordeaux, an indecent chocolate mousse and rich, warm fruit coulis she'd had to lick from her lips, the opulent décor and the seductive light thrown by the candles on the table, and the full moon, the complicit voodoo witchery invoked; all these things, with the main ingredient – laughter – fuelling the eager crackle of love's volatile kindling.

As the coffee cups were cleared, everyone else long gone, they reached a point where for a second the laughter exceeded the joke, where, whether out of nervousness or exuberance at the release, the momentum of their emotion overshot slightly, created a tiny backdraft of gravitas and skidded to a halt. They gazed at each other – pensive, gauging, the self-protective chess game of what-move-to-make-next apparent to them both. Expose too much and risk being hurt, or intuitively leap off the cliff edge, arms open wide, eyes closed.

Simultaneously, so it seemed, as if they realised there was nothing to lose, they both reached out a hand, fingertips touching, entwining, then tightening their grip, fusing, then leaning in close to each other, goofy smiles straightening to feather-light smiles, seeing their true nature, their souls raw, unguarded, their faces blurred around the anchor of their eyes, and their lips touched and they kissed.

The waiter's polite cough brought them back down to earth, blinking away tears and laughing.

Afterwards, to postpone the inevitability of the next move – foregone, but needing rational confirmation – they went to the Hive Bar. No different to clubs in Boulder or Nairobi – same colour, different pattern – there they sat by braziers under the stars for a while then, when he proffered a hand, ducked inside for a dance, both moving on the back-beat, Aidan hypnotised by her serpentine, silk-skirted undulations, while she smiled self-consciously, delighting in his admiration, letting herself go, so natural and unrestrained that any lascivious looks she got soon turned to grins of appreciation.

Catching his eye across the room she winked, gently blowing his mind.

Someone clapped, someone whistled, the tempo picked up, audibly, tangibly, drawing others to their feet.

Later, she had to nestle in close to him in the tuk-tuk, the night air chilly and abrupt after the close heat of the club. They felt their hearts fibrillate, knowing the other felt it, knowing it wasn't just the cold, both tightening their arms around each other, grateful for the racket of the two-stroke that rendered words redundant. No need for any 'Come up for a coffee', no awkward should-we-shouldn't-we, can-I-call-you-tomorrow; just up her ancient stairs, hand in hand, stopping at the screen door, turning, the slightest hesitation, the flash of moonlight on a glimpse of teeth and:

'Please,' she whispered, 'don't leave.'

Their skin merged, tonally variegated, anticipation that had mounted all evening ramped, just about held in check by the desire to draw out the pleasure, making their hands shake and their breath shorten, before succumbing to an overwhelming feral abandon as they entwined each other like the octopuses she'd described only two hours earlier. She was shocked, afterwards, in the post-coital aftermath, not by her lack of inhibition or how wantonly she had behaved, the *release*, but by how naturally it had come to her, how natural it had felt. They lay there, panting, while their universe reordered itself, supernovas delicately imploded and their vision stopped starring.

Later, giggling in the candlelight like teenagers, finger-tracing goosebumps and swooning on pheromonal updrafts, reconnoitring every new contour, mapping every dimple and lying nose to nose like nuzzling Inuit, they shared their secrets, their hopes and dreams, fears and doubts, until they fell asleep enwrapped in something more than just each other's arms.

That was six months ago.

It should have tapered off by now, she thought, but it hadn't, quite the opposite. This was the relationship she had dreamed of as a kid, the hand-in-hand, heart-to-heart companionship, the complicit smiles across crowded rooms, minute shared experiences, observations made at the same time so that they soon stopped pointing them out to each other, conveying whole sentences with a tilt of the head and a smile. The peace they felt in each other's company, complete and careless, telepathically wordless often as not. The touching. Unconscious nudges as they walked, hand on arm when making a point, the tucking of stray hairs behind ears, scratching forearms and neck napes, never out of contact for long. A steady drip of mutual pleasure.

Her soul thrilled.

In the two months since her contract ended they'd been inseparable, filling the days with trips into the mountains on a rented 250cc Honda, thudding through roller-coaster mountains, stopping at whatever village they found themselves near at dusk, taking picnics out to opaque, turquoise waterfalls deep in the forest, doing nothing, spending considerable time in bed. Not wasting a second. Then they took a three-day boat ride up river, branching off the murky Mekong onto the Nam Ou, whose clear emerald water splashed and chattered, full of animated life compared to the tired mother river, spent, dammed and drained from China and with half her gauntlet course still to run before the wide deltas of Vietnam. They stopped at Nong Kiaw, last outpost to roads and phones, then headed further north towards the Chinese border, the long thin speedboat careening through the rapids to a straining Toyota diesel engine and the whoops and cheers of those aboard.

At Muang Ngoi, a sleepy village of bamboo huts that teetered on stilts at the river's edge in the shade of the mountains, where kids splashed in the shallows, fishermen balanced precariously on tilting canoes as they flung nets into the stream, dogs listlessly scratched their mange, beady-eyed chickens scratched the dust and smoke drifted through the sandalwood trees, they stopped.

The villagers went into raptures when they discovered she could speak the language, and they were immediately surrounded by a gabbling throng of women who led her off for chai and chat while he tracked down somewhere for them to stay. Days slid by spent hammock strung in the afternoon sun – reading, basking in their love – a happy, somnambulant haze not entirely due to the opium tea they felt obliged to accept.

They fitted.

Her shoulder slotted neatly into his armpit when they walked, her gait matching his. Coitally snug too, their lovemaking rocked them together succinctly, breath merging, intuitively tantric in union so that the spiralling serpents of their kundalini wound around each other like a caduceus; their tempos matched each other, from the first, breath-baited sigh, through to the surge, to the shock of the drop from the top.

There was one area into which they didn't stray, and they'd had a minor blow out over it. Back in Luang, in a restaurant overlooking the river one evening. She'd become aware of herself waiting for him to see it – the world – the way she did, for the gentle rain of her love to wash off the scales of his cynicism and break the deadlock, to defy the curfew he'd imposed on his view of humanity.

'Listen, babe,' he said, leaning forward. 'Exponential population growth dependent on a global economy that *has* to grow, that cannot recede, that certainly isn't sustainable and that is, itself, dependent on finite, dwindling resources, is doomed – ta-daa – to collapse. And the power to do something about it lies, conveniently enough, in the hands of people who have a vested interest in the consumption of those resources, not their conservation.

'What really scares me is that since these motherfuckers aren't stupid, they must therefore know exactly what they're fucking doing, unlike the crowd on Golgotha, and, ergo, are *by definition* evil. Arms, oil and pharmaceuticals are the world economy's biggest money makers and are therefore propagated by war, consumption and illness. They want us at each other's throats, they want us buying shit we don't need and they want us ill. The loyalty of any corporation is to its shareholders, above and beyond all else, even if it means generating a market. Creating disharmony, nurturing discord. Starting wars and maintaining sickness.'

'It's human nature, babe,' she said.

'To destroy ourselves? Bullshit. I don't buy it. This is deliberate. Nature's too perfect. Admittedly we have put ourselves beyond nature, but even then it's not us, it's the twisted fucks that govern us, who tell us what to do. Who bent the Bible in order to convince us that we have "dominion" over nature as a birthright.'

'So what? We just stop consuming what we don't need? That simple?'

'Exactly. And stop listening to people telling us to breed more and more little consumers, usually religious leaders trying to boost their faithful or ministers of the new god, the allegedly "free" economic market, trying to create more demand. Nurture, that's all there is nowadays. We lost sight of nature a long time ago when we handed our souls over for flatscreen TVs, Prozac, porn and microwave dinners.'

'But we don't have to choose that, you and I, do we?'

'No, of course not, but we're part of one organism, part of the one life that is in turn part of the one world.'

'So you concede that by living outside of Mammon, Maya, whatever, with love, we can effect the whole.'

Both unwilling to cudgel the moment with a row, they sought common ground and agreed that everything was as it should be, the world was as it was for a reason, and that it was the grossest human arrogance to think for a second that humanity's puny machinations were anything but part of a greater scheme. It was always thus, from the moment the first lightning bolt hit the primordial soup, the first mud-skipper took a gasp.

'You do have some faith then?' she said.

'I believe that whatever happens is what's supposed to happen. But that's fatalism, or rather *realism*, and not pessimism, if you ask me. It's basic Gaia theory, that as a self-regulating organism the earth will seek to balance herself out, which with a global population that's three or four times over what's sustainable, doesn't look too rosy a proposition. To believe everything will be okay is much worse – blind optimism – and only means we become mired in our own inertia and don't try to do anything about it.'

'I'm not saying it's all going to be a bed of roses, or don't try to do anything about it! What I'm saying is that whatever we believe, at some level, whether here physically or wherever, happens. It's what we experience. That we create our reality by what we think – I've even heard you say it, that "we choose our mood", like Kai choosing to do what he did. She felt him tighten. 'You are choosing to see the world, and that means us, as doomed, and that will determine how you live and how we are.'

'But how can I justify bringing a kid into a world that statistically, logically and instinctively I see as being on her knees under the bloated, obese weight of humanity?'

'Aidan,' she said, 'just because it is doesn't have to affect how we live our lives. We don't have to live like that, don't you see? You don't have to look at it like that.'

'How, then?'

'By looking past the illusion, babe, and seeing things for what they are, by taking a breath and looking around you and seeing how beautiful the world is, how beautiful it can be, and by looking into my eyes and seeing how much love for you there is there.'

He gazed into her cool, pale blue eyes, full of light, love and laughter, and saw.

'Clever,' he said. 'That's *precisely* what I tell my patients. I just charge them five hundred bucks an hour for the privilege'

And slowly, like the sunrise, his smile grew and turned into a grin that exploded into a laugh she'd never heard before, unrestrained and infectious, and they were both laughing so hard their eyes ran, and the looks they got from other diners just made them laugh more.

'I love you,' he said, when they'd caught their breath. It was the first time he'd said it.

'That's lucky,' she said, 'because I just missed my period.'

Something in him had changed after that, like he'd shed a skin, his perma-frown lifted like a botoxed brow, and the weight he bore had lightened. Observations he made, normally tuned to plastic, progress, population and pollution, shifted to the slow shift of dawn through the coconuts, the rainbows that danced in the dewdrops and the delicate eroticism of orchids. He stopped grinding his teeth in his sleep, that sharp squeak of enamel belying tremendous pressure he couldn't possibly reproduce when awake. The shadows left his eyes.

A week later, entwined around each other in bed, he produced an antique silver ring, scored and dented with age, and so pure it possessed unusual density, and proposed.

'Yes, please,' she said.

Opening her eyes, she tracked a heron as it circled the hill and cruised off sedately over the soft tufts of bamboo. She turned to leave, taking the red-bricked steps two at a time down to the temple and through the waking town, returning, with her hands pressed together and a bow of her head, the *sabaidees* of pot-bellied men playing *pétanque*, women washing their hair and cock-a-hoop kids, arriving slightly out of breath at the Mekong Café where they'd arranged to meet for breakfast.

He was already there, head down in an out-of-date *Vientiane Times*. She slipped her arms around his shoulders and buried her face in his bed-scented neck.

'Mm. Stop. My fiancée is supposed to be here any minute,' he said.

'Sorry I'm late, babe.'

'I wish you'd woken me. I would have come with you. It would have been neat punctuation to say goodbye up there where we first met. Closure.' He gave the word a nasal Manhattan whine.

'You couldn't have got up if you tried. Anyway, I wanted to see what it was like to be apart from you for a minute.' She waved to the waiter.

'How was it?'

'Unbearable.'

'Well, just see that it never happens again.' They ordered scrambled eggs and coffee.

'Faz, I've been thinking about your grandpa's birthday. I mean, what the hell do you give a ninety-year-old who's lived the life he has?'

She was more concerned about how he'd handle the four aunts and uncles, eight cousins, three elder siblings and thirteen nephews and nieces, all of whom couldn't wait to meet him.

'You said he's a writer. Prolific, right? Well, how about this?' He pulled out an ornately covered notebook of handmade papyrus he'd bought from one of the numerous boutiques and craft co-operatives on the high street.

'Great,' she said, a little nonplussed.

'And . . .' With a flourish he tipped out the pen from a

small silk bag and handed it to her. 'How about this to go with it?'

'Oh, wow. It's beautiful,' Fazir said. 'Just perfect, he'll love it.' She turned it in the light, quite captivated. Unscrewing the cap she read the inscription on the nib. 'A Mabie Todd, Blackbird No. 8, 1933. *Really* perfect. 1933 was the year he left England to go to Kenya.'

Then she noticed the engraved initials.

She mouthed the familiar letters silently, letters surrounded now by many others, including her own, initials carved into a time-gnarled baobab in the dunes where she used to play as a kid, where her grandfather would sit and tell her stories for hours while she listened, rapt, the breeze ruffling the white mane of his hair, the horizon silvering his sun-slit eyes:

R.J.T.

# About the Author

Alex Wyndham Baker was born in England and has been pin-balling around the planet for the last twenty years or so, working variously as a barman in LA, TV reporter in Bangkok, magazine editor in Hong Kong, copywriter in Nairobi, mojito vendor in Barcelona, hotel inspector in India and English teacher in the Galapagos. He started writing *Cursive* after a climbing accident in Kenya incapacitated him for a year and currently lives in Somerset with his fiancée and a limp.

www.alexwyndhambaker.com